INTO THE NIGHT

MARIN MONTGOMERY

Marin Montgomery

© 2018
Wilted Lilly L.L.C.

ALL RIGHTS RESERVED
COVER DESIGN: LOUISA MAGGIO
EDITING: The Passionate Proofreader

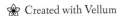 Created with Vellum

DESCRIPTION

When Blair and Bristol Bellamy's overprotective parents agreed to let their daughters spend spring break in Oahu, they never anticipated that only one of them would return. What should have been a week of soaking up the Hawaiian sun next to pristine blue waters takes an unexpected turn when Blair wakes up on the beach one morning with no purse, no shoes, and no memory of what happened the night before.

And worse?

No sister. Bristol had vanished into the night. Gone without a trace.

After months of tireless investigations and dead-end searches, Blair was forced to return home to the Midwest without her younger sister, and her life was never the same —until ten years later when a package arrives, the last of its kind.

For the first time since Bristol disappeared, Blair has a reason to believe her sister is still out there. But if she wants to find her, she'll need to return to the place where it all happened, she'll need to launch a dangerous investigation of her own, and if she's lucky, she might come out of it alive ...

For Bernie,
Friends are the most important commodity. Thank you
for supporting me on my writing endeavors and encouraging
me with kind words, not so-kind words that I sometimes need
to hear, and a quiet place to write.
For all the late nights, doggy play dates and dog-sitting,
take-out, and 'adulting' you've helped with, I appreciate
having you in my life.
Dashiell and I are two lucky blondes.
Thank you.

PROLOGUE

TEN YEARS PRIOR, ***March 1998***

Blair

SOMETHING WET TOUCHES MY CHEEK, gentle at first, the way our dog laps my shoulder with his slimy tongue.

I turn my head, signaling it to stop, desperately trying to brush it off.

What starts as a trickle increases, absorbing my body in a rush of cold that pulls me towards it, drenching my skin. Imagining myself floating on water, sinking down, the way I do in my bathtub at home, I let the feeling act as a guide. A surge of liquid washes over every square inch of me, enough to snap my eyes open. Color envelopes my line of vision, blue and white, but the brightness – it's blinding.

Closing my lids against the violent light, a sound like splashing and rolling waves hits my eardrums. There's a warm touch against my clammy skin, forcing them to flicker open. They feel gritty, like rough sandpaper's been dragged across my eyeballs.

A deep voice above me scares the shit out of me.

It's a man, speaking directly above my body. I assume he must be an intruder, breaking into our hotel room. Clenching my fists, he's prepared to drag me from bed and kidnap me, except as I shift my weight, there's not a firm mattress that moves beneath me, but something damp and sticky.

HEAVINESS WEIGHTS MY BODY DOWN, yet I feel a pull.

A waterbed – that's it.

That's what I feel like I'm lying on.

I remember the one my parents had when I was a young child. It shook underneath my small frame, the moving water mimicking an ocean, ebbing and flowing beneath me, the lull putting me to sleep.

Until one day it popped and flooded the whole bedroom.

Water washes over me again, this time hitting me directly in the face. Turning my head in agitation, I gasp.

Stop splashing water on me, asshole, I think but don't say.

I need to open my eyes, but I can't.

A firm grip tugs on my left arm.

Laying there, barely conscious, drifting off...

"You need to get up." It's the unknown male again.

"Get out of here, get out of my room," I murmur sleepily.

It's still not the sound I'm used to hearing in the morning. The voice of the brat.

My brain suddenly comes to life, the wheels spinning, processing what's happening.

Oh shit, a man's in the room – don't just lie there, fight!

Yell!

Hit back.

Flailing my arms, I hear a thud, then a moan.

When I open my mouth to scream, sand and bile choke me as I struggle to communicate my emotions.

My lids flash open, the shimmering light glaring in my eyes.

He's standing above me but has moved back a few feet, holding his elbow in protest.

"What the hell are you doing in our room?" I hiss.

"Room?" He shifts from foot to foot. "Honey, you're on the beach."

I shield my eyes from the glow as he comes into my peripheral. "You need to get up, you're about to get dragged out in the ocean."

I stammer, waving my arms wildly around me, like children do in the winter when they're making a snow angel, moving their limbs back and forth as the white powder creases into their shape below them. Instead, I bury myself in wet sand and thrash like a half-dead fish.

"Can you sit up?" He tries again to rouse me.

The feat of pulling myself up is a challenge. His warm palm takes pity, reaching out to grab my hand, slowly moving me forward into a sitting position. It feels too fast but really is gradual, the blood rushing to my head.

I rub my temples, disoriented, with no idea where I am.

Rapidly, I blink my eyes, my contact lenses scratchy and dry.

"Are you still drunk?" He squats down beside me, staring like I'm a new species of aquatic sea life.

I groan, twisting away from him, spitting out copious amounts of blue liquid. My esophagus burns as my body shakes violently, the nasty combination of salt and blue froth foreign to me.

"Where am I?" I hesitantly touch my face.

"The beach."

I look to the left, then the right. His sneakers are blinding, neon yellow, the Nike swoosh bright orange. "What beach?" I manage to whisper.

He looks surprised. "Waikiki."

"But where am I?"

"You're about fifty feet from The Waterfront, Waikiki Beach." The name of the hotel rings a bell, it's where we're staying, the brat and I.

A sigh of relief escapes my chapped lips. "Oh, okay." The gargantuan splitting headache takes the place of any cognizant thoughts I have.

"You need water." He's firm. "Let me go get you some."

I shake my head, noncommittal.

"Are you okay?" he asks, standing and taking a giant step back, giving me much-needed space. "Are you homeless?" I'm confused by his question until I notice tattered newspaper stuck to my bare foot, the aqua toenail polish adhered to a page on home sales in February.

"Do you need to go to a shelter?"

I pat the sand beside me. "I don't need a shelter." A tear tries to form but can't, my eyelids sucked into a vacuum. The man's salt-and-pepper hair and bare chest are above me, and his hands rest on his hips. Between his running shoes and his fire engine red shorts, there's no missing him on the beach.

"Where is she?" I ask.

"Who?"

"Bristol."

"Who?" He's perplexed.

"My sister." My sister a.k.a. the brat.

I focus on the jagged cut that hits right below my left knee, contemplating the reason I'm here in the first place. The man pulls me out of my thoughts when he says, "I haven't seen hardly anyone out this morning. I don't know about your sister."

"What about Nicholas?"

"No idea who that is."

For a moment, we don't speak.

"I'm going to go get some water," he repeats again.

"I have a purse."

He looks around. "Where?"

Panic sets in. "It has my room key in it. Cash. My daddy's credit card. He's going to kill me." I'm frantic, dragging my hands through the sand, unsettling and moving the black and tan flecks around. It's a small clutch, zig-zagged with patterns in rainbow colors.

"I'll help you look. Um..." He motions downward, his eyes locked on mine. "You need to adjust your top."

Glancing down, my halter top is no longer tied around my neck but hanging around my waist, both my breasts exposed. Quickly, I yank it up, my fingers fumbling to get it tied. I give up after ripping strands of hair out when it gets caught in the straps.

"Do you need help?" His voice is soft and low, a look of concern growing on his face.

I nod in response, keeping my eyes trained on my bare legs and cuts that I didn't notice yesterday.

Yesterday... yesterday was...

My mind drifts as he ties the cotton into a bow and then knots it. I go back to yesterday but there's a black hole, like an axe came down and cut a chunk out of the night, a piece of time.

Yesterday was Monday.

My sister and I took a surf lesson.

We met some boys, they had seemed nice.

And fun.

And older.

Had pizza, Margherita for him and I. Sausage for her and him.

Drinks. Lots of alcohol.

And then...

There's nothing.

It's like it never happened.

"Let's get you up to dry land." He extends his hand, waiting for me to make a move to take it. A neon orange wrist band is wrapped around my left wrist, the words *The Ocean Club* tattooed across it.

What was I doing in a bar?

After I stand, he slowly guides me, like you would an elderly person, a reassuring hand on the back but not too much pressure. He's gentle, never gripping my shoulders, just there in case I stumble.

Which I do.

HIS HAND COMES down to grasp my elbow as I wallow through the sand.

I think it's called 'sea legs', the struggle to keep your balance on land after you've been on moving water.

"WHERE ARE YOUR SHOES?" He realizes this is an illogical question based on the circumstances and bites his lip.

I shake the ripped paper off my foot, noticing a blister.

"I'm going to get you a drink." He's unyielding. "Let me help you to a chair on the beach." My white shorts are now dingy, covered in salt water and sand, see-through and wet now that they're drenched.

The lethargy is nothing compared to how every step feels in the embankment. Even without shoes, it's like each leg is a ten-ton bulldozer that I'm dragging through mud. Or in this case, a bottomless pit of sand.

We head the fifty feet to The Waterfront Hotel, which is a short distance but in my current state, it might as well be fifty miles.

Beads of sweat break out on my forehead as I painfully take one step at a time. His tennis shoes squish as he walks, his tanned skin glistening in the sun.

He points to a white and navy striped lounge chair by the pool, sheltered by a matching umbrella stand. "Let's head there," he says softly, directing me towards my final resting place.

I sink back into the cool plastic. The shade blocks me from the sun, yet my skin is covered in goosebumps.

"Do you have a phone?" I ask.

"I do. Do you need to call someone?"

Nodding my head as much as I can without aggravating the headache, I sigh. "My daddy."

"Here." He reaches into a fanny pack around his waist, handing me his cell. His face is etched with lines that seem to grow more pronounced with worry.

Dialing my parents' house, the phone rings, the voice-mail eventually picking up after three obnoxious beeps.

My father's voice speaks to me across the thousand-plus miles, soft and controlled.

"Hi, you've reached Pastor Bellamy. We are on vacation until March twenty-sixth. Please leave your name and number and we will return your call when we're back home. If this is about a prayer session or meeting group, please call Marcia, the church secretary at 402-717-8380.

Another beep.

I stutter, clicking the 'end' button, not bothering to leave a message for my absent parents.

That's right, they're gone as well.

They took a trip to Florida, their last hurrah before the adoption is finalized.

The man notices the look of disdain on my face, my mouth twisting in a grimace. Their cell phone number is not coming to mind – I didn't bother to memorize it since it's programmed in my own phone.

Shit.

As I mentally beat myself up, I realize it's not productive to speak to them at this moment in time. I'm her chaperone, entrusted with the brat's care.

First, I need to go to the hotel room, grab my sister, and we need to hunt for my purse and our daddy's missing credit card. My mother will ask to talk to Bristol and if she's not here, I'll be sent on a plane to a dungeon in the Himalayans or whatever they do with derelict girls instead of the private university I attend.

I can't very well explain to my parents that we got trashed and are both paying for last night's mistakes. Hopefully she's not...

"Do you need me to call someone for you?" he asks. "Another family member or friends?

"No." I shrug, pressing the phone back into his hands.

Settling back in the seat, my wet clothes cling to me. I shiver as water droplets trickle down my stomach.

The man clears his throat, searching my face. "I'm Peter, by the way. Peter Riggs."

My name.

At least I remember who I am. "Blair." I don't give him my last name.

His back turns and he heads up towards the hotel, pausing to glance over his shoulder to make sure I haven't vanished into thin air.

I stay seated in the same position, my limbs catatonic.

Peter looks down. I notice when he raises his head, his phone's lifted to his ear.

WHAT IF HE'S calling the cops?

I stink of liquor and bad decisions. Could I be arrested for underage drinking?

My mind wanders.

Would I go to jail?

And what about Bristol?

Would I be charged with providing alcohol to a minor? There's airplane bottles and empty vodka containers in our hotel room.

Things just went from bad to worse, and the gap in my memory annoys me.

I shut my eyes, trying to recollect my nighttime activities.

We *were* at a bar, the four of us.

They must not have cared we were underage.

Nicholas helped me stumble out.

My eyes drift to my toes. I try and remember my choice of footwear.

Wedges – I had brown pleather wedges on until they came off at some point during the night.

Did I fall?

That would explain the cuts on my knees.

Peter Riggs disappears into the lobby, his phone glued to his ear.

I watch his back and then realize I have to make a run for it.

1
———

BLAIR

BOTTLE OPENER IN HAND, I'm twisting the top off a Budweiser, my mind on auto-pilot, when the phone rings. I glance at the fluorescent clock that advertises Camel cigarettes from across the smoky bar.

3:20 A.M.

Sliding John's beer across to him, the sweat from the chilled bottle making it glide easy across the worn, scratched bar top, I let the phone shrill another couple of times. Must be someone's wife or girlfriend, eager to know if they're here drunk or out cheating. It depends on the woman what the greater offense is – some hate the drink, some despise the sex.

That's half the calls I get at the bar. I'm tempted to let it ring until the person grows tired of not talking to a person and hangs up.

As suddenly as it started, it stops.

I shrug, turning to the cash register to deposit the five dollars John leaves on the bar top as he stumbles to the pool table to shoot with his buddies.

A light blinks. The mounted camera that watches my every movement keeps me honest.

If only they'd invested in these more frequently in the past, I think.

Cooper's Bar & Grill, a small dive in Cooper, Nebraska, population fifty-three hundred, give or take the old folks that die off and the young ones that escape to the bigger cities of Omaha, Lincoln, or God forbid, get the hell out of the Midwest and flee to either coast.

Like I was supposed to.

I sigh, the tightening of my chest a subtle reminder that I had dreams once. I start to head down the dangerous path in my mind, but the shrill ring of the telephone cancels that trip down memory lane just in time.

It's for the better. Those flashbacks have been buried, but damn if they don't bubble to the surface like lava spewing out of a volcano. Speaking of fucking volcanoes...

Hawaii.

Dammit.

WHY CAN'T I just forget?

I've been punishing myself for a decade.

Ten years today.

It's why I worked a double shift. No sense in being alone on the anniversary of the day my life changed for the worse and everything went to hell in a handbasket.

She might've disappeared that day, but I've died slowly ever since.

It starts screeching again.

Shoving the register shut, the heavy metal clunking in unison with the annoying ring, I swipe the phone off the hook.

"Cooper's." I yell, louder than I need to. It's a Monday night and the place is practically dead. Besides the men playing pool, old man Bobby is at the other end of the bar, swaying his head to the ancient jukebox that's a relic at this point. He's stuck in another time, the seventies, I think, from his references to Woodstock and the drug culture that had him hooked back when he listened to Jimi Hendrix. Sometimes I think he forgets it's 2008, the way he rambles on about the concert he just attended or his days truck-driving the long stretch of Interstate 80.

"Blair." It's a statement, not a question.

I pause. "Who is this?" My hands grip the phone cord.

It's not like I don't know who it is, the tiny voice a distinct difference from the one I was used to growing up, but nonetheless still filled with anger and bitterness, just at a lower volume.

I'd know her voice anywhere.

"You know who it is." She sighs. "Priscilla."

"Okay." I shrug, more to myself since she can't see me. Even though she's not in front of me, I feel her invisible eyes boring into my back like a permanent shadow that's ubiquitous.

"I thought I could catch you here, with you being an alcoholic and all." Her tone drips sarcasm.

EVEN THOUGH I haven't touched a drop in five years, it's none of her business. I save my breath. It's a lost cause defending myself to a woman I've had a tenuous relationship with most of my life. "I'm working."

"Doesn't sound like it."

"It's a Monday. What do you want?" I balance the phone between my shoulder and ear, turning on the faucet to rinse some empty shot glasses.

"You don't have to pretend to work on account of me," Priscilla intones. "You know what day it is today."

"Yeah, so?" I use the sprayer since it's louder, hoping to drown out her voice...and maybe the memories of today, March twenty-fourth.

"How can you be so crass?"

"It's not like you've ever let me forget." I slam a pint glass down harder than I mean to. Wiping my hands on a dish rag, I take a deep breath. If anyone can get me from zero to sixty in record time, it's her.

"Oh, stop it. You're always the victim." Priscilla's bored. "She's the victim, not you. I wish you'd remember that when you're wallowing in self-..."

I interrupt. "I thought you were?"

Silence looms between us. There's been distance and reticence between us for years, not just in proximity but in her refusal to acknowledge I'm the other daughter.

The living, breathing one.

She breaks the lull. "I got a package."

"You always get a package."

"This one is different."

"How so?"

"She's dead." I imagine her petite frame shaking, a crocheted blanket wrapped around her frail body. "It came with a good-bye letter." Her voice has an air of finality to it.

"Priscilla, she's gone. She's been gone a long time," I murmur.

"It's done this time." Her voice quivers. "It's really done."

"Why would this one be any different?"

"Because of what the box contains."

There's a pause.

I knead the dishrag through my fingers, letting her gain her composure enough to continue. "I need you to see it."

"I'm working."

"YOU'RE AN HOUR AWAY."

"I can't just come to you when you dictate."

"It's not for me. It's for *her*. Wouldn't you want your baby sister to know you still cared?" Her voice has hardened again, the tears not enough to preserve a moment of fleeting sadness that isn't replaced by her war on me, a truce that will never be in the cards for us.

"She's not alive, Priscilla." I raise my voice. "There's no rush." I lean against the counter, turning my back on the trio of men staring at me, my sudden outburst causing an interruption to John's hunched stance over the cue stick.

She's firm. "Come see what they sent."

"You don't know it's a 'they.'" I whisper.

"Of course it's a 'they.'"

"Call the police." I stretch the phone cord as far as it will go to walk around the side of the bar. "You opening it is already tampering with valuable evidence."

"I didn't know what it was," she lies through her teeth.

"Every year you get a gift. Why would this year be any different?"

"You need to see this."

"I can't." I hang up.

A minute later, my cell buzzes in the back pocket of my jeans.

Yanking my phone out, her name pops up.

It's an attachment – a photo, grainy since my mother can't take pictures worth a damn, always shooting the image half out of the frame, cutting off limbs and heads in most shots.

My father was the designated picture taker of our family, God rest his soul.

It's a tan cardboard box, ubiquitous enough it could be a package from anyone. It's the kind you buy at any shipping store.

Except what it contains isn't from a concerned relative or an online retailer.

Priscilla's opened it up to reveal the contents of the package. Red tissue paper lines the inside of the box, reminding me of blood.

My stomach churns as my eyes drift over the items, and my pupils dilate in horror as I see what arrived this year.

Priscilla's right about one thing.

This year is different. How could it not be?

It's the tenth anniversary of her disappearance.

A tingling sensation overtakes my body as I'm transported back in time, my hands gripping the uneven edge of the counter.

I shut my eyes against the image, trying to gain control of my breathing, to slow down the inevitable panic attack that feeds on my body, the host.

Panic disorder, the doctor writes a script – it might as well be the narrative to my life. Anti-depressants, benzos, downers, uppers, and everything in between. Fumbling for a small peach pill, I sink against the wall, sliding down the rough wood paneling.

I've buried my past, but it always rises to the surface.

And in the box, a sense of tragedy and doom complete what I've known all along.

She's dead.

This package confirms it.

2

BLAIR

AFTER MY SHIFT ends at 4 A.M., I trudge up the stairs to my second-floor apartment. Not a bad commute, if you ask me. All I have to do is exit the stock room at the back of the bar and follow a small hallway, climb ten steps, and mine's the second door on the left. The right side has one other apartment, my employer, Marge, and her obstinate cat, Pickles.

I met Margaret McCallister a.k.a. "Marge' at Alcoholics Anonymous about five years ago, after my DUI – 'driving under the influence'. Losing my license for a year was the best thing that ever happened to me.

But not the worst. Go figure.

It's small – a studio, but that just means I can see every corner and crevice, even a spider crawling up the wall, the way I prefer it. The closet reaches the stretch of the six-hundred feet and a small bathroom has a pocket door with a combined shower and tub. A kitchenette's in the corner of the room, with a makeshift island that I use as a table, since I prefer to eat at a bar top.

This place was a fresh start for me, my old life in the rearview where it belonged.

At least, fragments of it.

I was sharing a house with my drug-addled party boyfriend who lived fifteen miles outside of town. We got in a drunken fight the night I got pulled over.

It was one of many, our time together consisting of his violent outbursts and my desire to bottle everything inside by drinking away the pain.

The numbing effect.

We had gotten in a physical altercation after too many shots of tequila for me and speedballs for him. Events of this particular night are hazy – the only difference from our other 'episodes' is that I had a broken nose that needed medical attention. It tweaked precariously to one side, broken vessels soaking the towel with blood. Hence the reason my driving was reckless, as I swerved with every curve of the road in my tormented fog to the hospital.

Tonight I remove my clothes, tossing them in a laundry basket, the smell of fried bar food and cigarette smoke remaining in their fibers, permeating my space. I spray air freshener on them, disguising the odor.

I lay down on my full-size mattress. A bigger one and the room would look cramped. My covers are scattered across the bed, disorderly. Ever since the morning I came back to the hotel and found our duvet cover intact, I hate the way a made-up bed looks, immaculate and untouched.

I'm certainly not pristine and unscathed.

My thoughts are as disorganized as my sheets. My hand reaches underneath the pillow to grab Bristol's old Hawks sweatshirt, the logo faded and the words cracked in the decade since I've had it. My mother sewed a quilt of her favorite tees and shirts, but I couldn't bear to reconstruct this sweatshirt into something else.

It's my security blanket. The last piece I have of her.

I shove my head beneath the faded flowered pillowcase and close my eyes.

Her face comes to mind, frozen at seventeen, instead of how old she'd really be now at twenty-seven.

As much as I don't want to re-live the turn of events that led to this juncture in life, I can't help but wander back in time, the way I always do on the anniversary of her disappearance into thin air.

I'm home from college, visiting our small Midwestern town, restless and bored. Even the ramen noodles and shitty cafeteria food I've become accustomed to make my stomach growl in protest. It's amazing how leaving your hometown, population under three thousand, gives you a different perspective.

It's almost the end of winter vacation, and I've been dreading the conversation with my parents when it comes to spring break.

A vacation is what I want. A vacation is what I need.

Not a road trip to Kansas City like I did with a group of seniors in high school, but a trip to Cancun, where a group of my Alpha Delta Pi sorority sisters are headed. It's all they can excitedly chatter about. Unfortunately,

I have never been out of the Midwest.

They whisper about sunshine and sand, boys and booze. My nineteen-year-old mind pictures washboard abs and maybe...just maybe losing my virginity to some Latin boy or an older guy, maybe mid-twenties.

Anything to make my friends jealous.

My parents are God-fearing conservatives that forbid talk of birth control and promote abstinence. Specifically my father, who pounds on the pulpit every Sunday as he leads our church in prayer and speaks of other fortuitous misdeeds with beads of sweat dripping down his forehead.

Stomach churning, I'm not only asking them to trust me in Mexico, I need their money to finance my trip. I have a part-time job at the mall, but let's be realistic, minimum wage and a clothing discount at said store only gets you so far. My money's filtered back into Abercrombie & Fitch with gusto every other Friday on payday.

"Daddy?" I ask on our way home from church. My tactic to go to the congregation without an argument, smile and sing loud in the front row, act like the pleasant daughter they swear they used to have before I became moody and withdrawn, has worked this Sunday.

Even the new tattoo on my lower back is covered by a sweater set.

"Yes?" My father's attentive, never moving his eyes from the road, always laser-focused on the task at hand.

"I'd like to go on spring break this year with my sorority sisters," I spew out, sitting in the backseat of our old beige Toyota van, my younger sister Bristol beside me. The words jumble together, quick to release from my tongue, hanging in the air, testing the waters and my parents' nerves.

My mother's incredulous. "With what money?" Her green eyes drift to the backseat, widening dubiously, matching Bristol's.

"Aren't you working a part-time job?" My father asks. He has the patience, well, of a pastor, and his tone doesn't waver.

"At the mall." Bristol smirks. I elbow her in the ribs, her annoying sing-song voice grating on me.

"Have you been saving for it?" My father ignores the peanut gallery.

"Wait," my mother interjects. "She's not going on spring break."

"I'm nineteen," I huff. "You can't keep me little forever."

"Blair..." My father intones. "That's not what your mother's trying to do."

"What's so bad about going on spring break?" I huff, blowing a chunk of brown hair out of my face. I even took out the hot pink clip-in extension for this visit.

"Because all you girls will act like sluts and get drunk." My sister mutters under her breath so only I can hear. She says this all with a plastic smile. I want to smack the smugness off her face, the brat.

My mother twists her body from the front seat, shooting me daggers. "Because nothing good happens on spring break trips with college girls."

"Except random boys," Bristol adds, eyebrows shooting up. I want to punch the freckles off her nose. "Bet you'll end up pregnant." She gesticulates a baby belly.

"How do you know I'm not going on a mission trip?" I deadpan.

"Is it a mission trip?" My father's confused, thinking of the usual volunteer groups going to El Salvador or a third-world country.

"Yeah, sure is." I bite my lip. "It's not through your church, Daddy, it's through a partner of the sorority house on campus."

"You're such a liar," Bristol yells, nearly bursting my eardrum since she's right beside me. Pinching her knee in rebuttal, she digs her pink polished claws in my arm. I swat her away, crossing my arms defiantly. "No, it's not a mission trip, Daddy."

"THEN WHERE ARE you thinking of going?" He drums his hands on the steering wheel as my mother glares at him in silent fury. He doesn't notice, his eyes focused on the highway, the barren landscape of ice-covered branches and frozen fields the only scenery passing by.

"Mexico." I take a deep breath. *"Cancun."*

"Absolutely not." My mother's stern. Her eyes narrow at the road, my father's denseness at her annoyed expression unnoticed. *"Girls get kidnapped there. You'll end up a lampshade or killed by a drug cartel."*

"If your mother says no, then no." My father turns the dial, the Christian music going up a couple decibels on the FM radio.

"Ha," Bristol sneers. *"I knew they wouldn't let you go."*

"Fuck off," I growl under my breath. *"I hope you get murdered in your sleep."*

How I'd come to regret those words, even a decade later. The way they were intended to sting, seems to only intensify with time. My headache throbs, reminding me I can't take them back. And there's so much I want to do-over, except life only lets you reexamine your behavior, not amend it.

3

BLAIR

"BLAIR." My father yells from the bottom of the stairs at our farmhouse. It's not technically our home, the church owns it, but we've been living here for the past seven years, since 1991.

Before that, the same – another small town, the farm on the outskirts of the county line, and a gravel driveway.

At first, I assume I'm in trouble. It's always *my* fault since I'm the older sister that should know better. Earlier, I could hear Bristol downstairs talking to my parents. The vents reside in the floor and carry sound upwards, my name repeatedly mentioned with that *tone*.

Before I graduated, I used to listen to every fight my parents had and every argument that involved my name.

Now I crank the volume on my music and ignore the world.

At least when I'm home. They pick at me, nagging me to be like *her*.

Bristol's an annoying brat that likes to stir the pot – she probably told my mother I said the *"f"* word to her. She's always the first to start a fight and eager to run to our 'parental units,' as I call them, when she doesn't get her way.

She used to be decent until my mother started coddling her, convincing her she's the most extraordinary girl in the world.

"Blair, get down here." His voice carries up the stairs.

I roll my eyes, standing up from my bed, the pillows haphazardly scattered.

"If it's about Bristol, she can..." I screech before I reach the top of the stairs.

"Stop yammering and come down here." My father's standing at the foot of the creaky staircase, arms crossed in exasperation.

Not the best sign.

He hides his annoyance well – not a trace of anger in his hazel eyes, so I might be in the clear, but he's got a great poker face.

I shrug, taking the stairs one at a time, my socks padding on the wood slats. Because this house was built in the early nineteen hundreds, it heats rapidly upstairs but has an arctic chill downstairs, the fireplace the only source of constant heat in the living room. Cold in the winter, hot in the summer.

My mother's seated on the faded flowered couch with my sister, knitting a new colorful sweater she'll inevitably donate to a shelter or raffle off at a church fundraiser.

Bristol's sitting cross-legged on the floor, answering church mail, her petite frame leaning against Oggie, our three-year-old sheepdog mix. They both weigh about the same, and sometimes I can't tell who's supporting who.

"What is it?" I'm wary, leaning against the doorframe between the kitchen and living room, keeping my distance.

If this is an intervention or I'm being ganged up on, I want an exit strategy.

My father settles in his La-Z-Boy, his reading glasses propped on his forehead, a Bible in his hand. He starts on next week's sermon after church, his mind already thinking of the next lesson he'll drill into the congregation's ears.

"We want to talk to you." He motions for me to come closer, his brows furrowing in frustration.

"Does she need to be here?" I nod in my sister's direction.

"It involves her." My mother looks up from her ball of yarn. Our tabby cat, Isabella, rests on the sofa behind her shoulder, taunting Oggie.

They remind me of Bristol and I, always trying to get the last word in, make the other get caught doing something they shouldn't be.

I sigh, annoyed, as I sink into the other side of the sofa. My mother grabs the remote and mutes the volume, the newscaster droning on about the latest forecast that's inevitably wrong.

Dark and miserable with a chance of flurries, I think.

Same as every day here in winter.

I just want out of this place.

California. That's where it's at.

"We've done some thinking," My father intrudes on my thoughts, placing his reading glasses on his Bible. "We want you to be able to have a college experience and memories that you can look back on fondly."

I'm half-listening until he says this.

My ears perk up.

"We want you to have a vacation," my mother chimes in. "Your father and I know you've worked hard to maintain a 'B' average, which isn't as good as your sister's..." I start to interrupt, but she holds up a knitting needle in protest. "Let me finish."

"We realize you're in college and she's in high school." She bites her lip. "So with that said, we've decided to allow you to go on a trip."

"I get to go to Mexico?" A wave of excitement overcomes me. I close my eyes for a moment, thinking of the white sand beaches I've read about in brochures and the piña coladas women in barely-there bikinis are drinking. My Alpha Delta Pi sisters have assured me everyone can drink in Mexico since eighteen is the legal age.

This is a golden opportunity to meet guys that speak fluent Spanish or fraternity boys from one of the coasts. I imagine a tan surfer dude teaching me how to paddle board or a sharp New Yorker whose parents have a house in the grandiose Hamptons.

My plan comes to a screeching halt when my father says, "Not exactly."

"What do you mean?" I narrow my eyes. "What kind of a vacation?"

"A camping trip," my sister grins, "in our mini-van."

"What the hell?" Cursing, I bang my fist against the chintzy fabric.

"With that attitude, you're not going anywhere, young lady," my mother lambasts at the same time my father says, "Watch your mouth, young lady."

"Fine," I pull my knees up underneath me on the sofa. "Can someone explain to me what the heck's going on?"

"Like always, you just took your sister's bait." My father shoots a dirty look in my direction. "One day you'll learn to listen first and then ask questions."

I know he means it in a good way. My father and I have

a much better relationship than the tenuous one I have with my mother.

She's constantly comparing Bristol and I.

I'm never pretty, skinny, smart...enough. Insert whatever adjective and that's me.

She catalogs my faults like she's writing a book on the 'worst daughter of the year' award. Every time, I'm the designated recipient.

"We've decided you can go on a trip." My mother smiles, but it's half-hearted. One of her fake smirks that are reserved for me. "But there're a couple of conditions."

I start to open my mouth, instantly shutting it, remembering what my father just said. Staring between them, I pause, hesitating. "What are they?"

"*One*, you're taking your sister with you." Mother ticks off on her fingers. "*Two,* you're not going to Mexico – it's too dangerous."

I suck on my lip, trying not to pout. "But Mexico has a drinking age of eighteen," I object.

She ignores me and continues, "*Three*, you'll look out for her and report back to us each night. *Four, no* drinking and absolutely *no* boys."

Looking at my father, I wait to see his response. I know they discussed this together, they don't make any decisions regarding my sister and I without being on the same page.

I cringe, afraid to ask what state we're allowed to visit. My bet's on a border state of Nebraska.

They must be in-tune with my thoughts. "We know you want a beach, want to get away for spring break." My father tilts his head at me. "Bristol suggested Hawaii."

"You let my younger sister decide on *my* college spring break trip?"

"Take it or leave it." My mother shrugs, clanking her knitting needles together.

"We can't go to Mexico but we can go to Hawaii?" I'm pissed. I shoot Bristol a death glare.

"You don't need a passport for Hawaii," my sister retorts. "I don't have one, do you?"

"I was going to get one." I turn to my father. "*She* has to go?" I don't bother hiding my frustration.

"Your sister's the reason you possibly get to go at all." Mother's barbed glance at my father annoys me. I'm always the ungrateful one, the troublemaker.

I look in Bristol's direction, her tongue flicked out at me. I'd flip her off, but my father's focused on my reaction. "She agreed to accompany you," he says.

"Why do I need a chaperone?" I moan. "I'm almost twenty."

"You just turned nineteen, Blair," my father reminds me. "Stop trying to grow up so fast," he admonishes. "We don't feel comfortable with you going out of the country with a bunch of your sorority sisters. Maybe next year. Let' see how this trip goes, deal? We know what happens on spring break. It'd be reckless of us to allow that."

I like to bait my parents, especially when they remind me they '*know*' something. To know would imply they actually had fun at one point in their lives.

I'm unclear when this ever was.

Certainly not after having children.

Pressing my luck, I play dumb. "What happens on spring break?"

"You know, the usual." My mother picks up her knitting needle, avoiding my curious scrutiny.

"No," I shake my head. "I don't. Can you please explain?"

She rolls her eyes at the yarn, knowing exactly what I'm trying to do.

"Drinking. Keg stands. *Intercourse,*" My father pounds his fist on his Bible. "Way too many temptations in Mexico. Hawaii is more tame for you young kids."

"You mean, since college students don't go there for spring break unless they're with their parents?" I infer. "Maybe we should just go to Disney and call it a day."

"You're a spoiled brat." Mother sighs.

"What did you guys do in college?" I wiggle my brows. "Oh yeah, you had me." I kick my leg out, touching my mother's thigh with my foot. My parents got married at nineteen, I was born a year later. "Just think, I'm the same age."

"Oh Blair." She shakes her head. "You're impossible."

"Keep asking questions and we'll revoke our offer," my father says mildly. "Bristol can go with a friend and you can work."

Point taken.

He glances between his notebook and his Bible, the universal signal that the conversation is over. His glasses appear back on the bridge of his nose.

"Okay," I agree. "I'll take Bristol. But I have my own conditions."

My father glances up, a warning look on his face.

"She can't act like a brat when we're there." I pout. "I don't want to have to hold her hand and have her ruin all my fun. I'm going for the beach, not to sit in some kiddie pool and babysit a toddler."

"Ha, that's funny. If I recall, I have more friends than you..."

"and"... she silently mouths, "a boyfriend."

Dating is forbidden in our household until college.

Except now that I'm a sophomore, it's a non-issue because I'm so scared of the opposite sex. I clam up every time I have to talk to a guy about a group project or homework. I'm awkward and out of place, my hands clam up and I sweat bullets.

Real attractive.

The only time I can seem to find my courage is when it's liquid – after I've pounded a few vodka sours.

This year is the first time I've given a hand job and it wasn't enjoyable...for him or me. I'm so far off the grid of being sexually enlightened that I might as well adopt seventeen cats and call them all by spices.

Cinnamon.

Clove.

Ginger.

Maybe even Peppercorn.

I'll become a hoarder – keeping yellowed newspapers as kitty litter and a collection of breakable dolls I bought on the Home Shopping Network.

"Why can't the two of you have sisterly bonding time?" Mother asks. "You two need to learn to get along. You're all each other has in this world."

"Oh, but we have you, Mom," my sister gloats.

She's the biggest suck-up in the world, a 4-H pageant queen, stuck-in-the-mud chorus girl who has everyone fooled about her cherubic persona.

My parents have us all wrong.

"Fine." I agree. "Let's start planning."

And just like that, my Mexico dreams turned into a Hawaiian nightmare.

4

BLAIR

OAHU'S the most populated of the Hawaiian islands, so my parents thought it would inevitably be the safest.

So did we.

Bristol and I stare out the airplane window in awe. The mountains, the volcanoes, the vast difference between the flat topography of Nebraska and the variations in the landscape entrance both of us.

We sit speechless for a moment, captivated. Maybe this won't be so bad.

My parents gave us a couple hotel options, all beachfront. We settled on The Waterfront, a resort that boasted of magnificent views of the Pacific, an infinity pool that touched the ocean, a slight variation in color between the lapis blue water of the pool and the cerulean blue of the ocean. If you stared just right, the two looked like they were one fluid motion, the brilliant blues captured in the sunlight.

Pool chairs were docked in three feet of water. Bristol and I immediately spread out in our bikinis and sunglasses, eyes closed to the impending sunlight.

The first two days we grab a latte from the local coffee shop and a croissant before posting out for our morning suntan. I can tell by Bristol's silence when I order a latte that she's impressed by my knowledge of espresso. Her usual routine is orange juice and buttered cinnamon toast, the same since we were children.

She senses a sophistication in me from my departure to college outside of our mundane, small town. Stuttering, the first time she orders from the barista, repeating my drink but failing to remember the slew of words like "half-pump and skim milk."

Lamely, her face burns as she stops mid-sentence. "I'll just have what she's having."

We take our breakfast and cozy up on the plastic white and navy deck chairs before the afternoon crowd fills the air with conversations in various foreign tongues and loud, squawking kids pounding beach balls at each other.

In the A.M., it's quiet – the only sound the water shifting. Speedboats pound the white foam, and an early-morning surfer straddles a board as they shoot over the waves like a cannon.

By day three of this routine, we're restless – our time was filled with walking the shops and buying useless trinkets. Both sets of grandparents and our parents have been sent souvenirs and postcards with slogans like, "The beach is in our sight," with a picture of the sun setting over the ocean, or, "Aloha, but we're never saying goodbye to Hawaii."

I try to heed my parents' rules, at least in the beginning.

But Bristol's a fish out of water, literally.

And so am I.

Our family vacations amounted to Midwestern lakes and ponds.

Fishing in Minnesota.

Scouring Lake Michigan for bottles and cans to donate to the needy.

Never an actual sunny place where we control our time and leisure. Left alone to our own devices.

"I'm bored." Bristol complains.

"You don't like the water anymore?" I ask, rubbing a red spot the sunscreen missed on my neck.

"I love the water, but we've been staring at the same stretch for days," she protests. Always one to be positive, her crankiness is a surprise.

"Let's go ask the front desk what's available." My father gave me his credit card with explicit instructions, only use if necessary.

The parental units sent us off with cash, but the hotel requires a credit card to hold the room, which I must show in person. My parents made arrangements with the resort and their credit card company, Visa, that I'm an authorized user for a week.

At least my father trusts me.

I still haven't opened my own line of credit for fear I will max it out at the mall.

Plus my parents forbid it.

My mother argued over leaving a teenager who has the responsibility of a flea in charge. I think the other part of her statement was 'sucking them dry' and 'bleeding them out of house and home', an expression I've never understood.

She didn't reference both of us in her statement. Bristol she kept out of any category that would cast her in an unfavorable light.

Me, certainly.

The front desk sends us to the concierge, a word I keep

repeating over and over. It has a nice ring to it, a word that screamed finesse.

A tall man in a burgundy top hat and matching coat with gold ornaments stands at attention.

Bristol stands behind me, suddenly shy.

"Hi sir, we'd like to do an afternoon excursion." I click my nails on the counter. "Any ideas?"

"Certainly." He smiles at us. "Off the island or on?"

"Here. One we can walk to."

"What type of activity?" He looks between us. "Snorkeling? Dolphin watching? Shark tanks?" I turn to eyeball my sister, whose eyes widen at the mention of great whites.

"Sharks," I deadpan.

She elbows me in the ribs.

"Just kidding." I shrug.

The man grins, his fingers flying over a keyboard. "How about surf lessons?"

"Oh my God, yes, yes, yes," Bristol squeaks.

"You want to learn to ride the waves?" I ask.

"Totally. Everyone will be *so* jealous." She puts her hands on her hips. "Can you imagine me on a surfboard?"

"No, not really." I say. "But I'd love to try."

"Two surf lessons for this afternoon?"

We nod.

The man's brass nametag says 'Jeffrey'. "Booking you for today, March twenty-third."

"Sure thing, Jeffrey." I smile at him.

At noon we head outside to a tiki hut to meet our instructor, a hot, college-aged Filipino. He's over six feet tall and sculpted, his broad shoulders carry a surf board easily, and you can tell he feels more at ease in water than on land.

"Hi, Will Loomis." He shakes both of our hands, pumping them up and down. "I'm the surf coach."

Bristol's smitten the second he smiles at her, his even white teeth brightening when he sees her petite frame in a yellow and white striped bikini.

She does have massive all-natural boobs for someone so small, drawing undivided attention to the twins with bronzer and glitter. Her tan has replaced the winter white we Midwesterners have. I pull from my father's side and have dark hair and fair skin, which tends to blister and burn if I'm not careful. Bristol has strawberry blonde hair, freckles, and green eyes, with olive skin that acquires sun in a matter of hours.

When Will hands her a red wetsuit to put on, she's crestfallen, hands on her hips in protest. "I can't surf in my bikini?"

"Of course...but it must go underneath your wet suit." He finds a reason to brush a hand against her back. "This isn't my choice."

She pouts. "I want to get a tan."

He turns to the small group gathered for surf lessons, but his stare's intent on her. "Does anyone know why we wear wetsuits?"

Everyone shakes their head 'no', pulling on the array of colorful wetsuits.

"The fabric's special, it's called neoprene. It basically protects you against the elements, keeps you warm, helps avoid cuts from objects, and keeps you buoyant in the water." Will shifts from one side to the other, playing with a woven bracelet on his wrist. "Does everyone know what buoyancy means?"

A teenage boy with braces and acne provides an answer to his question. I tune out, anxious to try something new, my bare foot tapping the sand impatiently.

Will's voice cuts back into my thoughts as he broaches

another subject, this time on the history of surfing. My sister foams at the mouth as he explains how surfing came to fruition after Lieutenant King James wrote about it in the late 1700s.

Bristol proceeds to ask a million questions as the rest of us grow fidgety. Will glances at his waterproof watch, startled at the time. "Okay, everyone, time to practice popping up and down before we hit the waves." He motions his hand in what we learn is a 'shaka' sign, the universal surfing term for 'hang loose.'

Bristol pretends to be unable to extend her thumb and pinky finger while curling her other three fingers in the palm of her hand. "Oh, I'm hopeless," she shrugs, "I guess I can't be good at everything."

Will snorts, grabbing her hand and placing it in the correct position. "See...you can do it."

Her flirtatious smile and blinking eyelids have him going gaga over her. She better cool it on the eye fucking or he's going to think she has an eye twitch.

I try not to gag, disgusted.

"Can we start?" A younger gentleman wearing plaid boardshorts and a beer gut yells out.

"Abso-frickin-lutely. Let's go through this one more time." We lay our boards in the sand and start running through the motions as Will strides to each surfboard and instructs us through the positions, his sinewy arms articulating every movement.

"Does everyone fall in love with surfing?" says a boy with a Southern accent in the group. I think Mississippi, but it's not like I've left Nebraska much.

"After you catch your first green wave, then yeah." Will waits for everyone to ask what that is, so he pauses as the chorus of "what's that mean?" and "what's a green wave?" flood in.

Both him and the brat are attention whores, a match made in heaven.

"It's an unbroken wave, one of the hardest parts of surfing since so much depends on the type of swell and winds." He squints at the sun. "As soon as you have an ideal wave, you'll keep craving it. You'll chase it, like a dragon."

Grinning at Bristol, she swoons with her hands strategically placed on her hips, elongating her short torso.

I have my feet planted in the sand, ready to get in the water and start putting into practice what we've learned about standing up and balancing on our boards.

After a couple hours with one-on-one instruction from Will as we take turns catching waves, he lets us do our own thing as his videographer films us.

Nicholas is his name. Last name Mercer. I call him Nick and he corrects me in a mild tone, he prefers *Nicholas*.

Another young guy, but polar opposite from Will.

He's blonde and blue-eyed – here from southern Utah. He's been in Hawaii going to school for the past couple years. This is his 'room and board' job, as he explains.

By the time our lessons have finished, Bristol and I both have a date lined up for the night.

I decide it's in our best interest to double date.

For once, she doesn't argue.

Looking back, I wonder if there would've been a different outcome if we had skipped the surfing lesson and sat at the pool all day, listening to music and reading magazines.

Would she still have disappeared?

AS WE GET ready to go out, you'd think we actually like each other, our friendship blossoming again. We turn on my iPod and blare the Pussycat Dolls as I sit on the edge of the bed. Bristol applies my make-up. Her cosmetic bag weighs as much as my suitcase.

"You have such pretty eyes," she compliments, swiping lilac eyeshadow on my lids.

"Me?" I'm surprised. "You got voted best eyes in your class."

"Yeah, but yours are a hazel color with green flecks. They're unique."

"Thanks." I give her a genuine smile.

She highlights my cheekbones with bronzer, the few days of sun giving me a nice glow, albeit still a light one since the sun hates me.

Singing along to the music, spirits high, I decide to take the sisterly bonding full-throttle and pry into her life, which I never do.

Our paths have diverged when they were once a linear path to each other. We used to share the same bed and our innermost secrets, now we're lucky to share a moment that's not a drag-down fight.

"You dating anyone back home?" I get the courage to ask, my voice neutral.

Her face reddens as she focuses on the rosy blush she's about to apply. "We're not allowed to date, remember?"

"Come on," I purse my lips. "No one follows that."

"You did." She smirks. "Oh yeah, not by choice."

"Shut up, brat." I throw a tube of mascara at her.

"Stop moving, you'll ruin my good work." She raises her brows. "And it was hard enough to turn you into a swan."

I stick my tongue out and she giggles. "Okay, okay. I'll dish." She smirks. "He's a senior. He's on the football team."

"What position?" I ask, as if it matters. I can tell she wants to play coy but deep down wants me to care and take an interest.

"Quarterback."

"Matt Eppley?"

"No."

"Brad Samuels' younger brother?"

"Nope." She puts the brush down. "Do you really want to know?"

I shrug. "Sure."

"Do you really care?"

"Only if he can carry the ball for a touchdown." She taps me with the bristled brush on the forehead. "You're such a brat."

"No, you are." I laugh.

"It's P.J. McGrath."

"Oh, I graduated with his sister, Samantha."

"I know. She hates you." She closes the case of blush. "Why does she?"

"Because she was popular and I wasn't?" I guess.

"True." She raises a brow. "Looks like you came out of your shell since college though."

I nod my head in agreement. High school had been rough for me. I wasn't a jock, wasn't a nerd, wasn't gifted at an instrument or academically inclined.

Average.

I was average.

Which is worse than being bad.

You're remembered for winning or excelling.

Hated if you lose or fail.

But being in the middle means you are invisible.

"Do you know where you want to go to college?" I stand up, brushing the flyaway powder particles off the cream duvet cover.

"I might just stay in town." She heads to the mirror to focus on her own make-up application.

"What?" I make eye contact with her in the reflection.

"Yeah, I think P.J. and I are going to get married." I assume she's kidding by her straight face.

"You're seventeen. You're kidding, right?" I remind myself to give her some slack or she'll clam up and stop talking, reverting back to her hormone-driven moods.

She shakes her head, fumbling for an eyeshadow in the cloth make-up bag she carries everywhere. "Mom and Dad got married at nineteen..."

"Why would you do that?"

"I'm not." She leers at me. "I'm going to join a sorority and be just like you." Her eyes roll in the mirror.

"Whatever." I thrust my hands on my hips.

"Don't worry, I plan to leave, if Mom will let me." Her eyes close as she swipes the small brush across the creases of her lids. "I can work at the church in the office and save money until P.J. and I can get our own place."

"Why couldn't you move out?"

"Mom keeps mentioning me staying at home, going to community college and helping with Isaiah." Franklin Community College is thirty miles away, a thirty-minute commute. Flat stretch of road, and it means she can stay put without wasting money on an apartment.

"Isaiah?" I'm stumped.

"The toddler they're adopting."

"They're adopting a child?" I lean against the counter, crossing my arms. "Since when? And why didn't anyone tell me?"

"You don't live at home." She shrugs. "I thought they had. It's not like it's a big secret."

I stomp to the phone, dialing my father's cell number.

He answers on the second ring.

"Hi darling daughter, how are you?" He's in a good mood, jovial.

I'm not.

"You're bringing a child home and didn't bother to tell me?" I pout. "Why do you always act like I'm not part of this family?"

"Your mother did talk to you about it."

"No, she didn't. I'd remember if a child just happened to 'join' our family. That's not a convo you just forget." I know my father longed to have a boy but instead got two girls.

But he had never seemed to mind.

"That's why your mother and I took a trip now – since the little boy's in Iowa, we have to finalize the adoption process when we get back."

I'm quiet, my brain going into overdrive.

"Blair, Isaiah's a child with no stability and in need of a better situation than he has – a child that has no control of his circumstances except a druggie mother who gave birth to him when she was fourteen. It's the right thing to do." He's collected. "Can you understand our position?"

I say nothing.

"Blair..."

"Put Mother on," I demand.

For once, he doesn't chastise my tone.

"Hi Blair..." my mother's voice trails off.

I repeat the same offense.

"You don't live at home." She's nonplussed. "Go back to your vacation and stop trying to ruin ours."

"Bullshit."

"I told your sister we would pay for her tuition if she helped with Isaiah. Daddy has a lot on his plate with running the farm and you're in Omaha doing God knows what, a seven-year plan to nowhere."

"Since when did college become a waste of time?"

"When you decided to attend and use it as an excuse to party." She's agitated. "I'm hanging up now."

The phone goes dead, the annoying static blaring in my ear.

I slam the phone down, disgusted.

Mother never suggested they help with my tuition. I couldn't get scholarship money because I'm an average student. They filled out the financial aid forms, but that's where the buck stopped.

Yet they want to bring another child home to raise.

"Bitch," I mutter.

When my parents talked to us about abstinence, these were the kind of stories they would point out as proof that having sex resulted in dire consequences. My mother forewarned that if I was to ever have a baby as an unwed teen mother, she would not be supporting it.

Yet Isaiah's from a teenage mother. Go figure.

My sister's trying to defuse the situation, hearing my end of the conversation.

"I'm not ruling out a state school. Might be fun to join you. You'll be a junior, so at least I'd have two years with you." Her eyelids are now a luminescent shade of coral, not too bright, the color bringing out the green. 'Unless you're on the ten-year plan." She gives me a sly look.

"We could buy a car and share it," I suggest, watching her line her rims with a charcoal pencil.

"Yeah, maybe. I don't want to rule anything out. I'll apply there and see what happens."

"What about your dream of becoming a fashion designer?" I reach for her prized necklace, the one she's trying to clasp back on her neck, the letter "B".

We both have one, a Christmas present from my father my freshman year of college.

He took pride in gifting them to us, enjoying the pleasant look of surprise on our faces. They're from an actual jewelry store, not the teen one in the mall that sells cheap merchandise that turns your skin green.

The small velvet box was wrapped in white and gold paper and tied with a bow. We were instructed to open them at the same time, my father glowing proudly as he saw our faces light up.

It was the most expensive present we've ever received. My parents say Christmas is about helping those in need – our focus should be on families in the community that need donations.

I connect the delicate gold chain, adjusting it so the 'B' sits in the hollow of her clavicle, the small indent, the pit of her neck. She only takes the necklace off if she's in the water, removing it right before our surf lesson. I didn't bring mine on this trip, leaving it in my jewelry box at the sorority house. My roommate Shay's trustworthy, or at least she's proven to be so far.

Her eyes drift up to mine. "Mom says that's impossible and I should focus on church, meeting a man, getting married, and finding a stable job."

"But is that what *you* want?" I gather her hair behind her, making sure it's not caught in the necklace.

"Look, I know you and Mom fight a lot and don't have the best relationship. She loves you and even though she's harder on you, it's because she knows you need more pushing."

"Why do I need more pushing?" I bite my lip, trying not to show my annoyance.

"Because you're lazy."

"I am not."

"You are. You have potential but don't use it." She turns to face me. "Blair, you can do so much, but you lack the focus."

"What do you know anyway? You're just a baby." I don't want to discuss my shortcomings anymore, so I tease.

"Shut up." She kicks a bare foot out at me, catching me lightly in the knee. She's wearing a white fluffy robe, the ones the hotels provide for your comfort.

"Well, don't throw your dreams away on account of anyone."

A decade later, I wish I could heed my own advice.

BLAIR

SHE CHANGES THE SUBJECT. "Can I borrow your plaid mini-skirt?"

"Okay, Avril." I reference the rocker chick, Avril Lavigne, notorious for her standard uniform of short skirts and skater girl attire. "What're you wearing on top?"

"White tank that I'm gonna twist in a knot at the bottom." She grins. "Gotta make it sexy."

"What should I wear?"

She tilts her head at me, wanting to give advice. Clothing's her specialty.

"What about the baby blue satin halter top and your short shorts, the white ones?" She winks. "I'll put some loose curls in your hair."

"What're you doing with yours?"

"Keeping it straight. Maybe even borrow your clip-in extension so I can have a pink streak in the front." She shrugs. "If that's okay."

I'm shocked. She's never acted interested in having a contrast in her hair between the hot pink and blonde. She's straight-laced and conforms to the standard norms.

"Yeah, sure, no problem." I point to the hair piece. "It just snaps in."

She giggles. "You know Mom will kill me if I dye my hair."

I pull our shared curling iron out of the tote bag in the closet. As I'm plugging it in, she yells across the room. "Have you finally had sex?"

I blush crimson. "Maybe." My hands focus on unwrapping the cord and pressing the ON button.

"That's a no...why not?"

"I haven't met anyone I like." I stare down at the slate-colored plastic, watching the red light flash. When it's ready, it stays a consistent red instead of intermittent blinks.

"You're gorgeous – you have lots of opportunity. I figured you did it with Dillon Penski when you dated him." She's referencing my first real boyfriend my freshman year of college. He was the same age, awkward and gangly, his head filled with calculus numbers and wet dreams.

"Nah, third base." I watch her drop her robe and slide into a pair of black lace thongs, more risqué than anything I own. "Wait, have you had sex with P.J.?"

"Maybe..." Her voice trails off.

"Why go out with Will tonight if you two are together?" I'm confused. My sister is the nun of our family behind Daddy, or so she pretends.

She volunteers every week at the nursing home in town, teaches Sunday school to the Pre-K class, and helps with fundraisers at our high school.

"I want to have some fun." She wiggles her fingers to prove a point. "Will's so hot and we're on vacation. Who knows when we will have this opportunity again? Plus, I need something to compare it to." She acts as if this is the most logical answer and I'm stupid for asking.

Walking over to the closet, I pull her clothing choices for me out.

"Fine, then let's make a pact. Whatever happens tonight stays between us." I step into my white cotton shorts and pale blue halter.

She ties it for me. "Absolutely." She snorts. "Plus, I have a surprise for us."

"Me too." I laugh.

"What's yours?" She's curious, adjusting her boobs in the nude bra she's wearing underneath the white tank top. Pulling the bottom into a knot, she shows off her tan stomach.

"I swiped some airplane bottles of vodka from the maid's cart earlier." I narrow my eyes. "I thought we could mix them with pop."

"Done." She's giddy. "I put some Mountain Dew in the fridge earlier."

"And..."

"And what?" She gives a nervous, high-pitched giggle.

"Seriously?" I nudge her. "What's your surprise, brat? Hello Kitty nail polish?"

"Sure." She's sarcastic. "If that's what you prefer..."

I stare her down, my older sister death glare she's come to know so well.

"Okay, okay. I got us fake IDs." She motions to the sink. "Let's get your hair curled so maybe your toes will curl later on Nick's bed."

"Nicholas." I correct. "He goes by *Nicholas*." We look at each other and laugh.

Sliding onto a stool in front of the mirror, my mouth twists in a grimace.

She's lying.

Has to be.

I thought about getting us fake IDs on my college campus but figured she'd tell Mother and they'd pull me out of state school, forcing me to become a housekeeper or maid.

"You're kidding, right?" It's too good to be true.

She shakes her head. "Will knows a guy. He'll have them for us tonight so we can go to a couple cool beach clubs. I gave him a hundred bucks."

"Where was I when you talked to him about IDs?"

"Trying to poorly surf." She points to her pink LG slide phone. "You spent so much time in the water I got a video."

I squeal in delight. "These last few days might turn out to be like spring break after all." We both start jumping on our king bed, slapping palms, giddy with excitement.

"This is the raddest thing you've ever done, you brat," I squeak.

"I know." She does a flip off the bed and runs to the mini-fridge. "Time for drinks."

I jump off the edge of the mattress, grabbing the hidden bottles from my beach tote. I pull the plastic wrap off the glasses and dump the Mountain Dew and vodka in.

This trip is turning out better than I expected, I think to myself.

We gyrate around, singing '*Loosen up my Buttons*' like the crazy teen girls we are, using a make-up brush and a Mountain Dew bottle as a microphone and shaking our asses as we dance around the seventeenth-floor room, a tornado of clothes and make-up strewn about like the miscreants we are.

Sloshing our glasses in solidarity, we stir the contents to mix them with a straw, taking a sip. I tilt my head back and take an impressive swallow, wanting to look like the more advanced and experienced sister.

I notice her taking small gulps as she tries to mimic me, mumbling under her breath.

"What?" I can't hear over the loud music.

"Thanks for letting me come." Her voice sounds small. "I've had a really good time with you."

I slam the rest of my drink and pour another one. "I've had a good time with you too." I give her a genuine smile, pouring her a second round.

She sits me in front of her on a chair, singing as she turns my straight dark hair into a mass of loose-flowing curls, the opposite of hers tonight. Bristol keeps hers straight, flattening it with a straightener and smoothing spray. I help her clip in the hairpiece, looking like a total rocker chick.

We take a final look at the floor-length mirror behind the bathroom door, whistling in appreciation. Her black and hot pink plaid skirt hits her mid-thigh.

Not long enough to get her out of the house under our parents' watchful eyes.

Enough to get her out of the hotel room under mine.

We smile at each other, exchanging mischievous glances as we wink.

She turns around and hurriedly hugs me.

Surprise registers on my face. It's a rare sign of affection between the two of us and because of this, noteworthy.

Etched in my brain.

The last time I remember hugging my sister.

WILL Loomis and Nicholas Mercer arrive on the seventeenth floor a few minutes later, rapping on the door with their knuckles.

Bristol gives herself a quick once over and nods at me. "Let's do this."

They're both dressed in what I would expect of Hawaiian locals, casual button-down shirts and khaki shorts, flip-flops, and casual jewelry. Will has his hemp bracelet, Nicholas a leather necklace with a polished shark tooth.

Both are attractive in their own ways – Will with his large chestnut-shaped eyes, thick eyebrows, and dark hair that curls wildly after he's in the water. His face is attractive, but a too large nose keeps him from being model perfection.

Nicholas on the other hand is average height, slightly taller than me, with a lean torso and limbs. He has fair skin and freckles in the sun, and eyelashes that girls try every mascara and serum to attain. I notice small scars trailing down his legs, unnoticeable at first glance unless you take a second look. His smile is disarming, perfect teeth except for the one crooked one, his lips plump and full.

"We come bearing gifts," Will yells as he walks in, a cup in hand, the lax environment perfect for public drinking and intoxication.

"Our new IDs?" Bristol's excitement is palpable. I want to bottle it up and contain it, except for an uneasy feeling twisting in my gut. I don't know why the turmoil, the boys seem harmless and aren't much older than we are. Will's twenty-two, Nicholas is twenty-one.

"You're at least eighteen, right?" Will peers at Bristol, lowering his eyes to her chest. It makes me uncomfortable the way he ogles her.

"Yes." She lies. I don't correct her, the small fabrication of her age not a big deal. In some states it's statutory rape since she's under eighteen, but we're just going to hang with them tonight.

"Then we can party." He brushes a thumb over her cheek as she smiles warmly at him.

"We brought you leis." Nicholas laughs. "Thought we could lei you right here, right now."

Bristol thinks this is hilarious, a throaty laugh escaping her lips.

I think it's corny.

Forcing a smile, a white and magenta flowered lei goes over my neck, courtesy of Nicholas, as he settles my curls around it in a halo. "Perfect." He steps back to admire his work.

"What kind of flowers?" I ask, fingering a petal delicately.

"Plumeria." He hands the other one to Will. "Put it on your princess."

Will does the same thing with her lei. Bristol glances

down, careful to make sure her necklace doesn't get twisted up in the adornment.

Nicholas notices the empty vodka bottles on the sink.

"You guys get a head start without us?"

I motion at his red solo cup. "Seems like you got further."

"That we did." He gives me a big smile. I notice one crooked canine that's endearing to me.

"Plus we're out of alcohol." Bristol points at the airplane bottles. "Not much damage we could do with that."

"Where are your cups? We'll refill them." Nicholas elbows Will. "You still got that bottle in your backpack?"

Will pulls off a khaki-colored knapsack with a drawstring that's on his back. "Yep, I got you covered." He loosens the top and pulls the contents out. "I've got vodka, pineapple juice, and..."

He points at Nicholas. "Drumroll please..."

Nicholas makes a staccato noise and bops his fingers on the nightstand. "Weed."

With a flourish, Will pulls out a blunt.

"And ladies and gentlemen..."

He opens his faded brown leather wallet. Two IDs with the state of Hawaii emblazoned across the top, a rainbow splashed in the background, are housed in the clear front plastic.

"Here, you are now...Haley Pritchett and Leslie Billings."

"How did you come up with those names?" Bristol eyes the plastic.

"They were what my friend had. Local girls." Will shrugs. "You each look kind of like one."

I don't argue, but I can't see any likeness between Haley Pritchett and myself besides our dark hair. Scrutinizing it closely, I see my birthdate is now October thir-teenth, 1977, which would make me twenty-one. According to these IDs, my younger sister is now a year older than me.

"You guys need to memorize the birth date and year. Make sure you can recite it if a bartender or bouncer asks." He unscrews the bottle. "I'm going to give you guys a refill. You both like pineapple?"

We nod in unison. Will heads over to the discarded cups on the bathroom counter and starts pouring.

Bristol turns to me. "Do you think I look enough like Leslie?"

I shrug. "Not really, minus the blonde hair," I examine her ID, "and it's platinum."

"Don't worry about it." Nicholas reassures us. "They don't look at 'em that close. We just need them for insur-ance in case you're ID'd. We don't want to get thrown out or arrested."

Memorizing the date on the license, I put into my memory bank Haley's address and note that she's an organ donor. Bristol and I take turns quizzing each other on our new birthdays.

Will brings our cups over to us. "Hang ten, ladies." He throws his hand up in the shaka sign. "Drink up, tonight's gonna be a night to remember."

A warning bell goes off in my head but I ignore it, focusing on swishing the contents of the cup together and taking a swig, the contents way too strong, the vodka drowning out any taste of fruit juice.

Bristol makes a face, mimicking my expression.

She gulps it down, quickly shooting it back, liquid drip-ping down her chin.

After we finish our drinks, the boys suggest we grab

some food. A pizza joint's within walking distance, like most places on Waikiki Beach.

The four of us scoot into a booth, staggering, our tongues wagging and our heads clouded with liquor.

We chat incessantly, Nicholas and I on one side, elbows touching as we sit next to each other. Will's more upfront about his feelings for Bristol, his hand resting on her bare knee. I want to scream at him to remove his fingers, she's only seventeen, but she seems oblivious. There's no indication of discomfort on her part. If anything, her body language betrays her – she's so close to him she's practically in his lap.

"Let us order the drinks here," Will says. "They really give the stare down at IDs since it's a restaurant."

"Won't four drinks be suspicious?" Bristol asks.

Nicholas laughs. "Nah, we'll order two drinks and share them and then another two."

"Oh," Bristol's meek. "Gotcha." I can tell she knows she asked a dumb question, so I give her a reassuring smile.

"What're we doing tonight?" I change the subject from booze to our night plans.

"I thought we could start at a bar close by and then end on the beach. It has live music and we can sit outside, perfect weather."

Will grabs Bristol's hand, lacing his fingers in hers. "Does that sound okay?"

She nuzzles his neck. "It sounds perfect."

When the waiter comes back, Will and Nicholas order double greyhounds.

"What's a greyhound?" Bristol runs her hand through Will's dark hair, tugging his earlobe.

"Vodka and grapefruit. But we doubled up." Will winks. "Everyone wins with more vodka."

I hope Nicholas doesn't get any ideas with me. I don't even know the guy.

Bristol and Will start talking amongst themselves, and I take it as my cue to turn to Nicholas and ask questions. "So you're in school here but moved from Utah?" I ask. "What's your major?"

"I'm gonna be a dentist like my dad," he explains. He moved from Utah four years ago to pursue dental school. It's his father's profession and he wants, or more specifically, is expected, to follow suit.

"I'd rather be a photographer." He's glum. "I love taking pictures."

"Is that why you're a videographer on the side?" I take a sip of the drink he pushes towards me.

"Yeah, I photograph a lot of beach weddings since there's such a demand for them. I haven't dropped out of school, but it's all I can do to keep going in a field I have no interest in."

He shrugs. "My dad said he wouldn't pay my student loans if I dropped out, so I guess I'll keep going. I just hate teeth."

"Hard to imagine for a dentist," I tease.

"I know." He hunches forward.

"It sucks. I can totally relate," I offer. "My parents are the same – mine hold the purse strings and don't support my passions in life. Parents can be such a drag."

He gives me a small smile. "I know. It's such a drag sometimes."

"Do they expect you to move back to Utah after school?"

"We haven't discussed that." He frowns. "I have no intention of moving back but if I can find a job here, I don't see a reason why they would assume that."

"Does your dad expect you to take over his practice?"

"Potentially, but my brother's two years older and will be graduating this year from dental school at BYU. He's slated to join my dad."

"Room for three?"

He shrugs. "God, I hope not. I want to live in Hawaii, surf, take pictures, and capture moments. I just have to be proactive and find a job here before it's expected of me to join them in practice."

I smile at him, noting how blue his eyes get when he talks about what he's passionate about – surfing and photography.

"What about you?" His eyes search mine, locking me down with his gaze until the waiter comes back with the next round. Taking a long sip, he waits until their back is turned before pushing the glass into my hand.

"What do you want to know?"

"What's your story?" He's curious.

"Sophomore year of college in Nebraska. Alpha Delta Pi sorority." I twist the salt shaker on the table. "Uh, I grew up in a small town, my parents are still there."

I'm rambling on about my family when he interrupts. "I don't mean to be rude," he motions, "but may I?"

Shaking my head, I close my eyes, expecting to feel his lips on mine.

I hold my breath, waiting, as he leans in close.

But I feel nothing except raw disappointment when I don't feel him connect with my face.

Until his finger touches my jaw and gently pushes a strand of hair off my face. "Sorry, that piece of hair is all I can focus on, it keeps getting in the way of your beautiful eyes."

It's the first time I feel such strong chemistry with someone, the desire and attraction building as his contact with my skin makes me tingle.

My unsettled feeling melts, my eyes are drawn to him, I twist his leather necklace, pulling him close, taking initiative I didn't know I had.

8

BLAIR

THE ALCOHOL HITS me full force, my feet uneven on the sand as we hit Will's suggestion for a good time, a beachside bar called *The Ocean Club*.

My face flushes crimson, yet my body trembles in a cold sweat. Grabbing the wooden railing, I drag myself up the ramp, the ocean calm against the lucid stars.

The four of us wait in a short line, and a bouncer with tattooed sleeves and ear gauges stares indifferently at us.

"Will." He nods.

"Sup." Pushing Bristol and I forward, he asks for our IDs, barely reading the small print on the license. Securing an orange band around my wrist that establishes I'm of legal drinking age, I breathe a sigh of relief.

That was easy.

Almost too easy.

The open-air bar is decorated like the bottom of a coral reef. An aquarium that's an infinity pool for fish makes up the bottom half of the bar top, winding around, practically invisible to the naked eye. It seems like the sea life will swim directly out to you, a glass partition the only separation between marine biology and natural selection. The neon spotlight throws a beam against the bright glow of the tank.

Despite the chill vibe of the atmosphere, a headache pounds at the back of my head, throbbing in turn to the music.

Bristol is embarrassed, whispering in my ear that she has to puke, so I pull her into the bathroom, holding her hair as she spews the contents of dinner in the cold porcelain, her tan knees shaking as she kneels on the floor.

"I feel awful." She moans, head leaning against my arm.

"Do we need to go home?" I'm concerned, standing over her in the cramped bathroom stall. I read the various comments on the bathroom walls, phone numbers for a good time, sexually explicit sayings, and nasty messages in black permanent marker meant for exes that did them wrong.

"No, I don't want to ruin your night," she murmurs.

"It's not a problem." I hand her some toilet paper to wipe her mouth. "I can always walk you back to the room."

"And leave me?"

"I'm feeling Nicholas." I grin. "I wanna see what happens."

"Are you going to sleep with him?" She's curious.

I shrug. "I don't know, but I definitely want to make out."

"I don't want to be at the hotel alone," she whines. "Will you stay with me?"

Remembering my parents, I did say I would look after her.

On the other hand, I'm finally feeling like a normal college student that can flirt and make eye contact with someone of the opposite sex. It might even lead somewhere. I've been yearning to get my "V" card out of the way. My sorority sisters are appalled that I'm still a virgin. They like to point out that guys don't like sleeping with newbies because they assume they'll get clingy and latch on.

"I'm not ready to go. Can you suck it up for another hour?" I brush her forehead with my hand. "Or better yet, can Will take you back to the room?"

"I don't want him to see me sick." She's appalled at my suggestion.

"Why? He digs you."

"Would you want Nicholas or any random guy seeing you throw up?" She shoves me away from her, annoyed.

Point taken. I can't even handle my father seeing me puke, let alone a stranger.

"Let's get you some aspirin and a wet cloth and see how you feel." Mother used to give us a warm washcloth to soothe our temples when we were sick. I soak a couple of paper towels under the faucet and gently pat my sister's face.

Her eyes look bleary and dilated under the harsh lighting.

Fishing in my purse for a bottle of medicine, I hand her a couple pills and watch as my cell phone screen flashes. It's our father.

"Oh shit." I say.

"What?"

"Daddy's calling."

"Don't answer," she shrieks. "He'll know we're drunk."

"But I promised him I would answer when he called."

"If you answer the phone, we'll be busted and he'll fly us home immediately and we'll never go anywhere again," she pleads. "Let it go to voicemail. Call him tomorrow, tell him the ringer was off or we were sleeping."

It's past 11 P.M. Almost believable.

"Can you hang for a bit more?"

She takes a deep breath, gripping the sink. "Hand me my lip gloss."

"That's my baby brat," I say, yanking out her pink sparkly tube. She swipes some across her lips, dabbing at it with a finger.

"Okay, let's go."

"You okay?"

"I'm fine." She gives me a weak smile.

I wish I could say I cared at this point about how she felt, that I noticed her eyes becoming more dilated, but I didn't, because I was too self-involved with Nicholas.

We walk back out to the bar, arm in arm, our steps awkward and forced.

"You guys okay?" Will asks, his eyebrows raised at our drunken stumbling.

"Yep." I help Bristol slide onto the stool next to Will, taking my place next to Nicholas on the opposite side.

"Good, because we got the next round." Nicholas pushes a blue drink over to me, and Will's thrusting the other at Bristol.

"These the girls?" The bartender, a man in his late twenties or early thirties, asks. He's wearing a gold wedding ring and a simple gold chain with a cross around his neck, nestled in the copious amount of chest hair he has.

I freeze for a moment, deer in the headlights.

Oh shit, are we in trouble?

Nicholas notices my hesitation. "David just wants to check your ID."

"What about our wrist bands?" I'm confused.

"I just have to double check." David glances at the loud cackling coming from a table behind us.

"Oh, sure." I try to act subtle. I grab my wallet out of my purse, pushing it in his hand, careful to act smooth.

Bristol does the same, albeit with a greenish-looking face.

He glances at the ID, a moment too long, then back up at me, then down. We lock eyes for a moment that stretches on forever.

Finally, he hands it back. "Here you go, Haley."

My hands shake as I slide it back in my purse.

"By the way, where'd you get your middle name, *Elisabetta*?" He starts pouring whiskey in a glass for another customer. "I haven't seen that name in forever. It's my grandma's and very old-fashioned." He's not unkind when he says it, more curious.

A test.

To see if I know who I say I am.

People that use other people's IDs probably forget to memorize the middle name.

"My mother hated the traditional spelling of Elizabeth. It was assumed I'd have that as my middle name, you know, since it's my father's mom's first name. She decided to switch it up a bit and keep everyone happy." The lie slips out easily.

"Makes sense." He sticks a lime in another cup. "Let me know if that drink isn't up to par." He motions to the fruity drink with maraschino cherries and an orange slice sitting in front of Will.

"Sure." I nod. He walks around the side of the bar, greeting another patron.

"What is it?" I eye the slightly foggy blue concoction.

"It's your favorite color." Nicholas says. "Isn't that enough?"

"Oh, this is one of those blue Curacao drinks, isn't it?"

"Better." Will smiles. "It's a Hawaiian specialty drink called Blue Balls."

"And what does that mean?" I give Nicholas a slight grin.

"It means that you're giving me blue balls," he murmurs in my ear.

I laugh, the sound more like a high-pitched hyena.

"It's a mixture of pineapple, orange juice, guava, and yes, Blue Curacao, rum, and vodka." He ticks the ingredients off on his hand. He could've been giving me a recipe for disaster at this point, I was so far gone.

My hand rubs his arm, moving up and down his skinny biceps. "Wow, you've got amazing arms," I compliment him.

"Thanks." He gives me a peck on the cheek. "You aren't half bad yourself."

"Oh really?" I bite my lip. "What's your favorite part?"

"Besides your personality?" He brushes a hand over my fingertips. "You have a killer smile. And those legs." He whistles in appreciation. "Damn, girl."

I stare at him, wanting him to push his lips on mine and kiss me, craving his tongue in my mouth.

Our gazes are locked until I see his eyes dart to Will.

He nods at him and gives a wink.

"What was that for?"

"Nothing, babe." He gives my hand a tug. "Aren't you going to drink up?"

Bristol mumbles something from a few stools over, her speech slurred. I can't make out what she's saying. Nicholas stares intently at me, gauging my reaction as I take a large swallow. The liquid doesn't taste good. It burns, not what I expect for a Hawaiian specialty.

"It's delicious, huh?" He grins at me, the one crooked

tooth snagging his lower lip. Once an endearing quality, now it reminds me of a rabid wolf.

I don't say anything, the bitterness a surprise.

"Keep drinking." He elbows me a little too hard in the ribs.

"You want a sip?" I ask, pushing it towards him.

"Nope, it's all you, babe." He shoves it back towards me.

Holding my head back, I swig the whole damn drink down my throat, gagging. The drink tastes off, something muddled about it that has nothing to do with the fruit.

Bristol is sampling hers, her face rancid.

"Drink taste weird to you?" I yell across to Bristol. She can't hear me over the din and the loud music blaring.

Mase comes on and the lyrics to "Been Around the World" bellow from the speakers. Puff Daddy and the Notorious B.I.G start rapping, the DJ spinning the track, going directly into "Getting Jiggy Wit it" by Will Smith.

"Oh my gosh, I love this song." Bristol stumbles off her bar stool. "Come on Will, let's dance." She pulls him out to the dance floor, a fall a sure thing had he not been holding her tight around the waist.

"You wanna get down?" Nicholas raises his eyebrows.

It's my moment to be bold, to ask for a kiss or just go in for one.

I move my face closer to his, closing my eyes like I read in magazines is the way to go.

Instead of feeling his wet lips, he pulls back, surprised.

"I'm sorry," I offer. It's a relief I'm tipsy because I'd be running out of here, sprinting, if I were sober and rejected in public. I see a girl at the bar staring at me from across the room with a strange look in her eyes. She must feel sorry for me.

Nicholas asks for a glass of water from another

bartender, ignoring my apology. "Nothing to be sorry about." He shrugs.

"Did I do something wrong?" I ask.

"No, but you're tipsy and so am I."

"So we can't kiss?" I pout.

"No, baby, we can kiss, we can do a lot of things. But not here. This isn't the time nor place," he makes eye contact with the girl, narrowing his eyes, "I know people here."

I go silent.

"Do you know her?" A feeling of jealously rises to the surface. Maybe this isn't a good idea.

He stands, ignoring my question, shooting her a dirty look.

I feel flushed and out of sorts. My eyes drift to the dance floor where Bristol holds on to Will for dear life.

"You wanna get out of here?" Nicholas rubs a hand on my nape, his touch sending spine-shivering tingles down my back.

Gulping the water down, I grab his hand for help off the stool.

I nod, unable to form words. I'm starting to feel woozy, like I could lay down and sleep for a million years.

"Yeah, let me go tell them." I say. "Where we going?"

"We can go to the hotel." He pushes me down as I try to stand. "No, no, you stay put. I'll go tell them. You're trashed."

I don't argue, mainly because I'm dizzy and I'm scared the floor will disappear under my feet. He stands up, all five feet eight inches, striding over to the dance floor to whisper in Will's ear.

Both give me a once-over.

Bristol squints, waving furiously at me, the pink extension in her hair whipping around as Will spins her on the floor.

In this moment, she looks content.

And as Nicholas leads my wobbling ass out of the bar, I see the clock on the wall of the bar.

1:17 A.M.

He holds my hand in his, leading me down the wooden ramp, dragging me across the sand. He's swaggering as he grips the iron rail. "Ouch," I groan as I trip on my wedges and fall face first in the sand. I wanted added height but didn't think of traipsing through the sand drunk.

He cackles, amused by my spill.

I don't say a word, brushing sand off my cheek.

"You okay, babe?" He kneels beside me, a lock of blond hair falling over his eye. I hold a hand to my forehead, the earlier headache feeling like a massive torpedo has invaded my brain, bombing it every couple of seconds.

I want to say no, but I feel paralyzed, my limbs made of rubber.

"Why don't you take those off?" He points to my sandals. "It'll be quicker and your feet will stop hurting." Helping me unbuckle them, he scoops them up under his arm.

"Are you sure the brat's okay?" I slur.

"Who?"

"My sis." I giggle, unmoving.

"Totally. They know where the hotel is and it's super close. They'll come back when they're done shaking their asses." He brushes my shoulder, "but in the meantime..."

This starts to seem like a terrible idea, but I can't form a coherent sentence.

He pulls me up, gripping my fingers tight in his. I want

to tell him he's hurting me, his grip surprisingly strong, but I feel like I'm standing outside of myself.

An out-of-body experience. As if I'm watching movie clips where I'm the main attraction.

Paranoia sets in. I stare glassy-eyed at the span of beach.

It all looks the same.

"Are you okay?"

I shake my head no.

Or at least it feels like I do.

"Such a lightweight." He chuckles, tickling my side.

"I guess." I sway, the sky tilts, the stars become dots as I blink, confused.

These are the last words I utter before I lose consciousness.

9

BRISTOL

AFTER I CAN'T BALANCE any longer, teetering on my sister's four-inch stilettos, I realize why my mom forbids me from wearing these. Not only are they uncomfortable, like walking on stilts, but add in alcohol, and it's a full-on hazard.

My mom doesn't know I drink or that I've smoked cigarettes, coughing up a lung as I inhaled the putrid air. But if she knew, she'd be relieved I'm not a fan.

I've tried marijuana a couple times, but I hate feeling sleepy when I'm trying to party.

I feel like a fraud, the straight As and the pedestal that I've been propped up on since a young age when my mom paraded me around town, using words like 'angelic' and 'pure'. Blair has it rough, her outward rebellion has dug lines in the sand that keep getting deeper with our parents.

A sinkhole.

Piercing her nose in tenth grade.

Check.

They made her take it out, grounding her for a month.

Making out with Jason Diller in a church pew on Ash Wednesday.

Check.

Extra chores for two weeks.

Getting a tattoo inked on her lower back in the shape of a butterfly on her eighteenth birthday.

Check.

When I asked her why a butterfly, she said she needed wings and courage to get the fuck out of our small town.

They haven't found out about that yet, and I'm not telling for that one.

She's taught me a lot with the two-year head start she has on me – exactly what *not* to do.

How not to act.

If you at least pretend like you're decent and whole-some, Mom leaves you alone.

The dance floor I'm exiting is dark and hazy, and smoke from the DJ's fog machine settles over us.

I can't believe my luck.

A tall, dark-haired, twenty-two-year old is leading me to the cordoned-off area where older people are gyrating and moving their hips seductively to the rap music that's mixed in with oldies.

EVERYONE IS 'OLDER' to me, since I'm seventeen.

And tonight I'm pretending to be another girl, a woman, a twenty-two-year-old woman.

Will's eyes catch mine as he pulls me close to him, a relief since I practically topple into his shoulder.

How embarrassing would it be if I fell...

MY LIMBS FEEL like rubber and I'm flushed. My cheeks are scorching as I wipe a hand across my damp forehead.

This started out feeling like one of the best nights of my life. Vacation, alcohol, a hot guy that acts like I'm the only girl in the room. And Blair, usually a total bitch, is being normal and nice.

"You wanna get out of here?" Will whispers in my ear.

I GIGGLE, his breath tickling my lobe.

Squeezing his hand in response, I give him my answer.

I'm at a loss for words.

The drinks are refilled as soon as I finish one. The last glass, some blue syrupy liquid that tastes funny, knocks me out. I want to spit it back in the cup, but I don't want to look like a total amateur.

My friends and I have stolen cheap vodka and beer from their parents. Not mine, of course. They have a strict no-drinking policy. It's hard to imagine them as anything but middle-age frumps. I've only tried alcohol a few times, and maybe this is some special Hawaiian vodka that has a different flavor. It's definitely not the cheap beer my boyfriend and the football team guzzle at a keg stand.

I follow Blair's lead since she swallows it down without complaint. She'll kill me if I draw negative attention to us or the fact we have someone else's IDs. I tilt my head back, gulping it, wrinkling my nose as Will smiles approvingly at me.

His seal of approval is what I want right now.

The room starts to slant.

People now look like blurred versions of themselves, like a drawing where someone's swept an eraser over the face but the image doesn't quite disappear. There's still a trace, but smudged.

I keep blinking, trying to adjust my eyes to the flashing lights and my ears to the noise level. My feet are killing me, my head pounds to the beat, and even though I threw up earlier, I feel groggy and tired.

Maybe I'm getting the flu.

That would be just my luck.

Sick in Hawaii. Ugh.

Will mumbles something in my ear, but I can't make out the words.

Instead, I smile, a tight line that never reaches the corners of my lips. My face feels frozen in place.

I stagger as I feel like people at the bar are judging me, staring from their stools. Our earlier bartender, David, glares at me. Some dark-haired skank shoots me daggers.

Or maybe it's my imagination.

Will's leading me out of the smoke and into the fresh air, thank goodness, since I'm losing my sense of equilibrium.

I tug on his hand to make him pause as soon as we hit the fresh salty air outside. "Where're we going?" I manage to screech, a foreign sound. My voice sounds high-pitched and shrill.

"My place." He brushes a strand of blonde hair off my face. I straightened it, but the humidity is making it damp and wavy.

"Um...do you mind if we stop by my room first?"

"Your sis and Nicholas are there."

"Yeah, I know." I don't want to tell him I want to see Blair, that the familiarity of her is what I need when I'm ill.

He'll think I'm weird.

Or maybe he thinks I'm going to ditch him by the way his

face twists into a frown.

Weird how someone can look so attractive until you see them upset. One change of their features and they turn ugly.

Hurriedly, I say, "I just want to grab my suit. I thought we could hot tub first before taking it to your place." I rub his arm, trying to placate his ego.

"Better." He sticks his tongue down my mouth. P.J. kisses soft and sweet, Will's advances are heated and sloppy. "Let's just skinny dip in the ocean." He nudges me, hard enough I almost lose my balance on the damn stilettos.

I'm freaking out inside, my heart thumping. I silently scream in my head, *"Just get me back to the hotel room."*

My stomach lurches as if I'm sea sick on a boat. I grab onto the iron railing that leads to the beach, one foot in front of the other.

My eyes want to close in protest. I've gone from wanting to go home with him to wanting the plush king-size bed at the hotel, my sister's dark hair on the pillow next to me.

He pulls his cell phone out to check his messages, humming as he concentrates on the bright screen. I can't hold my own weight up and I stagger, falling into a heavy pole that holds an awning.

My forehead strikes the metal.

Sinking to my knees, the world suddenly turns upside down.

He drops his phone when I crash, a cuss word on his tongue.

Will speaks, his voice jumbled. It might as well be carried away by the waves.

I CAN'T HEAR, so I nod.

Water soaks his phone as a wave laps it, carrying it out to the ocean. "Shit," he yells, trying to reach for it. He's not sober, his navy flip-flops catch on a stick or some object protruding out of the sand.

"Dammit." He kicks the damp ground. I can't focus, even when he appears in front of me. My eyes drift up as I rest my palms in the sand, unblinking.

"You wanna suck my dick out here, don't you?" he jokes, starting to unzip his pants. "Now that my phone's gone 'cause of you?"

I swallow, tears burning my eyes, my surroundings spinning like a violent tornado. I try to stare fixedly at my hands in front of me, concentrating on the pink nail polish, but it's vague.

Reaching a hand out, I halfheartedly swat him away.

He steps back.

"Must. Get. Home," I croak.

"Fine." His tone drips acid. "I should've known you just wanted to tease me. You're a *fucking* tease."

"I'm seventeen." I spit out.

"You said eighteen."

"I lied."

"Who cares?" He shrugs. "Your ID says twenty-two."

"Let's just get back to the room and we can use the pull-out couch." Unsettled, I want to stand and sprint back to the hotel without him, but I'm afraid I won't find my way back.

Especially to the seventeenth floor.

"What about them?" He pats his pocket in disgust.

I glare at him in the dark.

"Come on." He jerks me to my feet and I heave. Nothing but bile comes out.

The quick motion of standing to regain my balance has consequences – a mallet might as well be smacking me repeatedly. The headache makes me pinch my arm to detract from the throbbing.

We scramble back to the hotel, the beach parallel to The Waterfront. A sidewalk leads straight to the lobby. I mistakenly see my sister, but when I blink, she's disappeared.

I've never felt so exhausted in my life.

Maybe it's not the flu, maybe it's mono.

Wait, isn't mono the kissing disease?

How will I explain contracting that to my parents?

I'm not allowed to date.

P.J... is he making out with another cheerleader?

The thought slips away as suddenly as it appears.

"Seventeenth floor, right?" Will pulls me into the elevator, pressing the button to go up. He hugs me to his broad chest, a potent mix of sweat and cologne. His shirt's sticky, and my cheek is damp from resting my face there.

I nod into his chest, closing my eyes as we drift upwards.

I'm relieved we're the only two in here until he reaches a hand up my mini-skirt to cup my ass. "Don't you dare sleep yet." He tugs on my hair. "Wake up. We have a long night ahead of us."

My eyes flutter, the motion of the elevator yanking me into another dizzy spell. The movement of the floors slipping away makes my stomach bounce up and down, a rubber ball being slapped against my belly.

When the metal doors clank open, I shuffle out. The

arrows acting as directional signs confuse me, the numbers reading backwards.

"What room?" Will's voice is obnoxious.

I don't answer, covering my ears.

"Bristol, which way?"

My hands check my waist for the plastic card I stuck in the hidden pocket inside of my skirt. What did I do with the room key?

"Uh..." I squint. "Left. Seventeen ninety-eight." I'm lucky it's the same as the current year or I wouldn't remember.

Will grabs my hand and half pulls, half jerks me in the right direction.

There's a problem.

My pocket's empty.

"Are you playing hard to get?" He puts his hands on the band of my mini-skirt, caressing my stomach. "You need me to feel around and frisk you?"

"Stop," I murmur.

He ignores me, or maybe he doesn't hear me.

I start pounding on the door.

Will chirps, "Stop it, Bristol. You're gonna wake the whole damn floor up. Chill. I've got the room key." He pulls it out of his pocket, smug.

My knuckle keeps rapping the door, and his face twists in anger. He grabs my hair and twists it in his hand, my clip-on hot pink extension falling out in his palm. A look of horror crosses his face – probably the thought he pulled real hair out.

Something about this, his reaction, causes me to giggle.

I want to cuss at him, but it's too much work. How did he get a key? I shrug to myself – sleep is more important.

Slipping away...I'm slipping away.

He pushes the door open, slamming it shut behind me.

The only light comes from the blinds, which he yanks closed, shutting out the moonlight and water. He heads to the bed, and I don't follow.

Sliding my hands up and down the closed door, unable to feel the lock, I lean into the wood, my body giving in to slumber, as I fall slowly, like a slow-motion domino.

I curl up on the floor. His hands are rough as he shakes me.

"Leave me alone."

"Bristol." A hard tug as he tries to drag me towards the bed.

"Ughhhhh..." I moan. "Sleep..."

"Bristol." He grunts.

My hands move to my ears, partially to drown out his voice, partly because my head's spiraling out of control, like a train wreck that's about to crash, forcing me headfirst into a wall.

I shut my eyes, feeling his hands on me, all over my skin, running up my thigh and down my back. A hand cups my breast.

Must sleep.

I feel a kick.

A door slams.

I'm drifting off, slumped on the beige carpet.

Another crash.

I can feel myself being carried, no longer stationary on the floor.

"Put me down," I mumble.

Silence.

"It'll all be okay, little girl," a voice echoes.

——

10

BLAIR

AS I KEEP an eye trained over my shoulder for Peter Riggs, I ignore the curious glances of hotel guests and staff, frantically making my way to the front desk in the lobby.

My feet are cold against the diamond-pattern tile floor, and my wet clothes feel stifling. I want to rip them off and scream.

"Are you okay, miss?" The Asian woman behind the counter peers at me, examining my damp hair and clothing, and I assume my unkempt face.

Nodding, I take a deep breath. "I need my room key."

"You're a guest?"

"Yes."

"Sure thing, can I see your ID, please?"

I reach a hand in my pocket, checking both the back and front ones.

All I have is one that doesn't belong to me.

I sigh. "I lost it."

"Do you know where it is?"

"No."

"What's the last name on the reservation?"

"Bellamy." I sigh. "It's under my father's name. Bruce. Bruce B-e-l-l-a-m-y."

"Room?"

"Seventeen ninety-something."

She's suspicious. "You don't know the room number?"

I stand frozen, staring at her.

"Ma'am, as much as I want to get you a copy of your key, I need to verify it's yours."

"Can you just call the room then?" I lean my elbows on the marble counter. "My sister's up there."

She grabs the telephone off the hook and punches in a few numbers.

Her eyes scan the lobby, looking at anything but me.

After a couple seconds, she shrugs. "No one's answering."

"Try again."

Her eyes dart to the person standing behind me in line.

I soften my voice. "Can you please try again? My sister's probably still in bed. She's a heavy sleeper."

She hits a re-dial button and drums her fingers on the counter, impatient.

"No one's there." She sets the phone back in the cradle.

"I need to get my stuff." I explain. "Check on her."

"I can't just give you a key without any type of confirmation."

"My purse got stolen."

"When?"

"Last night or this morning."

"Do you have another credit card on you?" She gives me a plastic smile. "If the name matches the room reservation, that'll work?"

I shake my head, negative.

"Look," I exhale. "Can you or a bellman walk me up to the room?"

She looks annoyed, and the man behind me in line complains about my dilemma. "I can't just leave the desk."

"Never mind," I murmur. Turning on my heel, I head to the elevators, punching the 'up' arrow. A couple of Chinese tourists, cameras hanging from their necks, stare at me and talk animatedly amongst themselves, one going far enough to point at me, another snapping a picture.

Catching my reflection in the mirrored wall, I see why.

My lips are tinged blue from the drinks last night, my tongue's the same Smurf shade. A mixture of sand and mud are stuck to my cheek, as if someone swiped it across the left one in a circular motion. My eyeliner, expertly applied last night, is now shadowed underneath my eyes and smeared down the other side.

I'm a hot mess.

My face crimson, I hold my head high as the doors clank open, my bare feet stepping into the elevator.

No one follows.

IRRITATED, I wait for them to enter after me, but they pause.

My hand motions to the closing doors, but they shake their heads.

FINE, I think to myself, jabbing the button in frustration.

Snapping my fingers, I remember the room number – seventeen ninety-eight.

Crossing my arms, I tap my foot, antsy, as the elevator lands on my level.

Hanging a left, I head to our room.

My hand lifts to knock on the door, but something's off.

A PIECE OF HAIR, *my* fake hair, is resting on the neutral carpeting, sticking out from underneath the crevice of our door.

It's the hot pink extension she borrowed from me last night.

Her own fit of rebellion.

Even if it's not permanent.

Slamming my fists on the wood, I yell, "Bristol, let me in."

There's silence, no matter how hard I pound, the only noise is my fist connecting with the smooth white of the door.

My shrieks draws the ire of a neighbor, a fifty-something woman who steps out of her room across the hall. "What in the world is going on?" She's wearing a white robe, everything in this hotel monotone, her hair tousled from sleep.

"I need in my room." I'm annoyed by this interruption.

"Well, okay, but can you keep it down?" She shoots me a death glare. "Do you know what time it is?"

I shake my head.

"Seven A.M."

"Oh," I say dumbly. "I just need in my room."

She throws her hands up. "Then knock softly on the door."

"She's not answering."

The woman tightens her robe, muttering "kids these days" under her breath. I turn back around, and a door slams behind me.

Instead of quietly retreating, it makes me more hysterical, the clip-on in my hand.

"Bristol, wake up, answer the damn door." I thrash on the wood.

Nothing.

No footsteps, no answer.

Until I hear heavy footfalls behind me, and a controlled male voice snaps, "You're going to stop causing a scene and come with me."

Panic-stricken, I scream.

The man grabs my arm, yanking me away from the door and down the hall, my legs kicking out beneath me, but they don't reach the carpet as he hauls me out of plain sight.

11

BLAIR

"LET GO OF ME," I shriek, stumbling back against his chest.

His iron grip holds my elbow firm as he drags me behind a potted plant.

"You need to stop yelling, young lady," he commands. "We've had multiple noise complaints. This isn't a frat house."

He drops his arm from mine and I rub the sore spot. "But..."

"If you don't stop causing a scene, I'll be forced to escort you off the property. Would you like the police to get involved?"

I swing around. His tucked-in white polo says 'Security' in the right-hand corner. A brass-plated name tag says Mark Matsen. His ironed black pants are belted, black Doc Martens are shined up, and a...

Gun. Just riding on his hip in a leather holster.

I choke back any more sarcasm.

A solid name for a muscular dude. He's youthful-look-ing, blue eyes, shaved head to remove any grays, the five o'clock shadow salt-and-pepper, giving his age away. He's probably pushing forty-ish.

Swallowing, I bite my lip. "Uhh...no...but I don't know where my sister is."

"Is that your room, the one you're banging on?" He scowls.

"Are you an actual policeman? I ask. "I don't want the police involved."

He puts his hands on his hips. "Why, because you're an underage drunk?"

"No. Why does everyone keep asking me that?" I'm stymied.

He tilts his head at me. I ignore his speculative gesture.

"I handle security for the resort."

"I've lost my sister and my room key."

"Go speak to the front desk."

"I did," I lean against the wall, ticking off my missing items. "My purse was stolen and everything I have is in there – ID, credit card, room key, cell phone."

"Why didn't your sister answer the door?"

"I don't know."

"Are you sure she's in there?"

"No, but where else would she be?"

"How old are you?"

"Twenty-one." I lie.

"Where're you from?" He pulls a radio from his back pocket. "You here with your parents?"

"No, my seventeen-year-old sister. We live in Nebraska."

"Hi, this is Mark, floor seventeen, I'm taking an unidentified woman into her room..." He pauses as I mouth, "Seventeen ninety-eight."

A muffled female voice comes on the radio. "Yes, I

spoke to the young lady downstairs. She had no way of veri-fying her identity."

"I'm going to accompany her in." He looks at me. "What's your name?"

"Blair." I sigh. "Blair Bellamy."

"Who's the room registered to?"

"My father, Bruce Bellamy." He repeats this informa-tion into the radio, then says, "I'm going to check on the room and assist the young lady."

He pulls a universal key card out of his front pocket and motions for me to follow him, shushing me as I open my mouth.

His mouth narrows. "Stop talking for a minute."

Chastened, I stand behind him as he slips the card in the reader and it clicks open. Just like that, he's stepping across the threshold.

He puts his hand back, acting as a barrier between me and the room.

It looks just as we left it, except for a plastic key card on the floor near the door.

And the hair extension.

I feel a sense of relief the place isn't ransacked.

See, nothing bad happened here, everything's fine, I tell myself.

He narrows his eyes at the displaced clothing and makeup scattered around the sink and dresser, the carpet covered with mismatched shoes and plastic hangers.

My laptop's plugged into the wall outlet, my cell phone charger beside it.

Except I have no cell phone to plug in.

Our suitcases sit in the closet, zipped and tagged.

The security I felt a moment ago vanishes when I notice the bed and what didn't happen on it.

No one slept in it.

The covers should be rumpled, mascara and concealer on the pillow.

Instead, it's freshly made, the pillows untouched, only one crumpled when I smacked the brat with it as a joke the night before.

"Oh no," I put a hand to my forehead. "Oh no." The room starts spinning.

"What?"

"She didn't come home."

"How do you know?" He glances at the pulled shades on the patio doors.

I hold up her hair extension. "I found this outside the door." I point to the plastic card resting on the floor. "That's probably hers. Mine was in my purse."

He leans down and picks it up, testing it. It unlocks the door.

Taking the hair extension, he examines it first before setting it on the nightstand.

"Are you going to check for your purse?" he asks.

"It's not here." I'm certain of this.

He walks around the room, peeking out the curtains, checking the bathroom shower, the closet, and ending back at the center where I'm rooted to the spot.

"Do you have anything in the room that I can use to vouch this is your stuff?"

I point at the laptop. "That's mine."

"Is there a password on it?"

"Yeah."

"I'm going to power it on and I want you to enter your password so I can make sure it's yours."

I shoot him a dirty look.

"It's not that I don't believe you – I have to make sure I'm not letting a lunatic enter some poor girl's room."

"You mean a crazy girl?"

He ignores my comment, instead striding to the wall outlet, unplugging my laptop and placing it on the wooden dresser, turning the power button 'ON'.

As it boots up, he asks, "Where did you go last night?"

"A bar."

"How did your sister get in?"

"Huh?"

"You said she's seventeen."

I purse my lips, ignoring the question.

"Ms. Bellamy?" His tone is steel, like a younger version of my daddy when he's at his wit's end.

"Can I change?"

He sighs, noticing the goosebumps on my arms. "Yeah, just put your password in and I'll step out."

I type it in and press enter, stepping back as it chimes in confirmation, the desktop loading.

"Good enough." He nods. "I'm going to wait outside. Come get me when you're finished."

I want to collapse on the bed but adrenaline pulses through me, a weird tingling sensation as I stand, staring around the room as if the walls will start talking to me.

SLIDING MY WET CLOTHES OFF, I throw them in the bathtub to dry. The towel covers my skin, but the flesh is raised in permanent coldness no matter how hard I rub the water away.

Throwing on my ratty black sweatpants I wear as pajamas and a Creighton T, I double-check again, leaving no surface untouched.

My eyes drift across the room. All of her items are still here.

I check her suitcase, rifle through the drawers, nothing is missing.

Except for her.

Her clutch isn't here, neither is her phone or any evidence she came back to the room.

Except she did.

Her hair extension was outside, key card inside.

But she didn't stay.

Why wouldn't she stay?

I sink to my knees, the sobs bursting out.

BRISTOL

I WAKE UP ABRUPTLY, jerking forward into a sitting position.

Except I can't bring my arms where I want them. I pull, they follow, but are yanked back by a force.

"Ouch." I moan, constricted.

Bewildered, my eyes seek out light in the darkness, but there's nothing but pitch black.

Not a light, not a glimmer from the water like I'm used to seeing through the blinds on the balcony of our hotel room.

"Blair?" I look around, flustered. "Blair, are you here?"

Where am I?

"Will?" I shriek. "This isn't funny."

It's like a garage of some kind or maybe a windowless bedroom. I can make out four walls and the creaky mattress I'm on. Besides that, there are objects in the room, but they're shrouded in blackness.

Wrenching my arms forward, I can't seem to twist out of what's holding me hostage.

"Argh." I grit my teeth. "What the hell?" I scream. "Let go of me, Will."

Except when I look over my shoulder, I see the outline of a bed frame with no one behind me, forcing my arms back.

I'm being held against my will. My elbows bend and twist like a pretzel, but I can't turn over.

My wrists confined, I shake my legs. A feeling of dread tingles up and down my skin as I notice they're also restricted – my ankles are shackled to something. I can move, but not freely, and only enough to rile me up even more.

Panic sets in.

Don't panic, I remind myself as my breathing intensifies.

Blink once. Count to ten.

Blink twice. This time start at ten and go backwards.

This isn't the hotel bed, I can tell by the way the scratchy fabric underneath me rubs my bare skin raw. My legs feel itchy, like the wool socks my mom used to make me wear under my winter boots. The Waterfront has cream-colored, five-hundred-thread-count satin sheets. These have a type of pattern, I just can't make out what, maybe some kind of animal?

It's also not king-size, my petite 5'4 frame fills the entire surface. It reminds me of the twin-size trundle bed Blair and I used to share when we were little, before we had the independence of our own rooms.

Is this where Will sleeps?

Would a twenty-two year old really use such a small bed? I can't imagine his built muscles and tall body fitting.

I search for answers, but pieces of my evening are missing in gigantic chunks.

Am I in a guest room? Maybe a younger brother or sister's bed?

I'm trying to justify a reason I'd be fastened to a bed in the first place. Maybe Will let me sleep off what must be a hangover, not wanting to make me feel uncomfortable by sleeping next to me. Gentleman-like, I tell myself.

Except he took it too far. Was he worried I'd stumble and hit my head, harming myself because I was that intoxicated last night?

As for the sledgehammer pounding my head, I've heard my sister talking to her friends on the phone about the wicked effects following a night of drinking. She seemed dramatic, especially when she would come home from school and lay in bed, a pillow over her head, complaining of headaches and nausea.

If this is what drinking feels like, I'm never doing it again, I promise. I'll ask Daddy for his Bible and swear up and down.

My stomach feels empty but squeamish – like if I took a bite of food, I would retch all over the floor.

"Will?" I yell. "I'm up."

But why are my hands and feet bound?

Dread washes over me, adding to the discomfort my achy limbs feel. I can keep my hands at my side, but I can't shift over. The only position I'm able to lay is on my back, stuck in a spread-eagled position.

My eyes adjust to the dark, but there's still no light peeking in.

Glancing down, I stifle a scream.

I bite my lip hard, swallowing the taste of blood and my own yelp.

The outfit I wore last night is missing, the pink and

black plaid mini-skirt now replaced with a short-sleeve shift dress of some kind.

I move my fingers up my leg to my pelvis and in place of my black thong, I'm wearing some type of frilly briefs.

Is this Will's idea of a sick, twisted sex game?

I've read in magazines about fantasies that involve role-playing, but I thought it was for bored, married people.

Is this some kind of a fetish? I always considered fetishes to be whips and chains, but maybe it includes changing outfits. This isn't sexy though, more like drab.

Hollering at the top of my lungs, I beat my hands on the mattress at the same time I scream, "HEELLLPPPPPP."

Stopping and starting, I take short breaths in between, inhaling air in, exhaling air out, horror enveloping my lungs.

Feeling faint, my heart beats out of my chest a million miles a minute.

Can teenagers have heart attacks? You sometimes hear about athletes that collapse from an unnoticed birth defect. Does your body eventually succumb to death when you're tied up against your will? I feel like mine's going to jump out of my chest, a frantic thumping in my ears.

It could run a marathon right now without my help.

My howls echo through the gloomy room, but no light flickers on and I wonder if I'm in some kind of a lab, the kind you develop photos in.

A darkroom, that's it, like we have at school for our photojournalism class.

Tears run down my face, sliding past my cheeks to land on the collar of whatever the hell I'm wearing.

It doesn't matter. As much as I wail and pound the bed, silence fills the spaces around me. There's no hum of a refrigerator, no noise of outside traffic, nothing I can make out that tells me I'm around people.

I pause for a moment to listen – no thud of furniture, footsteps, or people moving below or above me. Waves don't crash and seagulls aren't flocking.

Where the hell am I?

"Blair!" I screech. "Blair, where are you?" I ball my fists up and sob, my body heaving as I shake on the musty mattress in clothes that smell like my grandma's attic.

I pass out, waking when a sharp bang smashes against a wall.

Shaking, I stifle my screams as a scratching noise thuds over and over.

The appearance of light filters through a crack. A door groans as it's pulled open, creaking in the blackness.

It must be a padlock or some kind of gadget meant to keep me in or someone out. I tremble on the dingy bed.

A flashlight, the low beam shining a path from the doorway to the bed, twinkles in front of a metal sliding door. I see a bulky form clothed in jet black that reminds me of the *Sleepy Hollow Horseman*, headless and faceless in the shadowy light. I can only make out shoulders and a broad torso.

Will?

I'm hallucinating, I have to be. This isn't real life.

Pressing my eyes shut, I swiftly count to five, except it's more like one and a half, fearful of the vague figure standing mere feet away.

Thank God.

Someone's here to untie me. I clasp my hands, waiting to be acknowledged.

Except it's hushed, the outline stands still, biding their time.

"Hello?" I scream. "Will, this isn't fucking funny."

I see the shadow coming closer, the massive frame

pausing to stare at my outburst. Disapproval covers the small space between us. "There's no need for language like that. Don't let me hear you cuss again."

It's a male voice shrouded in darkness.

The black lightens to a dull gloom, a small bulb the culprit.

A man stands in front of me, bathed in the pallid glow. His hand holds the flimsy string attached to the bulb in the ceiling.

"Who...who are you? I quiver. "Why am I here?"

He strokes his chin, eyeing me keenly. "Little girls don't use foul language. Do I make myself clear?"

I look to my left, there's a wall.

To the right, small objects fill the room, taking shape in the dimness.

When he comes closer, I can make out the lines of his face, the strong jaw and the towering limbs.

I scream bloody murder until I'm knocked senseless, my body sliding into self-imposed protection at the smash of his fist.

13

BLAIR

VOICES INTERRUPT my thoughts outside the door, definitely a female.

I hear a heavy knock on the door, a beep as the key card's accepted. The handle turns.

Bristol.

Thank God.

I sink back on my knees, ashamed at my overdramatic self – she was with Will all night, the tall drink of water she fell head over heels in love with.

At least for a night.

We can go back to the way it was, and I can refer to her as the brat again.

I'll apologize to the security guard. Heck, I'll even knock on the cranky lady's door and offer to buy her a coffee for waking her so early.

My face falls when Mark enters and not Bristol. He sees me crouched over on the floor and levels his gaze.

"Ready to chat?" he asks conversationally.

I nod at the floor, avoiding his gaze. I'm not ready to be interrogated.

Pulling out a chair from the small table, he sits down, settling back into the seat.

"I didn't do anything wrong," I whisper.

"Let's talk." He rests his hands on his knees. "I want to help you, I really do, but you have to trust me."

"Do you have any kids?"

"Yes." He pulls out his wallet, flipping through the photos in clear plastic.

"Daughters?"

"Two." He shows me their school pictures and one portrait of his family, smiling on the beach.

"How old?'

"Twelve and nine."

"You have a nice-looking family," I remark.

"Thanks." He shuts the wallet, putting it back in his pocket. "Now we need to focus on you," he says, "and your sister."

"I'm scared she's in trouble." I wipe a hand across my face. "And that we're *both* in trouble."

"With who?"

"My parents." I shrug. "Maybe the police."

"Why don't you tell me the story and we'll see if we can sort it out together?"

"Okay."

"But no bullshit." He's strict. "Don't waste my time lying to me."

"Okay, fair." I sniffle noisily.

"Come sit down, grab a tissue, and blow your nose," he instructs. "I'm gonna jot down some notes."

I rise slowly, making my way over to the other side of the table.

"If I need to involve the police, can we agree that's acceptable?"

"If I was your kid, what would you do?" I grab a Kleenex, wiping away the snot.

"As in what?"

"Punishment." I draw in a deep breath. "Like, would you ground me for life?"

"Let's hear the crime before the punishment's determined," he winks, "to make sure it fits. I think you're beating yourself up too bad. We've all done dumb shit involving alcohol."

"What did you do?" I want to detract from the situation. Partly because I don't remember, partly because I want to believe she's with Will.

"Irrelevant." He points at the room key. "Why do you think your sister's in trouble?"

I run through last night up until I leave the bar.

Then I abruptly stop.

His blue eyes pierce me. "What's wrong?"

"It's gone."

"What is?"

"The rest," I pause, "the rest of the night's memories."

"You remember nothing after leaving the bar with a young man?" He glances down at his scrawled penmanship. "Nick?"

"He goes by Nicholas," I say.

"What happened when you left the bar?"

"It's like a big blank in time." I groan. "It's foggy and then blank."

"Were you that drunk?"

"I don't know."

He gives me a 'don't bullshit me' look. "No, truly. I had a couple drinks, but I felt different this time. It was like I was on the outside of my body looking in."

"Where was Bristol when you left?"

"Still on the dance floor."

"Can I speak freely with you?"

"Yeah."

"I think your sister went home with the guy, Will. I know you're concerned, rightfully so, but it's a little after 8 A.M. If you were out late, there's no telling how much longer she was out, and I think she's still sleeping off her hangover."

"But what about her hair extension?" I ask lamely, motioning at the paltry pink hair piece, "and how do you explain her key being in the room?"

"She could've come back to the room, grabbed something, and forgot it."

I tap my fingers on the table, considering his point. "True."

"Are you sure the clip-on didn't fall out on your way to the bar?" He taps his chin. "It doesn't look like it secures very well."

"No, it was in."

"How 'bout this. Do you have the number for the guys you went out with?"

"No..." then I think of our surf lesson. "But I think I can get it."

"Can you contact them and check if Bristol's with Will? That should be the first step before going into panic mode."

"Sure."

"I'll let the front desk know you found your key but that Bristol will be requesting one when she comes back." He looks at his watch. "You need to stay put for a couple hours and see if she shows up. Can you do that?"

"What about my purse?"

"Call the bar you were at last night." He points at the phone.

"I might go search the beach later."

"If you left it in the sand, it's either in the ocean or gone. When do you fly home?"

"Friday."

"I'd work on calling for an ID and seeing what you can do about canceling the credit card."

I swallow hard. "I don't have any money. I had my Daddy's credit card and cash. It's all gone."

He pulls his wallet back out again, fumbling through his cash until he finds a large bill. "Here's fifty bucks." He slides it across the table, "and here's my card. I'm off at three this afternoon, but call my mobile if you need anything. If I don't answer, leave a voicemail."

Tears spring to my eyes. "Thank you."

He nods. "I have two girls. I hope someone would show them the same kindness." After he leaves, I settle on the bed and adjust the pillows against my back. What Mark said makes sense, she's probably still with Will.

Maybe they're having sex.

Eww... it's weird to think of my little sister, the brat, being intimate with someone. She's only seventeen.

But it's better than the alternative.

As long as she's comfortable with it and he didn't push himself on her.

I don't know why I'm worrying this much, probably because of how I felt when I woke up, a chunk of memory vanished, with no purse.

Dialing "0" on the keypad, I call the operator.

A man answers. "Front desk, how may I assist you?"

"Oh, I wanted to see if anyone has turned in a purse, ID, or cell phone? I seem to be missing all three."

"Oh no, let me check. Hold please." Annoying elevator music pierces the silence. He's gone for thirty seconds, but it seems like hours. I feel like I've heard an entire symphony as my annoyance and panic grows with every thrashing crescendo.

"Ma'm?"

"Yes." I hold my breath.

"No, sorry, no one's turned anything in yet."

"Okay." I sigh.

Staring at the phone, I continue calling Bristol's cell over and over.

It rings, then goes to voicemail.

I leave message after message. Some are calm, others frantic.

Heading down to the lobby, I avoid the gaze of the front desk woman who I spoke with earlier. Her eyes judge me across the room.

I notice the same man at the concierge desk, the one who helped Bristol and me book a surf lesson. He's standing at a computer, hands flying furiously over a keyboard.

"Hi." I walk over to him.

I pause, waiting for his fingers to stop clicking. He peers up at me. "I don't know if you remember, but I was down here with my sister yesterday."

He gives me a fake smile, one that implies he doesn't remember shit, but he'll play the overenthusiastic card and pretend he does.

"Of course, darling. How could I forget the two of you! So lovely. She's your older sister, right?"

"Younger."

"Arkansas?"

"Nebraska."

Our eyes lock and he decides to stop guessing. "Another excursion for the two of you?"

"No...well, actually, I wanted to find out the name of the surf shack we took lessons from and a phone number."

"It's cheaper if you book through me. The hotel can offer you a ten percent discount." He seems offended.

"Actually," I lie, "I took my favorite necklace off at our lesson and left it with them. I just want to see when a good time to pick it up is."

"Oh, certainly," his tone changes, "let me write the info down for you." He grabs a pen and piece of paper. "What was your last name?"

I tell him, and he looks through his previous reservations.

Scribbling the name and number down, he hands me the scrap of paper. "Here you go."

I delicately hold it in my hands, like it's the most precious commodity in the world. It might as well be Queen Elizabeth's diamonds.

As soon as you call this number, you'll talk to the boys, find out Bristol is with them, and this nightmare will be over. Done. You'll go meet them and it will be over. It's the not knowing that has me anxious and riddled with doubt.

When I get back up to the room, my stomach's knotted, as if it knows this can make or break how the rest of our vacation goes. I don't think in terms of life, or that anything permanent has happened to Bristol that can't be fixed.

I'm fearful, but I haven't gone into a full-blown breakdown.

Sinking onto the bed, I pick up the receiver of the phone, weighted in my hand, just like the potential outcome. Dialing the surf shop, it rings over and over as I pick at a loose piece of skin on my fingernail.

I hang up, then hit re-dial.

Same thing.

Clicking on the remote, I'm impatient, clicking through the channels, my mind wandering as the news and the daytime talk shows about paternity tests echo through the room.

After another fifteen minutes, I try again.

Nothing.

I grab a piece of hotel stationary and a pen, determined to retrace my steps last night and fill in the blank spaces.

A shrill ring fills the room, and I stumble, losing my balance as my foot catches in the duvet cover and I hit my elbow on the side table.

"Shit," I exclaim, yanking the phone off the cradle. "Bristol?"

"No, it's Mother," a voice on the other end responds dryly. "Where's your sister? Why isn't she with you?"

"She ran down to the lobby for some snacks," I fib.

"Why aren't you with her? You can't just let your baby sister wander around," she chastises. "Something could happen to her."

I swallow. Something might've already happened to her.

Not in the mood to argue, I change the subject. "How's your trip?"

"Florida is good, we're looking forward to getting home though."

"Everything good with the adoption?"

"Yes." She pauses. "Can you have Bristol call me when she's back in the room?"

"Yep," I mumble, "is Daddy around?"

Sniffling, "Let me get him."

"Blair, how's my girl? My two girls?" he adds.

"Good," I force the words out. I keep my voice light.

"Enjoying the beach, walking around and acting like tourists, using the hot tub here."

"You worried your mom," he says. "She tried both your cell phones and they both went to voicemail. Is everything okay?"

"Yeah..." I have to think of an excuse quickly.

Who would be the irresponsible one and lose their phone?

Me. Definitely me.

I exhale. "We went out to the beach and I was taking some pics. I dropped my phone in the sand and a wave took it."

"What? How did that happen?" My father moans. "We trust you to be responsible with your phone, Blair. I'm disappointed."

I close my eyes. "Bristol's is probably dead." As soon as I say the word *dead,* I want to retract it from my vocab. "I mean, her phone."

"I know what you meant," my father laughs. "Well, you girls need to do better. We haven't heard from you since before you went out and you didn't answer when I called last night. That's unacceptable and not part of our agreement." I hear Mother say something in the background. I don't ask what. She's most likely airing a grievance towards me.

"Yes, Daddy." I don't have an argumentative bone in my body at the moment.

We chat for a few more minutes but my mind is a million miles away. I want to get off the phone, what if Bristol's calling?

"Oh, Daddy, I gotta go." I mumble some excuse about the cleaning ladies trying to get in.

"Is Bristol back yet? Your mom wants to talk to her."

"I'm meeting her down in the lobby. She's going to wonder where I am."

"Oh, then definitely get going. We will catch up with you later. Make sure you call us tonight."

"Okay," I whisper. "What's the number for the resort?" Without my phone, their hotel is no longer on speed dial. He reads the number off to me and the room number. "Call us later. Love you."

"I love you, Daddy."

Hanging up, a tear pricks my eyes.

For the first time in a long time, I kneel beside the bed and pray. I pray for my baby sister and I pray that I don't have to lie to my parents about her, that we call them tonight and she's beside me, winking as we share a secret from our parents.

In my mind, there's no other possible outcome.

At least that's what I tell myself.

14

BRISTOL

WHEN I COME TO, the same man is perched next to me on the bed, his face hovering over mine. "You're up," he claps his hands. "I thought you might be by this time." His voice is cheery, like he's about to command a marching band instead of addressing a girl held against her will.

My position on the bed hasn't changed, my limbs achy and sore.

Suffocating a scream, I'm terrified of his close proximity and the way he's focused on me, one wrong move and I'm toast.

I lower my eyelids and glance over my shoulder.

I'm in a twin-size bed, a children's one. It's small, reminiscent of elementary school. The wooden blue headboard has a bouquet of multi-colored flowers stenciled across it.

A five-drawer dresser in the opposite corner matches the headboard, also a robin's egg blue color, with a single bouquet square in the middle of the three drawers.

My jaw drops.

In his hand, he's holding a plain paper bag.

He brings his face inches from mine. "Are you feeling

okay?" I can smell the peppermint he's sucking on as he speaks.

I hold my breath, pushing my butt as far back as it will go, only an inch left between the mattress and the head-board before I slam into the smooth wood. The bed's pressed against a wall covered in gray and purple panels that look like foam squares.

My eyes scan the contents of the room. It's a little larger than my bedroom back home – I'm guessing 12x12.

A small desk is to my right, painted bright yellow, and I can see markers and coloring books pushed in one corner. A couple of puzzle boxes and board games rest on the opposite end of the desk. A plush teddy bear missing one eye rests on the matching yellow shelf above, along with a clear plastic tray that has what looks like hair bows and rubber bands.

A matching yellow chair's pushed in to the desk.

The odd thing about the furniture – it's not adult-sized. Like the children's bed, it's meant for a kid. The chair would've fit me comfortably when I was ten or eleven.

I gulp, staring at the other wall.

It has a floor-to-ceiling bookshelf that doesn't fit with the décor. It's a custom built-in made of honey-colored oak and looks out of place with the rest of the furniture.

"Don't be scared." He reaches out to touch my hair, smoothing my head like I'm a puppy.

I pull my head back, jerking away. My mind drifts to my sheepdog mix. Oggie. Try to focus on getting back to your dog.

Bungee cords are the culprit of my inability to move off the bed, and I twist away from his touch as if he's trying to sear me.

"Now that's not nice. I came to bring you breakfast in bed and the rest of your outfit." Gasping, I look down. The outfit is not only a shift dress, it's the color of bubble gum, candy pink with a flowered brocade. A matching satin bow's attached to a white lacy Peter Pan collar, the short sleeves matching the frilly fabric. It's like I stepped out of the nineties into another era.

My eyes widen as I look around me. "Where am I?"

"Somewhere safe where no one can harm you." His cheeks flush. "You're mine, all mine, dear girl."

I start to cry, big, fat angry tears.

He looks taken aback, startled, like my sorrow is a surprise.

"Don't cry."

I cry harder.

"I saved you from the bad man," he confides.

Whimpering, I close my eyes. This can't be happening to me. It's all a nightmare. One big, ugly nightmare.

"If you keep crying, I'll have to punish you just like I used to." He gives me a bright smile, his bottom teeth slightly crooked.

Taking a deep breath, I stuff down my raw emotions, stifling the next sob.

"Good girl. I want to get you fed and dressed so we can discuss the rules."

"Rules?"

"Yes, why you live here."

"If it's all right with you, I have a home. My mom will miss me. You don't want my family to miss me, do you?" I ask.

He tilts his head, biting his lower lip.

"Why don't you let me go? Please, Please," I beg. "I think you have me mixed up with someone else. I didn't used to know you, I don't recognize you. I'm not from around here."

He shrugs. "But you look *just* like her."

"Her?"

"Marian." He pauses. "And the others."

"Marian? I stutter. "What other ones?" I peer around the small room. "Where are they?"

He shrugs, emotionless. "They're all dead."

My mouth goes dry and my body slack.

He's done this before? Kidnapped and killed other girls? This isn't the first time?

"Where's Blair?"

"Who's Blair?"

I shoot him a frustrated glance.

"Watch those daggers or I'll put you in time out." He sighs. "We have a lot of work to do with adjusting your attitude. You remind me of her already."

"Where am I?" I change the subject.

He doesn't answer, just starts humming a tune I've never heard.

"I'm really not a fan of you eating in bed since it brings bugs in, and since we're underground, it's even worse, but today it will have to do until I get a table set up. Would you like that?"

Would I like that? What the hell is wrong with this freak?

"I would like to go home," I murmur.

"Enough talk," he chastises. "Silence is golden."

He slowly opens the paper bag, and I'm almost more afraid of the contents. What if he wants me to eat dead rabbits or rats or some kind of exotic beetle?

My jaw relaxes when he says, "I brought you Rice Krispies and orange juice." The bowl he pulls out is already filled with cereal. Setting a plastic spoon aside, he dumps a small carton of milk over it.

"Snap, crackle, pop." He's giddy, mixing the milk and breakfast food together. "This was *her* favorite. And her favorite bowl," he adds. The ceramic bowl has the alphabet stretching across the faded purple surface in rainbow colors. I gulp, unsure I will be able to taste anything.

"I'm going to feed you." He dips the spoon in the cereal. "At least today I am. I can't always." Scooting closer to me, he reaches forward as I lean back, resting my head against the wood.

He's dressed casual, dark jeans with a brown belt and a red Hawaiian shirt, navy flip-flops on his feet.

"Eat, little girl. You need your energy." I don't bother to ask what for.

My lips are in a straight line but it doesn't matter, he shoves the plastic into the slits and crams it down my throat.

I choke, sputtering milk as it dribbles down my chin and onto the collar and satin bow.

"Dammit, you're ruining her favorite outfit." He slaps me with an open hand across the face. "Don't do that again."

He swipes a hand across my chin, angrily wiping the mess away with his palm.

Tears prick my eyes and my cheek burns.

The cereal tastes like stale cardboard. I can hardly swallow, my throat's closed up and I start to cough. He digs in the bag and peels a wrapper off a straw, slipping it in the orange juice container. "Here you go, have some Vitamin C." I suck greedily until it's half-empty.

I acquiesce as he feeds me spoonful after spoonful until the bowl's empty save for leftover milk.

"Do you want a cookie?"

"No."

"No what?"

"No, thank you."

"Good, good start." He strokes his chin, a single hair sticking out of a mole that's precisely to the right of his chin.

It reminds me of the wolf and the three pigs, the one who threatens to blow him down by the *hair of his chinny chin chin.*

He tilts his head, considering me. "I'm going to untie you from the bed..." I start to grow excited, my face giving too much emotion away.

"But if you make a peep, or raise your voice, you'll go in solitary confinement." He lowers his voice to a conspiratorial whisper. "And you don't want that. Oh no, you don't want that. I've been there before and it's not good. She taught me well."

Who is he referring to?

Certainly not another girl he took.

Or maybe she tried to escape and he killed her? My eyes widen.

I run my tongue over the suddenly parched roof of my mouth.

"In fact, you don't want any of her punishments. It won't make either of us happy campers." His face twists back into that fake smile. I notice a top tooth discolored from the rest. It reminds me of a buttered kernel of popcorn, standing out against the rest of his pearl-colored teeth.

"And I don't want to get out of control. I don't want to hurt you...permanently."

Don't go there, I say to myself, *don't even go there right now. Don't think about home, or Mom and Dad, or your life back home.*

"Do you understand?"

I can't speak, so I merely nod.

"Okay." He puts a finger to his plump lips. "Now shh..."

He starts with my ankles, untying the blue cords, testing if I try and kick him. I don't. There's no use since my arms are still restrained. When he reaches for my wrists, I turn my face away from his sickly sweet breath. Between that and the antique smell of the clothing I'm dressed in, I'm queasy.

"Is there a bathroom I can use?" I ask meekly.

"Good question." He undoes the cords on my left wrist, then starts on my right. "We will go over all of that." He giggles like a school girl. "You're so impatient, just like she was."

"Marian?"

"No, Leslie."

I sputter. The ID I had last night belonged to a girl named Leslie Billings. Could it be one and the same? Did I have a missing girl's ID?

Instantly, I freeze.

"Are you cold?" he asks, an air of concern apparent on his face. He reaches out to rub my shoulders, the lace fabric itchy on my skin.

"I'm okay," I say, crossing my arms, rubbing the raw skin where the cords dug in. I sweep my legs underneath me, scooting up against the rickety headboard.

"Okay, well, you have to tell me if you need something, little girl." He shrugs. "I'm not a mind reader."

If I need something?

I need my sister, a plane, and my parents. I want to rock in my mom's arms and have my daddy yell at me about underage drinking, and I'll gladly be grounded and live at home until I'm twenty-five.

I'll even become a nun.

Just *please* let me go.

He reaches into his back pocket, pulling out a small

black leather notebook. Folded-up paper is crammed in the middle and he carefully removes it, unfolding the squares.

I can't see what's written on it, but it's a list of some sort.

"Are you ready?" He glances up from the sheet, my eyes trained on the singular hair dancing on his chin. He doesn't wait for a response. "I'm going to hang this on a dry erase board so you can remember. At some point, it needs to go in here." He points to his forehead. "Memorize it, because one day the list will disappear."

I stare at him like he has three heads.

"Rule number one, there's no screaming of any kind. Not that it would matter, the room is sound-proofed.

"Two, every morning I will have an outfit laid out for you after I give you a bath. Bath time is always in the morning."

Does he work? I wonder.

"Three, you will read a book every day. I'll restock your book shelf every week with new titles."

How many pages are these books?

"Then you will read to me every night when I get home. I will sleep here sometimes with you to cuddle, just like she and I used to."

I shudder, my shoulders trembling.

"Four, you will need to keep your mind sharp. Puzzles, games, it's all at your disposal. You're the luckiest little girl, you get to be a kid forever."

Forever means eternity.

I'm puzzled. "How old am I supposed to be?"

He pinches my knee hard.

I recoil.

"I'm not finished talking," he snaps, then his voice goes back to neutral.

"You'll have two meals a day and a snack. Breakfast, a

piece of fruit, and then a simple dinner. I'll leave some water if you get thirsty. Today is special so you got cereal, but that's only on special occasions.

"I don't plan to keep you tied up, but that brings us to the punishment portion. I work on a strike system. First strike is a warning, then you'll have time out, then loss of privileges. This could be food, water, play time, it could even mean no bathroom breaks and diapers instead."

My eyes widen.

"I don't want to have to do that to you, but I will. I had to do it to her."

"The other punishments could be the box, being tied up again, maybe in a more uncomfortable position then you were, and branding."

"Branding?"

His eyes narrow. A darkness clouds over his blue eyes. He grips my chin firmly in his palm. "What did I tell you about interrupting?" Spittle flies onto my nose as he closes the gap between our faces.

"Sorry," I manage to moan.

"I'll ask you after if you have questions. You're lucky I'm so happy to see you today." He drops my chin and pushes my face away with the front of his palm.

"You might be more trouble than you're worth," he snarls. "Now, getting to the part about being a child. You'll respect me. You'll raise your hand to ask a question, and I'll decide if *and* when I answer it. Typically I allow five questions a day."

"The bathroom is the red pail over there." He points to the corner. "Today is an off day, so tomorrow we will start bright and early with your bath. I want you on a schedule, then you won't be so fussy." He caresses my cheek as I try not to vomit.

"Also, no spilling. If you do, automatic loss of a privilege. Or privileges. So don't do it. I'm trying to teach you manners and etiquette."

I start to open my mouth but shut it.

"Good girl. See, you're already getting the hang of it, thinking before you speak." He stares at me, his eyes burn into mine, and I'm forced to look down, his gaze undressing me.

I squirm, uncomfortable. Focusing on my hands,

the pink nail polish that's chipped off.

"Okay, now you can ask your questions." He holds up one hand and wiggles his fingers. "But only five."

Pausing, I consider what I want to ask.

Or what I want to know. It might be dangerous to ask certain questions.

Wearily, I ask, "Where's my sister?"

"Who?"

"Blair."

He shrugs. "No idea."

"Is Leslie Billings the girl you were close to?"

"Pass."

"How can you skip questions, that's not fair..." My voice trails off.

His mouth twists into a grimace. "Is that so?"

I realize I'm on shaky ground, but there's no backing down. "Yes," I say.

"Hmm... I'll think about it." He taps his nose three times.

"Can I call my parents?" I ask hopefully. "Let them know I'm alive."

"No."

"Where are we?"

"Where do you think we are?"

"You mentioned the underground. But where underground?"

"You're still in Hawaii."

"How old am I?"

"How old are you or how old do I think you are?"

"Yes, how old am I to you?"

"Twelve."

I start to ask another question, but he raises a hand to stop me. "That's five."

"But you didn't answer one of the questions," I argue.

"I'm warning you." He snaps a finger. "Tone."

I hurry on with my question, ignoring him. "Whose clothes are these? They look like they came from my grand-ma's closet."

His face turns beet red and the single hair stands on edge, like it's standing at attention. "Did you just do what I *think* you did?"

I narrow my eyes in confusion, tilting my head.

"Insulting my clothing choices and disrespecting me when I remind you of the rules?" He angrily pulls a chunk of my hair towards him. "Do you want to repeat what you just said?"

"I just want to know who they belong to," I whisper.

He ignores me, yanking the hair from my scalp. "Ouch." I try and pull back, it just infuriates him more.

Or maybe excites him.

It's hard to tell.

Pushing me over on my stomach, he shoves my head into the mattress and lifts my shift dress up and the frilly bottoms down. My necklace comes out from underneath the collar and I watch the 'B' as it moves against my clavicle.

"Do you want this?" I hear a belt being unbuckled under his shirt with his free hand.

Oh God, he's going to hit me with the leather strap.

"Noooo...." I raise my voice. "Please stop. Please please *please*," I moan into the scratchy sheets.

"What did I tell you about yelling?" His elbow balances in the hollow of my back, painfully holding me in place.

I hear a zipper being yanked down.

What the...

Before I can make sense of it, I feel a searing pain as a hard object pushes into my thighs.

The pink satin bow is soaked with my tears as it flutters against my cheek in rhythm with his movements up and down.

He grunts. I bawl into the pillow as he finishes, a wet mess between my legs.

"Look what you made me do," he chants over and over.

I say nothing, my eyes shut tight against his monotonous voice and the deadness I feel inside.

"Guess bath time will come early tonight, little girl."

Unresponsive, he pulls my head back to grip the nape of my neck, pinching my shoulder blades, his fingers digging into my back. Holding my head under the pillow, he chokes me until I'm gasping for air, the 'B' pressed so tightly into my skin that it becomes a purple bruise.

Oxygen deprived, I pass out.

_____

15

BLAIR

THE REST OF THE AFTERNOON, I pace the room, wearing down the carpet as I pad over it, from one side to the other and back again. The dullness of the beige carpet matches my mood –depressed and bored.

Willing the phone to ring, I stare at it incessantly.

It doesn't.

Around noon, I call the surf shack again.

On the fifth ring, I hear a click.

"Hello?"

"Aloha. This is Drew."

"Hey Drew, this is Blair Bellamy. I took a lesson yesterday. Are Will or Nicholas around?"

"Nicholas isn't, he was filling in for me, and Will isn't slated to be in, but he usually stops by regardless."

"By any chance I can get Will's cell number?"

"Uh, we typically don't give that out to customers."

"Understandable, it's just that I think I left my phone in his car last night."

"He doesn't have a car."

Thinking on my feet, I say, "Yeah, not his – one of his

friend's." I plead. "I really need my cell. I don't live on the island and I have to call my parents or they'll *kill* me."

The word hangs in the air.

When I only hear silence, I assume he's hung up.

"Umm...here, got something to write it down with?"

"Yep."

He reads Will's cell off to me and I scribble the numbers down.

"Thanks."

"Yeah, mahalo."

Hanging up, I take a deep breath, picking the receiver back up. My hands tremble and I punch the wrong numbers.

I hang up, try again, forcing myself to slow down, pressing one digit at a time.

Straight to voicemail.

I call the surf shack again. "He's not around, any chance I can get Nicholas's number?" He seems annoyed but still gives me his cell.

What if he doesn't pick up?

"Hello?" A tired voice answers.

"Hey, Nicholas, it's Blair."

There's a pause.

"Yeah, hey, Blair, how's it goin'? You feeling better?"

"Nah." I say. "Last night was rough."

"Tell me about it."

"Why did you leave me on the beach?"

"You were fighting me pretty hard, making a scene." He's contrite. "I didn't want drama or the cops to get involved."

I'm annoyed by this, but it's not why I'm calling. I shove my emotions in the back of my throat.

"Have you talked to Will today?"

"No. Thought he was at your hotel. He didn't come home last night."

So Will's missing too?

Bristol and him have to be together.

My voice borders on hysteria. "What do you mean? She never came back to the room last night."

"I'm pretty sure they did." He laughs. "He didn't even bother charging his phone. It's dead, went straight to voicemail when I called."

"Well, they aren't here."

"Maybe they got their own room? Did you even think about that?"

"You don't get it..." I'm riled up.

"No, you don't. Geez, Blair, calm down, they're probably just having fun together. You should try it sometime." He speaks to a woman in the background. "I'm busy, gotta go. Mahalo."

I stay in the room the rest of the afternoon, my nails bitten to the quick as I switch between pacing the floor, staring at the phone, drilling holes in the wall with my eyes, and glaring at the television.

When I try and focus, my mind continually races, drifting back to last night.

My stomach growls, testing my limits, angry that I've ignored it for hours and left it hungover and empty.

At 4 P.M. I can no longer stand being cooped up in the room, helpless. I grab the key card and decide to retrace my steps.

I pause at the door.

What if Bristol comes back to the room and I'm not here?

Would a message help?

It seems futile, a gut feeling tells me deep down that

evil's lurking. Bristol would never not find a way to call the hotel, and for all our differences, she's an annoying younger sister, not a mean, vindictive one.

But maybe her phone's dead too.

Jotting a quick note, I fold it so it's half sticking under our door in case she comes back. I don't give my where-abouts, I just tell her to ask the front desk for a key.

Walking out the lobby, I hope the sight of the beach and the umbrella I collapsed under will jog something in my memory.

Wearing a pair of flip-flops, the earlier absence of people has been replaced with the sounds of tourists and locals, sunbathing and drinking, surfing and boating, laughter a constant as I walk towards *The Ocean Club*.

If anything untoward happened here, the sunshine and salty air cover it like concealer over a beauty flaw.

Hawaii – it's difficult to imagine this place as anything but vivid and lively...and safe.

The bar from last night is about fifty yards away, strange-looking and lonely, opposite from the clamor of the beach. It's empty, primarily a night club and bar, it hits its stride after 9 P.M.

I leave the sand and walk up the wooden steps. A covered patio with light strands straddling the palm trees and tiki torches, shaded cabanas line the other side of the entrance, unobstructed views of the Pacific stretching for miles.

How could anything bad happen here?

It feels ominous to step inside during broad daylight, the dance floor and DJ booth empty, a janitor sweeping the concrete floors and mopping them.

There's a young woman, probably a year older than me,

who's dressed in black shorts and a white tank standing at the hostess stand.

I walk up, almost shy. "Hi, did you happen to be working last night?"

She eyes me curiously. "No, I was off," she grins, "I had a hot date last night."

"Is anyone here that was working last night? I misplaced an item." I want to add, "It's big, huge, actually, and it's my sister."

"David should be in shortly, he's always late but his shift started five minutes ago. Also, Dylan and Kylie." She sees another girl, this one covered in tattoos and piercings. She motions her over.

"Hey Kylie, this girl has some questions about last night."

"You the girl that left your phone behind?"

My phone is here?

I stammer, "Yeah, I probably did."

"Some nice patron found it in the sand near the front entrance, stepped on it, but it's not broken. At least I don't think so."

There's a chance it could be hers...or mine. Or someone else's.

Think good thoughts, think good thoughts, I order my mind.

"Let me grab it, it's behind the bar."

The hostess smiles at me as I follow Kat Von D's dead ringer to the middle of the bar. A guy walks in, blond, blue-eyed, and dressed in black pants, black shirt, and a black belt. Clearly the dress code is consistent.

Bingo. The bartender from last night.

Kylie reaches behind a shelf and pulls out a white LG phone.

It's mine.

Thank God, what if Bristol called it?

I try not to snatch it out of her hand, cradling it carefully in my palm.

Quickly, I press the ON button and power it up. Battery's at ten percent.

"Thank you." I smile at her, clicking on the voicemail button. I have two from Daddy – one from last night, one from early this morning.

A text message from my roommate Shay.

My heart sinks. None from Bristol or Will.

"No prob." She busies herself with refilling the straw holder. "There's David if you want to talk to him." The dirty blond thirty-something strolls to the bar, the same attire he wore last night – all black except for his gold wedding ring and chain.

"What's up?" he says to Kylie, giving her a peck on the cheek. "You talk to Steve?"

"Yeah, we broke up again." She rolls her eyes. "He's a piece of shit and tried to lie about..." She notices me watching them and stops mid-sentence. "Hey, this girl wants to talk to you about last night."

"About?" He turns and looks at me. "What's up?" He drums his fingers on the counter. "Aww...yes, the one with the unique middle name. I remember you."

I smile. "Yep, Haley E., that's me."

"Couldn't stay away, huh?" He twists the cross on the gold chain.

"You got me," I nervously titter. "Actually, I'm missing something."

"Oh yeah, what is it?" He starts to reach under the bar. "We always have items found by the cleaning crew."

His jaw drops when I say, "My sister."

"Oh shit." He leans on the counter. "Was that the other chick here with you?"

"Yeah, we came with two guys." I describe them. "One is tall, dark eyes and hair, the other blond and blue-eyed. My sister is strawberry blonde, green eyes."

"Oh yeah, I know Will Loomis. You were all pretty trashed."

"Did you see her leave, my sister – the blonde?"

"Yeah, she left with Will." He grimaces. "He didn't even pay the tab."

"Oh shit, what happens when someone doesn't pay?"

"We have Will's card on file, so no biggie." He smirks. "Between you and me, I'm giving myself a big tip."

"Do you know him well?"

"Not really, he's not the type I associate with."

"You mean because he's a surf instructor?"

"No, because he's trash. Total lowlife." He grips the edge of the bar, his voice stilted.

"What do you mean?"

"Never mind... I'm surprised we haven't permanently kicked him out. Him and some of his friends."

"The other guy in here?" I ask. "Nicholas Mercer?"

"Nah, I've never seen that guy cause problems. Will usually comes in with a red-haired dude and leaves with whatever chick he picks up that night." He notices my face turn crimson and he murmurs, "Sorry, didn't mean to make it awkward if you guys have something going on."

"No, it's not like that."

He nods. "Let me guess, you took a 'lesson' from him?" He says with air quotes.

"Yeah, my sister and I did, but she didn't come home last night."

"Everyone has a mobile device these days, where's her phone?"

I shrug. "No idea. I assume with her." I continue. "Did you by any chance notice the time they left? I saw her at 1:17 A.M."

"Um... no, I don't. Probably shortly after because the DJ quits at 1:30. Last half-hour is just radio."

"You said we were trashed. Like out of the norm?"

"Odd question." He smirks. "This is a bar. You were all pretty intoxicated, stumbling around like idiots. The usual." He shrugs. "You included."

"I know." I run a hand through my hair, whispering, "I just don't know what happened last night..."

"Sit down, let me buy you a drink." He points at a stool.

Shit, he assumes I'm of age because I had a fake last night.

"Actually, a water would be great. I need to hydrate."

"You were that bad, huh?"

"No, it's weird." I slide onto the stool. "It was more than that."

HE SPRAYS water from the nozzle into a glass, sliding it across to me. "What do you mean?"

I bite my lip. "I don't know how to describe it other than an out-of-body experience last night, and then today I woke up with zero recollection, like an alien had scooped out twelve hours of brain function."

"Do you think he drugged you?"

"Who?" I chug a sip of water. "Will?"

He leans his elbows on the bar top. "Can I ask you something?"

"Yeah."

"You're not twenty-one, are you?"

My face flames. Looking down, I shake my head.

"Neither is your sister?"

"No."

A pudgy man, balding and wearing a shrunken t-shirt three sizes too small, walks up. "We need to talk, David." His fat fingers shove a toothpick in his mouth. "Tardies. Your shitty attendance."

"Sure thing, George." He grabs my water glass. "You better scoot. If you're caught in here underage, we'll both be in trouble."

Slowly, I stand, watching the middle-aged man with a heavy gold pinky ring stand at the cash register, counting bills. "Kylie said a bunch of young girls came in the other day underage. You know anything about this?"

"No, sir." David's respectful, avoiding my lingering gaze.

"You look young." The weasel peers over the register. "How old are you?"

"Twenty-two," I lie. "Thanks for the application, David, I'll stop in next week." I decide to add that part so I seem like a local.

"Yeah, no problem."

The owner gives me a second glance, whistling. I hear him telling David to hire me based on looks alone. Ugh.

I turn to go, feeling both sets of eyes on the back of my skull.

Walking about ten feet, I stop, turning around. The owner grabs a cash bag and heads in an employees' only room.

Waiting until he's out of sight, I ask. "One more thing. Why'd you ask if we were underage?"

He takes a ragged breath. "I don't want to scare you."

"Say it, please," I plead. "My younger sister is missing."

Lowering his voice, he whispers. "We don't want trouble here, this can't get around." He looks over his shoulder to make sure his boss hasn't sneaked up behind him. "Word is that Will and his posse like to drug young girls. They provide fake IDs or IDs they find to sell and get girls wasted."

"For what purpose?" I ask, my stomach churning.

He looks at me like I'm dense. "What do you think?"

"Got it." I shiver involuntarily.

"Yeah, he likes to mess around with them when they're blackout drunk." He looks down at the row of bottles lining the bar shelf. "Some people are into weird shit."

"Why doesn't anyone do something about it?"

"We've threatened to stop serving him before since so many girls were leaving shit behind – clothes, phones, purses. It became an issue."

"What does he think?" I nod in the direction of the weasel.

"George?" A bitter smirk plays across his face. "He doesn't care what Will does as long as the tabs get paid. He brings in a lot of business, if you catch my drift."

"But Will didn't pay his tab last night..."

"Yeah, but we charge his card and he never complains or argues about the amount."

"Does he go anywhere else?"

"No idea. I've just heard a couple girls mention having no memory of their night out with him. Some have gotten arrested for public intoxication after having one or two drinks here. The police used to threaten to hold us responsible for serving clearly-intoxicated individuals, so I had to lay into Will about that last year."

"And he admitted to drugging girls?"

"No, I didn't accuse him of that. I just asked him to cool it with the fake IDs. I talked to him like we were pals looking out for each other. I want him to take his biz elsewhere so it doesn't draw attention from the cops. That's the last thing he would want as a felon anyway."

"Felon?"

"Yeah, rap sheet a mile long." He leans his elbows on the bar. "I wouldn't tell anyone you got in with a fake or someone else's ID. The police will jump all over you. If you're underage, they'll totally make an example out of you."

"David?" The weaselly boss yells. "Let's do inventory before it gets busy."

"Gotta go." He gives me a crooked smile. "Good luck, but I'm sure she'll turn up. Probably just embarrassed because she had a rough night."

I nod, overwhelmed, because I'm starting to realize I'm in way too deep and that means she is, too.

Walking towards the hotel, I keep my eyes peeled. It's as if I'm seeing the horizon in a new light.

Every crowd, I scan for her face.

Glancing towards the setting sun, I trudge through the sand, slipping my flip-flops off so I can walk barefoot. Keeping my eyes on any man-made holes and the long row of sand castles, I accept my purse is by now long gone with my wedges.

But Bristol – she's not an inanimate object. She can't just disappear into thin air, can she?

My stomach lurches as I consider another scenario.

What if she passed out on the beach and wasn't as lucky as I was? Got dragged into the current and didn't wake up until it was too late. Could she have drowned in the Pacific?

She's a strong swimmer and has great upper-body

strength but with the amount of alcohol we drank, she could've been washed away.

Will her body eventually float to the surface, bloated and purple?

Nauseated, I cover my mouth.

Staring over the shimmering water, waves churn with fury farther out, crashing and burning. Beautiful but in the wrong setting, deadly.

But what about what David said?

His lackadaisical attitude concerns me about drugged girls – what if Will raped her? She's not from around here, he could've just dropped her off somewhere when he was done with her. She'd be disoriented in a new city and lost.

Putting a hand to my forehead, I shield myself from the glare of the sun. I've gotta get back to the hotel. I convince myself she's there, sitting in our hotel room, my note in hand, waiting dutifully for me.

Holding my breath as the elevator rises, same with my apprehension, my stomach undulates every floor we pass that takes me closer to our room. When I arrive back on the seventeenth floor, the metal grinds to a halt and I step forward, almost banging my head into the door, willing it to open, wanting to know my baby sister's safe.

Except the hall's eerily empty, and I don't see her blonde hair covering her face in front of our door, clenching my note as she laughs at my unfounded fears.

A wave of terror washes over me, a gut feeling that something's just *not* right.

I shakily insert the key card, barely making it past the threshold before sinking to my knees. Cradling my head in my hands, a panic attack sets off a chain reaction as I struggle to breathe. Hyperventilating, I'm convinced I'm dying, my heart galloping as if it's going to explode once it reaches an invisible finish line.

Tears flood my cheeks and I know I have to do something, like involve adults.

Tell my parents.

I look at the digital clock on the side table, it's now after 6 P.M.

Calling Bristol again, it goes straight to voicemail. I can't leave a message, it's full.

Scrolling through my phone, I look for any missed texts or calls. Nothing new.

I decide to call Will again.

Same thing. Voicemail.

I'm able to leave him a message. It's nonsensical and rushed, but I repeat my number, blubbering the digits, in case he misses it the first time.

Mark. I have Mark Matsen's card. I dial his cell.

He picks up on the second ring. "This is Mark."

"Mark, it's uh...it's Blair Bellamy. Room seventeen ninety-eight."

"Yeah, I remember." I hear the television in the background and kid's giggling. "You called to tell me your sister's back?"

I pause.

Silence.

"No."

Another lull.

"Mark?" I let out a shaky breath. "I don't know what to do... if I should call the police? I talked to a bartender from where we were last night and he said Will's bad news."

"Bad news in what kind of way?"

"Drugging girls." I stammer. "Forcing himself on them."

"Have you told your parents?"

"No."

"You need to call them. Are they at home?"

"No, vacation."

"Are they reachable?"

"Uh-huh."

"I'm going to head over. Stay put. I work with a lot of people on the Honolulu police force. I'll look up Will's record and address."

"Thank you." I'm relieved he's going to help.

"He teaches surf lessons right down the beach, right?"

"Yeah, Aloha from the Surf."

"Did the bartender remember anything else?"

"Will and his friend didn't pay the tab, but both are local. Said he brings in out-of-town girls. It's like a game for him."

"What's your sister's full name, birth date, and age?"

"Bristol Anne Bellamy. She's seventeen, junior in high school, birthday in June. June eighteenth."

"Okay. I'll do some checking. Sit tight, should be there within an hour or so."

"Thanks."

"And Blair?"

"Yeah?"

"Call your parents."

My silence echoes through the phone line.

"I know you don't want to, but you have to."

"Is this because you think she's missing now?"

There's dead air, he's already hung up the phone.

And as I put the phone back on the cradle, I realize I don't want to know the answer.

16

BLAIR

MY PARENTS' number is on the pad of hotel paper, staring at me in black ink.

I pick up the phone, then slam it back down.

Bristol's fine, I tell myself. She's just having a good time. Why get them upset over nothing?

Mentally, I can't force myself to call them. I can't tell my mother her favorite child is misplaced. The word 'missing' too much of a negative connotation.

They will interrogate me with a ton of questions, none of which I have the answers to.

Standing, I stretch my arms over my head, ignoring the hunger pains in my stomach.

If she can't eat, neither can I.

I chastise my empty belly, willing it to settle down.

Searching through her luggage, I tell myself that maybe I'm ignoring a clue. Her favorite sweatshirt, a black and yellow one with the words *Hawks Cheerleader Squad,* is folded neatly in her suitcase.

I pull it out, sniffing it. It smells of the laundry detergent my mother uses at home, a mix of spring time and fresh laundry.

Taking my Creighton one off, I replace it with hers. I settle under the covers and wait, the clock ticking down the minutes in my head, until I hear a knock at the door.

My ears perk up, considering it might be her.

"It's Mark," the deep voice bellows.

I hop up, opening the door as he stands there, this time in khaki pants and a red hooded sweatshirt. "I brought someone with me. This is Detective Paul Goodman." I can't see him at first, Mark's height blocking him from sight. He must be 5'6 or 5'7, rail thin, and dressed in a Hawaiian shirt and black shorts with boat shoes.

"He's off-duty," Mark adds, noticing my eyes darting up and down Goodman's island attire.

Goodman flashes a badge. "Hi, I'm Detective Goodman. Mark and I go way back, high school actually, and he told me your sister hasn't returned, is this correct?"

I nod, my hands gripping the door so hard I'm afraid I'll remove them to find splinters in my palms.

"Mind if we come in?" Goodman asks, peering behind me into the room. Sunglasses hang from an elastic around his neck.

"Sorry," I mumble, rubbing my face. "Come in." I hold the door open as they brush past me, both examining the room and making mental notes, their eyes darting from corner to corner.

"Why don't you have a seat?" Mark says, holding up a paper bag. "I brought you some chicken nuggets and fries."

Surprised, I sink into a chair at the small wooden table.

"I figured you hadn't eaten all day." He pushes the bag over to me.

"I haven't," I say softly. "Thanks."

His eyes are kind. "Eat something and then Goodman will want to ask you some questions." I open the bag, the smell making my mouth water, but my insides coil. There's a bottle of water from the hotel and I use it to swallow the food, every bite getting stuck in my throat.

Goodman checks the sliders on the patio, steps out on the balcony, scans the views from our room, and looks down onto the cement sidewalk seventeen floors below. His eyes flit back and forth over the railing and the metal patio furniture. He steps in our bathroom, our closet, and then goes back outside to walk the hall. I hear him knocking on the neighbor's doors. I should warn him about the grumpy woman I woke up.

When he leaves, Mark takes the chair opposite mine. "What did your parents say?"

I take a sip of water, my mouth parched. "I...I couldn't call them yet," I whisper. "I don't know what to say. They'll ask a million questions that I don't have the answers to."

He stares at me, his eyes never leaving my face.

"I feel helpless," I add.

"Does your sister like to run off?"

"No. Never." I say. "She's the star of everything. Popular. Nice. Involved in activities, volunteers."

"Does she have a boyfriend?"

"We aren't allowed to date in high school." I play with the plastic bottle top, avoiding his curious stare.

"That doesn't answer my question."

"She's dating someone," I say, "someone at her high school." But I hurriedly add, "My parents can't know. It's their rule."

Mark leans back in his chair. "I'm not worried about him. He's not here, is he?"

"No, he's back in Nebraska as far as I know." I look

down at my ragged hands. "Unless he went on his own spring break trip."

"And your parents, you mentioned they're on vacation?"

"Florida. I don't want to interrupt them."

Mark takes pity on me. "I'll call them with you. They can talk to both Goodman and me."

A tear falls down my cheek. "I'm so scared and I don't know... this isn't like her." He's searching for kind words to say, but I see a troubled glimpse cross his face. He won't say it, but he's starting to worry.

Goodman comes back inside, a notepad and pen in hand. "You get enough to eat?" He asks me.

"Yeah, thanks." I rub my stomach, ignoring the sick feeling.

"I'm going to ask you questions about your trip here, what you've been doing, your relationship with your sister, some generic questions that will be easy to answer, some more personal."

"Okay."

"I brought a tape recorder, but I'll also take notes to keep track in case I miss anything. I don't want you to have to keep repeating the same answers over and over."

"Yeah."

"You aren't going to like all the questions. Some aren't going to be easy to answer. They will be about boys, sex, drugs, and anything else that might be relevant to the case."

I look down at the half-eaten box of chicken nuggets as heartburn fires up in my chest, sudden and brutal.

"It's important I tell you this because I don't want you to shut down. You have to realize that this is to help find your sister."

"I want to help find her," I offer.

"I'm sure you do, and most likely this is nothing but a misunderstanding." He sits across from me. "Okay, Blair, this isn't going to be easy, but let's first establish a pattern of trust."

Angling my head at him, I say, "I don't understand."

"I'm going to let you in on a secret." He raises his brows. "But you can't tell anyone."

Confused, my eyes swivel to Mark for verification of what I'm being told. Pulling my legs up underneath me, Goodman's locked in on my face.

"You're not in trouble, understand? Whatever you say, even if it's illegal, you're not in trouble. You're not getting arrested. The purpose is to locate Bristol. Got it?"

"Yeah." I pick at another nail, the polish crumbling.

"Okay, so for my secret, in high school, I got drunk and wrapped my car around a tree. I lied and told my parents that my friend had been driving my car and I wasn't with him. They still think he crashed it and that I was at my girl-friend's house at the time."

I peer between him and Mark.

"They still don't know the truth." He points to the phone. "You could call them today and they would have no idea I lied."

"Yep, they think it was me." Mark grins. "And they *still* hate me for it."

Goodman sits on the edge of the bed, his hands in his lap. "Am I making myself clear, Blair? You're not in trouble, but even the hard details, we have to know. It could help find your sister."

Mark adds, "If she's even in danger. She could just be partying it up with a new friend."

Goodman turns on the recorder, asking me basic ques-tions like do I have his permission to record statements I give. Starting with the date and time, he proceeds to ask questions like my age and birthdate, where I live, where I grew up, and then the same about my sister.

Next he asks about our parents, if we have siblings, our parents' professions, what I'm studying in college, and why we came on this trip.

The first couple days I can describe in detail, up until we reach the bar.

"So you were drinking in this room, seventeen ninety-eight?"

"Yes."

"With both Will Loomis and Nicholas Mercer. Anyone else?"

"No."

"Drugs?"

I hesitate and he pounces. "Weed, pills, harder stuff?" He names them off. "E? Coke?"

"Not on purpose," I mumble. "Except for a joint."

"Did Will and Nicholas have access to your drinks?"

"Yes. They brought vodka in a backpack and Will poured it for us."

"So it could've been anything?"

"Yeah, I guess. I didn't feel sick then."

"At what point did you start feeling intoxicated or out of it?"

"When we arrived at the bar, my sister puked in the bathroom. Then she seemed fine. It wasn't until I had another drink that I started to feel like I hadn't slept in days. It was weird, like I was slipping away."

"And then what happened?"

"I can't remember leaving the bar until a stranger woke me up on the beach this morning."

"Who was the stranger?"

"A man running on the beach. He helped me to the hotel."

"Any chance you caught his name?"

"Peter. He said his last name, but I don't remember. Rhodes? Ridley?"

"Have you been drunk before?"

"A couple times, but I just puke or have a nasty hangover the next day." I elaborate, "I don't like how I feel, so it hasn't happened much. I live in a sorority house and we take turns acting as the sober sister."

"Do you typically remember your actions or what happens when you're drinking?"

"Yeah."

"But in this case, a good chunk of time – at least eight to nine hours, has just vanished?"

Defensive, I cross my arms over my chest. "I'm not lying. I wasn't that drunk that I would just pass out on the beach."

He changes tactics. "How did you get in the bar?"

I repeat his question. "How'd we get in the bar?"

"You're underage," he states, looking at his notes. "Nineteen and she's seventeen."

"Yeah." I look down at my hands.

"Where'd the IDs come from? The boys?"

"Uh-huh."

Goodman and Mark exchange another perplexed look. "Usually they require wrist bands to serve. I'll have to check into this."

"We had them."

"Did you ask Will and Nicholas for the IDs?"

"I didn't have the conversation with Will."

"So Bristol did?"

Hesitating, I don't want her to get into trouble.

Goodman reads my mind. "She's not in trouble."

"Yeah, she asked Will for them during our surf lesson."

"Do you know what Rohypnol is?" Mark asks.

I shake my head.

"Also called roofies, Mexican Valium, or the 'forget pill'?"

"No, is it like heroin?"

"When the bartender said Will likes to drug people, what did you think he meant?"

I stare at my hands. "I just assumed an injection or something."

Goodman shakes his head. "People can inject all sorts of drugs, you're correct. Roofies are different, they're a pill that can be crushed up or dissolved in a liquid. We need to take you to the hospital in a little bit so we can test your urine. It has a limited shelf life, meaning it only shows up for about seventy-two hours."

Biting my lip, I think of the bar, the blue drink that seemed off. "Does it taste funny?"

"It can."

"My drink tasted odd, like it was diluted or something."

"Did you finish the drink?"

"Yes."

"Did your sister drink out of your cup or have her own?"

"Yeah, she had her own, but it was the same drink. A Blue Hawaii or something like that."

"Did you leave your drinks unattended?"

I pause to think. "They were waiting for us when we got back from the bathroom."

"Same guys with you?"

"Yes."

"Let me explain roofies to you. It's more potent than Valium, do you know what Valium is?"

"Um, I think my daddy took one after a surgery."

"Yep, probably. It's a sleeping pill, but very strong. That's why roofies are used. They cause temporary amnesia."

"And this is a thing people do?"

"Yes, it kicks in fast, and causes you to forget everything that happened during a period of time." He watches my face closely. "They can do what they want with you and you won't remember."

Inadvertently, I shiver.

"Have you showered today?"

"I rinsed off."

"Any tenderness down below? Pain? Soreness? Are you sexually active?" Goodman taps his pen to his notepad, pausing for my response.

I squirm in my seat, blushing. "No to all."

Sulking, I say, "I'm uncomfortable with these questions."

Mark nods his head, holding his hand up as Goodman starts to speak. "Paul's asking because the drug does what it says – it's called the date rape drug because it makes you forget things, things like being raped."

There's silence for a moment, all of us waiting on me to answer. "I don't know...I don't think so."

"Your sister's boyfriend back home?" he asks. "Was she having sex?"

"I don't live at home, I don't know... she's dating that guy, but I don't know if they have gone...if they have gone all the way." I'm being untruthful, but it's not like P.J. is involved in her disappearance. I'm not giving away her secrets. I have to adhere to the sister code.

"I don't want to scare you, but we're going to need to take you to the hospital for an exam."

"Huh?" I'm shocked. "The hospital? What kind of exam?"

"Have you had a pap smear before?"

I shake my head. "My mother said I don't need one until after marriage."

"This will be a full-body exam. They'll check your urine, but we want to make sure we get blood work, make sure no one... make sure no one violated you."

A pop of red appears in my nail bed.

Blood. I tense up, trying to smooth the pain that I've caused.

"Would you be more comfortable with a female doctor?" Mark asks.

"Yeah, I guess, but why... do you think something happened to me?"

Exchanging glances, Goodman shuts off the recorder.

"We need to call her parents first." Mark says to Goodman. "Just to let them know Blair is safe and Bristol's whereabouts are unknown."

The fear of having someone prod around my private parts seems like a walk in the park compared to telling them I can't find Bristol.

"The number's there." I point to the pad of paper near the phone.

"Why don't you call them and speak to them first?" Goodman instructs. "Then Mark and I can take over."

Slowly, I rise from my chair. Mark scoots over to make room for me on the bed.

I'm nervous, compounded by the fact they're both watching me, their eyes drilling into my every movement.

My hands shake, concentrating on the numbers, asking the front desk woman at their resort to connect me to their room.

When my mother answers, my voice loses control.

"Blair?" she says. "You're stuttering. What's going on?"

"I need to talk to you and Daddy," I manage to squeak out.

"What's wrong? Did you hurt yourself? Where's your sister?" She asks rapid-fire questions. I close my eyes for a second. "Can you please just get Daddy? Now," I add, an edge to my voice.

It cuts through her continued questions.

My father comes on the line. "Blair? Blair, what's wrong?"

I lick my lips.

If I say the words, they will come true.

They will be true.

Like gospel.

"Is this about your phone?"

"No." I sigh. "I found my phone."

"I thought you lost it in the water?"

"False alarm."

My eyes shift to Mark and Goodman, both intently watching me. I better get this over with. Shakily, I whisper, "Bristol's missing. We can't find her."

I wait for the screams, the yelling, my mother to have an outburst.

Nothing.

"Did you hear me?"

"Your sister is missing?" My father enunciates every word.

My mother chimes in, "What do you mean *missing*?"

"You were just with her this afternoon." My father's confused. "Did you two get separated? Can you ask a policeman for help?"

"I wasn't with her this afternoon."

"So you lied?" Now my mother's tone turns acrid.

"Yes."

"When did you last see your sister?" My father asks, my mother starting on a war path behind him, her voice rising an octave. "Catch me up."

"Last night." I take a deep breath. "She's been missing since last night."

"Wait, back up. Didn't you two stay in the hotel room?"

"Did you get her drunk? I knew it. I knew you would find some way to corrupt her. Oh my god, my baby!" My mother starts launching into a tirade, I have to hold the phone away from my ear. "Is she with someone?"

Goodman pulls the receiver from me after my mother starts yelling what a harlot she has for a daughter.

That would be me.

My father's calm, but he can't talk over my mother's ire.

"Mr. Bellamy?"

"Yes, who's this?"

"This is Detective Paul Goodman. I'm with Mark Matsen, head of security for the hotel. Your daughter contacted us immediately for assistance."

"Wait, the cops are involved?" I hear my mother wail in the background.

"I need your wife to take a breath so we can have a conversation, it's very important you both hear this. Can you help her calm down? I realize this is all very fresh and with you being halfway across the country, even harder to stomach."

"Yes, can you hold a moment?"

"Absolutely."

My father must've put the phone down as Goodman covers the handset and says to Mark, "I'm going to have you take Blair outside for a minute while I talk to them."

He nods, motioning for me to follow him out.

I slide into my flip-flops, hearing words like, 'hospital, exam, rape, drugs, and Blair.'

Goodman is fielding their questions, but he has no answers for them.

Mark opens the door for me, ushering me out into the hall, my mother's screams following me out as I shiver underneath the Hawks sweatshirt.

17

BLAIR

AT THE HOSPITAL, Goodman rushes me into the emergency room entrance, speaks to a nurse, and then sends me back with her to an exam room while Mark has a seat in the waiting area.

"Hi, aloha, I'm Elaine," a middle-aged woman with a black braid secured by a hair clip says.

"Blair Bellamy," I mumble. "What exactly are you going to do to me?" I'm nervous, wringing my hands apprehensively.

"I'm going to be right by your side tonight, okay?" She has a clipboard with pages of forms. "This looks overwhelming, but we will go through it page by page."

I nod, exhausted just looking at the sheaf of papers.

She asks me if I've had a vaginal exam before. I stare at her, unsure exactly what they do with my private parts.

Just a physical, I tell her.

She sees the frown lines across my forehead, my brow furrowing in confusion.

Explaining what the exam entails, she also adds, "We're also going to do a rape kit, also known as a sexual assault kit.

This includes a urine sample, physical exam, and blood test."

"I don't think I was raped," I offer.

Wouldn't I feel different? Shay told me she bled the first time she had sex. Other sorority sisters have said their first time was painful and uncomfortable. I'm not experiencing any issues down below, just memory loss. I mention this to the nurse.

"I understand." Her kind eyes are warm. "This is a long process, but we want to be thorough. I understand you might have been drugged last night, and that's why we're doing this." She lightly pats me on the shoulder. "Hopefully you weren't raped, but this can help with determining if you were under the influence of drugs and alcohol."

She goes through my medical history, prescriptions, and asks me more personal questions than I've ever even asked Shay.

"Okay, the doctor will come in and assist. Luckily we're able to grab Dr. Kalani. She's sweet and gentle... and a woman."

Elaine fills out some paperwork and walks me to the bathroom, holding a cup with my name and date of birth written on the side in permanent marker.

"I need you to pee in the cup and then bring it back out to me." She smiles, her teeth small and even. "Take your time, and just make sure it's filled up to here." She points to a line on the cup.

"Will this tell if I was drugged?"

"Yes." She's candid.

I struggle on the toilet. Peeing on command causes me to have stage fright, just like when I was in a community theater play as a middle-schooler and forgot my lines during opening night. I froze, the bright lights causing me to break out in a sweat, the audience watching me expectantly for my dialogue.

That was awful.

But it's nothing compared to this.

After I manage to trickle out enough to reach the designated line in the plastic, I meet Elaine in the hall, warily handing her the cup. Her light blue scrubs and white sneakers glow in the dim light. She leads me back to the exam room and instructs me to change into a pink paper gown.

I hesitate, not wanting to take Bristol's sweatshirt off. Elaine notices how I falter when I start to remove it.

She gently guides my arm back down. "Keep it on for now. Make sure everything else is off. Were you wearing underwear last night?"

I nod, puzzled by the question.

"We will want you to leave it behind." She points to a clear plastic bag, the words *evidence* written on it. "What happened to your clothes from last night?"

"They got wet from the ocean, they're hanging up in my hotel room."

"Okay." She pats my knee. "Dr. Kalani and I will be back in a few. Just disrobe from the waist down and slide onto the table."

The flimsy fabric covers my lower half, my bare legs shaking as I wait anxiously for the doctor. My pediatrician always had magazines in his exam rooms, even The New Testament in one.

I wiggle my toes, the aqua nail polish reminding me of the blue concoction of God knows what last night. There's a clock hanging on the bare white walls. I watch the seconds tick by, growing more impatient and petrified the longer I wait.

What if something did happen to me?

What if I'm pregnant?

Caught a disease?

My mind wanders to stories my high school friends told me about pap smears. "A cold metal object's shoved up your insides, twisted like a knife in your ovaries." That's how one girl in my class described it.

My thoughts are interrupted when the door opens and Dr. Kalani enters, followed by Elaine.

"Hi Blair," she says, reaching out to touch my shoulder. "I'm Dr. Kalani, and I've been with this hospital for over a decade. I understand something traumatic happened to you last night?"

She waits expectantly for me to nod my head.

"If you've never had intercourse and aren't experiencing any pain or symptoms like blood in your urine, there's a good chance there wasn't penetration. In that case, we'll just keep the evidence to check for any drugs in your system."

My face goes ashen.

"Are you taking any prescription medications or street drugs?"

We go over my night again in detail, ending with my sister still missing.

"I'm going to do a quick examination of your pelvic region. Have you had one before?"

"No," I utter, twisting my hands on my paper-laden lap.

She pulls two metal stirrups out of the table, explaining what they are and how to position my feet in them.

Elaine hands her some long, cotton swabs. Instinctively, I close my eyes after she squirts some lube on her gloved hand. "I'll also take a quick peek over your entire body, but you can keep your sweatshirt on until the end."

The speculum is cold, but not as cold as the K-Y Jelly coating it.

Squeezing my eyes tight, I imagine Bristol and I lying on the beach the other day.

Was that really yesterday?

Already it seems like last year.

SILENTLY, I say a prayer, asking God to help my sister, protect her, and bring her back to me, uninjured and unharmed.

It only takes the doctor a few minutes, but in that time, I feel violated. I shiver as she feels around my insides, poking and prodding.

Something inside me snaps, and I cry out in pain.

Elaine moves to my side, stroking my hair, tears running down my cheeks. She dabs a tissue, wiping my dripping nose like you would a child.

"All finished." Dr. Kalani rolls her stool away from the exam table. "Now let's quickly check out the rest of you."

"This will be quick." Elaine senses my trepidation at removing my sweatshirt. She helps me undress, setting the worn shirt next to me.

Dr. Kalani grabs her camera, telling me why they take pictures – in case there's evidence something happened. "This can help with prosecuting a case."

A blood test is next.

The phlebotomist comes in and silently administers the needle as I turn away from the prick draining blood into a vial. Elaine never leaves my side.

More paperwork.

By the time I'm sent back to the waiting room, I'm

mentally and physically drained. I don't want to answer any more questions, my brain hitting a wall.

Detective Goodman is seated, Mark is gone.

He offers an explanation before I can ask. "He had to go home."

I get it, he probably has to work in the morning.

"Are you okay?" He glances at my dejected face and slouched shoulders.

"I guess." I shrug. "If it helps bring Bristol home, I'll do whatever I can to help."

In the unmarked car on the way back to the hotel, I think about being alone in the hotel room. What if someone comes back to get me? The other key card is missing. Could they track it to our room somehow?

Sweating bullets, I wipe a trickle of sweat from my brow. My armpits are wet with perspiration.

As if he can read my thoughts, Goodman says. "I have an officer that's going to be outside of your room all night. I'll walk you up and introduce you to her."

I breathe a sigh of relief that a woman's going to be near. Does she carry a gun, I wonder? Could a man overpower her?

He's on his phone when we arrive back to the hotel, barking orders, mentioning a lot of words I don't understand and names of people I don't know.

An overweight black woman with short hair and a permanent smile on her face is standing alert when we arrive, a cup of coffee at her feet.

"Blair, this is Officer Chapman."

"Moira." She flicks her wrist at him. "You call me Moira, honey."

"She's been doing patrol for five years."

"I got you, baby girl." She gives me a smile. "I'm going to

protect you from the crazies, okay? I'll be out here all night. Just don't ask for no fairytale story."

Goodman walks me in so he can do a sweep of the room, checking the balcony and the bathroom, looking under the bed and in the closet. He doesn't know this, maybe he suspects it, but I'm relieved at his thoroughness. I notice a bag in his hand, my clothes removed from where they were hanging in the shower.

"I'll see you in the morning." He turns on the bedside lamp. "Get some rest. If you need anything, ask Officer Chapman."

I nod, shifting my weight to my other foot.

"You're brave," he says, seeing the uneasy look on my face. "You did the right thing confiding in us." He pats my shoulder, turning the knob behind him, leaving me alone with my thoughts again.

I hear murmurs as he consults with Moira. Typically, I would listen, pressing my ear against the door. Tonight, I do the opposite, hiding under the covers instead.

In spite of my fatigue, the events of the night, I can't sleep, turning over restlessly as I imagine Bristol, tossing in the open water, bait for a shark in the night.

Then I see her being held down, thin wrists flailing as Will uses his weight against her.

Howling, I sit up so suddenly that the room spins. My body's drenched in sweat, the covers soaked. I think I'm still screaming, but it's the shrill sound of the phone.

"Bristol." I reach a hand to my chest, my heart beating. I grab the receiver, breathless. "Hello?"

"Blair?" It's my mother. She sounds distant.

I play with the phone cord, twisting it, watching it meld into shapes as I wait to hear what she has to say.

"How could you?" Her speech is slurred.

"Mother?" I rub my eyes, confused.

Her voice breaks, I hear the tears. "Blair, did you ask for forgiveness?"

"What?"

"Forgiveness from God for being sinful."

"Mother, what're you talking about?"

"The officers told us what happened...were you being lustful?"

"Mother, you're scaring me."

I hear a rustle, a murmur, then my father's voice. "Blair, honey, are you okay?"

"No." I whisper, gripping the receiver. "No, I'm not."

"We're on our way – we're at the airport now."

"What is she talking about?"

"Don't listen to her, she's struggling, incoherent." His voice sounds uneven, like he's as lost as I feel. "She took something to calm down. It's making her loopy. We'll see you in the morning. We're coming straight to the hotel."

I start to hang up when I hear him say, "Blair?"

"Yeah?"

"Blair, are you feeling okay? Like physically?" He's struggling to form words. "Did someone hurt you?"

"No, Daddy." I grip the damp covers, clenching and unclenching my fist.

I can't say anything else. My brain can't process anything else right now.

Moira knocks on the door, asking if I'm okay. I lie, lying back down, jittery and agitated. I turn the television on, then off, then on, then mute the sound, the screen flashing as I try and sleep.

Nightmares plague me, one after the other, Bristol on the dance floor with Will, her back to me, but when she stops dancing and turns around, her face no longer looks carefree and happy, it screams in terror, her eyes alarmed.

"Help me," she yells. "Somebody please help me."

When I try and reach her, people keep getting in the way, separating us, my hand reaching out and grasping at air. I'm frustrated, calling her name, loud and shrill.

Finally the crowd parts, but there's no sign of her.

She's disappeared into the night.

18

BRISTOL

WHEN I COME TO, I'm startled by movement. A jerk of my head and my eyes flicker open. The children's clothes I woke up in earlier have been removed.

I'm now naked and cradled in his arms. Trembling, I remember why I'm stripped bare. My attempts to push away from him are futile. Terror-stricken, my eyes widen in horror as he holds me tight to his chest.

"You're okay," he soothes. "I'm just taking you to have a bath." He softly kisses my forehead. "Let me help you up."

A large metal drum is now perched in the corner of the room. He must have moved it in when I was out cold.

"Bath time in morning," I mumble.

"Usually is. Except when we have this problem." He pushes a hand between my legs. "We have to clean you out. It was wrong what *you* made me do. We can't let that happen again. It's wrong."

What *I* made him do?

He instructs me to wrap my arms around his neck, my legs around his waist so he can carry me to the makeshift tub.

"You're bleeding." He pulls his hand away from my inner thigh, disgusted.

Sure enough, there's a dark red stain on his jeans.

I shut my eyes, willing the tears to come later, or away from his watchful eyes. I don't want to anger him, I just want him to leave.

"Can I bathe alone?"

"Never." He's matter-of-fact. "I don't want you to drown. I couldn't live with myself."

"But I'm seventeen," I murmur.

"What did you say?" He abruptly stops, shaking me in his arms like a rag doll.

"Twelve, I'm twelve."

"That's better." I go limp in his arms.

There's a spigot with a hose that's filling up the tub. I shiver, wondering how cold the temperature is. I want burning hot water to take away the feel of him pushing inside me.

Shuddering, he sets me down. I curl up in a fetal position, wrapping my arms around my legs. Rocking back and forth, I taste the salty tears as I cry out for my parents.

"You know the rules." He shoves me on the back, his hand jabbing into my spine. "Stop. I'm not going to remind you again. No wailing."

Taking a deep breath, I will myself to calm down, counting numbers in my head.

"Come sit by the tub while it fills up," he commands.

I obey him, sinking down onto my knees. "Will the water be warm?" I whisper.

"Raise your hand." He motions.

I repeat my question.

"Yes, it's a self-heating tub. See the coils underneath?"

He smiles at me, with the ugly tooth and even uglier mole. "I built it."

I decide then and there I'm going to call him the Mole.

He busies himself with setting toiletries by the red pail, humming as he unpacks a cardboard box.

It's then I notice the titles of the books on the shelf. They're all classics like *The Boxcar Children, Nancy Drew,* Laura Ingalls Wilder's *Little House on the Prairie,* Lois Lowry, Judy Blume.

"Is there anything you need to see to read, like glasses?" He notices my eyes trained on the built-in unit.

"No," I answer.

"Good, because tonight I want you to read to me in the tub. Your choice on the book."

You have to be freakin' kidding me. I cringe. He rapes me then wants story time?

"I brought you floss, a toothbrush, and toothpaste. I need you to take good care of your body so we don't need to go to the doctor." He points to the pail. "I told you about your toilet. I'll be in charge of emptying it for now."

Wait, would he take me to a clinic if I got sick...

"Because there's no doctor visits. If you get sick, you're out of luck. I'll let you die." He says it jokingly, but there's a blatant seriousness to his statement.

"What if I get pregnant?"

He looks horrified, like I just told him he has two weeks to live. "You can't get pregnant, you're too young." His voice goes into a high-pitched sing-song as he chuckles. "You're silly, little girl."

I clench my hands beneath my bare legs. The Mole is not only a sociopath, he's delusional. I might have lied and told my sister I had sex, but it was only to seem like I'm mature. She's older and experiences everything first – drinking, college, tattoos.

I wince, but his violation is not consensual, I remind myself, and his attitude towards unprotected sex are at odds with everything I've learned about unplanned pregnancies. I know where babies come from. My parents weren't dense enough to tell me they came from a stork or baby Jesus just dropped them on their front porch. That's why they preach abstinence.

"Come pick a book." He turns to the hose, shutting off the spigot. "And get in the water before it gets cold." I stand up, pain shooting from my pelvic region. My hand instinctively reaches to cover my privates. I tip-toe over to the shelf, my head swiveling to keep an eye on him.

He starts to undress and I hear the clasp of his belt buckle come undone for the second time, my insides twisting. I vomit, liquid OJ is all that's coating my stomach. Sinking to my knees, I heave, wiping my mouth with the back of my hand, tears burning my eyes. What if he tries something in the tub?

He turns his back on me in disgust, muttering, "Does my little girl need me to take her temperature?"

Appalled, I stagger up to the shelf. I don't want to think about where he would put a thermometer in me. My breathing speeds up and I have to lean against the shelf to steady myself.

"No." I groan. "I'm fine. Just dehydrated."

"You can clean it up after I'm gone." He shakes his head. "Pick out a book and then brush your teeth," he demands. "Hurry up."

I grab a book off the shelf, not even bothering to read the title. Grabbing the toothbrush and toothpaste he brought, I gag on the cinnamon taste. Brushing my teeth, I pause, waiting until he sinks into the tub to creep back over. It almost overflows as his hairy body disappears into the water. He's not fat, but not skinny, just a tad on the pudgy side, average, I'd say, but still tall.

Slowly stepping around the tub, he reaches a hand out, twisting his fingers around my wrist. "Don't forget the wash-cloth." A ratty striped washcloth is between two towels. All look like they've reached their thread count expiration date. We donate nicer ones to the shelters, new ones, I think.

I pick it up, trying to take my time to avoid sitting in the makeshift bathtub with him. Maybe he'll get cold and quickly retreat. "Get in." He motions to me. "Careful when you step inside. I don't want you sloshing water everywhere."

Slowly I hand him the secondhand book and the wash-cloth, gingerly lifting my leg, not wanting to raise it more than I have to. Noticing the dried blood on my inner thigh, I start to quickly lower myself until I'm seated in front of him. He tries to push me down and forward, and I have to sink until I can clasp the edges of the metal. Gritting my teeth, the lukewarm water hits my sensitive spots, sore and bruised

I wish it were hotter, scalding enough to burn him off of me.

The Mole wraps his arms around me, pulling me back towards his chest.

My body shivers, his touch unwanted and repulsive.

He doesn't notice or care, humming another annoying tune. "Ready to read to me?" He nudges it in my hand along with the washcloth. "Dry your hands before turning the pages, we don't want the book to get wet," he instructs. I have to bite my lip to keep from pointing out that the pages are already waterlogged by their streaked print.

I wipe my hands, hand him the cloth, and stare at a

cover of two boys, *The Bridge to Terabithia* by Katherine Paterson. Turning the page, I clear my throat, attempting to read. My voice is shaky at first, my position against his naked body awkward, hunched over as much as I can in a makeshift bathtub with a deranged stranger.

First The Mole makes a couple of comments, but as I read he stays surprisingly quiet, his head leaned back against the drum. The first twenty pages I breeze through until my stomach cramps and my left foot falls asleep.

Then I stop, looking over my shoulder at his drooping eyelids.

At first I think he's asleep, there's no movement, just his heavy breathing over my shoulder. I try and scoot forward in the water, but he breaks the silence, tightening his grip around my waist.

"Did you know I saved you?" He sits up, adjusting me in front of him.

I freeze, his flaccid penis against my buttocks.

"What do you mean?" I whisper.

He brings the washcloth up to my skin. Goosebumps race down my flesh, a combination of his undesirable touch and tepid water. Starting to wash my back in a circular motion, he ignores my question for a minute. It's a test, he wants me to pry, get pushy so he has a reason to punish me.

I stare straight ahead, focusing on the metal door that's a fortress against my freedom.

"Aren't you curious?" he asks, his fingers tracing the back of my neck. He changes the subject. "What's this necklace?" He pulls the thin chain around, examining the diamond-encrusted 'B'. "Very pretty," he murmurs. "This from a boyfriend?"

Biting my lip in agony, I'm mute for a moment as I consider how to respond. It's all I have left of home, of my father. I don't want to tell him it only leaves my neck to shower or swim. If he knows it's priceless, he'll take it away from me.

"It looks expensive. You shouldn't wear it in the tub," he chides. "Let me remove it for you."

Reaching a hand up, I cringe, grasping his fingers. "Let's not tonight. I'm more curious to hear how you saved me. I love heroes and white knights in shining armor." I attempt a half-hearted giggle. "Just like the fairy tales I love."

I freeze, waiting to see if he's bursting with anger or beaming with pride.

He's neutral, pulling his fingers out of my grip. "Okay, but just for tonight. Next time, don't argue. Just do what I say."

Shaking my head, I stare again at the panels on the wall. Why are they covered in foam?

He resumes washing my shoulders and back. "You really want to know?"

"Of course." I feign interest.

"The guy you were with, what's his name?"

"When?"

"Don't be stupid." He tugs my hair. "At the bar."

"Will."

"I was watching you." Clearly, if he knew I was at a bar with a guy. I don't point out the obvious. My eyes drift to the corner, focusing on a flashing light.

It's a camera.

Licking my lips, I wait for him to continue. "You came in and were perfectly fine, but when you went to the bathroom, I saw him slip something in your drink. Both you and the other girl."

"Blair," I moan. "My sister."

"She's probably worried about you."

I shake my head. "Can I call her? Let her know I'm safe?"

His hand pauses on the dimples in my lower back, and I'm worried I've offended him. "That feels really good," I murmur.

"Does it?" He sounds surprised. "I used to wash her. She liked it except when I went too low." He gives a strangled laugh, reaching forward, using the washcloth to reach in between my legs. They're closed tight, but he forces them open. "Stop, little girl. I have to make sure we get all of me out of you." He repeats again, "It's just not right what we did, we can't do it again. She would be so mad."

"Who?" I ask.

"Doesn't matter," he whispers in my ear. "You're safe now. With me. As long as we can wash away your impurities." A hum comes out as he keeps the washcloth between my legs, forcing the coarse cloth up my vagina, irritating my already sore spots. It's like a Brillo pad's being scrubbed on my insides.

"Ow..." I scoot forward. "Stop. Please stop."

He keeps humming, I think he doesn't hear me at first, his voice like a trance, the motion the same as he ignores my request.

I try to stand, hoisting myself up, anything to stop the uncomfortable feeling.

"What're you doing?" he remarks, snapping out of his thoughts.

Changing tactics, since he seems to like giving me pain, I respond. "I'm cold. You were right, it's been a long day."

"Oh...yes it has." He considers this. "Yes. Please stand up."

My teeth chatter as I slowly rise, water dripping down my legs. I'm miserable, hot tears burning my eyelids. I bite my lip to keep from having a full-on sob session. I don't want to feel the wrath of his anger, my body broken in one day.

He stands behind me, then steps out. "I'll dry you off and then you can do me." Taking the worn towel, his touch is the opposite of the harsh washing he just gave me, now it's light and gentle. "I've got a robe for you. It was hers."

Of course it was, I think dryly.

Except this might be the only item not from another time period.

It's a typical robe, fuzzy and pink. A butterfly on the pocket. It smells cheap, but doesn't have the mothball scent of the shift from earlier.

"Thank you," I say, covering my body as quickly as humanly possible. I wrap the belt around me, securely closing any gaps.

"I have a nightgown for you that I expect to see you in in the morning." He purses his lips. "You aren't allowed to sleep in anything else. Do you understand?"

He forces me to look at him and say 'yes' out loud.

"Good girl. Now my turn."

Tentatively, I take the towel and start drying him off. I go as lightly and quickly as I can, his eyes half-open. His body's supple, the arms, legs, and chest covered with golden tendrils, like a porn star from a Playgirl a friend from school's mom had shoved under her bed. My girlfriends and I snuck it into her room and looked through it, curious about the big bushes that men and women seemed to have back then. He seems to be stuck in another time all together.

I can't bring myself to touch his penis, even with a towel covering my hand.

"You forgot an area." He opens his eyes, attentive, waiting to see how I'll respond.

Playing dumb, I ask him what he means.

HE POINTS DOWN. "Make sure it's dried good. It needs to be clean and dry."

I want to close my eyes and imagine I'm somewhere else, but he's watching me with a twisted smile on his face.

"Of course." I force a strangled laugh as I rub the moisture between his legs, thinking of my hometown, my bedroom, the band posters on the wall.

Abruptly, he startles me out of my thoughts. "That's enough."

With that, he stalks off to the dresser, opening the bottom drawer. "This is your nightgown." He removes a thin piece of pink material. Something a little girl would wear. It's long and Pepto-Bismol colored, a small, dainty white ribbon at the top with three buttons that're decorative only.

"You'll wear this." His statement brooks no argument.

I nod.

"Remove your robe."

I hesitate, my hand grips the rigid belt around my waist.

We make eye contact, his blue-green eyes staring into mine. The displaced hair in the mole is like a third eye.

Quivering, I undo the belt and slowly slide the robe off my shoulders, letting it fall to the ground. I try and shield my body from him with my hands, covering up as much as I can with my palms.

"Little girl..." His voice trails off. "Arms up so we can get your nightgown on. You're trying to seduce me, and I don't like it." He steps forward, gripping my chin. "Is this what you want?" He pulls my hand from my breast and puts it on his genitals.

I shut my eyes, appalled. "No," I say flatly.

"Then listen. It's time for bed." The Mole interrupts my thoughts. "You're moving too slow. Hold your arms up."

Instinctively, I move them behind my back, terrified he's going to tie me up again, that I'll be forced to sleep spread-eagled.

"I must never come back in the morning to see you wearing anything else unless I say differently, do you understand, little girl?"

Nodding my head, my hands tremble slightly as he pulls it over my head, brushing his hands lightly over my curves.

I sigh in disgust, staring at a spot on the ceiling. It doesn't have the typical texture of popcorn or smooth paint, or canned lights. It's flat, but has a weird pattern.

"And these." He fidgets through the top drawer, handing me white underwear that go up to my belly button. "Put these on. It's unclean to sleep naked. We don't want anyone touching you."

Except for you, I think bitterly.

"Also, after every bath, you have to spray this on you." The pink bottle says *Love Baby Soft*, and he opens the top drawer and motions for me to hold out my wrists. "You need to put a dab on each wrist and then spray it on your neck."

I cough. The powdery smell overcomes me as I inhale it.

"You don't like?" He steps back, offended.

Gagging, I quickly say, "No, I'm just not used to the smell."

He tilts his head. "What would you prefer? Something more sensual?"

"No, no, this is perfect." I add, "It reminds me of my childhood."

He's satisfied with this answer, turning back to the dresser as he sets the bottle back in the drawer.

But no...there's something deeper that creates this time travel back to another age. Blair took an abnormal psych class her freshman year in college, and she used to tell me stories on different mental illnesses. She was explaining a fascinating story about this man who was raised by his grandma and after she died, he became obsessed. He never removed her from her bed, continuing to act as if she were alive, and from that moment forward, time stopped in his mind.

I wish I knew the ending.

My mom interrupted Blair's story, telling her it was 'dark and twisted,' and then cut off her response to talk about my accomplishments on student council.

Typical Mom.

Blair thought I liked the attention from our parents, and it's true, at first I did, except it became overbearing after she went to college and Mom had no one else to dote on. Her interest never wavered, and it's impossible to please a mother that needs to be involved in my day-to-day and live vicariously through me.

It's like I can keep very little for myself and to myself.

The Mole takes my hand and leads me to the bed, pulling the thin blanket off and helping guide me under the sheets. He flattens the pillow underneath my head, softly kissing my forehead again.

He kneels on the floor next to me, his warm breath on my face.

"Just remember, I can see you at all times," he says. "I'll know what you do, and I'm right next door." He pushes my head down until there's an indent in the pillow. "If you ever try to escape, I'll kill you."

My eyes widen in horror, but he pushes my lids closed, like you would a dead person that accidentally died with them open.

"Go to sleep, little girl. And don't forget your responsibilities in the morning."

He smooths the covers over me, leaving my side to grab the ratty brown teddy bear from the shelf. He shoves it underneath the crook of my armpit, a hole where the stuffing is missing.

I press my eyes closed, pretending I'm in the hotel room, back pressed against Blair's. But sleep doesn't come, not after he lays down on the carpet next to the bed and hums lullabies until he thinks I'm asleep.

Not after he pulls the string to the lightbulb, shrouding me in darkness again.

Especially not as his flashlight clicks on and he slides the metal door open and closed behind him, reminding me exactly how alone I am.

19

BLAIR

MOIRA'S REPLACED by another officer by the time I wake up, and Goodman and Mark are both back in the room when my parents arrive. Jet-lagged and tense, both have aged overnight. Lines etch their faces and their movements are jerky and robotic. Both have coffee cups in their trembling hands as they sink into the chairs at the table.

Both explain to my parents a timeline that's constructed to the best of our abilities. My parents ask about the boys and their potential involvement.

The phone rings and I rush to answer it, my parents holding their breath. We're all thinking the same thing – maybe it's Bristol.

Except it's not, it's Will.

He acts as if nothing's wrong. "Hey, you called yesterday." He's chipper. It grates on my nerves the second I pick up the phone.

He's guilty.

"Took you long enough to call back," I mutter.

"What do you mean?" He's apathetic. "I lost my phone."

"Sure," I say.

I can feel everyone's eyes staring at my back, waiting to hear the outcome.

"It got lost in the ocean."

"Yeah, let me guess, a shark swallowed it." I twist the cord in my hand.

"Why the 'tude?" He's annoyed. "What do you want anyway?"

"Bristol's missing, as I'm sure you know." Bitterness laces my words.

"No, how would I know?"

"Because you were the last one with her." My voice drips with sarcasm. "And you're phone apparently just 'disappeared.'"

"Well it did, and I'm sorry she's gone, but I don't understand what it has to do with me."

"Did you physically come into the room with her?" I keep my voice even. "No one's upset, we just don't know why she wasn't here."

"Yes." He pauses. "She went inside and I left. That's all."

"You sure you didn't leave her outside?" I ask. "Or on the beach?"

"Nope, seventeenth floor."

"Did you actually see her go inside the room?"

"Yep." I hear his name being called. He murmurs to someone in the background asking him a question.

"Did you force yourself on her?" I can't help myself. "Rape her?"

A hand touches my shoulder. It's my father.

"Jesus, Blair, calm the fuck down." I hear a girl's voice giggling. "I gotta get going."

"Nicholas said you never came home. Where were you?"

"Go to hell, Blair. I don't know what happened to your sister." He slams the phone down.

I hit redial, but the phone rings and rings, and no one picks up.

The room's filled with tension, my mother cowering in her chair, my father pacing the room. Mark and Goodman talk to my parents, then they both leave.

The three of us sit in awkward silence, my mother staring out at the water, the seagulls, people walking below, anywhere but me.

I play with a straw wrapper, balling up the paper, twisting it, watching it meld into shapes.

"How could you?" she speaks.

I glance up. "Huh?"

Her eyes are still focused in the distance, not on me.

"Leave her with a boy. She's not like *you*." Her eyes glower at me.

"Like me how?" I rip the wrapper in half.

"A slut. A harlot," she scoffs. "She's a church-going girl. She doesn't know about drugs and boys and whatever nonsense you told her she had to do for a good time."

"She knows more than you think." I meet her eyes, defiant.

Standing, she walks over to me.

I feel it before it registers, a sharp crack where her palm slaps me. "Don't you ever speak about my baby like that."

My hand reaches up to my cheek, rubbing the offended spot.

"I never should've trusted you," she repeats. "You're the reason she's missing. Don't ever forget that."

"I know. Don't you think I know?" I cry out.

My father's eyes are vacant, he says nothing at her outburst, his hands on his Bible, glasses tipped precariously on his nose. Any movement on his part will send them crashing to the floor.

Goodman comes back later, scraping his knuckles on the door. He was able to interview Will and Nicholas at the surf shack.

The bartender wasn't kidding – Will does have a rap sheet.

Goodman tells us that Will's brushes with the law are primarily juvenile shit – hot-wiring a vehicle, underage drinking, and speeding.

Until he mentions 'arson and involuntary manslaughter'.

Will was sent away to a boy's home when he was only twelve.

He was baby-sitting his twelve-year-old sister and thought it would be genius to set his mom's boyfriend's house on fire to collect insurance money. He didn't count on the fact that the boyfriend didn't have insurance or that his sister would be trapped in her bedroom. She locked in her closet for stealing food from the pantry since they hadn't eaten in a couple days.

I'm sick to my stomach, butterflies clawing at my insides.

Will acknowledges to the investigators he was with Bristol but claims he brought her back to the hotel. The cameras in the lobby substantiate this-they were spotted getting on an elevator and he was spotted coming back down, alone.

He left her at our room, the key card inside confirms this.

"He couldn't have escaped with her out the window?" Mother asks.

"Seventeen floors?" Goodman raises his eyebrows. "Highly unlikely."

"But what about after they came up to the room?" My father asks. "Surely there're cameras on every floor?"

"Only in the lobby and the elevator banks." Goodman frowns. "We've never had a situation like this."

"Surely she isn't the first girl who got...lost." Mother refuses to say "kidnapped, missing, or runaway."

"Usually they're found drunk, sleeping off hangovers." Goodman surmises. "This is an extremely rare case. Both boys have cooperated with our investigation thus far."

After a week, the hotel suggests moving us to a suite so we'll be more comfortable but Mother refuses, so the three of us share the room.

The pull-out couch becomes my makeshift bed.

THOUGH I DON'T SLEEP.

None of us do.

We pretend, but we toss and turn, the days drag on into overwrought nights as we wait...and wait. We stay on the island another two weeks, helpless as hamsters circling a wheel, frantically spinning but without purpose.

Tensions rise between my parents, the adoption of Isaiah put on hold, their grief twisting every word and gesture. It escalates between my parents and I. Between Will and Nicholas and all of us.

Will's cooperative at first, then he refuses additional questions and interviews, citing 'work.' He's finally hauled in after they issue a search warrant for the surf shack and him and Nichola's apartment.

At the beginning, Bristol's case receives primetime news coverage, helicopter searches, pleas for public assistance, and reward money. Local news turns to national interest – the story of Bristol Bellamy, a farm kid from rural Nebraska gone missing on spring break.

The media loves to sensationalize the case, painting Bristol as this naïve girl out of her element in the big, bad city of Honolulu. I shudder at how they portray me, an out-of-control sorority girl that pushed my baby sister into drinking underage and clubbing.

The atmosphere is nuclear – my mother's bottled-up anger rises to the surface and then explodes until the next thought becomes a new obsession.

"Why would you just leave her?" My mother shrieks, "and with a felon?"

Then, "You were always jealous of her." Shaking her head disapprovingly.

My father tries to interject, his hands kneaded on his lap or his worn Bible as he stares at the floor, his voice monotone.

But it's pointless, her tirades continue.

ONE MORNING, I'm on my side, curled up, my anxiety shooting through the roof, as I huddle on the pull-out couch.

I try to slow down my breathing.

Mother wakes up, the room still dark, and her eyes drift over to the sofa. "Bristol?" A smile tugs at her face.

"No, it's me." I sigh, taking a deep breath.

The disappointment in her voice stuns me. "Oh." The smile immediately dies as she lambasts me for every character flaw and mistake I've made.

MY FATHER REACHES a breaking point when she throws the television remote across the room, narrowly missing my shoulder.

"That's enough," he says, pushing his glasses up his forehead. "Damn it, Priscilla, that's enough." I've never heard him cuss, even 'Hell' is off-limits unless he's using it in one of his forceful sermons.

He's been extremely patient, coddling her as she cries, picking her up when she falls apart. But this is too much even for him.

My mother stares at him like he's a stranger, unrecognizable.

My father tries to play the intermediary at the beginning, reminding her that I'm struggling with my own guilt.

"She's having a hard enough time," he murmurs. "It's her sister that's missing."

But what burns down my throat is what she says next. Under her breath, she mutters, *"It should've been her."*

The days seem to stretch on, minutes ticking by, and every morning, there's renewed hope, but by evening, despair. It's a constant mind game, the possibility she'll be located, then with each passing day, it becomes less and less likely.

We never speak of the statistics, though Goodman has tried to prepare us that she might not come home.

The investigation continues – the hotel staff are interviewed, pizza place employees and patrons. At *The Ocean Club*, the bartenders and DJ are interviewed, verifying the boys were there, but they deny seeing us.

David the bartender confirms two girls were with them.

Leslie Billings and Haley Pritchett.

The other workers say the same thing.

There's no recollection of a Bristol and Blair Bellamy.

My parents assume I'm lying, or that I got the bar wrong.

Leads pour in, but they're from unreliable witnesses or do-gooders who want to help but can't provide a shred of evidence.

The only solid fact we know is that Bristol was alive when I left... but after 1:17 A.M., it's like she walked off the face of the earth.

There's no trace of her after Will left her at the hotel door.

Or so he says.

20

BRISTOL

I FINALLY FALL asleep but wake up disoriented, forgetting I'm in a twin-size bed. During my thrashing, I roll over the edge, crashing to the floor with a thud.

The teddy bear and my elbow take the brunt of the fall.

Eyeballing the blinking camera, I quickly climb back in bed, rubbing the sore spot. I don't want The Mole coming back in here and trying to snuggle me to sleep.

Or worse.

I wish I knew the time, but there are no clocks in here. It's like I stepped back in another time period. Someone else's childhood and someone pushed 'pause'.

When I fall into a restless slumber, I'm awoken by the clang of the door being thrust open. I keep my face to the wall, pretending to be asleep.

If I thought that would keep him from humming and turning on the single lightbulb, I was wrong.

In fact, he plugs in a floodlight that illuminates the foam walls and forces me to shut my eyes against the blinding glare.

"Rise and shine, little girl."

I groan. "What time is it?"

"Time for you to get up. No need for a bath this morning since you had one last night. Just wash your face. I brought your breakfast." He's wearing navy coveralls, like the kind car mechanics wear. Maybe this means he's on his way to work and won't stay long.

Rolling to my other side, I sit up slowly.

He's humming, his back to me, standing at the yellow dresser. I slowly step out of bed, tiptoeing across the room. He's searching through the contents, murmuring to himself.

If I thought today's outfit would be more consistent with the 90s, I was wrong.

"Here you go." He pulls something out of a drawer, it looks like a brown turd. "Today's outfit." It's a drop waist dress, UPS brown, with orange frills down the front. To complete the look are cream stockings and black Mary Jane patent leather shoes.

"Well, hurry and come over here," he chastises. "You need to wash your face and put your Baby Soft on." He uses the spigot to wet the washcloth and hands it to me. "Soap's by the tub. You can rinse your face in there and brush your teeth."

I follow his instructions, wiping the sleep out of my eyes. I have to pee, but the thought of him standing over me while I try to force my bladder to go sounds painful.

"Underwear. Dress. Stockings. Shoes." He ticks them off. "I'm thinking pigtails today." Handing me each article of clothing, I remove my nightgown, trembling at the thought of him examining my naked body.

He doesn't even notice my hesitation, his attention turned to the tray that holds the hair brush and rubber bands.

Cringing, I change in silence, his eyes darting back to

my face. He watches like a hawk as I move to the dresser to grab the Baby Soft. I dab the required spots and turn to look at him for my next instructions.

"I'm pleased by how eager you are." He claps his hands together. "Go sit at the desk and eat your breakfast. I'm going to do your hair."

The chair's low to the ground and uncomfortable, I have to slouch to fit on it. He sets an apple and a carton of milk in front of me. "Breakfast is served."

I hate apples – the annoying skin gets caught in my teeth. My stomach growls as I concentrate on drinking the milk, hoping he'll ignore my hunger pains and scorn for the fruit in front of me.

He busies himself with brushing my hair, the bristles running over my tangles.

"Why aren't you eating?"

"I'm not hungry," I lie.

The brush goes deeper into my scalp.

"I brought you an apple. You will eat it."

Sucking down the last of the milk, I'm pulled against the wood slats of the chair as he pulls the plastic through my hair.

"Ouch," I exclaim.

"Do we have a problem already this morning?"

"No," I groan.

"I didn't think so." He reprimands me, hitting my shoulder with the plastic head of the brush. "And call me 'sir.'"

"No problem, sir."

Sinking my teeth into the red of the apple, I purposely take a large bite.

"That's better, little girl." Back to gentle strokes. Then he parts my hair and ties each side into pigtails.

"What is the agenda today?" he asks.

I start to answer, chewing, as he thumps me again with the brush. "Swallow before speaking. Manners."

Gulping, I pause. "Puzzle and books."

"Yes, you better read. Tonight you'll read to me out loud." He strokes my cheek with his smooth palm. If he works on cars, I'd be surprised. Maybe he wear gloves? His hands don't match a manual labor job.

I'm mid-bite when he takes the apple from me. He points to a paper bag. "Your snack is in there. Water jug as well. A cup's on the dresser. I'll empty your bucket and be right back." He pats my shoulder. "I'd like you to draw me a picture today."

Luckily I only peed last night.

I half-heartedly raise my hand. "Of what, sir?"

"What you imagine when you think of the beach." He leaves me sitting. I twist to watch over my shoulder as he grabs the bucket, humming again, watching the metal door.

There's blackness behind it. No lights, just dark.

He's back in a little over a minute. I count it down in my head.

Does he dump it outside? Maybe a trash can?

"Okay, little girl. Have a good day." He tugs on my pigtail. "I'll miss you. Will you miss me?"

"Yes," I whisper, fighting back tears.

"Can you sew?" he asks out of nowhere.

I shake my head no. He snaps his fingers. "Darn. She could." He gives me a pinch on my cheek. "Oh well, I can look for that in the next one." He turns to leave, sliding the door open.

"What do you mean, next one?" I ask out loud.

"What did you say?" Swinging back around, he crosses the room in three quick strides.

I look down at my hands, avoiding his flared nostrils.

"You heard me." He grabs my chin, tilting my face from side to side. "What did you say?"

Before I know it, I'm screaming at the top of my lungs, the mole on his face lunging at me as he presses his hands on my throat.

Choking me, I squirm under his grip until I go limp, my arms falling to my sides.

When I wake up, I'm in a place worse than the room.

21

BLAIR

AFTER WE GET BACK to Nebraska, we go our separate ways – my parents to our small town, me to university. I only have a couple months left of the spring semester before I'll be a junior.

My parents and I stop talking, except for Sunday calls after my father preaches at church. And then, it's only him calling to say hi.

I throw myself into my studies, but I can't focus, chewing through the pencil, tapping the keyboard wordlessly, or finding every reason not to study.

So I start going out at night. Partying. Binge drinking. I don't let anyone get close to me, I'm just there to numb myself.

Men are all lumped into the same category – potential threats to my safety. I don't trust them, even co-ed college boys that ask me to dance or hold hands. Even though I drown myself in alcohol, I watch my drinks carefully, never letting one go unattended.

The self-loathing doesn't work – I can hardly be alone

with my thoughts, the images violent and graphic, my sister always at the top of my mind, but in trouble.

Panic attacks plague me.

I'm scared of the dark.

Terrified to be alone.

Goodman calls me. A body washed up on Waikiki Beach of a young girl. They're speculating it might be Bristol, trying to prepare us all in advance.

It's not.

Someone else's daughter, someone else's loss.

This time, a nineteen-year old girl from Nova Scotia. Her demise was from drowning-

falling off a catamaran after a storm rolled in. It was never reported in the States because her family didn't realize she was sailing. Worse yet because she couldn't swim.

What if Bristol *did* drown?

At least it would be swift and immediate.

It becomes an obsession, picturing her body out in the ocean, caught on plankton or sunk at the bottom like buried treasure.

This sets off a chain reaction.

I become so fearful of water that showering gives me the willies.

My best friend and roommate, Shay, tries to help, but I'm withdrawn, a shell of myself. Most mornings I stay in bed crying, the thought of showering, making it to class, or studying a steep impossibility.

Besides my fear of water, I'm worried a man will come and take me.

I leave the door open to the bathroom when I bathe. Never turning my back, nervous, my eyes glued to the hallway. I spend maybe a minute, sometimes two, tops, washing and rinsing off, shampoo dripping into my eyes as I struggle to keep them open at all times. If I close them, let down my guard, that's when I'll disappear.

The other door to the bedroom is locked since I can only watch one entrance at a time.

When I bother to shave, I sit on the toilet and use water from the faucet and a wet towel.

Night terrors invade my fitful sleep. Most nights I scream until Shay wakes me or my alarm pulls me out of my intermittent hibernation.

One morning, I'm in the bathroom, my usual routine of keeping the plastic shower curtain half-open, my back towards the wall, eyes trained on the door.

I hear voices, stilted and tense.

Shay's from Chicago, Southside, a family of twelve. This means she has a loud, booming voice, since she never felt she was heard in such a crowded house. Because of the size of her family, she has an affinity for crowds. Part of why I love her is her ability to immerse herself in groups of people she doesn't know and walk out with fifteen new friends.

I used to love her potential for being the center of attention.

NOW I DESPISE IT.

Turning the shower off, my eyes tear up from unrinsed conditioner. Tentatively I step out, pausing as her speech becomes raised and more pronounced.

My towel hangs on the rack, I share the bathroom with her and the sisters across the hall, two sophomore girls.

Shutting the door, I dry and lotion my skin, throwing on baggy sweatpants and Bristol's sweatshirt.

SHAY'S back is turned to me when I tip-toe back into our room, her shoulders hunched. "She's not okay though, Mrs. Bellamy. That's what I'm trying to tell you."

She pauses, listening to what's said on the other end of the line. She doesn't like the response, shaking her head in silent frustration.

"Okay, then can I talk to Mr. Bellamy?" There's an edge to her tone.

A lull follows as she waits, a cuss word murmured that only I can hear.

I'm silent, rivulets of water from my wet hair drips down my back, then my legs. I don't utter a sound, wanting to hear this.

"Hi...Mr. Bellamy? Yeah, it's Shay Carbona, Blair's roommate at the Alpha Delta Phi sorority house."

He says something and she pulls her shoulders back.

"I don't think she *is* safe." She shakes her head. "No, I don't mean she'd hurt herself, I mean, she's not okay."

"I know you're all not okay," she says lamely. My father responds, and that's when she turns to glance in the direction of the bathroom. "She's in the shower... oh wait, she's right here." Her face drops as she realizes I'm eavesdropping.

She looks at me, her black hair pulled in a tight bun. "Your father's on the phone." She thrusts the phone in my direction, "He wants to talk to you."

Reaching for the cordless phone, I say, "Hi Daddy."

"Hi Blair, how's school?" he asks. "Two weeks until you're a junior. How 'bout that. You ready?"

"Sure."

"Are you coming home for the summer?" he lowers his voice.

"Yes," I say listlessly. "Is that okay?"

"Of course. I'm just worried about you. Shay says you have constant nightmares and don't sleep," he muses. "I know it's hard, baby, but you gotta keep it together, be strong for us, for her."

I stop listening.

"Okay, honey?"

"Sure."

"See you in a couple weeks."

But the next weekend, Shay brings a guy home, one she meets at a local watering hole. They're drunk and stumbling, but I sleep with one eye open anyway. I never get to the stage where I'm well-rested. I'm tired all the time, eyes open or shut.

I turn my back to them, ignoring the grunts he makes and the sounds of sex. It reminds me of farm animals. The bed pounds against the wall, the wooden headboard shakes.

Pressing my eyes tight, I try and force the images of Bristol being violently raped out of my mind.

Shay starts crying out, saying "Stop, don't do it," and my protective mode kicks in.

Before I know what I'm doing, I jump out of bed, grabbing the baseball bat that's replaced my body pillow.

The room is dark, but her twin bed is no more than ten feet from mine, separated only by a nightstand and our plethora of books and marked-up term papers.

Jumping on the dude's back, I start smacking him with the bat, pulling his hair at the same time as Shay flails beneath us.

They're both screaming, Shay's hands reaching out

above her, trying to shield the back of his head from my outburst.

"Stop, Blair, stop it!" She shrieks. "We're just playing."

It's like I'm outside of myself, watching from above, as I hit the back of his knees, his bare back, and a final strike on his chest as he rolls over and pins me down. Shay holds my arms above me. The two girls from across the hall sprint in, both in various stages of undress.

It takes all three of them to get me off him. They yank me to the floor and clench my arms.

"Let go of me," I huff.

The guy wrenches the bat out of my hands, tossing it across the room where it rolls to the wall and hits with a thud.

"What the fuck are you thinking, Blair?" Shay's crying, her mascara bleeding down her face. "You could've seriously hurt him."

I'm dazed, my eyes adjusting to the dark. "Who?"

Brittany, the sophomore from across the hall, drops my arms to stand and flip on the light switch.

"I thought you were being attacked," I murmur.

"I wasn't." Shay's kneeling beside the guy, his long ponytail loosened by my fury. "We were just playing."

"I'll get you an ice pack." Brittany motions to the dude. "I'm sure we've got a first-aid kit somewhere."

He nods, trying to cover his junk, pulling Shay's comforter over his body. He scoots back towards the edge of the bed, shooting daggers at me.

"Are you okay?" The other girl, Monica, asks Shay.

"Yeah, I am. Thanks for coming in." She gives her a tense smile.

"Yeah, thanks," he sputters, "for saving me from this crazy bitch."

"She's not crazy, she's sick." Shay throws her hands up in the air. "Don't say that about her."

"Whatever, she was acting crazy." He locates his boxers, jeans, and sneakers from under the bed. "I'm out."

"Do you want my number?"

"Nah, I'm good." He rubs his head. "I don't want this fuckin' drama."

Shay rolls her eyes. "Nice to meet you, Calvin."

"Kelvin. It's Kelvin."

"Whatever. Bye."

Brittany walks in with a freezer bag full of ice, and she hands it to him with the look of a championship winner who just knocked out her only competition. "Here." She thrusts it at him.

"Thanks, you're cool." He nods at her, pulling his pants up.

"Walk him out, will you, Monica?" Shay motions. "I'm going to talk to Blair."

"Sure thing." Monica takes the hint and Brittany follows.

The next day, my parents arrive. My mother refuses to come in to the sorority house, sitting in our Toyota, fingers clasped tight in her lap.

My father, his shoulders hunched, helps me finish packing. Shay had called him and told him I wasn't well, that I was a threat to myself and others.

He tries to make small talk in the van, but our pain's insurmountable, and it's hard to have a conversation that doesn't revolve around Bristol. Mother's silent the whole way home, the only sound the click of her knitting needles.

When we pull into the drive, my mother slams her door, stomping inside the house.

Over the summer, the sorority sisters vote to have me removed, concerned about my 'violent tendencies.'

My failing grades make it impossible to keep my financial aid.

And to add insult to injury, the clothing store fires me. Showing up drunk and only half the time doesn't work.

It's for the best, I'm unable to care about what kind of cargo pants or sweaters look great with your eyes and body type, my inability to hold a conversation or make a sale a detriment to the store.

When I ask someone what they're looking for, I have a canned response that doesn't go over well with customers or management.

"What're you looking for today?"

"Oh, I'm trying to find something to wear for pictures."

"Great, I'm trying to find my missing sister who's probably dead. I hope you have better luck."

With a depleted bank account and major depression, I become a prisoner at the farm.

But it never feels warm, welcoming, or like home again.

Not with my mother looking at me every day, reminding me how unwelcome I am, that her 'preferred' daughter shouldn't be the one missing, it should be me.

And definitely not with my father commenting that he never got to bring home the son he always wanted.

22

BRISTOL

WHEN I OPEN MY EYES, the first thing I notice is that I'm sweating, the air stifling hot. I'm not bound, but when I stretch my arms out, there's not enough room to hold them parallel to my body.

Sweat drips down my back, but I can't reach underneath to wipe the perspiration away. I'm in a small space. My hands swipe above, scraping against a surface that feels like wood. It's sharp and prickly against my skin. Compared to some of the smooth varnishes, this is rough and jagged.

My fight or flight response kicks in, I rap my knuckles until they're raw against the top and sides of whatever I'm in, shouting for help.

Alarmed at the tight quarters, I start hyperventilating, my breathing ragged, the sense that I'm dying controls my brain as it spirals into a dark place.

I suffocate, my body paralyzed in fear.

Too much oxygen makes me dizzy and weak, enough so I pass out.

When I come to, my body is stuck to the hard surface, sweat trickling down my eyelids and into my mouth.

I taste salt and baby powder.

The pain and inability to wipe my face or move my limbs is excruciating. There's a stickiness on my hands – it's blood.

This must be the box, I realize.

The 'box' is really a makeshift coffin.

I shudder, realizing it's the perfect length and width for me. I fit snugly into it, with no room to squirm.

Closing my eyes, I try and sleep. It's impossible, the heat and lack of air force me to lie there, cramped.

My hands tingle, then go numb.

I get a painful twitch in my left leg.

It feels like I'm stuck for days, it's more like hours. Long, tedious hours of torture.

My mouth feels like I've eaten a tub of peanut butter, my tongue stuck to the roof of it, bone dry. I mumble to myself at first, but my energy's depleted, stuck in this dazed zone where I'm aware of my surroundings but cannot do anything.

A loud knocking causes me to shriek, at first I think it's coming from inside the box.

It's some type of tool, whacking against the outside.

Did he nail it shut?

I ball my hands into fists, trying to convince my blood to circulate so the temporary paralysis will subside.

The clamor continues, one deafening pound at a time.

Then a scraping noise, the top of the box sliding off, darkness above me.

I'm no longer sealed in the box.

My eyes stare at a blanket of stars, hundreds of them.

Bewildered, I blink.

The Mole shines the flashlight directly in my line of vision. I reach a hand up, covering my face.

He pushes my hand down, blue eyes glinting. "I see you've become acquainted with the box."

I gawk at him, unmoving.

"You can speak, no need to raise your hand." He pulls my right arm, raising it, letting it fall back at my side.

Silence.

"Let me help you up." He lifts me out of the box and places me on grass that's tall enough to be weeds. My body tramples a patch as I lay on my back, staring at the ink-black sky. Gingerly I move my limbs, rubbing my hands to force life back into my extremities.

"Where am I?" I look around, confused. It wasn't apparent as I laid in the box that I was outside. My sense of smell was muted, the tight quarters making it impossible for me to pick up on scents beyond the narrow space.

"Okay, I know you get five questions. But first, I have a question for you." The Mole feels for my pulse, humming.

I lick my chapped lips, waiting in agony.

"What did you think of your coffin?" He claps his hands, gleeful. "I made it specially for you. It's one of a kind." He raises his eyebrows, the mole standing out against the moonlight.

Grabbing my throat, I motion for water.

He ignores my request.

"I guess you don't have any questions..."

I croak, but nothing audible comes out.

Shrugging, he continues, "Now you know what the box is. Hopefully we don't have to use it again. Do you think you've learned your lesson?"

He doesn't wait for me to answer. "Next time, I might not leave the air holes open. Can you imagine suffocating to death in here?" He taps on the wall of the box.

"What a painful death..."

I roll onto my side, dry heaving.

"I don't picture you dying like this, it's not the way I imagined it in my head, but Mother says I have to do what she tells me. She told me to put you in there." A slight frown rests on his face as tears silently run down my cheeks.

He reaches a hand out, softly brushing them away. "Marian, don't cry." He taps his nose three times.

I'm naked, the cool air damp against my skin. He places a hand against my clammy forehead. "We better get you bathed and into bed. It's been a long day."

All of a sudden I feel a sharp throb, then it subsides almost immediately. "Shh...little girl, you're going to sleep well tonight. Just relax and let me carry you home."

He stands, grunting as he picks me up.

Immobile, I close my eyes, my last cognizant thought before I drift off is how I despise the minty freshness of his breath.

When I wake up, I'm back in the room, alone.

I wish I could count down the hours, have a sense of time, but it doesn't work that way in the room. With no clocks, the only thing I can track are the number of days.

Sharpie in hand, I think about marking the underside of the mattress, but it's a ballsy chance I don't want to take. The blinking light of the camera reminds me he's watching.

Judging.

Memorizing my routine, my patterns, waiting for me to screw up so he can punish me. I'm fearful of the box, the mood changes, the deviant personality of The Mole.

As afraid as I am of him, I have to test if the camera's real or a 'dummy' one. Except it doesn't work in my favor, and it leads to another punishment phase called 'branding.'

I remove my shoes one afternoon, or at least I think it's

later in the day, preferring to be in my stockings. The shoes are too small and pinch my toes.

Within a short time span, maybe an hour, he's standing in front of me, mouth twisted in a sneer. "You're in deep trouble, little girl. Walking around, getting the bottoms of your stockings dirty?"

Nonplussed, I ask, "Don't I get a warning?"

"Raise your hand," he growls.

Conceding, I throw up both arms.

"I told you that shoes are mandatory at all times and you disobeyed me."

"They hurt," I whine.

"I can assure you, little girl, the recourse will hurt worse." He ignores my pleas, removing my stockings in one smooth motion. Pulling a cigarette lighter out of his pocket, he presses it to my ankle. Flicking it, the smell of burning flesh fills the air as I wail at the stinging pain.

"Shut up," he warns, "or I'll continue up your legs."

Thrashing violently, he brands me, marking every few inches with a singe of the lighter. I lose count, the scorching of my bare skin enough to warrant me throwing a tantrum, my arms flailing as he holds me down.

He stops on my inner thigh, huffing, his energy zapped from my outburst. "Stop moving." Grabbing a fistful of hair, he pulls, ripping it from my scalp. I stare, horrified, at the chunk of blonde hair now visible in his palm.

As if branding me and causing hair loss aren't enough, he pushes me over the bed and lifts up the plaid skirt I'm wearing, this time pushing himself deep in me as I holler, my fists pummeling the mattress.

Yanking my head back violently, he hisses. "Shut up, you filthy whore," in my ear. I close my eyes, my fingers grasping the sheets. He heaves against my back, his seed running down my legs. Before he even exits my body, he orders, "Get in the tub."

In shock, I'm limp against the bed.

"Get. In. The. Tub." Another mark to my skin, this time my left butt cheek. I jump out of bed, losing my balance as I scramble to escape his touch.

"Don't just stand there, get in," he commands.

Stepping into the metal basin, he hoses me down like you would a farm animal. Spraying me in the eyes, the face, shoving the nozzle between my legs. My tears mix with the cold water, running down my cheeks as my hands try to push the stream away.

I'm rewarded with a hard slap across my left cheek and the wrath of The Mole.

"Look what you made me do." He pounds his fist against the cold metal, his anger radiating through his bulging pupils. He savagely lifts me out, my head narrowly missing the tub as I'm turned over and beaten with his bare hands. My skin is slippery, he doesn't bother to dry me off before pummeling me, hitting any limb he can grab.

I don't know who makes more noise – the sobs wracking my body or his screams about what she's going to do to us when she finds out.

Marian, he must mean Marian.

After his tangent subsides, I'm on the floor, dripping wet and panting. He's unglued, seated underneath me, his fingers digging into the carpet.

Stunned, he throws his hands up in astonishment, as if he stepped outside of himself for a minute and has re-entered his body.

He hunches over, ashamed, covering my eyes with his hand, unable to regard me with anything but contempt. He absentmindedly rubs the bald spot on my head, pushing my face down. Next he murmurs instructions at me to stand in the corner, nose pressed to the wall.

My body's on fire, pain has replaced the numbness I feel. Bruises are forming on my legs, welts on my left butt cheek and inner thigh. I don't have to look to know the burn marks are red and ugly.

He helps me stand, never removing his hand from my face, keeping his eyes trained on the floor. I close my eyes, picturing myself flying through the air in front of the crowd, the cheers erupting for my perfect basket toss in cheerleading. Water trickles down my back, running down my legs. The carpet is damp underneath me.

He tells me to stay in position for an hour.

I wait, counting backwards, but after what feels like an eternity but is only a couple minutes, I hear the door scraping and then a thud.

The Mole leaves, his aggression and humiliation following him out.

Then there's silence.

I don't test the camera theory again.

To track my time, I at first use a coloring book.

In the pages, I aimlessly fill in the objects, sometimes drawing outside the lines, sometimes laser-focused, sometimes not. Incorporating a number into the shape, I go through the book in order, assigning every page a subliminal number.

Every day begins the same.

Bath.

Warm water if he's in a generous mood.

Cold if he's in a rush or upset.

A piece of fruit and juice or milk. Mangoes. Pineapple slices. Kiwi. Honeydew. Strawberries. Watermelon.

Tangerines. The list goes on and on, depending on what's in season.

My clothing options are old-fashioned, reminiscent of the Brady Bunch era. It all smells the same – mothballs and lingering cigarette smoke. I catch a whiff of Baby Soft saturating the fabric.

Shift dresses, polyester, plaid, baby doll outfits with large bows and billowy sleeves. Satin ribbon and bright colors.

The only constant are the white granny-looking underwear that stretches up to my belly button. That never changes.

His hair-brushing technique varies depending on his hostility.

He sits me in the yellow chair and will gently brush out my tangles, careful to not pull if he's in a loving mood.

If he's irritated or bored, the strokes become rough, the bristles digging into my scalp, his annoyance building as he rips through the strands.

The worst is when he wrenches the brush through my blonde locks, acting as if my head is a scratching post like cats rub their claws on. Scabs form on my scalp if he's after punitive measures.

He like pigtails, ponytails. Straight hair is allowed but he despises buns.

I'm relieved he hasn't shown up with a curling iron, sure he would find another way to brand me.

I read voraciously, the only activity that makes me forget how pathetic I am, the written words reminding me of my father reading to Blair and I as children, curled up on either side of him, safe and protected. He would always lead us in prayer before we drifted off to sleep, my lids heavy by the time we whispered "Amen."

The Mole leaves puzzles, most are easy and geared towards children, consisting of shapes or food items. I sit at the small, round table, also child-size, that he brings in. That's where I take my meals.

In a couple of the books, I notice a dedication to a girl named 'Sonia'. There's nothing else written but her name, except he calls her '*Sonia-Poo, my little darling.*'

I'm scared to ask at first about Sonia, unsure of his reaction, wondering if it's adulation for another girl or if he has a kid.

Maybe neither – it could be secondhand and come from a garage or used book sale.

Sometimes I sit on the floor, against the foam wall, or on the bed. Often times I lay stretched out, daydreaming I'm in my own bed, at a picnic, or sprawled across the grass of our lawn.

Every day ends the same.

Routine. Monotony.

I daydream about my parents.

My dog Oggie.

Even our annoying farm cat Isabella.

What's Blair doing? P.J.? My friends?

Every night I pray to a God I had always thought existed, it was second nature to me to believe in a higher power, as natural as rain or tying my shoes.

Now I wasn't so sure.

One night, The Mole wanted to sleep in my bed. Lucky for me, he'd been retreating to wherever it is he goes instead of staying.

"I'm going to lay with you tonight." He kisses my cheek, his stale breath igniting a feeling of dread in my body. "You've been such a good little girl lately."

Shit.

He curves his torso on the bed, tucking me into him, our limbs barely fitting on the narrow surface.

I close my eyes, cringing at the suffocation I feel, my hair tickling his chin. He laughs, the mole probably sprouting another single follicle of hair.

"Tell me a secret," he says, rubbing my arm. "Something you haven't told anyone."

Silence.

I'll never open myself up to him.

He continues. "I want us to be close." He nuzzles his face into the nape of my neck. "She and I used to be real close. We shared everything."

"Your sister?"

INTERNALLY, I shut down.

My mind races. What can I make up that's untruthful that he'll never know about?

"I accidentally ran over a neighbor's cat once." I don't know why I say it, but it springs to mind.

"On the farm?"

I bite my lip. He knows I grew up on a farm?

"How did you know about the farm?" I stammer.

"I know a lot about you. I have to, you're in my space." He kisses my earlobe.

My body shrivels inside.

"You hurt a living, breathing object?" He's surprised.

"Not on purpose." I say. "Sir?" I try and hold my arm out, like I'm raising it to ask a question.

"Silly, you can relax," he says. "Don't move."

"What about you?" I ask.

"What about me *what*?" he hisses. "Have I killed anything or anyone?"

I meant secrets. Maybe they're one and the same.

"I think you know the answer to that." He threads his fingers through mine.

"Who is the *her* you always mention?"

"Marian?" he asks.

"Or," I hesitate, "Sonia."

He squeezes my hand.

"Who is Sonia?"

"How did you hear about Sonia?" He's not angry, but curious.

Shyly, I say, "I saw her name in a book."

"She used to be here, right where you are." He hums.

"And...?" For some reason, I don't hesitate to keep going.

"She didn't make it." A trace of sadness in his voice. "She couldn't cut it as my little girl."

"Why do you like little girls?" I ask.

"I don't *like* little girls," he chides. "I protect little girls from her."

Baffled, I stare at a raised mark on my arm, unsure how to respond.

He puts a finger to his lips. "Shhh...sleepy time. We have our whole lives to talk about why I like what I like, don't you agree?"

I'm not so sure.

A lock of dirty blond hair falls over his cheek as he peers at me, his blue-green eyes change depending on his mood. They're more green right now.

When he's deep in thought, they turn greenish.

Blue for when he's angry or perturbed.

If he's in a neutral mood, I see both colors reflected.

And every day, when he stares at me, another piece of me dies inside.

23

BRISTOL

WHEN THE MOLE'S GONE, I pace the floor incessantly, my only exercise. Of course, with my stockings or socks covered by shoes. After bath time, he's okay with my bare feet, and in bed, so it must just be a control issue.

Sometimes the claustrophobia sets in, my heart racing, as I pound on the door for a breath of fresh air.

It never comes. What I would give to smell rain, fresh cut grass, even the manure pile on the farm. I miss Blair's perfume, my mother's homemade strawberry pie, and my father's laugh, always slow to come but easy on the ears.

I picture my room, the sloped ceiling, my bed.

Every morning I play a game in my head. I make a mental list, checking off each item I miss. I try and keep adding to the list, memorizing my answers and then repeating them out loud. It's the only way I know how to keep my memories safe without choking on the regrets of a life I'm barely surviving at.

When The Mole is in a good mood, I raise my hand to ask if we can go outside.

He pretends to consider this request, tilting his head.

Then as quickly as he pauses to think about it, he shakes his head no.

"Too risky," he says.

"But I'd like to go outside," I complain.

I'm rewarded with a slap across my cheek and another burn mark, this time on the bottom of my foot. I limp for a day. The other marks have scarred in places, some healing better than others.

Since I'm seventeen, I can't avoid the inevitable, my monthly cycle. I used to dread the cramps and bloated feeling in my stomach. Now I'm relieved when my period comes, thanking God.

When The Mole sees my bloody underwear, he freezes. "What's this?"

I'm confused.

"What's wrong with you? Are you sick?" He puts a palm to my forehead. "Little girl, you need to lie down."

"No, it's just my..."

HE CUTS SHORT MY ANSWER, following it with a death glare.

"This kind of thing does *not* happen to little girls, understand?" Before I know it, he's ripped off the offending underpants and shoved a diaper between my legs, fastening the adhesives over each hip bone.

"YOU'LL WEAR these for times like this." He points to the bed. "You'll also be on bed rest. We can't take any chances that you'll get more ill. Clearly, you're sick."

When I protest, I'm dragged by my ponytail to the bed,

my wrists bound to the headboard, and left for at least a full day.

He comes back as if nothing happened, untying my sore wrists and humming, appalled that I would lose control of my bladder.

"Lucky we have these." He's cheerful, removing the soiled diaper, pushing me towards the tub which he fills with frigid water. "Mother says you have to be alone right now, you're unclean." I settle in the tub and he perches on a foot stool, demanding I tell him about the farm I grew up on.

"What do your parents do?" He's curious.

"My father's a pastor." I stare at my ripped cuticles. "My mom stays at home, runs the house, helps in the church office."

"Then you know that what we do is not for others to know about." He gives me a warning with his eyes. "It's wrong. You should know better. This is why you're being punished right now."

He gives me a few minutes to rinse off, tossing a wash cloth at me. After I dry myself off, he makes me wear a black nightgown to impress upon me the fact he thinks I'm dirty. I'm taped into another diaper, this time with my wrists and feet bound.

He leaves me in the bed, shivering and terrified for longer than usual this time. The cramps I experience are nothing like the stomach pangs that supersede.

This time he avoids me for a week, leaving me protein bars, apples, oranges, and canned soup with the labels missing I'm forced to eat cold.

Eventually, he hangs up a dry erase board that has my chores and daily activities, but also a calendar so he can track my period.

I'm left to my own devices and while it takes the pressure off of me, I know he's watching. The thought of him sitting alone in a room staring at me gives me the creeps.

Fitting, since I'm a caged animal, that I start reading Maya Angelou's *I Know Why the Caged Bird Sings*.

His once-consistent visits become erratic. Sometimes there's a consistent routine to follow, other times he abandons me for extended lengths of time. Since I eat so little and infrequent, my weight continues to fall off my already rail-thin body.

Sometimes he's wearing casual clothes, other times coveralls, sometimes jogging pants and a windbreaker. Or he's dressed like he's attending a funeral.

A little voice in my head wonders if he is – maybe for another missing girl.

His moods are unstable – multiple personas, his voice sometimes childlike and playful, other times stern and authoritative. As soon as I think I have a read on him, his Jekyll and Hyde personality changes from one extreme to the other.

One morning, he comes in extra early. I know this because he's holding a flashlight and it seems like I had just drifted off to my troubled dreams. I used to go to sleep with visions of being rescued and returned home, that I would wake up in my bed with no recollection of how I got there, just that I was finally safe. Now I have tormented nightmares that end with me running for my life or being tortured until I succumb to a painful death.

"Wake up," he whispers, shaking my shoulder.

I'm curled up in a ball, my long nightgown tucked around me.

"I have a surprise for you." I don't move at a particularly

alarming rate, the word 'surprise' ruined by the fear that it will mean a form of torture.

"Hurry." He strides to the dresser. "You can leave your nightgown on, but you'll need wool socks."

Is he taking me outside?

I should be thrilled, instead I'm filled with nervous anticipation.

A dark object's in his hand. "Coat." He motions as I hold out my arms and he helps me shrug it on. He clasps each brass button on the olive green wool coat. It reeks of dust and mothballs. Tugging a woolly knit cap on, he covers my head, tucking in the loose strands.

Raising my hand, I tremble.

"Yes, little girl?"

"Where are we going?"

"It's Christmas today." He gives the middle of my lip a gentle poke. "I thought we could celebrate. I have a present for you."

Solemnly taking my hand, he asks, "Are you ready?" I push my feet into the uncomfortable shoes, made inches smaller by the heavy stockings.

I nod, hopeful I'll see the way out of this underground confinement. *Maybe I can get help*, I tell myself, pumping myself into thinking positive.

"I'm going to blindfold you." He pulls a dark handkerchief out of his pocket. "I don't want to ruin the surprise."

He turns me around a few times, like a game of pin-the-tail-on-the-donkey, my eyes shielded by the thick fabric.

"If you try to run," he murmurs, "I've got my gun. You won't get far." With that, he presses a cold metal object to my hip. "Now let's see how well you really listen."

I hear the thud of the metal door, and then he leads me

down a level hall, my steps even as we walk. I assume it's dark, no light penetrates the material over my eyes.

He pauses for a moment, shoving open what must be another door. "Stairs," he instructs. "One at a time." We walk, my footfalls timid as I raise one after the other. My legs ache, this exercise a rare occurrence.

By the time we reach the top, I'm winded. I reach out for something to grasp but feel nothing.

HE'S DOING SOMETHING, his arm slack on mine.

Another click, and I feel the difference.

Air.

Cold air.

A breeze.

I breathe it in.

Then out.

Over and over, filling my lungs.

Just like that, he's opening a squeaky door, I assume for a vehicle, and I'm lifted onto a seat. It feels like ancient leather, lots of ridges and cracks as I rub the texture with my hands.

"Don't move," he breathes in my ear. I feel his cheek brush my lips, and he's leaning over me, clicking my seatbelt into place.

I hear a lock.

Then another door opening, the driver's side, I presume.

A key turns in the ignition, and the engine buzzes to life.

His hand holds mine, the sound of the radio pouring out of the speakers.

The news.

I haven't heard the news in so long.

Before he can shut it off, I hear the announcer say, "Happy holidays everyone, wishing you health and happiness as we wind down 1998. It's 5:37 A.M., and we'll be back to talk about what the holidays mean to you in just a moment."

He turns the dial, oldies filling the space.

The wheels pound the pavement. At first it's rocky terrain, I can tell by the forceful thud underneath me, the shocks rocking back and forth. Then a slight incline and it becomes smooth, signaling we must be on a well-traveled road or highway.

"Sir?" I ask.

"Yes?"

"Can you roll down the window please?"

He sighs but a moment later, a cold rush hits my face. It's like an arctic blast. I shiver, but even in the chilliness, I want the moment to last.

"Thank you." I lean my head towards the window, his hand still holding mine, his touch warm against my clammy one.

We drive in silence, the music and his humming the only sound besides the roadway. I don't hear the ocean, but in my mind, I imagine it.

I wonder if my family's celebrating Christmas without me, and the thought causes bitterness – are they gathered around our tree, did Blair put the snow angel at the top, standing on her tip-toes on our rickety stool, my usual job?

Tears clog my eyes. The bandana catches most of the wetness, the others trickle down my cheek. I bite my lip to keep from sniffling.

I've been here for almost nine months. And I'm no closer to freedom, except now I can taste it in my tears and in the whiff of air that dances around my nostrils, pulling me in, willing me to find a way to escape.

We finally come to a stop, the sounds of the Pacific no longer a question. I hear the roar of waves pounding in my ears.

Is he going to drown me, right here right now?

Or let me walk the beach?

Maybe neither?

He unbuckles my seatbelt, tugging on my arm. I lean to the side, almost falling out, but he catches me in time.

"I'm going to let you lead and then remove the bandana," he says. "I'll tell you when to step up or down."

I stand still, arms at my sides.

"You trust me, don't you?" He's hurt by my silence.

I nod, glad my eyes are covered.

We walk, I stumble, my feet unable to predict the uneven terrain. He lets me fall once, my knees and palms hitting the ground. I'm pretty sure he pushed me, but he yanks me violently up. "Pay attention," he commands.

I'm parched, my body in need of hydration. I'm scared to ask for water, worried he'll push me off a cliff into the ocean or turn me back around and take away the only taste of freedom I've had.

I can't wrap my mind around how long I've been stuck in that room. I never thought I'd make it more than a week.

Then a month.

March Twenty-Fourth.

December Twenty-Fifth.

"Duck," he says too late.

My head smacks into a jagged piece of what feels like rock. A knot forms above my eyebrow, a trickle of blood starts to descend down my face.

He pulls on my arm, motioning me to stop.

I hear a cap unscrewing and then him sipping, swallowing liquid.

Nine months, one day.

He's taunting me, waiting to see if I'll dare ask for a drink.

Moving forward, I keep walking, my steps becoming heavier. The shoes are too small and ill-fitting, my toes are pinched and I feel blisters on my heels. This isn't the right atmosphere for patent leather Mary Janes.

I feel a hand on my neck, now damp and sweaty.

"Stop," he directs, tugging on my coat. He stills behind me.

"Okay," I croak.

"You thirsty?"

I nod.

He twirls me around, untying the bandana on my forehead.

My eyes adjust, the sunrise starting to peek through the top of the tall trees. These are different than the palm trees, they cloak whatever forest or trail we are hiking, letting in minimal light. The air is cool and brisk, but we've come to an impasse.

Straight ahead, a cavern is in our path.

There's nowhere to go but in.

"Go ahead." He shoves me forward. "I'll let you drink when we reach our destination."

All I can think as I take a step ahead is if I'll ever leave this cave again.

If I wasn't being rushed into another space by my tormentor, I'd have liked this hike with Blair. I picture her dark hair, the way she'd touch the natural formations in awe.

It's beautiful, what I can see of it.

It's dark at first, a narrow opening that feels small and confined. Walls jut out and anyone over six feet tall would have to stoop to enter. The Mole ducks, holding onto the back of my coat, clutching the fabric securely with his hands.

Like an illusion, the cave expands, the ceiling reaching higher and higher. The cramped space becomes an open room. One chamber leads to another, the dirt floors uneven in spots, my breathing ragged.

The Mole pushes me forward, impatient, his steps heavy behind my limping pace.

The cragged rocks reach out to me, spindly fingers that seem to point in one direction.

How much longer, I wonder, before I pass out from exhaustion and thirst?

"Almost there," he says, reading my mind.

The distant sunlight pitches in and out, the weak glare becoming brighter as it rises and shines across the rubble. We reach a narrow pathway and have three choices – straight out I can see the lapping waves and smell the salt spray of the ocean. Instead, he shoves me to the left, bumpy dips combined with heavy boulders require us to climb single file, until he grabs my waist, stopping me mid-step.

"Over there." He nods in the direction of a concave wall. A long slab, formed like a bench, summons me. I sink down, resting my sore limbs. I can barely muster the energy to raise my arm, but I see his face twisted, testing me to disobey him. "Yes, little girl?"

"Can I have a sip of water please?" There's not much left in the bottle, and he drinks most of it before wiping his mouth with the back of his hand.

"Sure."

I say nothing, exploring my surroundings. He thrusts

the bottle in my hand when's he done taunting me. I drink greedily, careful not to spill any down my chin.

"This place is special to me." He leans against a depression in the rock. "I found this exploring one day as a child."

So he did grow up on the island.

"My sister and I got lost in here." He stares off in the distance. "A hiker found us, but we were in big trouble."

"By your dad?" I realize too late I didn't raise my hand.

His eyes are glazed, luckily he's not watching me.

"No, our mother." He's quiet for a minute, crossing his arms. "I never met the man who was my sperm donor. He got her pregnant and left." He pauses for a moment. "I saw pictures of him, and could see him through a peep hole. My mother would lock us in a closet when he showed up. She was scared he would take us from her."

"What about your sister?" I murmur. "Was she okay?"

"We were twins." His eyes drift back to my face, mouth tense. "Don't think I didn't notice you didn't raise your hand." He runs his ice-cold gaze down my body. "I'll deal with you later."

I MUMBLE AN APOLOGY.

He accepts, changing his tone back to neutral.

"Is your sister okay?"

"She is now," he shrugs.

"I brought you down here so you could see what was so special about this place." He doesn't wait for a response, doesn't need one. "My favorites are buried here."

I raise my hand, he pushes it down. "What do you want to know?"

"What favorites?" I manage to choke out.

"Leslie. I buried her here. Nothing left of her now but

bones." He shrugs. "Wild animals eat the corpse, everything but the bones. That and decomposition happens."

I shudder. "Leslie Billings?"

"Uh-huh."

"I had her ID." I'm frantic. "How did I get her ID?"

"Why are you asking me these questions?" He's bored. "How would I know?" He taps his finger on my nose. "All I know is she ran away from home. That's what happens to girls who leave their nest before they're ready." A maniacal laugh escapes his lips, spittle flies on the tip of my nostrils.

I change the topic to the sister he mentioned. "What's your twin's name?"

He rubs his chin, hitting the mole. "It doesn't matter."

"Why not?" I tilt my head.

"They're all right here, when I want my own visiting hours." He touches a hand to his heart. "I feel close to them. Marian's also here. I took her here to get her away from Mother. She always thought this cave was beautiful."

"Who's Marian?"

"You're Marian." He brushes a strand of hair back from my forehead, tilting my chin to inspect my face.

"I am?" I whisper.

"Yes, but I come here to visit *all* my girls." He walks forward, his hands running along a crevice that snakes around a corner. Brush sticks up in sparse patches, and he prods a finger in an indentation, pushing on something in the wall.

He smiles, humming, as he pulls out a long piece of cartilage. I always imagine bones to be bleached white, fully formed, and clean, images of Halloween skeletons coming to mind. Fun and silly, the dancing rib cage twirling a hat.

Wishing I would've paid more attention in biology, I try and remember the largest bones in the body. This elongated one might be a femur or fibula. Cracks and small holes cover the yellowed surface, reminding me of something that's left out in the sun too long. Dirt and debris cover the exterior and I stay put, refusing to cry out in anguish.

"This makes me feel complete." He rubs his forefinger over an indent as he holds the matter up to examine it. "My good girls."

"If they are so good, why are they here?"

"Because they turned bad." He whistles through his teeth. "Let this be a lesson to you. This is what happens to naughty girls." Bringing the bone to his mouth, he touches it to his lips, lightly kissing it.

I shrink in my seat, disgusted, watching him return it to its hiding spot.

"Let's go." He's brusque. "It's Christmas and we have a lot to do."

This time he anxiously leads the way. I silently attempt to memorize the trail, telling myself I'll lead the police here one day to recover the remains of the missing girls. The least I can do is return them to their concerned and heartsick families.

Am I still considered a missing person or have I been relegated to a deceased status?

The idea that my family has stopped searching for me, believing me to be dead, causes me to abruptly stop, hitting my head on a low part of the overhang.

I'm sick to my stomach, imagining them packing up my room and selling my belongings, erasing every trace of me from memory.

Help me, I plead, *please help*.

I spend the rest of the way praying to run into a nature lover or a tourist taking early-morning photographs.

The Mole is smart, knowing the only time to avoid

being seen is at dawn. By the time we arrive at the entrance, the bandana is out of his pocket and back around my eyes. My last image is of the massive banyan trees before I'm cloaked in darkness again.

We ride in silence, the radio mute. The Mole doesn't go directly back, braking to put the vehicle in park. He rips the bandana off before anyone can see me, keeping my hat on to cover my unkempt hair. We're in a drive-thru line, the only place open on Christmas. I wait for him to ask if I want something, but he doesn't.

"Don't say a word or I'll drive you back to the cliff," he hisses. "Keep your head down." I can feel his eyes watching me like a hawk, his iron grip swallowing my hand.

The bored cashier takes his order and collects his money, their interaction brief as I stare at my feet. It's a truck, which I figured from how high up I sit. The carpet mat is gray and I peer at the dashboard, careful not to raise my head. He has one of those miniature dancing Hawaiian girls-the ones that sways their hips settled there.

The smell of food makes my mouth water, chicken nuggets, beef patties, and potatoes cooking, an overload of salt on the fries. I haven't inhaled anything so glorious, my meals small and unfulfilling. Nothing that involves a stove or fryer, no delicious aromas wafting through the room. Counting in my head, I focus on the placid tiny dancer that's at a standstill while we wait for his order.

He pulls away from the window and into a parking spot, blindfolding me again, the only sound the rapid movement of his mouth as he chews and swallows, then the annoying suck of a straw.

Antagonizing me, I don't react, which is what he wants. I sit silently, hands now folded in my lap until we drive off again.

When he parks, he shuts off the engine, humming a tune as he drums his fingers on the steering wheel.

I WAIT.

This time, he doesn't bother leading me, carrying me instead, the jerky movement of him thrusting me up and over his shoulder causing a dizzying headache. His breath reeks of Coca-Cola and mustard.

He fumbles with keys and I want to start hitting him with my fists, catch him off balance.

Run.

But the more I think about it, the more I tense up, my body rigid.

The poor girls.

I don't want to end up like them. But I need a plan. Because I don't want to be buried in some obscure place where I might be discovered in another century, fossilized like dinosaur bones.

When we get back to the room, he slams the door behind us, dropping me on the rough carpet without warning.

I wince, my left side slamming onto the floor.

"Get undressed."

Slowly, I take my clothes off as he runs a bath.

"Get on the bed," he instructs. Scanning my blisters and cuts, he smirks. "I guess you weren't cut out for hiking."

"It's the shoes..." I trail off.

Roughly, he grabs my neck. "I didn't ask your opinion." Squeezing my throat, my B chain becomes entangled in his grip as he jams his fingers into my clavicle.

Tears burn my eyes, his thumb rubbing over my cheek.

"Besides, if you don't behave, next time we go back, you'll be nothing but a cadaver."

Goosebumps cover my flesh and I shut my eyes as he takes what he calls his 'Christmas present', my mind drifting back to a past childhood holiday when I was six – the one I got a Cabbage Patch doll and a matching outfit to wear that my mother crocheted.

He calms down after, his tone softening, holding me against his sweaty armpits. I cringe, his eyes drifting over my body in appreciation.

"Why so pensive?" He runs his thumb down my bare shoulder, hitting a burn mark.

I want to stab him in the eyes.

"What?" I ask, unsure what 'pensive' means.

Quickly, I add 'sir' to the end.

"You look like you're deep in thought. What're you thinking about?"

Ending your life, I want to say.

Instead, I start out with a compliment, or I can thank my personal request good-bye. The Mole needs to be coddled and loved at all times. "I love being with you, it just makes me sad my parents don't know I'm alive..."

"I know you are, and that's all that matters."

"I know...it's just that...I want them to let me go, sir."

"How will they let you go?" His lip curdles. At least his yellowed tooth is hidden behind his sour expression.

"We could send them a letter," I force a smile at him, "saying we ran off together. Something like that. Then they'll stop looking, if they haven't already."

"They're not looking for you."

"How do you know, sir?" I walk straight into his trap.

"I keep tabs on them." He's confident. "They adopted a

little boy and seem happy. At least their Christmas card did." His eyes never leave mine.

My face loses all trace of color.

"Oh," is all I can manage to force out.

"Let me think about the letter." He closes his eyes, mulling it over.

Popping his eyes open a second later, he agrees. "Merry Christmas." He touches my cheek.

I stir against him, ready to sit up and write them a note from a coloring book on the desk.

"Wait," he raises his arm, holding me down. "Tomorrow," he says. "You can write them tomorrow. I'll even bring you a card to send to them."

Shutting my eyes, I go to sleep, picturing next year, Christmas morning with my family, presents under the tree, and my sheepdog Oggie at my feet. It's made perfect by the fact I wake up in my own bed, The Mole dead and buried.

Better yet, I have no memory of his existence.

"Merry Christmas, sir," I murmur excitedly.

24

BRISTOL

A COUPLE DAYS after Christmas but before the new year, snow's falling outside, covering the ground in white. My parents barely speak to each other as Daddy finds solace in his Bible, Mother with knitting. She's twisting the yarn into a sweater. The needles jab at the stitches, an extension of her anger. The divide between them grows wider, first Bristol, then my mother's refusal to follow through on Isaiah's adoption, wanting to focus on finding my sister.

The mailman knocks on the door, a deviation from his usual stop at the mailbox at the end of our long drive.

My mother answers it, stepping outside to thank him for making the trek to the house. She rubs her hands together, numb from the cold, a shawl wrapped around her gaunt frame.

I think she's shaking because of the winter storm, but her face has a look of distress. I glance down to see a piece of mail.

A red envelope.

She holds the letter in her hand like it's going to bite her.

Block handwriting in black magic marker.

A late Christmas card, I wonder?

She rips it open, not bothering to use the letter opener.

Postmarked 'Lanai' instead of Oahu, another one of the Hawaiian islands.

Inside is a single greeting card, a red cardinal on a frosted tree branch, with the heading *Happy Holidays*. The heavy paper itself is faded and yellowed around the edges.

HI MOM AND DAD,

I miss you all.

Blair, I'm sorry I scared you by running off. It wasn't your fault, so please don't blame yourself. I'm alive and I'm fine. I met someone and am in love. I ran off because I was scared you would try and change my mind.

I know it's been almost a year today. Give Oggie a belly rub. I'm still thinking of you.

Love, Bristol

THE POLICE CHECK TO see if they can authenticate where the card was purchased. It's a dead end – this particular card hasn't been made since the 70s. The note brings attention to her case, and a new search reignites for her. It's a blessing in disguise since the media attention is needed, but more so locally, not in Honolulu.

At least for a moment in time.

Parts of Lanai are searched, but there's so many volcanoes and plantations, nature in all its beauty. Unfortunately, it makes it hard to search.

Handwriting analysis authenticates the writing is Bristol's.

Odd, but the only other fingerprints on the letter are from a dead girl – Sonia Sutherland.

After that, quacks send us mail and items claiming to be hers. They either give us a false sense of hope she's alive or a sickening fear she's dead. Crazy nuts like to fuck with Priscilla's head, impersonating Bristol. We even get ransom letters from fake kidnappers requesting monetary assistance. None of these can be proven accurate or legitimate.

The police reprimand us, instructing us not to open any more suspicious mail but to call them, so they can test for fingerprints.

A majority of our mail is handed over to the authorities.

It goes nowhere...all dead ends.

Until the only mail that arrives are bills, advertisements, and condolence cards.

The baseless claims even come to a standstill after a while.

You would think my family would become closer, pull together to find her. Or in spite of her.

The opposite happens.

Mother spirals into a deeper depression, reading Bible verses all day, making weird grunts, and spending her time in bed. The times we do see her, she shuffles around in her house coat and slippers.

My parents want me to work, contribute to the household, and save for my own place, so I offer to manage the church office, but both of my parents immediately nix that suggestion. I get hired on at a gas station, working as much overtime as I can muster.

When I see old friends from high school or Bristol's friends, I freeze up, my body wracked with guilt. I know they wonder why it was her and not me.

So do I, I want to scream.

A weird energy passes between us, like I'm a plague everyone wants to avoid. People stutter through questions or refer to me as the 'sister of the missing girl' or the 'freak sister of the missing girl.'

Eventually, I turn and walk away if someone I know comes in, hiding in the stock room.

That or I punch in numbers on the register, avoiding the curious stares.

When a night position opens up, I gladly take it, sleeping during the day, less intrusions at night, plus I hate the dark. I might as well be in a well-lighted store with the occasional customer, keeping busy.

At home, I sneak into my sister's room to sleep in her bed, my hands wrapped around her body pillow, feeling her in spirit.

Mother walks in one afternoon when I'm still asleep, her voice waking up my daddy as she hollers, "You get the hell out of her room, out of her bed, right now. You're tainting it. You're the reason she's gone, you're never to come in here again."

The next day, a metal padlock's attached to the outside of her door.

I never find the key to it, no matter where I search.

The jewelry armoire, the junk drawer, the glove box of the vehicles, the bathroom linen closet. I only find empty glass bottles of vodka.

Mother's done a good job of hiding it.

We hold our breath to see if another letter follows, but it doesn't.

And once again, we lose hope.

THE AFTERMATH

CHRISTMAS IS FOLLOWED by New Year's. The Mole goes silent for a few days, leaving me to my own devices and a perpetually empty stomach.

I assume he's out drinking with friends or celebrating, wearing a tiara that lights up the numbers 1999, listening to Prince, and blowing on one of those squawkers that makes noise as the countdown ends and a new year begins.

I realize how little I know about him.

Does he party? I try to imagine his average body dressed up in a tuxedo, sipping champagne and caviar, dancing with his hands on a woman's hips.

Maybe a girlfriend? A wife?

Squeamish, I suck down the image of him acting like a person and not The Mole.

The realization that I've passed into January without being found fills me with dread and terror. How much longer do I have to live in this room? What if I'm never found alive?

New Year's Resolution. I have to start getting him to

open up to me. It's the only way I'll be able to manipulate him, figure out his weaknesses, and escape.

During the day, my brainstorming sessions begin.

Everyone has flaws, and I have to start uncovering The Mole's.

One evening after he rapes me, he fills the tub as usual, agitated about his actions, or in his head, my behavior that drove him to have this reaction.

He's murmuring, repeating the same sentence over and over, but it's babble to my ears.

Reaching into his pocket, I freeze, wondering what he's pulling out.

A peppermint.

He unwraps the plastic and sucks on it. It soothes him when he's in one of his moods. I wish I could hand him a bag every day, force feed him until he chokes.

Swallowing the pent-up rage, I re-focus.

Giving him a shy smile, I ask if I can sit behind him in the water instead of in front.

He's visibly nervous. "Why?"

"I would like to wash you, if that's okay?" I pick up the washcloth. "You always are so gentle with me, I'd like to make you feel good."

"Okay," he finally agrees, scooting forward in the water. "But I have eyes in the back of my head." He chuckles as I sink in behind him, my legs sliding around his limbs. I've lost all my muscle definition, my body shrinking from malnourishment.

I examine the back of his head, noticing another mole behind his left ear.

Dipping the washcloth into the water and soaping it up, his frame becomes slack as he leans forward, hands on his knees.

"Mmm... that feels good," he murmurs.

"I'm glad." I stroke the cloth in a circular motion, memorizing his back and shoulders, the taut skin pale in the dim light, the freckles that show under his tufts of hair.

We sit in silence, my eyes drifting around the room as I think of how to engage him.

"Okay, that's enough. Switch spots," he says. "I want to hear you read."

Standing, I step over his legs to sink in between them, sliding back against his chest in the tub.

I pick up the book we're almost finished with, holding it over my mid-section. I've read and re-read every page on the shelf, even the author biographies and the dedications.

Continuing the Lois Lowry book, it has a theme that ties in perfectly to The Mole. In '*Find a Stranger, Say Good-Bye*', a college student searches for her birth parents.

I rub his leg in the water with my other hand, curling my fingers in his blond hair.

He tightens up in surprise.

I stop, raising my hand.

"Do you have a question?"

"Yes." I say. "This book makes me think about parents and families..."

"Like your own?" he finishes for me.

"No. Yours actually." I press on. "Your father. Did you ever look for him?" I'm on treacherous ground, and I know this. It could go either way – offend him or inspire his ability to confide in me.

He kneads a circle on my shoulder. "My father was a bad man."

"Did he hurt you?"

"Yes." He doesn't elaborate.

"I'm lucky you saved me."

"You feel that way?" Now he traces a heart shape.

"Yes. You saved me from parents that treated me like I wasn't good enough, that I was a failure." It's not true, but I know Blair feels this way, rightfully so. "It's so much better spending time with you."

HE SEEMS THRILLED at the idea of being a hero. "I knew it, I knew you needed my help." I hear him groan. "I couldn't save her but I can save you."

"If you hadn't come when you did..." I take a deep breath, inhaling for full effect. "Those boys could've hurt me."

"A voice told me to save you."

"Where were you sitting?" I ask, "or were you on the dance floor?"

I feel his body tense up behind me. Not a good sign.

"I just want to know how you came upon me, what made you pay attention to me?"

Treading carefully, I keep my voice low. "I don't remember seeing you that night."

"Hmm...well, I was in a corner watching." He drops his hands from my back, sliding them around my waist, nuzzling my neck, his minty breath tickling me.

I used to like peppermint, now I cringe at the smell.

"Well, thank you for saving me," I manage to croak. "I'm so grateful to have you."

He squeezes my shoulder.

"Little girl, that's nice to hear."

"Your father..." I whisper. "Did he get in trouble with the law... or hurt your mom?"

Pausing, his hand stops mid-trace.

I close my eyes, waiting for an outburst or a confession. I

wish I could see the pigment of his irises, it will tell me which way we're headed.

"He was a deadbeat. Didn't want to work. A drunk. Worthless." He shifts his weight in the tub. "He used to call her names. Beat her. She tried to protect us, that's why she kept us hidden away. Sometimes in a closet, sometimes the cellar." His voice hitches. "The worst is when she forgot to let us out."

"You and your twin sister?"

"Yeah." He covers his mouth with his hand, yawning. "There were more children after us. We were the special ones, the only ones that mattered, she said." He shrugs. "She had multiple miscarriages. He would come home, force himself on her, impregnate her, then leave. When she was expecting, he pushed her down the stairs or put her in the hospital."

I don't point out the similarities of him forcing himself on me. I have to focus on him, not my own pain.

"What happened to your siblings?"

"The state or her sister came to take them away." He toys with a lock of my hair. "You look so much alike."

"Who?"

He nods. "My twin."

"What happened to her?" I ask. "Does she live on the island?"

"No," is his only response, then, "Keep reading."

I read a couple paragraphs, then stop. "I'm beginning to enjoy this," I say.

HE SUCKS IN A BREATH, yanking the nape of my neck against his jaw line. I feel his lips brush against the side of my face. Thankfully, he's never kissed me on the mouth, only the forehead or cheek.

My eyes flick up to the ceiling, worried I've gone too far. "I just like spending time with you," I add.

"You know it's not right what you make me do." His speech pattern changes, becoming one big syllable. "If you wouldn't make me so mad, do bad things to my boy parts, this wouldn't happen. You can't say what you just said. Take it back. Mommy will find out again."

Wait...what?

I've fallen down a rabbit hole I didn't intend to.

"You know what happened before..." He relaxes his grip on my neck, twisting my hair up and letting it fall.

Apologizing, I say, "I'm sorry I make you do bad things." I pull my face away from his chin, the mole and its friend in close proximity. "But why is it bad if it feels so good?" I leave the bitter out of my voice, aiming for neutral.

"Brothers and sisters don't act like this. Mommy told us that last time." He splashes water in my face. "You have to behave or she'll lock one of us in the closet."

"Why the closet?"

"Because I'm scared of the dark and she knows this."

Bingo.

No wonder he turns a flashlight on to go just a few steps into the room before he reaches the light bulb string.

"What was her name?" I whisper, looking over my left shoulder.

"My sister?" He tugs on his earlobe. "Marian."

I try and keep my voice neutral. "Your sister's in the cave?"

He struggles to push away from me, his eyes tortured. "No, no, why would you say that? I told her not to hurt you." Agitated, he pinches my arm, the flesh becoming pink, then bright red.

It will turn purple, a bruise, I assume, my teeth gritting down as he twists his nails in my skin. I ignore the pain as I force the cries down my throat.

Gradually he releases his fingers, the tender skin mottled.

He tries to soothe it, but I clasp his hand in mine, never missing a beat.

After my bedtime routine, he wants to spoon me, his weight sinking against mine. I finish reading the book to him, his eyes drooping.

Now for my plan of action.

I close the book with a thud, sighing. "It's too bad."

He moans half-asleep. "What?"

"I've read everything on the shelf two and three times. It'd be nice to have more books."

"I can find more books," he says. "Not a problem."

"Would it be too much trouble to go to a bookstore?"

"New books are expensive."

"What about the library?" I suggest. "I love the smell of paper."

"We aren't going to the library."

"Will you go?"

"Little girl, you're starting to annoy me. Stop poking the slumbering bear." He elbows me in the ribs. "Or you'll end up as my dinner." He mimics eating his prey. I'm silent for a moment, unable to keep my mouth shut.

"What if there's one in particular I want?"

"Little girl..." he swats me. "Sleep."

But he's intrigued. Unable to help himself, he chastises me. "You can't read anything risqué. Age-appropriate only."

Nodding, I agree. "I'd like to read you Huckleberry Finn."

"Ahh...Mark Twain." He snuggles in closer. "I'll see what I can do."

But the days pass and he doesn't mention it again, and neither do I.

26

BRISTOL

THE MOLE DOESN'T bother with an updated calendar, preferring to make me 'guess.' By this point, I assume he's got my monthly cycle down to a science.

The pent-up energy, the strain of being in confined quarters for so long makes me feel like I'm losing my mind, stuck as a child that I'm not, the monotony overwhelming at times.

Besides my family and friends, I miss pizza.

Television.

Music.

Gymnastics.

Even snow.

The list goes on and on.

I sometimes practice the splits and cheerleading moves when I'm ready to lose it. The bed is perfect for backflips and I make up routines to pass the time. If I'm wearing pants, I'll do handstands against the wall, barely able to hold my bony arms up.

At first, the idea of The Mole watching me on camera gives me the willies, but then I reach a breaking point.

Sometimes I pace listlessly, touching the foam walls, turning in circles until I'm dizzy.

Other times I lay on my back, shutting my eyes to focus on twinkling stars in the sky, our farm the perfect place to look up and find peace in the quiet.

I picture Blair at school, her sorority car washes and late-night cram sessions for exams.

Her hair's probably long.

I wonder if she's added any more tattoos to her collection. I daydream about what I'd get inked on my skin, now, if only to cover up the scars from the lighter.

Jealousy hits when I imagine Isaiah. Did he replace me as the second child, the boy they always wanted? Is my father taking him on tractor rides, showing him how to catch fireflies?

I think of my father's sermons, my mom sitting on the sofa, knitting something sensible, socks or a new scarf. Even baby clothes.

Balling my hands into fists, I imagine everyone moving on without me. The anger is so raw sometimes that I have to clench and unclench my knuckles, counting to twenty.

When I assume we've hit September, I'm agitated, a foul mood hangs over me.

My senior year.

I would've made head cheerleader, been in the running for homecoming queen, and TP'd the town, riding in the back of a flatbed pickup. I draw pictures of what my homecoming dress would look like, a hot pink sequined number trailing over silver high-heels, the one time I could probably convince mom to allow it. Compromising with a cover-up since bare arms aren't proper.

The days run into each other.

I lose track, my life structured and routine-oriented,

until The Mole disappears and leaves me wondering if he's even alive or coming back. He seems to know just when to pop up, when I'm so starved I can no longer sleep, the gnawing stomachache the only constant.

Another birthday, another Christmas, another New Year.

I'm tired of stale lunches and The Mole's humming and the four walls that're my obstacle against freedom.

At times when it becomes unbearable, I want to die, praying for God to just call me to Him in my sleep.

The summer creeps up, I try not to think about the fact I should be preparing for college, for the start of my adulthood.

August comes.

My fellow classmates are leaving for their chosen universities or to start new jobs, their cars packed to the brim, parents in panic mode that they've forgotten to bring a winter jacket or fill their car up with gas, preferring to leave the tank half-empty.

Blair's done with college now. A graduate of Creighton, off to start her life and a new career, probably L.A. or San Diego. I bet she's got a glamorous title and has a sweet pad near the beach or maybe Hollywood. I'm envious as I think of her leaving our small town behind, making her dreams come true.

The Mole visits, noticing my flippant responses and listless eyes. I don't even care if he withholds food or makes me do extra chores. I might as well be dead.

The only thing he instructs of me is to take my bucket to the bathroom next door. At the beginning he would empty it, but now he watches me from the hallway. I'm only allowed to go to the right, the corridor pitch-black.

I dump the pail in the rusted-out toilet, flushing it. The

bathroom is really just that – a toilet that has no seat, a tiny pedestal sink, and cleaning supplies. The floor's concrete and bare. Every time I'm allowed in there, I scan the room for any sign of where I'm at, makeshift weapons, or ways to escape, but it's windowless and cramped.

The Mole blocks my path, standing between the hall and my room, squinting his eyes at me, arms crossed.

After I walk back into my prison, he turns the key and leaves without a sound.

This time, he doesn't come back for a couple weeks. He left dry ramen, cans of tuna fish, and old fruit, the bananas rotting with black spots.

When I've eaten it all, I'm prepared to starve to death, getting my half-hearted wish. When he returns, it's as if twenty-two days hadn't passed.

MY EYES ARE CONTINUALLY TIRED, eyesore inevitable. Having nothing to do but read, color, and piece together puzzles is wearing on them.

I have to find a new task.

LAYING ON THE FLOOR, pretending to daydream or sleep, my eyes search for seams or loose ends that I can pick at in the carpeting. I manage to lift off a corner and notice thick padding underneath.

It becomes my hobby, trying to figure out a way to get to the underneath, which is likely concrete. You hear of people digging tunnels and escaping from prisons to other countries, from captors...

It's impossible, but I have to have a goal.

Or else I'll lose the ability to live.

One day when he comes in from the outside, he's dressed up in a suit and tie, hair slicked back, a three-hundred-and-sixty-degree turn from the jumpsuits and coveralls I'm used to seeing.

"What's the occasion?" I ask, after raising my hand to be called on.

He seems preoccupied, adjusting his navy and yellow striped tie.

"It's a special day." Noticing my yellow shift, this one covered with embroidered flowers, he squeezes my chin gently.

"We're celebrating."

I'm confused.

It's not my birthday.

Not the day I disappeared.

Not the birthday of anyone I know.

Is it a holiday that I don't celebrate? Passover? Rosh Hashanah?

"It's her birthday." He smiles at me, the yellow tooth greeting me.

"Who?"

"Jean."

Puzzled, I lick my lips. What does this mean for me? Is Jean a missing girl that made a bad decision and wound up tied to a bedpost?

"You're dressed appropriately." He's thrilled by this. "We're going to take flowers to the cemetery and put them on her grave."

I manage a nod.

So she's now a dead girl that was once tied to a bedpost. I press the unease down and focus on the positive. This excursion means fresh air and hopefully sunshine.

Maybe an escape route. Today could be my lucky day.

The Mole hands me a bouquet of white lilies and purple gardenias.

HE'S IMPATIENT, grabbing my hand, talking a mile a minute.

I wait for him to blindfold me, which he does, but when he picks me up in his arms, I expect we'll go for a ride in a vehicle.

Instead, he shoves open a door, the whoosh of the steel closing rushes past my ear, brushing my cheek.

Abruptly he sets me down.

I hear him grappling with the flowers, the blossoms caressing my skin.

Pausing, I move my head to speak to him, even though I can't see. "Aren't we going somewhere?" Now I'm scared, maybe this is one of his tricks.

"It's a walk, silly. Hold my hand," he rebukes.

A light breeze rustles my ponytail. I breathe in the outside air, calming myself with each inhale, my diaphragm rising and falling, holding his hand as if it's my lifeline.

And by this point, I know he is. He can kill me, he can save me.

He plays God.

Smelling fresh-cut grass, the earthen stench of dirt, and the scent of perennials, I shyly raise my hand.

"Yes, little girl?"

"Did Jean like these flowers?"

"Yes. These are her favorite flowers and colors."

"Is this a happy celebration?"

"Of course."

"Sir?" He loves when I'm submissive.

"Yes, little girl?"

"How old was she when she...when she passed?

"Old. Fifty-Eight."

"Oh," I say, "so not a child."

"Nope." He tugs my wrist. "And not an accident either."

"Was it a tragedy?"

"Aren't all deaths a tragedy in their own way?" he muses.

I consider this. "I guess so."

He's quiet. I hear his footsteps on the hard surface, cement, I presume.

"Was she one of your girls?"

"Enough questions for today." He's staunch. "Let's enjoy our walk."

We stroll in silence, birds chirping, my ears on high alert. I wish I could see something other than the four foam walls that house me. My eyes long for color, vividness.

Something new.

He hears my cries of desperation, even in my head. "Would you like the bandana off?"

"Yes please." I don't want to act excited or he'll change his mind.

"You've been a good girl lately." He claps his hands. "This is a privilege, remember that."

"Yes, sir."

He removes the cloth. My eyes hurt for a minute, the room dim and windowless, light a rarity.

I blink a few times, my eyes adjusting to the sun, the sky, and the pine trees that look out of place here. I sigh, running my hands over my face, my skin luminescent, all traces of color barely visible except for the marks he's inflicted.

A small hill dips where we walk, the grass overgrown. There's a pond but no ducks, only junk cars – no people, and nothing but trees and lawn decorations made out of old car parts – rusted radiators, fuel pumps, and tires filled with dirt and shrubs.

It's a personal cemetery.

My heart drops. Will I be buried here one day?

He gives me a sideways glance, reading my mind. "Not today."

I nod, unable to speak, lost in thought.

Pointing to a makeshift grave that's nothing but a wooden cross with faded lettering, the name says Jean, beloved mother and friend, October 7th, 1939 - September 30th, 1997.

She's been dead a couple years.

He motions for me to kneel beside him. "Is she related to you?" I whisper.

Setting the white lilies and the purple gardenias at the foot of the marker, he nods. "My mother."

"I'm so sorry." I bow my head, mimicking his motions, pretending to pray for her soul.

And for her son, because he's going to hell.

"She was my best friend," he murmurs. "But she had an evil side."

Shocked, I stare at the latest burn marks on my hands, this time running the length of my index finger.

"What do you mean?" I don't expect him to answer.

"She hurt me." He scowls. "She hurt her."

I bite my tongue, tracing the scabs that will become jagged scars. He threads his fingers through mine, his voice shrill. "So she had to go." He's certain of this, shaking his head up and down. "It was time. We all have a time and a season."

He shrugs. "Soon you'll have a time." He says this so matter-of-fact, my hand goes limp in his palm.

Focus, I tell myself, focus on him.

"Did she kill your sister?" I barely breathe, a blade of grass tickling my bare knee.

"Yes." He squeezes my fingers painfully. "So I had to take matters into my own hands." He's quick to add, "but I didn't mean for it to go that far. She was all I had."

"What happened to Marian?"

"She died." He yanks on his tie. "So Mother paid the price and joined her in heaven."

"How did Marian... ?" I stutter. "How did she um, pass away?"

"Mother locked her in a closet and she never came out." Sadness pains his eyes.

"How come?"

"Because she didn't like that we were close, that I wasn't Mommy's little boy anymore. That Marian and I had a bond, she was my other half."

Marian.

His twin.

"She couldn't let us be."

"Why would she hurt your twin and not you?"

"Because I was her favorite. Both of their favorites. She was jealous of my sister."

Jesus. This is deep. Imagine if my mom was this psychotic about Blair and I. She might be more critical of her, but crap, this is heavy.

"She made me help." A fat tear rolls down his ruddy cheeks.

I'm silent. His range of emotions tire me out, the constant change a testament to his deep-seated issues.

PATTING HIS SHOULDER AWKWARDLY, I soothe him by whispering kind words and condolences.

He seems to appreciate the gesture, his body relaxing against mine.

I hold his hand, mine pale and marked, his tan with flaxen hair.

We sit like this, the questions piling up, but I'm too scared to ask, another swing to his mood and I'll be in a shallow grave myself.

"She said it was wrong," he moans.

"Who?"

"That we were too close." He bows his head. "Mommy didn't like it."

"What didn't she like?"

"That we would lay in bed together."

"Did you share a room?"

"Yes." His eyes are sorrowful. "We shared everything. She was my best friend."

"How old?"

"Twelve." He sags against me, burying his face in my shoulder, the mole out of sight.

I'm aghast, my face turning ashen, his admission closing the gap in a story I've long wondered about-his obsession with the age of twelve and another decade.

When he leaves the room, he's in present time, but when he comes in, he leaves it behind for the past.

I'm her.

And he will keep killing young girls until he's caught or murdered.

Because we all age, even in a room of your own making.

This realization stuns me.

I close my eyes, pretending to listen to his desperate attempts at emotional maturity, but I'm shriveling up inside.

Why doesn't anyone care that I'm still missing?

He blubbers for a few more minutes, his snot running down my cheek.

I say nothing.

His touch can't hurt me anymore, the wounds inside a cesspool of self-loathing that even I can't reach.

When he stands, his tribute to his dead mother over, he leads us in a hymn. Instead of singing, he hums. I silently mouth the words, his fickle tendencies at the forefront of my mind.

I notice a grass stain on the knee of his pants but I say nothing, his mood tenuous. I can see the wheels turning in his brain, and that means I will be on the receiving end of his tyranny.

As we walk back, I get maybe five hundred feet before he covers my eyes, wrapping the bandana around.

It's tight, too tight, and he moves his hands to my neck, squeezing.

I cough, air filling my lungs, his anger now directed at me.

The tension cuts the air as we walk, his steps hurried and uneven, mine laced with trepidation. I'm running out of time.

When he closes me back in the room, I lay down on the floor, balling myself up, the fear and uncertainty eating my insides.

There has to be a way out. Alive.

27

BLAIR

WHEN I TURN TWENTY-TWO, I head back to Hawaii, drugged up on benzos to get me through the plane ride, my body's chain reaction a wave of panic attacks at the idea of going back to the island.

Not only that, but flying over open water causes my heart rate to increase and my palms to sweat profusely.

It's like anticipating a plane crash you know is coming.

You don't want to go, but you have no control over the outcome or the emotions you feel.

The same goes for Waikiki Beach. It's ruined, the beauty marred by my baby sister's disappearance.

I'm obsessed Will Loomis is guilty, that he's hiding her somewhere, using her for his own gain, pimping her out.

I rent a car to follow him, wearing oversized sunglasses and an auburn wig, chain smoking cigarettes one after the other.

He works at a mechanic shop during the weekdays, his weekends spent teaching surf lessons at the same locale. I watch him from a distance. His extracurricular activities still include riding waves. I'm amazed at his ability to merge with the ocean, coasting over them in one fluid motion.

His mode of transportation has upgraded, a baby blue moped or a souped-up truck, walking home not enough to trick young girls into coming with him.

I'm jaded and angry, a bad combo. The three years that have passed haven't been kind – a strained relationship with my parents, no college degree, and a career path as a cashier in a convenience store.

Bitter is what I am.

Permanently tainted to the island.

At night, Will still spends his time at various bars, he ages but the girls stay the same, young and naïve.

I watch him from a high-top table, disgusted by the way they fawn over him, their childlike expressions and blind trust in him a poignant reminder we were once that innocent. My blood starts to boil as I seethe in the corner.

The last night on the island, I stop in at *The Ocean Club*, noticing Will's stupid blue moped parked outside on the strip.

I don't bother with the wig, the inside dim and murky. I glance around but don't see his tall stature and dark hair. He must have started at another location tonight.

THIS TIME, I have a seat at the bar. David, the old bartender, pours someone a whiskey. I try to make eye contact with him, but there's not a flicker of remembrance. No expression, his eyes flat, the gold wedding ring still wrapped around his left ring finger. I know I must look different – my hair's long now, past my shoulders, a lighter caramel color with honey-streaked highlights, and I'm filled out, not as lanky. I'm legal, my ID real this time.

Blair Priscilla Bellamy.

He scans my ID, his eyes never leaving the card to examine my face before he slides it back to me. He squints at the name. "Drink?"

"Michelob Ultra." I decide on beer, less chance of being drugged if I watch the cap pried open. "Bottle please."

He removes the top in one swift gesture. Sliding it across to me, I swig it.

"You live in Nebraska?" he asks. "What's that like?"

"Cold," I say. "Nothing much to do. Lots of corn."

"Cornhuskers, right?"

I give him a small smile, lighting a cigarette.

Shit." He whistles. "Midwest. I've never been."

"Middle of nowhere," I say, blowing a ring of smoke.

"You know you can't do that in here, right?" He reaches for my lighter, tossing it in the trash.

I exhale, stomping it out on the floor as he winces.

"What part of Nebraska are you from?"

"Would you even know where?" I twist the neck of the bottle. "Are you familiar with the state?"

"Yeah, my friend lives there." He shrugs. "Omaha."

"Where did you grow up?" I ask, feigning interest.

At that moment, Will walks in, followed by a blonde with spiky hair and a lip piercing. If her jeans were any tighter, she'd need pliers to remove them.

And this is coming from my twenty-two-year-old self.

I watch him out of the corner of my eye, my pulse racing as I struggle to maintain composure.

"You see that guy over there?" I nod at Will, since it's rude to point.

"Yeah." David shrugs. "He's a regular."

"What do you know about him?"

"Not much. Surfer dude."

"He come in a lot, *a lot*?"

"Few times a week. This is his home away from home."

"This your full-time job?" I make conversation, my eyes glued on Will as he orders a drink from across the bar. The girl doesn't sit, instead she heads to the bathroom.

"Nah. I do this for fun. It's a great way to meet people."

"Excuse me..." I interrupt, "I'll be right back."

Following the young girl to the bathroom, I watch her enter a stall. I pretend to wash my hands, rinsing them repeatedly under the faucet.

She comes out a moment later.

"Hi," I say, handing her a paper towel. She looks puzzled, unsure why there's a bathroom attendant all of a sudden.

"Hi," she gives me a sideways glance, unsure if she should know me.

"How do you know Will?"

"We go way back." She looks in the mirror at me, glassy-eyed. "Why?"

"Oh, I used to know him." I shrug. "Not a big deal except he *killed* my sister."

"Huh?" Her mouth drops open. "What're you talking about?"

"Never mind." I shrug. "Have a good night. Hope you don't end up as another missing girl." I raise my eyebrows. "The body count keeps piling up."

She stands woodenly as I turn to walk out, never moving an inch.

Smiling at David, I slide back onto my stool and order my next round.

Raised voices cause me to turn. Will and the blonde are in a shouting match, her finger pointed directly at me.

I flip back to the front, scrutinizing the bottles of liquor on the top shelf.

Swallowing, I turn my attention to David. "How long you married for?" I eye the gold band.

"Long enough." He laughs. "I met her in middle school."

"Seriously?" I gasp. "That's a story right there."

He nods his head in agreement. "You're telling me."

"She mind you working nights?" I'm curious, as bartenders are night owls and it must make relationships hard unless they have similar hours or occupations.

"Nah, she's preoccupied a lot." He grins. "She likes her space away from me."

"Fair enough."

"You married?" he asks, leaning on the counter, eyeing my naked finger.

"Just because I'm a small-town girl doesn't mean I follow the trend," I tease.

'True." A drunk co-ed wearing a tiara comes bum-rushing the bar. "Need. Shots," she yells, her blonde hair cascading down her back in waves.

Will's female companion grabs her purse off the table, storming out, her heels clicking on the floor.

Then his voice behind me.

"What the fuck?" He slams his hand on the counter directly in front of me. "Who are you?"

I turn slowly, my eyes drifting to his bronzed face and dark hair. "Hi Will."

It takes him a moment, but a flicker of recognition appears.

"Blair?"

I haltingly nod my head up and down.

"Why're you telling people I killed your sister?"

David's confused, his eyes darting between the two of us.

"It's true."

He punches the air with his fist. "It's a lie and you know it."

"Then why so defensive?" I reach in my purse, gripping the pepper spray. "Get the hell away from me."

He looks at David. "This girl is psycho." He points at me. "Just remember, you're in *my* bar. I didn't seek you out, Blair. And Bristol's been missing for a few years. It's time to stop focusing on old news."

Tears sting my eyes as he turns on his heel, heading to the other side of the establishment, shooting daggers over his shoulder at me.

My thoughts are interrupted when a waitress rushes over, helping the drunk blonde sit down, the tiara falling on the table as she passes out facedown. "David..." She sighs. "We gotta get this girl outta here."

"What do you expect me to do?" he asks her. "Get the bouncer?"

"Is it always a shit show like this?" I roll my eyes at a group of co-eds squawking a Journey song horribly off-key.

"It's mildly entertaining." He shakes his head in amazement. "The shit people do to shake loose."

A short, petite, dark-haired girl walks up, leaning over the bar to whisper something in David's ear. I can't hear what she says but immediately he lines up a row of shot glasses.

"Hey, want a shot?" He starts pouring tequila. "I gotta make 'em for that bachelorette party. Might as well make extra."

"Nah, but one more beer please." I watch him stick lemon wedges on the tray with the liquor.

Glancing across at Will, he's not pouting too hard, staking his claim at another table with a wasted group of girls. It's impossible to tell who's the most inebriated of the foursome.

A red-headed man sits on his other side, beard scraggly, voice slurred, loudly gesticulating.

We have a winner, I think.

Sipping my beer, I watch the way Will slides his hand up the girl's thigh, her skirt hitched up to her waist. The blonde laughs at something the ginger says.

He must've made a joke, the giggles loud enough to overtake karaoke. Will reaches out a hand, pulling her towards the dance floor, grabbing her tight around her waist.

I slam my last bottle down hard on the counter, the glass rattling, imagining him and my sister, the way he put the moves on her.

Déjà vu all over again.

She's happy, or punch-drunk happy as they say, while anger courses through my veins like heroin through a syringe. Once it's injected, the feeling of despair and half-truths destroy me, seeping through my bloodstream, just like a drug.

Out on the dance floor, their moves are sloppy and jerky, hands fumbling for each other in the dark. I'm half-perched on my stool, eyes glued to their every move, David glancing at my sulky expression with interest.

He's too polite to ask why I care so much. Probably assumes I'm a bitter ex-girlfriend. I might as well be.

Will and the girl leave together, their mouths pressed against each other's lips.

I hurriedly drop forty dollars on the counter for my tab, thanking David for his hospitality. He eyes me suspiciously, watching me follow them out of the bar.

Staggering, they both walk to Will's moped, my long legs keeping up with their inebriated pace.

"We better not," she says, running a hand through his curly hair.

"No, we better." Grinning, he caresses her bare shoulder.

"Nah, it's a bad idea." She halfheartedly pushes him away.

He stumbles, reaching to yank her by the hair. "Stop talking and let's ride." Grabbing her hand roughly, he pulls her towards the bike, pushing her leg over the seat.

My temper boils over. I clench and unclench my fists.

Another girl he discards for his own amusement, his advances unwanted, yet he forces himself on her.

Before he can react, I close the gap, my fist landing on his jaw. A look of surprise registers on his face, his chestnut-eyes dazed as he recognizes me as the assailant.

The woman screams and reaches in her pocket for her phone, dialing 9-1-1.

She must think I'm trouble. She doesn't know who I just saved her from.

Goodman shows up, surprise registering on his face when he sees me. His partner separates me from Will and his lady friend.

Except from the bits I hear that drift over to me, I learn she's not being harmed, only berating him for wanting to drink and ride. The argument stemmed over his unwilling-ness to take a cab home.

He gladly presses charges for assault and I end up in court.

My trip is prolonged as I have to make an appearance in front of a judge. I call Mark, infuriated at the injustice that

Will thinks he can act innocent to everyone else. He's quiet as he listens to my tirade.

Will shows up with his attorney to the hearing, and they agree not to press charges if I agree to stay off the island for a period of three years, plus stay five hundred feet away from him for the same amount of time.

It's a blow, considering my sister is still missing.

The judge listens to me plead my case.

Her tone is kind but firm. "Ms. Bellamy, Mr. Loomis hasn't been indicted or charged with kidnapping or any other crimes against her person. In fact, it's unclear exactly what happened to her. Have you considered she left the island of her own volition, drowned, or was picked up by someone else?"

Tears streak my cheeks as Will looks on, smug in his pinstriped suit.

I stand, "Your Honor, may I address the court?"

She agrees, her arms crossed as she hears me out. I explain the situation as Will has the audacity to look bored.

"I concur that this is a terrible loss, Ms. Bellamy. I encourage you to undergo counseling, in fact, the court demands it, and anger management as well." She raises the gavel, signaling the end of my pleas.

Mark waits for me outside the courtroom, his biceps barely fitting in his three-piece suit.

"Blair." He gives a frustrated sigh. "I hate meeting like this."

"I know," I say, "but I'm not sorry. He knows what happened to her." I attempt a small smile. "Plus I get to see you for old time's sake, that's not half bad."

He tries to keep a straight face, but a twinkle's in his blue eyes.

We walk out of the courtroom and stand against the

wall. "I'd tell my teenager the same thing I'm telling you." He pauses, making sure he has my undivided attention before he continues. "You can't always assume the innocent are guilty and vice versa."

"What're you saying, Mark?" I'm thrown by his statement. "That he didn't hurt Bristol?"

He shakes his head, defeated. He taps the toe of his wingtips against the bench I sink into.

I cross my arms in defiance. "You know he knows something. Or *someone*. This doesn't just happen like this."

"Maybe." He's contrite. "But I've never found any evidence linking him, and neither has the PD."

"They've never worked the leads or gave a damn." My voice escalates. "You know they're so focused on tourism and keeping a clean image, that's all anyone cares about."

Mark's wounded by my vitriol. "I don't agree with that statement at all."

I bite my lip, resentful of everyone and everything in this courthouse. I stalk out, my legs carrying me to a waiting taxi.

And Mark...the only person I've entrusted with this case is now divided on the perpetrator.

"You've gotta let this go." He tries to grab my arm, but I yank it away.

"Why, because it's so easy for you?" I scowl at him.

"Blair..." he throws his hands up. "Come back here."

"You want me to let my sister die in vain?" I toss over my shoulder, sliding into the backseat of the cab.

"No, but I want you to live life." He softens his tone. "You're drowning."

"What does it matter when no one saved her?" I argue, waving my arms emphatically at the courthouse steps where

Will's talking to his attorney, a dark-haired woman in a wrap dress.

I'm headed back to Nebraska, to a home I don't have, a life of big dreams and bigger goals thwarted by this cocky asshole.

Mark gives me a small wave good-bye, his figure shrinking in the rearview, defeat in his weary eyes.

We fall out of touch.

I'm now completely alone.

It takes time, but I have to hit rock bottom before I can pull myself out of the black cloud that envelopes me.

It comes a couple weeks later when I'm perusing the news online, scanning the Oahu paper.

Another girl has disappeared.

When I see her picture pop up on my screen, a cold chill runs down my spine. I'm 99.9% sure it's the blonde girl in the tiara celebrating a bachelorette party.

28

BRISTOL

WHEN I FINALLY PICK ENOUGH AT the carpet to get to the padding underneath, it's foam. Thick, almost bouncy. Definitely for sound-proofing.

I spend my time memorizing every corner of the room.

Time passes, hours, months, all go by at a snail's pace.

Years certainly, but I don't have a birthday to celebrate. It's like my age has paused in here. It's never acknowledged, I'm forever twelve to him.

The Mole's either jovial and talkative, or disagreeable and sadistic, a true split personality. I've learned the color of his eyes reflect the oncoming storm, determining whether it will subside or turn into a hurricane. This helps to prepare me for the severity of punishments, though it never gets easier. I just become numb.

One evening, or at least it feels like night, he shows up after being absent for a period of time.

Freckles stand out against his ruddy complexion, a sure sign he's going to blow a fuse. His eyes darken.

Sure enough, he flips out on me because the bed's not made to his exact specifications, a corner untucked.

Dragging me by my long braid to the door, he kicks me in the ribs.

Face flushed, eyes bulging. "You're gonna scrub the bathroom." He pants.

"Why're you upset?" This is a pointless question, and I know better than to ask.

"You take me for granted. I feed, clothe, and give you shelter, you ungrateful whore." He screams, kicking me again, this time catching my chin with the toe of his sneaker.

I ball up in pain, holding my knees to my chest.

"Get up." He snaps his fingers.

Balling my fists, I use my hands to pull myself up the wall.

"I'll be right back." He steps around me, sliding and locking the door shut behind him.

Catching my breath, I start to cry. They're furious tears, angry and repressed.

When he comes back a minute later, he sets a pail and toothbrush at my feet.

"You're going to scrub the bathroom...with the tooth-brush." He thrusts the door open, pushing me out and to the right.

"I'll be right here waiting." There's a metal folding chair set up in the hall. "I'm going to write while you get to work." He pulls out a small black notebook and ballpoint pen.

As I take the first step, he reminds me to change the toilet paper and scrub the porcelain bowl. "Oh, and little girl, don't think about using anything else to clean with besides the toothbrush and soap."

When I enter the bathroom, I turn on the barely-there light, the wattage so minimal that a flashlight could do a better job. Changing the toilet paper out of the bulk inventory stored near the cleaning supplies, I notice the trash can is full.

There's no mirror over the sink, so I can't watch the hall behind me, but an imprint of it remains. The Mole probably removed it so I couldn't use the glass to stab myself...or him, I think dryly.

Getting on my hands and knees, I fill the pail up with soap and water, pretending to scrub the faded linoleum. I move closer to the trash can. Holding my breath, I rummage through the contents. A crumpled newspaper's shoved in the bottom underneath a bunch of used tissue.

The date's in the upper left-hand corner in black print.

Overwhelmed, my hand automatically grabs at my heart.

The year makes me nauseous.

It can't be. It just can't be.

It's 2004.

I've been here over six years.

Nervously, I scan the contents of the newspaper, glancing over my shoulder every few seconds. Buried between the obits and an editorial piece, there's an article that catches my eye, about a college student who went missing six months ago. She's been happily reunited with her family after a massive manhunt.

Her name's Charlene Meadows, aged twenty, from Long Island, New York.

She was drinking at a bar, and the name sounds familiar.

The Ocean Club.

According to the paper, a bartender saw her stagger out after a night of drinking at 1 A.M. but claimed she was alone.

Her friends mention a red-haired, freckle-faced, twenty

something she was flirting with before they left to continue on to the next bar. Charlene insisted they go ahead, she would catch up, liking the guy enough to stay put.

I almost disregard the article until one of the girls mention what they had done earlier in the day. The owners of the condo had left a guidebook with suggestions on water activities.

They chose surf lessons.

My heart rams in my chest, thudding sharply against my ribs. There are a million surf instructors, could Will Loomis be theirs?

One friend sent Charlene a text at 12 A.M., she responded, saying she was still good at *The Ocean Club*. Assuming she went home with him, it wasn't until the next afternoon when warning bells started going off with her friends. She hadn't come back to the shared condo and her phone continued to go to voicemail, text messages showed undeliverable.

No one could find her, or her cell phone and purse, it was like the night had swallowed her whole when she vanished.

Distraught, her wealthy family offered a handsome reward to the tune of five hundred thousand dollars, begging for information. This was after the detectives had no leads and the case dried up for a couple months. Shortly after, a man found her naked and curled up in a fetal position, near a popular cliff diving spot on the island. She was near an entrance to a cave and would've been missed had she not been mewing loudly like an injured animal.

Wobbling underneath me, my knees shake as I read the next paragraph.

Charlene's memories are vague, the night in question plucked from her memory, except when she wakes up, she's a prisoner, tied to a bed in a small room. She has such traumatic PTSD that detectives glean little other information from her.

With no recollection of the night she disappeared or her captor, the case goes cold.

My heart plummets when they mention a couple of other missing girls that have never been found.

Shockingly, my name's absent from the list.

Silently crying, my tears slide into the pail, my existence in question.

Doesn't anyone care I'm still missing? I want to pound the dirty floor with my fists.

Digging through the rest of the trash, it's mainly strips of toilet paper, tissue, and gum wrappers. I find a broken shoelace and an apple core. At the bottom is a torn, cream-colored business card for a car dealership in Honolulu. It has a salesman's name on it.

Dean Morgan of Island Chevy.

This gives me renewed hope that I'm still close to where I was last seen.

Frantic I'll forget the information, I consider hiding the paper and business card on me, patting my baby doll dress for a place to disguise it.

What about in the band of my white underwear?

No, not a chance.

It's a certainty that he will find it when he either undresses me or makes me change in front of him.

Practicing mnemonic devices to remember the girl and area, the car salesman and location, I scrub the floor with renewed perseverance, my tears now dry.

At least I'm still on the island.

When The Mole comes to retrieve me, humming

another one of his annoying tunes, his blue eyes narrow as he checks my work.

"You missed a spot." He points at the back of the porcelain bowl.

"That's rust," I explain. "It won't come off."

"Are you calling me a liar?" He takes a step forward, I move one back, shaking my head.

"I didn't think so." He gives a menacing stare, his height lumbering over me.

When he reaches a hand to yank me back towards the hall and the room, I begin to violently shake. It's not because of his strong grip or his fingers digging into my neck. It's the realization of how much time I've spent here and the other girls that went straight to their deaths, never given a shot at survival.

Grunting, he rips my dress off and pushes me face down on the bed. "You see anything in the trash?" He pushes my head further into the mattress.

"Huh?" I close my eyes. "What're you talking about?"

"There was a newspaper in the garbage." He straddles me. "Read anything good?"

I open my eyes, voice muffled. "What?"

"You see the date?" He chuckles. "You see how long you've been here?" He runs his hands down my body, searching every crevice for signs I'm hiding something.

"You've been discarded." There's a twinkle in his greenish eyes. "They don't even mention you in that article about the poor missing girls." He shrugs. "You're dead to everyone. Lucky you have me, your own family doesn't even look for you anymore."

HE PINCHES MY CHEEK, hard. "You're dead to them." He motions to the bathroom. "Garbage. Leftover trash."

Holding my pain and emotions in, I nod in agreement. "I know."

Cocking his head, he doesn't expect this response from me. He's not used to me submitting so easily.

I sense disappointment in his body language.

"IF YOU DIDN'T SAVE me, I'd have no one." I give him a small smile. "Can we read a book tonight? I know you're wondering what happens next."

This suggestion turns off a switch in him, the battle brewing in his head starts to calm, his touch softening.

He must've forgotten about the business card or not known it was there.

I haven't prayed in a while, but I do that night.

Thank God I left the paper and card where it belonged.

The Mole tried to trick me, break me.

It almost worked.

29

BRISTOL

OVER THE NEXT FEW YEARS, I'm on my best behavior, following the rules the first time, stroking his ego, and doing chores before being asked.

All in good time, I tell myself.

The Mole shows up one afternoon, a smile glued to his face. "I have a surprise for you, little girl."

Not bones, I hope.

It's a plastic bag.

I assume it's a sweet treat, his usual reward of gummy bears or chocolate bars.

It's a caramel apple. I hate apples, even with caramel covering their nasty skin. He's testing me, circling his prey, ready to attack if I don't roll over.

"Thank you." I beam. "I can't wait to eat this later." It's hard to say with a straight face as my stomach grumbles in protest.

"How about now?" He gives me a sly look.

"What about dinner?" I bite my lip. "I don't want to ruin my appetite."

"This is in place of dinner." The yellow tooth grins at me. "I thought you deserved something special."

"You are so thoughtful," I spit out. "I'm not hungry right now. Mind if I save it for later?"

"Actually, I do mind." He reaches back in the bag. "I thought you could enjoy it with a book."

I can't believe my eyes.

He's holding five books in his hand.

Library books.

All with bar codes and the actual library name stamped inside.

"Eat first. I don't want you to get the books sticky." He's impatient as he sits on the edge of the bed.

Sliding onto the small chair, I start licking the caramel on the outside. The Mole's tapping his foot, waiting for me to bite into the skin. In my rush, I crunch down hard, except it's not a bite of apple that's shooting pain, it's my back tooth.

"Shit." I groan, letting a dirty word slip, my hand reaching inside my mouth.

"What did you just say?" The Mole's eyes bug out.

"I hurt my tooth," I mumble, feeling around, a bicuspid now loose.

He abruptly stands. "No books."

"What?" I whisper, holding my cheek.

"I'm taking them back." He wags his finger at me. "You know better than to cuss."

"My tooth, I need a dentist." I plead with my eyes as he shoves each book back in the plastic bag, one by one.

"Guess you don't deserve a special treat." He closes the bag and sets it on the table. "Let me see your mouth."

"No, it's okay." I snap. The last thing I want is The Mole poking around, playing dentist.

"Open up." His tone brooks no argument.

I try and scoot back in my seat. He jerks the chair, toppling me over.

"Don't fight me. You'll never win."

He gives me a hard slap on the knee. "Now open up." His fingers push their way into my gums, jabbing at the tissue.

I'm tempted to bite down, the idea of clamping on his hairy fingers, causing pain to him, running through my mind.

The consequences aren't worth the action, I decide.

He nimbly stretches my lips open, blinking rapidly at the detached tooth. "Don't worry, I wanted to be a dentist." As if his want of being one justifies his intent to practice on me.

"Be right back," he claps his hands.

I'm still lying on my back, my feet in the air.

WHEN I HEAR the door click, I realize this is my shot.

Sliding off the chair, I fumble for the plastic bag on the table. Pulling out one of the books, I notice the date on the check-out slip.

It's 2007.

I don't have time to let it sink in, instead I grab a blue magic marker that rolled under the table earlier. I scrawl a note on one of the pages.

MY NAME'S Bristol Bellamy and I was kidnapped in 1998.

Please help me. I'm being held in a room in Honolulu but I don't know where.

It's 2007 and I'm alive.

Tell my family please.

THE KEY TURNS in the lock and frantic, I shove the book back in the bag, careful to keep my back turned to the camera. He might rewind the video and see I took a book out, but hopefully not that I wrote a note inside.

A glass bottle's in one hand, pliers, cotton, and a flashlight in the other.

"This is gonna hurt." He thrusts the vodka in the air. "We gotta remove the tooth."

"No, no, please." I protest. "I'll be okay. It'll come out eventually. I'll just keep wiggling it."

He stares at me, unconvinced.

I hold my hands up. "Let's just take a bath."

"We haven't done anything to take a bath." An evil gleam crosses his face. I'm at rock bottom if him violating my body sounds better than his idea of surgery.

"Then what're you waiting for?" I stand, starting to unbutton my denim dress.

"Stop." He holds up a forceful hand. "You're not going to make me sin again." He steps towards me. "You have two choices. Surgery or I put you in the box." He squints at me. "I can't promise you'll be alive when you come out though."

We stare each other down, his blue eyes unblinking.

I break eye contact first. "Surgery," I murmur, the fight gone.

He taps his nose three times. "I knew you'd make the right choice." He pulls rubber gloves out of his back pocket. "Go sit on the bed. I'll get everything ready just like a dentist would."

With a sinking feeling, I lay down on the mattress, hands folded across my chest, despising him. He hums his way around the room until he ends up at my side, his mouth sucking a peppermint.

"Okay, first things first. You'll take a shot of vodka now. Then one after." He pauses to reconsider. "Actually, two now, two after." He pours it directly in my mouth.

Unprepared, I sputter as it burns down my throat.

"This way you'll hopefully pass out from the vodka and not the pain."

Petrified, I move my hands, gripping my upper arms, holding them tight. I can wrap my fingers, circling the width of them, my skin translucent and gaunt.

I don't want to close my eyes, wary of the 'surgery'.

I swallow the poison, my first drop in years since I was taken.

It burns its way down, settling in an uneasy pit at the bottom of my stomach.

"Round two." His peppermint-laced breath hovers over me.

CLOSING MY EYES, I gag.

HE THRUSTS MY CHIN BACK, clutching it. "Don't spit it up."

My body convulses but The Mole ignores it. "Okay, now for the removal of your tooth." He winks. "Should the Tooth Fairy pay you a visit?"

He grabs the pillow and pushes it over my eyes, removing the sight of him. "Be a good girl and hold this tight," he instructs. I don't know if I should be relieved or terrified. I hold each end, arms pressing it over my lids.

"Open your mouth wide," he guides my mouth. "No, wider."

A hard object's shoved in my mouth...what the...it's the flashlight.

"This reminds me of playing doctor with Marian," he muses.

My head starts to pound, the vodka making me dizzy and nauseous. Or maybe it's a combination of both the alcohol and the back-alley surgery.

What if I can't hold still and I move while he's removing my tooth? The thought fills me with dread. He could seriously injure me, leaving me without any medical help.

My fingers tighten on the faded edges of the pillowcase, hugging it to my forehead.

I barely have time to consider this when cold metal's shoved in my mouth.

Choking, he chastises me.

"Shhh...don't fidget. I don't want to cut half your face off."

So he's considered this outcome too?

He starts to hum, his gloved fingers feeling around inside my cheek. He's playing with the tooth, yanking it back and forth.

The pounding in my temple becomes a splitting headache. I can feel my face flushing, my temperature rising. Helplessly, I start to tremble.

"Calm down, little girl." The Mole strokes my earlobe, tracing his finger down my neck, latex on my skin making me shudder. "Marian used to listen to my heartbeat, the plastic stethoscope we had tickled, and then she would give me my yearly exam."

Something wet's rubbed on my gums.

It tingles, anesthetizing the spot – I realize it's numbing cream.

"I polished her teeth, or at least I pretended to, when we played dentist." He pushes a wad of cotton in my cheek, his fingers poking the ball into place. "We'd use toothpaste as the tooth polish."

With no warning, a sharp tug pulls at the tooth, the rusty pliers twisting it from the root, exiting my mouth in one quick motion, a twinge replacing the jagged hole.

Blood, the taste metallic on my tongue, fills my mouth, soaking the cotton.

My throat's dry and I'm unable to swallow.

Tears leak into the fabric pillowcase. The Mole starts speaking again, his pace rapid and indignant. "We had fun until she caught us. Then she locked her in the closet...this time for a couple of days."

Running my tongue over the void where the tooth was, jumbled thoughts twist in my head but I'm unable to speak.

"I tried to sneak food to her, but Mother found out, and I had to eat kitty litter for a whole week."

Nervous laughter fills the silence that follows.

The Mole's going to lose control if I can't calm him.

Pushing the pillow off my forehead, I watch his facial expression as he examines his handiwork. His mouth gapes, the yellow tooth visible. Wrinkles form across his forehead, the lines around his eyes pronounced. He needs a haircut, the sandy blond shaggy on the sides.

"Good girl." He pats my cheek, handing me a cup of water to rinse with. "You were so brave." He pulls a handkerchief out of his pocket, wrapping the bloody tooth in it to take with him.

"What're you going to do with it?" I mumble.

I know I should go back into character, thank him, build up the hero complex he's imagining in his mind, but I can't.

He feeds me a pill that must be Vicodin or a similar type of strong pain med, his hands caressing my hair. "This'll help you sleep," he reassures me. "Let's get you ready for bed."

"But what about Marian?" I ask. "What happened after she went in the closet that time?"

He doesn't respond, instead he moves, drifting out of focus.

I start to repeat myself but something's wrong, my vision blurs, numbness crawling up my body, leaving me paralyzed.

Startled, he slaps me gently on the opposite cheek, calling my name. I can't respond, I try forming words, nothing comes out.

I shut my eyes. Go to your happy place, I tell myself.

Complying, I let myself wander into my bedroom, imagining the posters on the light yellow walls the color of buttermilk, snuggling with Oggie underneath my flowered daisy comforter.

It's a childlike memory, but right where I left off at home.

30

BRISTOL

MY HAND FLIES to my face. A tingling sensation starts in my cheekbone and gnaws its way down to my mandible.

I'm still positioned on the bed, my ankles shackled but my arms free.

My mouth aches, swollen and throbbing.

LOOKING DOWN, I'm still wearing the denim dress from the day before, but half the buttons are missing.

Did I do something when I took the pain pill I wasn't supposed to? Is that why I'm being restricted to just my hands?

I don't know how long I lie glued to the spot, changing position to sit up before resignedly flattening on my back.

My mouth tastes like dust, the absence of saliva reminding me how dehydrated I am.

I'm in a weird place – too weak to scream, too tired to cry.

Thinking of my list, I go over what I would add in my mind.

I wish I could have ice cream right now, chocolate chip cookie dough. Or maybe cookies n' cream.

My stomach grumbles, but the meds have worn off. The pain increases, a fiery sensation radiating down the left side of my face.

I'm half-asleep when I hear metal clicking later, the scraping sound as it shuts. Keeping my eyes closed, the mattress creaks as he sits down beside me. Flicking my wrist, he speaks. "Do you know why you're in this position?"

I don't have to open mine to know his eyes stare at me intensely.

Too weak to respond, I point to my cheek. "Help," I moan.

"That doesn't work today," he sneers. "Do you have something you're hiding from me?

My mind races to the hidden corners I've been refusing to confront, compartmentalizing what I can't control, as if it will just go away on its own, like a bruise.

Except a swollen belly doesn't go away, it becomes more obvious as time drags on.

My eyes dart to the wall of supplies. Did The Mole notice my period hasn't come, that the diapers are still stocked on the shelf?

I avoid his question.

"Can I have some water?" I whisper.

"No, you absolutely *cannot* have some water." He rubs a hand over his face. "Do you know what you did?"

"I didn't mean for it to happen... I cry out. "It was an accident."

"Look at me." He punches my arm until his face comes into focus. There's a look of pure hate, glinting from his ominous stare.

"This is no accident." He's enraged, a vein pops in his forehead, even the mole seems to darken in color as his fury builds. "You tried to get us caught."

His open palm lands a smack across my hurt cheek. "I read through all of the library books, *all of them*. I saw your nice inscription."

Twisting, I try and cover my face against his blows, a crack against my temple as he aims his next shot there.

"I should've left it, added my own note that said 'now dead.'" He grabs a fistful of hair and yanks, my skull prickling at the rough movement.

"Lucky for you, I ripped the page out and returned all five books." He grabs my shoulders, shoving me violently into the headboard. "You just passed the threshold between good and naughty. Do you know what happens to naughty girls?"

One of my eyelids starts to swell.

I blink, his face inches from mine.

He's about to strike me again, this time aiming with an open fist for my stomach, when I raise my hands in front of me as a shield.

"Stop! I'm pregnant," I shriek, my voice giving life to what has become my biggest fear.

I just haven't wanted to vocalize it.

GIVING BIRTH HERE, in this room, with him by my side, causes heart palpitations. If he isn't scared of performing surgery on a tooth, I can only imagine what would happen with childbirth. He'd want me to grin and bear it, probably forcing me to drink a bottle of tequila as my epidural.

The Mole recoils, whipping his head back, surprised, as if I returned a left hook to his face. "What?"

The word strangles to come out again. "I'm pregnant."

His eyes simmer. "I don't understand..."

"What did you think would happen?" I tremble. "We've never used protection."

HE STARES at me in disbelief, as if I'm speaking to him in tongues.

"This...this can't be happening, not again." He buries his face in his hands. "No...not again." He sinks off the bed onto the floor, sliding down with an audible sigh. "You're too young."

"Maybe you can take me to the doctor, we can ask how to prevent this from happening next time," I suggest. "Then we won't have to worry."

My attempt at coddling him doesn't work. "There won't be a next time." There is finality in his voice.

I shudder, deep down I know what he means. I've outlived my welcome.

Reaching down to stroke his arm, I keep rubbing the same spot, terrified of his silence as he sits huddled on the floor.

If I can convince him to take me to a clinic, I might have a chance to escape.

He doesn't respond, his arm flinching as I try to soothe him.

"We just have to be more careful." I put my other hand to my stomach. "I'm scared about dying in this room without a doctor...that's all. I don't want to leave you."

The Mole examines my belly with his eyes, confused, the outline of my hip bones and ribs defined from malnourishment. I'm amazed I can support the weight of another human being in this shape. Must be why it took so long for my body to take to a child, that and the stress.

"I don't believe you." He taps his nose three times.

"What?" I'm incredulous. "What don't you believe?"

HE STANDS, leaning over the bed, the lingering smell of fresh mint gum on his breath. "You aren't pregnant." He holds my arms stiffly at my sides. "Don't ever say that again."

I swallow my rebuttal, afraid I'll end up in the box or slammed up against a wall. A child's growing in me, another life to consider, even if we don't make it outside of the room. I have to at least try for their sake.

"Do you understand?" He pushes his elbow sharply into my stomach.

Terrified, I reply. "Yes sir."

"There will be no more talk of babies," he reprimands. "This isn't appropriate conversation for us to be having, little girl."

"Will you hold me?" I croak out.

He wordlessly unshackles my ankles before he lays down next to me on the bed.

Nuzzling under his arm, I hide my face in his long-sleeve shirt. He smells like aftershave and dandruff shampoo.

"Will you tell me your last memory of Marian?" I ask quietly.

"That would mean she's dead." His voice falters. "I couldn't save her from Mother."

"Did you help your mother...kill her?" I can barely get the words out.

Shaking me like a rag doll, he's furious. "Of course not. I didn't want to help."

"Was it an accident?"

"It wasn't my fault, I told Marian it was wrong."

"What was wrong?"

"That she would find out."

"Your mother?"

"It doesn't matter." He lifts his head. "She's not a threat anymore. She can't hurt me or you."

"How long ago did Marian pass?"

"A long time ago."

"Do you miss her?"

He gives me a shaky smile. "No, that's why I have you." Tweaking my nose, he lifts his arms, my face buried in the crook of his shoulder. Now I smell peppermint and gasoline.

"I'm not going to let you die in a closet or the room," he groans in my ear. "Even though you're acting just like her. She tried to tell me the same thing. She told me she was getting fat in the belly, that something was wrong."

Dumbstruck, I swallow hard.

"How was it your fault that your mother found out?"

"Because I told Mother. I didn't understand what was going on, and Mother kept asking why she was gaining weight. I didn't know it would happen." He snaps his fingers. "Poof, just like that, she's pregnant."

I'm quiet for a moment. "What did you think happened?"

"That she was with another boy." He shoves his hand in mine. "I didn't believe her when she said she wasn't. I couldn't control the jealousy, the rage I felt."

"Why not?"

"Because she was such a flirt at school, disappearing on the playground, chasing boys to make me upset. She would act like I was invisible at school or call me names. I hated it."

He sucks in a breath. "I hated her."

Furiously he shakes his head. "Mother didn't believe her."

"Why not?"

"Because we were just kids."

"But you shared a bed."

"Yeah, but we were twins."

"What happened?"

"She locked her in the closet, called her a lying tramp, and withheld food from her." His eyes fill with tears. "I brought her scraps, leftovers from the dog."

"And?"

"Mother found out and padlocked the closet."

"The same way you lock me in here?" I try and draw a correlation for him, make him see my point. If he understands, he feigns ignorance.

"Eventually she stopped breathing."

"How did you know if you couldn't get to her?"

"The smell." He taps his nose. This time only once instead of three times. "It seeped out and poisoned the whole house. Mother wanted me to bleach everything."

"Is that how you covered up her death?"

"Uh-huh."

"Then did you move Marian?"

"Mother asked me to set the house on fire."

"What happened?"

"I couldn't do it." He shakes his head sadly. "She belonged to me. I wasn't going to hurt her any more than I already had."

"Already had?"

His eyes show a human side, compassion, rare form for The Mole.

"By leaving her to die, all alone, while we went on without her."

31

BRISTOL

THE MOUNTING EVIDENCE of pregnancy can't be ignored. As much as I struggle with my changing body, my breasts becoming swollen and tender, my hormones causing acne, I can't disregard the life growing inside of me like I could before.

My belly protrudes out as the months pass which is crazy to me, because the rest of my body's skeletal. It doesn't get very big, just a little bump. I don't even need larger clothes.

Still, The Mole's disgusted by these obvious changes.

His punishments are silent now.

Withholding food and going weeks without visiting, leaving me to fend for myself and the unborn baby. I wouldn't mind his absence, except I'm worried about the lack of nutrients I'm feeding my body.

THE POSITIVE MEANS he doesn't bother punishing me for my infractions.

I'm also responsible for picking out my own clothes.

Luckily, a majority of the items are shift or A-line dresses, the material hugs my belly instead of swallowing my skinny frame.

Much to my relief, he doesn't bathe or violate me, choosing to keep his distance.

But after he sees me on camera giving myself a sponge bath and rinsing clothes in the tub using hand soap, he shuts the water off.

I keep track of my pregnancy by using a color-coded system and a coloring book.

When I'm six months along, I wear a nightgown, watching as he wordlessly drops off bare essentials – apples, rotten vegetables, old, stale bread.

"Can we talk?" I ask softly.

He gives me an overeager smile. "What's wrong?"

Uh-oh, no little girl follows his response.

"Can I get some reading material about pregnancy?" I ask, "It'd be nice to know what to expect."

He glares at me. "No."

Biting my lip, I change tactics. "I miss you..." I pretend. "Will you come lie down with me?"

His eyes drift to my belly, and he looks at me like you would a bug you wanted to squash. I feel a kick to my gut, I know it's more than just the baby.

Turning away, he busies himself with restocking toilet paper and baby wipes.

"Can we go to the doctor for a check-up?" I follow him across the room. "I think you'll be excited if we see an ultrasound. It'll feel more real."

"Real? You want *real*?" His head bobs around. Squeezing my neck, he pushes me backwards toward the bed. Tears burn my eyes as I stare at the hatred in his dark blue eyes. "Is this *real* enough for you?"

I sink onto the sheets.

"WHAT ELSE?" He drops his hand from my throat. Noticing the gold chain, his eyes narrow. I've gone this long without losing it to him.

"Nothing." I whisper.

"It's about time we got rid of this." He yanks the 'B' necklace off in one fell swoop.

My hand flies to my throat, the sobs coming in waves.

"What?" He shrugs. "I need a present to remember you by."

Scooting back towards the headboard, I'm out of breath, my belly heaving.

His voice becomes soothing, a hand reaching to rub my stomach. It's all I can do not to puke, bile rising as he touches me. "I have a surprise for you," he says. "Someone I want you to meet."

Baffled, I look at him in amazement.

"I know you'll be thrilled." He licks his lips. "A quick change from my original plan." For a moment, I'm hopeful, wondering if it's anyone that would help me.

"A friend of yours?" I ask. "Someone you work with?"

"No." He stares ashamedly at my enlarged breasts, the nipples peeking out of the thin material of the gown.

What if...oh no. It can't be. "Please tell me it's not another girl?" I plead.

He shrugs, noncommittal. "How long until the baby?"

"I don't know," I lie. I've been keeping tabs, but I don't want to give him a due date that could signal my own expiration date.

Standing, he leaves, another week of uninterrupted solitude, a jug of water and a couple saltines my only sustenance.

When he finally reappears, I'm so starved with hunger, I'm bedridden, gnawing at my fingernails, watching the small rivulets of blood seeping in my cuticles.

At first I think my eyes are playing tricks, like what happens when you hear about people stuck in the desert with no water, how they hallucinate and imagine cacti are talking to them.

Blinking, I open and close my lids a few times, a bulky item nestled in his arms.

I want to pretend it's a garbage bag with food and toiletries, but the object has long blonde hair.

Please no, I pray. Maybe she's just a doll to replace the old ratty teddy.

EXCEPT as The Mole moves closer, he pushes tangled hair from her face, her life-size body slack as he sets her on the floor of the room.

Another girl to replace the dead ghost of Marian.

And eventually, me.

SHE CAN'T BE MORE than a teen, the age I was when I was captured. She's unconscious, mouth duct-taped and eyes closed. A skimpy black dress hangs off her shoulders, feet bare. A silver toe ring and lavender nail polish stand out against her bronzed skin.

Purple eyeshadows smeared down her cheek. There's a tiny messenger bag hanging over her body, the chain wrapped around her stomach.

After he straightens from setting her on the floor, he

brushes his hands together like he's completed an arduous task.

"Bristol, meet Bridget." He makes the introductions, glancing between a comatose girl and a starved one.

"I must have a thing for B names." He's giddy, smoothing her strawberry blonde hair down, "and blondes."

She could be my twin, now that I've been here almost a decade, a reminder of my life outside of the room.

"Is she the new Marian?" I ask, my hands shaking as I try and sit on them so he doesn't notice. I'm sure there's not a good answer either way.

"*New* Marian?" He's upset at this comparison. "No one compares to Marian, certainly not you, and *not* her."

"I just mean is she coming to replace me?" I back down, too exhausted and swollen, my hands settling on my enlarged stomach.

"You could say that," he agrees. "You're of no use to me anymore."

I tilt my head. "How come?"

He ignores my question.

"It's lunchtime. I brought you a sandwich. Thought you'd be hungry..." Reaching into his duffel bag, one of her red heels proceeds to fall out. He tosses my lunch on the table along with a bottle of water.

"Go sit over there," he instructs.

"I can't fit in the chair."

"Then sit on the floor." He rolls his eyes. "It's not my fault you got fat."

Before I can stop myself, I spit out, "I'm not fat, I'm pregnant."

His tan face goes white. "What did you just say to me?" Venom laces his words. "Are you telling me I'm wrong, that you're not obese?"

I look away, withdrawing my statement. "No."

"Sit on the floor and eat your food." He's stern, attention waning. He goes back to Bridget, his hands starting to undress her.

A vibrating sound causes him to pause, confusion knitting his brow. He pats his pocket and then fumbles in her bag for the source. Pulling out a cell phone, I'm tempted to throw a chair at him and use it to call the police.

It's so close, I tell myself. *So close, your freedom, take it.*

"Dammit, I forgot to leave this," he mutters, throwing his hands up. He's flipping out, ranting about location services, and immediately presses a button to turn it off.

"I'll be back." He's callous. "Eat your food, that'll be it for a while."

Stomping to the door, he yells over his shoulder. "That water better be gone when I get back."

I stare at the listless girl.

Bridget and I are alone.

Her purse still rests across her lifeless body.

I wonder about the contents.

The camera's blinking, so I wobble over to her and pretend to check her pulse. Leaning in to hear her breathe, I flip the lid of her purse open. Her items are scattered at the bottom. There's the usual – breath mints, a tampon, pink lipstick, and loose change.

She has two cards – one debit, one credit.

Taking the credit card, I leave the other.

She's got seventy-six dollars in cash and her ID.

Bridget Masterson, eighteen, St. Louis, Missouri.

Will The Mole notice if I take this too?

I slide the cash, credit card, and ID into my stocking, pretending to adjust them as I keep my back to the blinking light.

Hurriedly I sink back onto the floor, eating the dry sandwich, tasting the water he brought. It's off, there's an odor that's out of place.

I sniff again. Is it the pregnancy hormones?

No, it's not from a heightened sense of smell.

She's your replacement, and he's either poisoning or drugging you.

Turning the clear bottle around, it has a sheen to it, like oil mixed with water. It's not crystal clear but sits on top, separate.

The tub? Can I toss it down the drain?

No, he'll see it on the camera.

PRETENDING TO DRINK IT, I turn my back, sitting on the pail. Peeing at the same time, I dump the water between my legs into the plastic. I pray he doesn't have time to watch the video or that he's preoccupied with another task right now.

When he comes back a few minutes later, his jerky movements signal his agitation. "We have a real problem." He drums his fingers on the small table, his shoulders hunched.

"What's that?" I mumble, my mouth full.

"I think you'll find my solution reasonable."

"I'm unsure what problem you mean...if it's about the chair, I can just sit on the floor until the baby's born."

His fist hits the table, bread and lettuce scatter to the floor. "This is what I'm talking about. You'll never learn to respect me. I've given you so much and you just take, take, take, and lie, lie, lie." He squats beside me on the floor, mimicking me. "You're unsure what the 'problem' is?" Spittle flies from his mouth. "Is that so?"

My eyes widen in fear, my back against the wall.

He grips my wrists, holding them tighter than the bungee cords, pushing my head down.

"Try again."

SILENCE.

HE SHOVES a hand in my face, his finger thrusting in my sore mouth as he jabs his finger where my tooth was.

Instinctively, I bite him.

He roars, his hand pulling back, striking my cheek.

"You bitch." His face turns from red to a weird purplish color. Striking the other cheek, he claws at me. I'm no match as he holds me down, cupping my mouth as I struggle to breathe.

There's a loud moan as Bridget stirs.

He releases me, his attention on her, a sick smile lighting up his face. "Did you ever think I'd bring you a pet?"

A punch to the gut, I can only shake my head no.

"I've gotta get to work." He walks to Bridget, tapping her with the tip of his shoes. "Make her feel welcome. Teach her the rules."

"Yes sir."

He gives her a sharp kick to the ribs. She doesn't groan or move. Turning to me, he shrugs. "Maybe I used too much this time?" I watch him turn and walk out the door, whistling a tune today instead of humming.

My heart beats in my chest, a flicker of hope. Two of us have to be able to outsmart and overpower The Mole.

Removing the blanket off my bed, I tuck it around Bridget's shoulders, lifting her head to place the pillow underneath it on the floor.

Sleeping on my back, I drift off until I hear a tiny voice, confused, say, "Where am I?"

I don't bother to move, staring at the ceiling, I cross my arms over my chest. "You're in a room."

"What room?" She jerks her body forward, her eyes darting around the small space. "This isn't our room."

"One we can't get out of."

"Excuse me," she asks, "who're you?"

"One that's been missing for a long time." I sit up, "I'm Bristol. Bristol Bellamy."

My name must not ring a bell. "Bridget," she says in a whisper.

RISING TO STAND, she smooths a crease out of her ripped black dress. "I feel awful. Sick. So hungover."

She doesn't realize yet what's going on, her new reality hasn't sunk in.

Stumbling to the door, she tries first to find a handle, then a pull, her fingers running along the smooth metal, trying to rattle the door off its hinges. She can't locate anything other than bolts.

When that doesn't work, she pounds on it, frustrated, yelling until she's hoarse. Hollering cuss words, she kicks the door with her bare foot, a useless task, injuring her toe on her second try.

Wobbling over to where I lay, she sits on the edge of the bed, carefully watching me.

"Why aren't you helping?"

"I don't think you understand..."

"Understand?" She's pissed. "Are you part of this whole thing?"

I ignore her question. "You've been drugged and kidnapped."

"But...no...no, this can't be happening." She rests her head in her hands. "I was here for a fun trip. This is what happens to runaways."

"I wasn't a runaway," I say. "I was also on vacation, spring break."

"My parents will find us." She's overconfident. "My dad's a powerful man, he knows a ton of people and has lots of money."

"It's not that simple."

"Ransom money? They'll gladly pay up." She breathes a sigh of relief. "At least they can offer to do that."

"He doesn't want your money."

"He has to." She notices my belly for the first time. Her mouth drops in horror. "Wait, he kidnapped a pregnant girl?"

The look on my face tells her all she needs to know.

Gasping, she releases a shrill scream. Her moment of realization has arrived.

32

BRISTOL

"HOW LONG HAVE YOU BEEN HERE?" She hesitates, unsure if she wants to know the answer.

I lie, telling her twelve months, not wanting her to feel as hopeless as I have for a majority of my twenties.

For a couple days she screams and cries, throwing her body uselessly at the walls, the metal door, acting like she's in the middle of a nervous breakdown.

I've been in this dark place, the adjustment period of the walls closing in on you, the reality that you have no control over your life, you're merely The Mole's pawn.

Bridget at first is standoffish, unsure if she can trust me. She spends her time pacing the room incessantly at all hours of the day.

She tells me the year and I have to be careful what to ask so I don't give myself away.

I want to know what's happened in the real world – fashion, music, politics, people. I'm so removed from what's hip and new in pop culture that I sound ignorant. Passing the time, she tells me stories about high school. It's relevant since I was about her age when I went missing, that time period all I have to remember.

The Mole's gone for a few days before he returns.

"Is he always like this?" she moans, the door creaking open.

I shudder. "He's unreliable."

I'm hesitant how to act around Bridget in front of him. I don't want to make our plight worse. Does he want us to get along or act like bitter enemies vying for his attention? What will be the least upsetting to him and with two of us, will he drop his guard faster? Will he forget the rules and punishments or will we both pay if one screws up?

"Bridget," he claps his hands, "I see you've met Bristol. I've left you both to get acquainted, you can be sisters for now." Unloading a bag of supplies on the table, he starts on a tangent about his expectations. I tune out.

"You can shadow her." He points to me. "See what I like, how to act. Bristol will be your mentor while she's here."

Bridget's suspicious. "Where's she going?"

"Oh no. No, no, no." He taps his nose three times. "You can't ask questions. Let me give you a quick lesson." He slaps her across the face, her startled expression turning into one of hate.

"Better?"

Silence as she rubs her cheek in surprise.

"When I ask a question, you *will* answer me." He snaps his fingers. "*Immediately.*"

Her eyes drift down to her lap.

"As if your life depends on it." Standing in front of her, he touches her neck lightly, starting at her throat and working his way down, his pointer finger barely making contact with her skin. "If you find this too difficult, we can try another arrangement. Do I make myself clear?"

"What's the other arrangement?"

She's not getting the hang of it. I sigh.

The Mole turns to me, exasperated. "Am I not making myself clear?"

"Since you're new here, I won't start out with punishment. I'll give you until next time to get your act together." He shrugs. "Consider this the transition period."

"Little girl, let's take a bath," he says to me. Turning to Bridget, he points his finger at her. "You can sit in the corner and watch."

Bridget's eyes go wide, unsure what she's about to be privy to. She visibly relaxes when she sees it's a bath, settling herself in a corner, her eyes wide with disgust and fear as she watches the bedtime routine. He ignores her the rest of the night, pretending she doesn't exist. After he tucks me into bed, he whispers something in her ear before leaving.

SHE PAUSES A MOMENT, listening for noise in case he comes back, then crawls over to the bed.

"Bristol," she moans, "he's a psycho. What're we going to do?" She starts to sob, her shoulders shaking. "I can't stay here."

"Come and lay beside me." I pat the narrow space next to me.

"CAN I BE NEAR THE WALL?" I nod, understanding that with me between the door and her, she feels a layer of protection from him.

Scooting over, she slides underneath the covers.

"Tell me about yourself." She touches my arm. I almost don't know what to say, speaking more to her in a couple days than I have in almost a decade.

Choosing my words carefully, I tell her about my family in Nebraska, the pets I have, my cheerleading squad, and my boyfriend.

Before long, I hear even breathing next to me, her back to mine as she sleeps.

A hand closes around my heart, a kick from the baby in my belly. I'm reminded of the way Blair and I would sleep, backs touching, each lost in our own dreams but still connected.

Silently, I let myself cry.

Over the next few weeks, Bridget goes between hysterically crying and sitting catatonic in the corner. I try to be strong for her, letting her know she'll adjust, that our bodies adapt to horrendous events in mysterious ways.

I tell her about The Mole, his rules and punishments, the routines he insists upon, the best way to stay under the radar.

She chooses instead to get under his skin, test him, just like I did at the beginning.

The final trimester has resulted in sluggishness and combined with the lack of consistent meals, I'm tired constantly, and impatient. Bridget notices how quick I am to snap at the smallest infractions. I apologize to her for my shortness, reminding myself this is all new to her.

I'm napping one afternoon, hunger pains and spasms in my leg making it impossible for me to fall asleep. Bridget eagerly offers to rub my feet and I let her.

My eyes close as I try to drift off. She seems calm and less fidgety, so I don't sense the storm about to come.

I hear a thud and at first, I assume it's The Mole entering the room. Not bothering to open my eyes, a loud crash follows, then a splintering sound.

I'm fully awake.

Sitting up abruptly, Bridget's flailing her arms, picking up and breaking everything in sight, flipping the small wooden table over, pulling books off the shelves in droves.

"I wouldn't do that," I warn her.

"I don't care," she screams.

"He'll come back..." I tilt my head towards the camera. "It's not worth it. Plus, he won't replace the items you break."

"I don't care," she hollers, "I don't care what he does. Stop making this easy for him."

Within a few minutes, the room reminds me of the aftermath of a stadium after a concert or baseball game, the leftover ticket stubs, bottles of water, trash, and paper littered on the ground.

I try to calm her, patting the bed next to me, begging her to read me a story.

She ignores my request, choosing to slam a broken leg from the table into the metal drum.

The door flies open so fast I think the police are breaking in, a moment of false hope as I watch instead The Mole's angry stride. Incensed, her rebellion of ripping pages out of books and breaking furniture comes to an end when he picks her up so fast, she doesn't have time to spin around.

I watch in horror as he carries her over his shoulder to the tub, dropping her like a wrestler does to his opponent, a body slam to the bottom.

She lays there, startled, hands grasping the edges. The Mole turns the hose on in the tub, his mouth a grimace as he watches it fill with cold water. He beats her with his fists, pushing her face down into the water, using one of the busted table legs as his implement.

Bridget screams, her body writhing in pain, trying to helplessly kick her legs up at him.

Internally, I'm helping her restrain The Mole, taking away his power, but outwardly I know if I come to her defense, it will only enrage him to hurt her more.

And the baby.

Covering my ears with my hands, I try to drown out her horrified screams and the noise of his abuse.

After he's done punching her, he kneels by the tub, forcing her head beneath the surface, waterboarding her. He repeats this over and over, shoving her face roughly down, holding her there for ten to fifteen seconds, her arms struggling for leverage. I notice her body becoming lifeless, a rag doll, as he pushes her under and then pulls her up.

I have to calm him down before he kills her, whether accidental or on purpose.

Silent, I tip-toe behind him. "I'd like to read you a story," I whisper.

"I'm busy." His hands are dripping wet, eyes narrowed as he looks over his shoulder at me.

"How about a bath?" I reach out to touch his back, knowing he will either press pause on his anger or lash out at me.

"Stop." Disgusted, he shakes his head at me. "I know what you're trying to do."

Naïvely, I say, "What?"

"Keep me from killing your new pet."

"Yes," I say. "Let's not go too far with her yet, sir."

Resigned, he grabs her by the hair, mouth sputtering as she coughs up liquid puke. Terror looms in her bright green eyes as she waits for the next round.

Lucky for her, it doesn't come.

"I'm done." He rises to stand. "This place better be cleaned up by the time I'm back."

Trying to trick him into letting us know when that is, I ask, "When should we have it done, sir?"

"No idea, so do it now." He glares at the ripped and shredded pages scattered haphazardly around the room. "You can thank her because I'm not replacing anything. I guess you'll have to stare at the wall now for entertainment."

He stalks out, not bothering to turn back around. I heave, knowing it'll be weeks before he comes back.

Before we're fed again.

33

BRISTOL

I RUSH TO HER SIDE, helping her stand, her body shriv-
eled like a prune. She shivers uncontrollably, covered in
bruises and contusions. A nasty cut's jagged on her forehead from the metal drum.. "Shh..." I whisper. "Everything's going to be okay."

Tears swim in her eyes, her bottom lip cut and swollen.
She's got a rug burn on her cheek, the skin red and bumpy.
A depth of pity I haven't seen yet overtakes her contorted
face.

"You have to learn to behave for him," I say, "It takes
time but if you don't, he'll kill you."

Before she can rebut that, I add, "See, this is where you
do have the power. You have to decide how long you want
to live before you die."

She's puzzled for a moment until a flash of understanding registers in her sage green eyes.

After this, we settle into a steady routine, both helping
each other come to terms with our own predicaments – me
bringing new life and her adapting to this room.

We make our own fun, and for once since being

kidnapped, I'm not so alone. Writing our own plays, we act them out based on what the popular shows on television and movies are. Bridget fills in the details and we ad-lib scripts and scenes. The cast and locations are real or imagined, diving into our own memories for examples to base our characters on.

I share stories with her about my life until I turned seventeen, never telling her the exact age or time I've been in the room. It's more painful for her to tell me about her life, the wound raw and gaping open. She struggles to maintain a sense of composure as she talks, biting her lip to hold back tears. When I speak about mine, it's so far removed that I feel like I'm talking about another girl.

Listening to her recount her childhood, I learn she's an only child, the apple of her parents' eyes. She was their miracle baby, her mother struggled for years to conceive her. She grew up in Overland Park, Kansas, an affluent suburb, her sixteenth birthday present a cherry red Ford Mustang.

I tell her about The Mole, the trade secrets I've learned.

"Do you know his name?"

"No. He's never given me his first or last name."

"Where did he take you from?"

"My hotel. But he was watching me earlier. I think The Ocean Club."

"I haven't heard of that place. I was at The Sandlot and the Island Breeze with a group of friends." Bridget focuses on hatching a plan to break out. "We have to escape." She taps a finger to her chin. "There's gotta be a way to catch him off guard."

"With two people, it should be a lot easier." I give her a small smile. "I'm glad you're here."

"I'm not." She gives me a gentle squeeze on the shoulder. "But I'm glad I'm not alone."

She asks me lots of questions about the baby, but I'm pretty clueless about childbirth and what to expect. I just know what changes I've seen in my body.

At night, she rubs my feet or massages my back, trying to help me get comfortable as every position becomes awkward. "What do you think he's going to do when you go into labor?"

"I don't know. I'm trying not to think about it."

"Will he let you keep the baby?" A look of horror crosses her face, "He won't *like* kill it, will he? Or take it somewhere and dump it?"

To hear her vocalize what I've thought about so many nights makes me squirm with worry. I fear the unknown, his reaction to the baby unsettling to begin with. I don't tell her how scared I am he'll dump both of us in the ocean, the baby and I becoming fish food.

Nightmares plague my sleep as I get closer to the impending due date. She notices my discomfort and tries to re-focus my efforts on something else. To pass the hours, we play charades and make up word games, sometimes making up new definitions. Since her outburst, The Mole's been firm on his resolve to not replace the damaged items.

This frustrates her enough that the next time he comes back, she's polite and responsive, The Mole pleased with her change of heart.

We turn a corner, his visits continual, hands full of bags containing fruit and cereal, watered-down ramen, and oatmeal.

I can tell he's pleased with her progress, bringing *To Kill a Mockingbird* on his next visit.

As he leaves, he stops in his tracks. "I also brought *you* a gift." He gives me a light peck on the cheek. "I want you to try it on for me right now."

TRYING TO HEAVE MYSELF UP, my breathing ragged, I watch him sort through the bag he brought. Pulling out a long, white sheer nightgown, pink satin bow at the top, pink satin slippers for my feet, I shiver.

He lovingly caresses the fabric. "This is what you'll wear tonight." He adds, "and don't forget the Baby Soft."

TEETERING TO THE DRESSER, I rub the perfume on. The scent becomes revolting the more my hormones shift. Pulling the nightgown over my head, the hem drags to the ground, the sleeves poufy and bell-shaped. I remove the credit card, ID, and cash out of the stocking, carefully covering it with my foot in the bottom of the pink slipper.

"Such a very special outfit for such a special day," he claps his hands in excitement, "your burial outfit."

I waddle to the red pail, vomiting a string of spit into the bottom. Nauseated, I wipe my hand across my mouth. Bridget's sitting on the floor, staring at me in concern. The Mole looks repulsed, his back turned to me.

"Say goodbye, Bridget," he tells her. "Thank her for helping you learn the ropes." Her mouth drops in awe, realizing that this isn't a semi-good-bye, but a permanent one.

She's my replacement.

A new version, untouched by him, not carrying a child.

His child.

I walk over to where she sits. She stands to hug me, body trembling. Tears roll down her face as she buries her head in my shoulder.

"You're my kindred spirit," she whispers.

"Be strong." I kiss her gently on the cheek. "You'll be

saved, I know it." I squeeze her arm, willing myself to believe this, to place my belief in the words I say.

"How can you..." she starts to raise her voice, her anger directed at The Mole. Stepping back, I hold her at arm's length, gesturing with a flick of my wrist over my throat.

There's no point in her getting him riled up. It will only make it worse for me.

She stops, heeding my advice, her hand grasping my elbow as I turn to leave. I have to pull my fingers away from her death grip as she stares at me in trepidation.

The Mole watches our interaction with amusement, getting off on the fear in her eyes and the abandonment in mine.

"Let's go, big girl." He touches my shoulder, leading me to the door, out of the room and my prison. I give one last backwards glance to Bridget, her hands clasped in front of her as she watches us go.

Mustering up all the courage I can, I smile wide, wanting her last image of me to seem happy. We both know I'm not coming back, but I don't want it to seem that way.

34

BRISTOL.

CLASPING MY HAND TIGHTLY, eyes blinded by darkness, the door slams shut behind us.

The key grinds in the lock, another victim to dispose of.

In the dank hallway, I lose my composure. "Wait," I exclaim, "just wait."

"There's nothing more to say." A look of sadness crosses his face. "You aren't my little girl anymore." He motions to the door. "She's going to be my new Marian."

I hiccup, frantically trying to think of a way to distract him.

I claw at his chest, trying to wrap my arms around his waist. "Can't I help with Bridget?" I beg. "I can teach her everything she needs to know."

GENTLY PUSHING ME OFF HIM, he pulls the blindfold out of his back pocket, his eyes darting down to my swollen belly. "No," he strokes my hair, "you've done a good job with her." He glances down at me in surrender. "It's impossible to manage both of you. More risk, less reward." Binding my hands with duct tape, he shoves a wet rag in my mouth to stifle my questions from bubbling to the surface. He pulls the gray tape tight over my mouth. I stare at his facial mark, the strand growing longer, curling out of the follicle. He shakes his head, frowning. "This isn't the right environment to raise a child."

"If this hadn't happened..." his voice drifts off. "You should've known better than to bring a baby into this."

I'm surprised it didn't happen sooner. But I'm lucky my body rejected the idea – the starvation, the stress, and the fact he didn't make it a habit all saved me from a quicker demise.

How many of them got pregnant, I wonder?

Probably all.

Unless he killed them first.

I concentrate on putting one foot in front of the other, reluctant, as if I'm navigating a gauntlet. Before I'm able to press my padded foot on a step, I become airborne, my breath whooshing out of my chest. Headfirst, I'm hanging over his shoulder, the woolly flannel of his shirt rubbing against my cheek, then rough denim.

GRUNTING, he stumbles for a second. "You're too heavy." He pauses, regaining his balance.

We take a couple steps backward.

He turns, walking about ten feet.

I hear four beeps in quick succession before a shrill alarm goes off, his pace quickening until he stops, pressing another button.

He moves forward, a loud click and the sound of steel

clanking shut. The floor moves out from under us, my weight still distributed unevenly over his shoulder. The sudden movement throws me off guard, my position awkward as I count three floors until there's a beep and he slowly steps out.

A door opens and slams, followed by a breeze that rustles my hair.

Wanting to breathe it in, I can't, the gag making it impossible.

Metal scratches against what must be a lock, then I'm pushed onto a seat, smooth hands strapping the seatbelt snugly around me, a door slamming to my right.

The rag tastes of sweat and moisture, my lips chapped around it. Being unable to see is terrifying to me, but also unable to speak, to communicate my fear, makes the isolation petrifying.

The other door cracks open, then whooshes shut. His seatbelt clicks into place, the engine turns and purrs, the radio abruptly goes silent.

"No music today," he says, "but it's a beautiful day out."

I feel his hand fondle my belly.

Reeling in disgust, I shake my head.

Isn't it nighttime?

He ignores my gesture. "I can't wait until you can see it." Drumming his fingers on the steering wheel, he starts humming. "I've got a special place for you."

I wonder where he's taking me, if we're going to the same cave or a new spot. I pray it's where we already were and not a different place.

Frantically, I try and remember the cavern – it had an entrance that went straight to a walkway above the ocean.

All I know is this is my last chance at escaping. Whatever the outcome, I have to be ready to die for my potential freedom. My thoughts are slamming into each other, reality setting in –

I've been captive for almost a decade and now I'm going to die?

After all I've endured?

And pregnant, my baby without a chance at survival.

The baby's foreign to me, it grows and kicks.

Internally, I'm terrified it will grow up to be him. I'm resentful at first, the fact his DNA could procreate, and angry at God for letting this happen.

My first trimester I hoped to miscarry, the circumstances dire for a child. I was terrified it would look like him, that I'd die giving birth, or that he'd deny me pre-natal care.

When I felt the first flutter in my belly, I lost a little apprehension. I started rubbing my belly, speaking to it, singing, reading, and daydreaming about being a mother.

You could say I even got a bit of baby fever, someone to talk to, look after, a purpose in this isolation.

By my last trimester, my fear had increased for the newborn's safety, and my fury subsided. It's a living, breathing miracle of life.

And I'm responsible for it.

For not letting The Mole hurt it.

But I don't want to lose him or her.

And now, I won't live to see childbirth. I'll be thrown into the ocean to be eaten by sharks or die in a remote cavern.

Or maybe, my heart sinks, he'll torture me, cutting me up or doing some crazy shit to me, pain he knows I can feel before I go unconscious.

He is, after all, a sick psychopathic Mole.

The drive before was terrifying and unknown. I imagined I'd be going somewhere better than the room. This time it's ominous, my mouth tense around the spit-soaked rag.

We bounce over a rough road before hitting smooth terrain, the wheels squeaking in protest.

This can't be it, I tell myself.

I'm desperate.

Are we speeding too fast?

Maybe a cop will pull him over. You always hear stories on the news about a dumb mistake a kidnapper or thief makes – they either leave incriminating evidence behind or get too cocky.

The Mole, for all his flaws, is not stupid.

Stay present, stay alert. I pinch myself.

"You getting tired?" I feel a nudge, then hear him chuckle. "Oh yeah, you can't speak." We spring over a pothole, another groan from the tires.

"Almost there. Then you can sleep." His hand grazes my cheek. "You'll feel better soon. Well-rested and able to dream."

Mumbling, I cough, the rag sucked into my lungs.

"CAREFUL," he chastens. "You don't want to choke to death. What good would you be to me then?" He pets my head, his fingers on my earlobe, tugging it gently.

I cringe, starting to shake as the vehicle slows down, crawling to a stop, then proceeding up a steep incline or hill.

LANGUID, my back sinks into the seat, thoughts starting to weave in and out of consciousness. Whatever the rag's soaked in, it's making me sleepy. *Count*, I instruct myself, *play a game in your head*. I start with one, the numbers blurred in my mind, jumbled together like the letters you shake during a Boggle game.

Again the truck halts before circling into a wide turn. I presume he's twisting into a parking spot, the engine idling for a moment, humming before it shuts off.

CRANING MY NECK, I listen for sounds – people speaking, birds, water rushing, anything that can save my life.

His door opens, thuds shut, and heavy footfalls on the ground as he makes his way around to my side. My hands are on my lap, the tape pulling at my wrists.

I move my hands to the side, fumbling for the lock.

"Not so fast." He laughs, pulling open the passenger door. The seatbelt snaps off, his arms grab me under the armpits as he sets me down on the uneven pavement.

"Same as before. You'll walk until I tell you to stop."

I raise my arms in front of me, signaling I have a question.

"No need for words, the time for talking is over." He clutches my hand, impatient.

I'M WOOZY, the steps feel awkward and cumbersome, his pace excruciatingly fast compared to mine. He tugs me along. I stumble, rocks and foliage nipping my heels, biting my legs underneath the nightgown.

The sole of the slippers is made for smooth surfaces, not for bumpy pebbles. Tripping, I feel myself hit the ground, my hands unable to pull myself back up. Staying on my knees, tears trickle down my lids. Snot drips down my nose, my lungs struggling to breathe as the panic sets in.

Without sight, I know I'm in some type of wilderness or outdoor area, but I have no sense of my surroundings.

Frightened, I cower, too scared to stand.

"Up," he hisses.

I don't move.

"I'm warning you..." A heavy object hits me in the chest with a thwack. I realize it's his foot kicking me. "Get up now."

His voice rises at the same time he pulls my hair. "I will drag you if you don't get up now." He's forceful, causing me to lose my balance and fall backwards. He doesn't let go, gripping my strands as tight as possible, the hair now falling past my shoulders, his breath hot in my ear.

My cheeks are soaked, perspiration dripping down my forehead. Adrenaline courses through my veins, fighting off the sinking feeling of whatever the rag's covered in. I have to try. *Think of your sister, your mom, your dad*, I internally yell.

A cuss word escapes his lips. "Shit," He grabs me from behind, yanking me backwards as loud voices carry over to us. I wonder how far away they are?

I attempt a scream, but it catches on the rag.

The Mole's trying to take deep breaths, his hands firmly planted on my shoulders. "Don't move," he instructs. My fingers grip the rough bark of a tree, the duct tape loosening slightly.

I don't want to draw attention to the slackened adhesive. I rest my palms on the surface, waiting as the sounds grow emphatic. "Look over here," a male voice yells.

At first, I think he means us and my eyes widen behind the bandana.

I'm about to be saved.

I sink down lower, resting my head against the bark, relieved.

"Mushrooms?" Another booming voice.

"Yeah, these are rare," a different male says.

Shrieks pierce the silence.

The Mole crouches beside me, his warm breath on the nape of my neck.

I shudder, willing the men to spot us.

A trickle leaks from my left foot. The Mole must notice, a sharp intake of breath as he contemplates my injury.

"Hey," the voice grows stronger. "You over there. You got a light?"

The Mole, frustrated, hits me in the shoulder, his sign for me to be quiet.

I hear rustling and then footsteps as he walks towards them.

"Hey yourself," he says. "I don't have a light. Quit years ago myself."

"You see these mushrooms?" the other voice asks.

"They're really something." The Mole's losing his patience, the strain apparent in his voice.

"You from around here?" One asks him.

I grab at the tape, stripping it away from my gaunt wrists, the pain like a Band-Aid being ripped off, except it lasts longer.

My hands are now free, except my foot is asleep, the awkward position I'm angled at causing a pins-and-needle sensation.

THE MEN'S voices are farther away, The Mole leading them to another place to hunt for mushrooms. Away from me.

Stumbling, I reach out in time before I crash into a tree branch, my skin being sliced as I feel a sharp pain and more blood.

The Mole's voice is getting closer to me instead of more distant.

I turn, running in the other direction. My legs can't manage a full-on jog, weakness causing my muscles to cramp.

Pushing the bandana up, I can't untie the knot at the back of my head. It stays around my forehead like a crown, the sunlight forceful even in this dense of a forest.

Yanking the duct tape off my lips, a burning pain follows the flaking skin. I spit the rag out, my mouth bone dry.

The men have stopped talking, that or I'm farther away from them. I can't see their outlines or hear any sound. Did The Mole hurt them?

"Where are you, honey?" The Mole hollers in the distance.

"Oh, was someone with you?" The man's voice penetrates the air.

"My teenager," he lies.

I hear all three men screaming, my ear drums piercing as they hoot and holler.

"What's her name?"

"Marian."

All their voices consecutively yell for me, calling me the wrong name. Looking over my shoulder to gauge where they are, the hem of my nightgown catches on a fallen tree branch, pitching me forward. My elbow splits open, the pain sears as I groan. My belly hurts, the baby thumping in protest, kicking my inner walls as I push sticky strands off my forehead.

Gritting my teeth, I pull myself up, cradling my arm.

"There you are," a calm voice says behind me.

Swallowing, my fingers wrap gingerly around a broken limb.

"It's time to calm down. Let me take you home." His blond hair's sticking straight up, the mole glowering at me.

"Oh, you found her. Phew." The man stops right behind him, screeching to a halt, the dried mud on the ground damp from recent rain. He's dressed in camo pants and an olive green slicker.

"Marian, let's go home." The Mole smiles at me, his tooth stands out, distinctly yellow.

"I don't want to." My eyes wild, I turn to look behind him. The dark-haired man's concerned. His eyes skim over my disheveled appearance – my white nightie that's now mud-stained and ripped, the blood and bruises covering my body.

Oh, and I'm about to give birth.

"Are you okay?" the stranger asks me, stepping forward.

"She's fine." The Mole speaks for me.

"No. I'm not. I've been kidnapped." I'm weak, my elbow gushing red. "Can you please help me? I need medical attention. And the police."

"What's your name?" His kind eyes never leave my face. The other man hollers in the distance. "Hold on, Rob," he screams, "I'll be right..." Before I can give him my name, before he can finish his sentence, a flash of metal glints.

A loud cacophony echoes through the trees, disbelief as I stare at a burgundy stain that swells on the man's chest and grows bigger, his hand lifting to cover the gaping hole. His eyes flinch as he sinks to his knees.

"Rob..." he whimpers. "Get help." These are his last

words, The Mole hit him directly in the chest, as if he were the bulls-eye on a target.

He falls forward gradually, his forehead smacking the dirt floor in a final bow. The Mole's giddy, ecstatic about warranting his shot, hitting him with the butt of the gun for full effect.

Rob, hearing a gunshot, starts wailing for his friend, panic tinged in his shrieks.

The Mole gives me a glazed look. "See? This is what happens when you don't listen. This is all *your* fault. You killed an innocent man." He wipes his palms on my nightgown, the red a contrast to the starkness of white. "Make it two innocent men. I can't leave the other one behind, now can I?"

I feel faint, the smell of gunpowder filling my nostrils, a crumpled man's body before me. I just want to lay down, my lids heavy, any chance at freedom dead in front of me, lifeless like the innocent bystander.

The Mole walks in the direction of Rob's shouts, his .22 caliber gun aimed in front of him. Closing my eyes at the burst of gunshots, I quiver, my hands reaching to protect my ears, drowning out the surprise, then the revulsion. A flight of birds scatter as the sound reverberates through the trees.

Turning to run, his voice is behind me, deadly, "If you run, I'll shoot you in the back."

Resigned, I stumble towards him instead of away. The branches of the thick limbs heave and shake, motioning me to turn around.

I'M REWARDED with an icy stare. "Let's go. You haven't seen the best part yet."

I wobble closer, his impatience closing the distance

between us and my plodding feet. Heaving me over his shoulder, he whistles as he lumbers toward the caverns and away from the brush.

"Got a little sidetracked." He pats my butt. "But we're almost there."

My eyes flicker and shut, his heavy footsteps a trance as I drift in and out of consciousness.

35

BRISTOL

I PICTURE BLAIR'S FACE, her dark hair and brilliant hazel eyes staring back at me, willing me to keep pushing, to fight. It's like she's here rousing me awake, knowing if I give in to sleep, I'll never wake up again.

We reach the shallow opening, the sunlight balmy against my back, replaced by cool air once the roof of the cave blocks us from warmth.

My eyes scan the walls, the rocky flooring, every nook and cranny, until the path becomes laden with boulders. The Mole's having a hard time carrying my extra weight, stumbling, his breathing laborious.

Catching the wall just in time, my body slides into a handstand pose, fingers grasping for a firm grip so I don't tumble on my head. He manages to grab one of my legs before I hit the jagged rock face-first. Instead, it gashes my stomach, pain settling in my belly.

"You gotta walk now." He's gruff. "I'll give you some water once we reach the end."

We both know it's a lie, that the end is finality in this

case. There's no purpose in arguing with him or pointing out his flawed logic.

I'm dead when we reach our resting spot.

The divide's coming up and if I can't manage to flee as soon as we reach the tunnel that splits off, I'm a goner.

"In front of me." He points, standing aside.

I step around him, slow and calculated. I'm drawing on sheer will to propel me forward. I need the last of my frenzied energy to sprint.

The Mole grabs the back of my barely-there nightgown, "I don't want you getting any ideas."

We move at a snail's pace, my eyes playing tricks, going in and out of focus, my mind trying to guide my panic-stricken brain.

I see infinite blue up ahead, the water and sky blending into one limitless expanse, the sun casting shadows as it bounces off a rock formation.

It's too beautiful a day to die, I think. As much as I want to bolt, with only one shot, I have to wait for an opportunity, a chance when he's not as in tune with my movements.

Opportunity presents itself when The Mole hears a smacking noise, stopping short as his eyes dart over his shoulder to confront the sound.

It's now or never.

I raise my foot, kicking it behind me, high enough to connect with his kneecap. Caught off guard, he rips the rest of my nightgown, splitting it at the seams as I lurch forward.

Spinning around, I aim for his crotch, a fluid movement as I bash his nose with my fist at the same time, anger and frustration taking precedence over the effects of the liquid-soaked rag, at least for now.

Grabbing a fistful of hair, he angrily pulls me towards him.

Howling in protest, I claw at his face, the ugly mole staring at me as it becomes a casualty underneath my broken fingernails, chipped and torn, black and dirty.

SCREAMING at the top of my lungs, I take off, though it feels like little more than a hurried walk, my injuries and weakened state preventing me from sprinting.

Unfortunately for me, the walkway winds around the cave, but there's no railing to shield against the waves that lap up the side, pulsating high against the algae-covered rock. Droplets of water splash and thunder as they crash into the boulders.

THE MOLE'S BEHIND ME, his face beet red, nose bloody. Dirt mixes in with the cherry color dripping down his face.

Eyes pop out of his head, like a cartoon. "There's nowhere to go, little girl."

Frantic, I dart to look at the water, the rocks, and The Mole closing in on me.

HE'S RIGHT, there's nowhere to go. "You're dead no matter what. You jump, you're dead. And if you don't bash your head on the rocks, if you live, I'll find out and kill your sister. I know everything about her."

"No, you don't," I shake my head in denial.

"No?" He tilts his head at me. "Blair went to Creighton University, graduated with honors, got married at twenty-five, no children yet. She now lives in Burbank, California. I even have her address."

My mouth drops in horror.

"You'd be surprised what you can find on the Internet since you disappeared."

I pause.

"And your parents?" He shrugs. "They're still on the farm."

Licking his lips, he reaches for me. "If you survive, your sister will have the same fate you did. Except I'll cut her open while she's still alive."

I shake my head.

"YOU KNOW I WILL." He manically laughs. "You've seen the other bones.

And what about poor Bridget?" he adds. "No one will ever find her. You're the only one who knows where she is, that she's even alive. If the cops arrest me, or I disappear, she'll die slowly, starving to death. If she doesn't kill herself first."

He wiggles his eyebrows. "And the others I'm keeping? No one will ever find them either."

"The others?"

"Yeah, girls in other rooms. You have so much power right now to do the right thing." Wiping his brow, he pulls his gun out of his waistband. "You're already responsible for two deaths today, two innocent civilians."

Tears prick my cheeks as he continues. "I don't like to shoot my girls, but I will if I have to, since you're being extremely difficult today."

"Why?" I whisper. "What do you want?"

"Marian," he says simply.

His hand reaches for me, his dirty nails pawing at my wrist.

We make eye contact, his eyes an in-between shade of

blue-green today.

My bare skin prickles, I have no choice. Die at the hands of a freak or jump in the ocean, drowning, if I even make it to the water before hitting every cragged rock on the way down.

Making a split-second decision, a huge leap backwards, I make sure to step off the cliff at the very edge, my body eerily still as I wait to make contact with either the rocks or the water.

A gunshot rings out and I feel a whoosh as something passes me.

A bullet.

The Mole's scrambling in front of me, yelling, his words gibberish. They get lost in the wind as he stomps his foot.

I reach my fist out to try and grab at something, anything, the waves coming faster than I expect. In movies they always have time to think about their decision before they jump, plan out their escape, knowing exactly how they'll hit.

Unfortunately I have neither time nor an exit strategy.

Misjudging the clearance, I'm thrust onto the side of a heavy boulder, hitting the serrated edges of loose rock. Slamming my head into the side, the sudden crash knocks me unconscious, my body floats on air, before it goes down with a flourish.

Straight down.

My eyes closed tight, I see my family, waving, welcoming me home, the farm in the distance, the red barn and corn fields surround us in a blaze of sunshine.

I'm confused, wondering why they're dressed in all white as The Mole looks on, holding me down as I struggle to reach them. As much as I try, he holds me at arm's length, never letting me touch them.

The world spins and goes black.

I STARE at the moldy ceiling, another leak evident as my eyes trace the brown stain inching across the off-white drywall. This place isn't a dump, but it's close.

It's clean but old and decrepit. The floors are hardwood, which I love, but they're loud and squeaky. I've scattered area rugs on the floor to help with the sound of my footsteps, but I usually don't wear shoes inside, preferring to be barefoot, even in the winter, which everyone says is weird.

I can't stop thinking about Priscilla, my mother.

Closing my eyes, I attempt sleep, but it's useless.

I grab my phone, scrolling to look at the last message she sent.

The grainy pictures.

Damn her.

Out on the farm, I've buried the memories of that night.

A box holds all of my secrets, even the ones I didn't tell the cops. They wouldn't help find her anyway. Scared of negative press on their precious island, they buried Bristol in the back of newspapers, barely keeping her memory alive.

Agitated sleep finds me, the old nightmare I hadn't had in a while wrapping itself around me. I'm being pulled into the ocean and held down by a hand pressed firmly on my back.

He pauses so I can choke water out of my mouth and nose.

Yet as soon as I inhale, I'm pushed back under.

This keeps repeating, my breath coming in shallow waves.

This is how I continue until I wake up gasping for air.

Waking up on sweat-soaked sheets from nightmares involving Bristol at precisely 1:17 A.M. every morning.

By 7 A.M., I can't take it any longer.

I'm on the road, headed back to the place I grew up.

It's not home to me.

I left at eighteen and never looked back.

WHEN I MOVED BACK HOME at twenty after my mental breakdown, my mother was combatting her own depression.

After she had permanently locked the door to Bristol's room, at least to me, I tried to gain entrance by breaking and entering. The pounding on the door wasn't welcome, neither was the hammer I used. When I tried to explain to Priscilla that I needed some things out of her room, she yanked me outside, threw me my car keys, and told me to get the hell off the farm and never come back.

So I haven't.

Father took the brunt of her anger and grief, but he's only human and had his own meltdown. He spiraled down-hill, his steadfast belief in God shattered after she went missing. Even though he counseled others on their mourning, this was different, this one personal.

HE UNDERSTOOD me better than Priscilla, but I know he blamed me for Bristol's disappearance. It never came out of his mouth, it didn't have to. I saw it when I looked at him. His eyes were blank when they stared, they seemed to look through me, not at me.

The foundation he wholeheartedly believed in crumbled, and he started burying himself in the bottle.

It resulted in destructive behavior, his hands shaking at the pulpit, not from his passion for the sermon, but from alcohol withdrawals.

He'd slur his speech, miss meetings and church functions, eventually stopped showing up all together. The congregation tried to pull together, intent on saving him. He was, after all, one of them, and their leader.

But his dysfunction scared them. If this could happen to him, then what did that mean for their souls?

No one could save him.

And I went right down with him.

When he died, it was awful and unexpected and tragic and miserable.

He crashed his car into a telephone pole seven and a half minutes after leaving a bar. The engine exploded, causing a fiery scene that left burn marks you can see if you're close enough, the concrete charred in places.

Priscilla claimed it was a broken heart he died from, caused by me. Said it should've been me they buried. If only she knew how close I was at times to ending it all...

But I can't. Because she still hasn't been found.

I missed Daddy's funeral, not that I didn't try to attend.

She forbade me from coming and had a local sheriff stand guard at the church entrance. I stood at a side door, dressed in black, my own private funeral.

ALIVE OR DEAD, I'll take it, but I know it'll be bones. The remains of her, the beautiful girl that had so much life ahead of her.

I squeeze my eyes shut. Fuck. I have to get it together.

MY HANDS SHAKE and I pull over at the next gas station, in another small town, population close to zero, for a pack of cigs which I tell myself every other day I'll quit.

In my defense, my other bad habits I've given up. I still cuss like a sailor and I still smoke on occasion, but this seems justifiable.

Rummaging in the glove box of my ancient maroon car, one I've had almost as long as Bristol's been gone, I find a green BIC lighter. Opening the box, it takes a couple tries to get the damn light to take, my hands trembling in protest. I can't decide if it's rebellion against seeing Priscilla, the farm, or smoking a Camel cigarette.

I'm only an hour from the town I grew up in, but it might as well be another continent.

She asked me to stay away, so I did.

Doesn't mean it wasn't hard or that I didn't cry myself to sleep, abandoned by my family at twenty.

The town is marked by a small wooden sign, no bigger than a cemetery plot. I know this because Bristol's got one that's been waiting on her all these years. Of course, Priscilla didn't *buy* her a plot, that would mean they had given up hope, that she was truly dead.

But the town mayor declared a 'Bristol Bellamy day' complete with a town meeting and a pancake breakfast that raised money so she could have a proper headstone.

Morbid, but necessary, he said.

Priscilla hemmed and hawed on what to write, finally completing the inscription.

To our daughter, the light you shine comforts us as Jesus guides you on your path back to us.

Love, your devoted parents & Oggie.

There's no mention of me, her sister.

I was written off as if I had disappeared right along with her. Sometimes I wish it were me that had been kidnapped or killed or drowned or....

They would've had their favorite child, Isaiah would've come home, Daddy wouldn't have died, and Priscilla could still play the victim since she lost a child.

Deep down, only she would've known it was the throw-away kid.

The farmhouse is about five miles out of town, depending on how fast you speed through the four stop signs and three stoplights.

I expect progress since the last time I was home, but disappointment shadows my face as I take a long drag of my cigarette, the pack now half-empty.

Good thing I bought two.

The town hasn't evolved, I guess it hit pause when she went missing, same as the rest of us. The high school on my left hasn't even expanded. The circular parking lot and hawk out front just has one additional monument – a statue dedicated to my sister in front of the high school, captioned with, *"Bristol Anne Bellamy, a kind-hearted soul, the one we strive to be like and befriend. God bless your soul."*

It's surreal to see her face carved in stone, a school photo the image they used to reconstruct her smiling face in marble.

Moving my eyes back to the two-lane highway, I keep speeding by the open pastures and the cattle grazing, a red barn in the distance. The farm we settled on wasn't ours at first, it was the church congregation's. After Bristol went missing, then my daddy died, the church congregation felt sorry for Priscilla, paying off the mortgage and passing the deed to her.

The gravel drive is up ahead, where the pavement ends and the treacherous, winding driveway begins. It curves up to an almost full "P" before it stops in front of the house.

Thank God the neighbors can't make out the house from the highway – two large maple trees stand in front, shielding Priscilla from the prying eyes of outsiders and those that think she needs to move into town, with no reason to stay out here all alone.

"When she comes home, she needs to know where to find us," Priscilla always said. The paint's crumbling, once snow-white now faded and gray, the harsh winters and spring showers tattering the outside. Even the front door is lackluster yellow, once sunny and bright.

I park, taking a final drag on my cigarette. Grabbing my cell and purse, careful to lock my car doors even in the middle of nowhere, I peer at my surroundings, a nervous habit since that day she went missing. I stub out the cigarette, leaving the butt on the ground.

When I step up the rickety stairs to the front porch, a fake bouquet of flowers greets me in a stand. I brush my feet off on a faded welcome mat, the welcome worn out ten years before.

I inhale, holding my finger above the doorbell.

Pausing, I gather my thoughts.

Here goes nothing. I press the bell, waiting as it chimes.

She must've been waiting for me on the other side of the door, opening it immediately as if she'd been standing behind it, holding the knob. Priscilla is tiny, her and Bristol both 5'4. She doesn't look much different, still underweight, just a little saggy for her age. Her face has taken the most beating – wrinkles cover her forehead and her eyes are creased, years of tears and constant worry, I think.

Her eyes are still bright, the brilliant green color Bristol had, and the same lip shape. Her strawberry blonde hair tinged with grey underneath a bandana,. her velour track-suit and tennis shoes on as if she just got back from a walk.

"Oh...Blair," she says, reaching a hand to her chest. "You scared me."

"You look like you were expecting someone to come," I say pointedly.

"I just didn't think it would be this fast."

"Are you going to let me in or should I stand on the porch?" I'm in no mood for her passive-aggressive tendencies.

"Come on in." She steps away from the door, holding onto it for support in case she loses her balance. She looks gaunt, smaller than usual.

I feel like I'm in a stranger's home, everything the same as when I left, yet everything different. The kitchen is small and clean, laminate flooring and a huge walk-in pantry to store all the jars that she cans for the winter, a project her and Bristol liked to do. New appliances are the only change, and the light over the kitchen table.

A puzzle is out, the *Bridges of Madison Country,* a fifteen-hundred piece puzzle, or so the box proclaims.

"Looks like you got a lot of work to do to complete that." I motion to the scattered pieces.

She nods.

"Where's the box?"

She grunts, ignoring my question. "You saw the picture?"

"Of course, why do you think I'm here?"

I pull gloves out of my purse, sure she's already tainted any evidence. She gestures towards the dining room. "It's in there."

The living and dining rooms are combined, my daddy's reclining chair still in the same spot. She got a newer couch after Oggie died, our old neighbor informed me of that. The television's been upgraded since a decade ago, seated on a stand next to the same mahogany dining table. A mantel over the fireplace showcases photographs of Daddy and Bristol.

I'm nowhere to be found. I swallow a lump, striding to the table.

"Did you forget your manners?" Priscilla asks. "Shoes. Leave them at the front." She wrinkles her nose. "You smell like grease and smoke." I make sure to move closer to her to squeeze past, brushing her shoulder. She twists her face in a frown. "Those cigarettes are going to kill you."

"Something has to," I say evenly. Sliding my sandals off, I tiptoe back into the kitchen, watching her sink into a chair at the dining room table.

Noticing my hands, she snorts. "Gloves? Is this an episode of that CSI show?"

"No, Priscilla, it's so any evidence or fingerprints aren't disturbed." I glance at her. "Except I'm sure you already did that."

She makes a ho-hum noise and drums her fingers on the table.

The box is plain, no marks, red tissue paper inside, and the latest gift.

I take a deep breath before peeling away the tissue. Her B necklace and a tooth are nestled in the bottom, the gold chain starting to tarnish in places. It looks like a front tooth, one of her bicuspids, but I'm unsure.

Laid next to the box, what looks to be a tattered page out of a children's book, edges jagged like it was carelessly ripped, has a note written on it. I know Bristol's handwriting and this belongs to her. Trying to swallow, a massive rock might as well be lodged in my throat, the struggle to breathe coming in short bursts.

It's written in blue magic marker, dated 2007, a plea for help from Bristol.

Except now a message is scrawled over her print.

My hands shake, the red letters that overlap her writing are slanted, heavy and coagulated like dried blood, the message short but omnipotent. 2008 *DEAD*.

"This must be the final package." I say, resting my hands on the table.

"No, her body coming home would be," she admonishes.

"That sonofabitch." I mutter.

"I need to see her remains to believe she's really gone." She glares at me. "Not all of us can be so quick to write off our children."

Sarcastically, I mumble, "You wrote off both your children, so I guess you win."

"You left," she spews.

"You kicked me out."

"We did it for your own good."

"You did it because you couldn't bear to look at me."

"It was hard." She stares back at the box. "This is *too*

hard. No mother should have to watch her daughter suffer and be helpless. She needs to come home to us. I still can't believe she's really gone."

A pause lingers between us. "She can't be dead." She says stiffly, as if her words settle the matter once and for all.

"All of the other girls are dead." I say. "Why would Bristol be special?"

"How can you come in here and act so damn ignorant? Your sister *is* special."

"That's not what I mean..." I inhale. "Why would he keep her alive and not the rest?"

"Because..." Priscilla doesn't elaborate. "She's your sister."

"I'm going to call the police. Have them come take the box to the lab for testing." I head to the wall phone. Priscilla's one of the only people to still have a landline.

Same idea, same comment. "What if she calls home and can't reach us?"

I CALL THE STATE POLICE, they're familiar with our case and have been for years.

The packages come on the anniversary of her disappearance.

Every year.

First anniversary, her half-empty tube of lip gloss arrived, a piece of her strawberry blonde hair twisted around the wand inside. It doesn't matter how small the object, they're always in the same size cardboard box.

Her clutch the second year, the lining ripped inside.

Third came my pink-and-black plaid skirt, the one she was wearing the night she disappeared.

Bristol's Nebraska ID, her age still seventeen, the

picture faded and laminate torn was our fourth year surprise. It was wiped clean, no prints, not even hers.

Fifth, her knotted white tank top, ripped and now a yellowish-color.

A lock of hair the sixth year, it's a huge chunk, a trace of red like blood, confirmed to be hers.

Stilettos, the ones she could hardly walk in, the type Priscilla forbade. That was the seventh year. Everything was stored as evidence, but always the same issue, finger-prints wiped clean or no latent ones could be found.

Ninth, a ripped-out page from a library book, her written plea inside.

Detective Osborn's been handling the case since Goodman retired, at least on a local level. The Honolulu police are in charge of the open investigation into the disap-pearance of Bristol, but the items my parents receive are collected by our local jurisdiction and sent to the crime lab for processing.

"Osborn." A man answers, his voice has a Texan lilt since he came from Dallas.

"Hey Osborn, Blair Bellamy here."

"Blair, hi, what a surprise. Haven't heard from your kind in a long time."

"Yeah, I know."

"Though it's never good."

"True, this isn't either. Priscilla got a package that has a single tooth and Bristol's necklace."

"Necklace?"

"Yeah, we had matching ones that my daddy gave us the Christmas before she disappeared."

"Oh, geez, I'll be over this afternoon to grab it."

"Thanks."

"Tell Priscilla hi and I'll see you later."

"Okay." I hang up. Priscilla watches me like a hawk, ready to pounce.

"I need to get in her room," I say after hanging up.

"Why?"

I glare.

She nods. "Fine."

WE HEAD UP THE STAIRS, her walk more pronounced as she holds onto the railing for balance. I almost feel sorry for her, but I can't.

At the top of the stairs, you hang a right and there are two bedrooms with a Jack and Jill bathroom between them – our rooms and bathroom.

As soon as I left, my room turned into a Find Bristol/sewing area, my bed scooted into a corner, the rest of my furniture moved into storage or sold.

The other bedroom up here's a guest room now, it was slated to be Isaiah's room, but after Bristol disappeared, that was off the table.

Carefully, Priscilla slides her necklace off, twisting the key in the door handle.

The lock clicks and I'm hit with a musty scent. It's pungent, and I cough as the stale air fills my lungs.

I feel as if I've stepped back into time, 1998, the posters untouched, her bulletin board, the small desk she did her homework at. A Destiny's Child, K-CI & JoJo, and Backstreet Boys poster cover one wall. The pictures pinned up on the corkboard are of her and her friends at various locales – school, church, volunteering. There's an award for cheerleading, debate team, and a Certificate of Excellence at the nursing home she worked at a few hours a week.

Bristol Bellamy, loved and revered by everyone.

I step into the room. An eerie silence follows, her comforter still the same daisy one she had when we left on our trip, her bean bag chair still in the same spot. Hell, her chemistry textbook is still open to page three-hundred and seventeen, the homework assignment only half-finished, signaling she thought she'd come back from spring break and finish it.

I sigh.

Priscilla doesn't know everything.

Underneath Bristol's desk, we found a loose floorboard. We cut it in half with our daddy's hand saw so we could have a secret hiding place. We slid a rug over the spot, the desk over the rug, and no one was the wiser.

SHE'S EYEING me suspiciously as I grab the desk and tug, grunting as I pull it away from the wall, sliding the daisy area rug away from its permanent location.

"What in the world are you doing?" She's annoyed. "You can't come in here and move stuff around."

I ignore her, sinking to my knees to pull out the floorboard.

Her eyes glare at my back as I yank at the slat, exposing a gap in the floorboard with a small box hidden.

"What's that?"

"Everything I've saved from the case."

"You have information you didn't give to the police?" Her eyes narrow, hands clenched at her sides.

"No, this is all saved from back then. In case we ever needed it." I shrug.

"Why is it here?" She motions for me to give it to her.

I hold it out of reach. "Because I put it in a safe place here and you locked me out, then kicked me out."

No response.

"So now what?" I ask, pulling the smooth box onto my lap. It has a lock on it, the key safe in my apartment.

"Now you have to find her." She's dead serious. "You have to go back to the island and find her."

"She's gone, Priscilla."

"No, she's not."

"Ten years is a long time."

"You're telling me." She sinks onto the yellow and white comforter. "I know what it feels like. I've been with her the whole time."

"You want me to go back to the island and what? Ask people from a decade ago the same questions, except now all this time has passed and their memories are blurred? Why would they remember anything differently?"

"Because time has a way of sorting through things for you."

"Maybe they will remember it wrong."

"Maybe. But I think you know a lot more than you ever let on."

"I was drugged, you know this. Dammit, why do you keep picking at these wounds, Priscilla?"

"Stop calling me Priscilla, I'm your fucking mother." She's calm as she says this. "These wounds have never healed, nor can they, because we have no answers, that's why."

"And what can I do the police can't?" I brush a tear angrily from my cheek. "The FBI, the police, psychics, private investigators. They all tried and failed."

"They weren't there that night."

"Neither was I."

"Have you tried hypnosis?"

"Yes. Nothing."

"You know something."

"I do not."

"Who were those boys?" Priscilla picks at a loose thread on the comforter. "Did you meet them at a bar?"

"No, they taught us surf lessons." I'm impatient, we've been over these details and this story a million times. She always asks, wanting a different answer.

"How'd you get in the bar?"

"Someone else's IDs."

"You gave her someone else's ID to use? Of all the asinine..."

I interrupt her. "I did no such thing."

"Where'd she get it then?" She's accusatory. "I know you didn't bring them with from here. I searched your luggage before you left."

"She bought them from Will Loomis."

"Bristol would do no such thing."

"Okay, Priscilla. I have no reason to lie." I smirk. "You have to stop putting her on this pedestal like she's not just a teenager."

"You just want to run her name through the muck, don't you?"

"Don't you get it? You can't keep making her into a saint, Priscilla. Bristol was a great kid. She still was a teenager."

"*Was?*" Priscilla puts her hands on her hips. "Watch how you speak of her in this house."

Disgusted, I murmur, "No wonder she wanted away from you."

"She wanted no such thing. She was going to help with Isaiah. You had to ruin that, though. Your daddy's only shot at having a boy."

"I wish it were me that was taken."

"Me too." She huffs, her hands twisted in her lap. "What's in the box?"

"Just notes I wrote from that first week, people I encountered."

"Haven't the police interviewed all these people?"

"Yes."

"We need to go back to Honolulu."

"What're you talking about?"

We went together once as a family when they thought they found her body, but it was another girl. Her name was Sonia Sutherland, and she had been missing from Mobile, Alabama. Her and Bristol looked eerily similar – strawberry blonde hair, green eyes, smattering of freckles, and same body type and height.

This was a little over six months after she'd been gone.

I know it's selfish, but I had prayed it was Bristol. That she wasn't suffering, that she'd found peace. Also that I would have closure, some peace, and that I could stop living in the past. That maybe my parents would forgive me.

"We have to go back, search the island."

"Why?"

"Why not?" Priscilla shoots back.

"No one's seen a trace of her in ten years," I answer.

Priscilla looks at me, really looks at me. The first time in forever, she sees me instead of looking through me. "I'm dying."

"What do you mean, dying?" I ask.

"I have cancer."

"Yeah," I shrug, "a lot of people have cancer and survive."

She swallows. "I have colon cancer, stage four. Doctors gave me less than a year to live. I'd like to know what happened to my baby girl."

"What about your other girl?"

"She's sitting in front of me." She strokes her chin thoughtfully. "I've always known where you were. You did nothing with your life, wasted it away. You weren't hard to track or find."

"Then why bother me now?"

"Because you can do something with your life, Blair. You can find your sister and prove you have some worth before I die."

"You act like I don't want her found." I shake my head in disgust. "What the fuck is wrong with you?"

"I'll sweeten the deal, Blair," Priscilla says. "I'll make you an offer you won't be able to resist."

"What're you talking about? I don't want anything from you."

"You have nothing, you've shit for brains, working at a bar, living in a dump, jumping from man to man who you think will fix the broken parts of you. You're broken, Blair, accept it. Permanently broken. Stop trying to find someone to put you back together."

"Why're you so mean?" I stand. "I've got to get going." I nestle the box in my arms, cradling it like I would a small child.

"Why won't you show me what's in the box?" Priscilla grabs the rail, slowly pulling herself down the stairs.

"It's locked."

"Where're you going?"

"Back home."

"You're not waiting for the officer?"

"No, you have the package. Give it to him when he shows up."

"What about my offer?"

"What about it?" I grab my purse off the counter as she jerks at my sleeve. "Hear me out, Blair."

"I want nothing from you, got it? Don't you think I know you and Daddy would've preferred that I had disappeared? Don't you think I wished the same thing? How my life turned out? You act like you're the only one that's suffered."

She ignores my statement. "If you find Bristol, whether it's her alive or... you know... I will leave you the house and money to fix it up."

"And if I don't?"

Her voice drips poison. "I'll leave you nothing. You'll be dead to me even when I'm gone."

"I've been dead to you living, Priscilla. Nothing will change." I open the door, turning to face her. "I want to find Bristol because she's my sister, not because you demand it and promise your land."

"Good enough."

I start to slam the door in her face.

"Wait," she yells. She thrusts an envelope in my hand. "Here's five thousand dollars. Instructions are inside." I try to push it back in her palm, but instead of taking it, she slams the door in my face.

I hear the deadbolt chain.

When I sink into the worn cloth seats of my car, I wait until I've headed down the gravel road before I pull over and scream at the top of my lungs, pounding my fists on the dash and steering wheel.

Priscilla's a fucking lunatic. What did I do to deserve her as a mother?

You lost your baby sister, I remind myself.

I open the manila envelope, holding it away from me

like a snake's going to strike me, injecting venom from its bite into me. No different than Priscilla.

A typed note is inside.

BLAIR,

I want to go to sleep and die knowing Bristol has been found, whatever the outcome may be. I'm not worried about an eye-for-an-eye at this point, God will take care of anyone who was involved in her disappearance.

$5,000.

First, you must buy a plane ticket. I want an emailed receipt so I know the date you are leaving. I suggest it be a one-way ticket since you're not to come home until you have answers.

Second, the same goes for the hotel. Emailed receipt so I know where and how to reach you. Room number emailed to me upon arrival.

If you can manage to finish something in your life, make it this.

Mother

LIGHTING A CIGARETTE, I burn her note.

The nerve of her, trying to buy me off, my sister not some pet project. I'm not some sinister type who purposely dumped her with a crazy person. I watch the flame lick up the paper, shriveling it, the ends a burnt crisp. The bits fly out the window, trailing behind me as I drive off. I leave the windows rolled down, hard rock vibrating against the speakers, the bass and treble making my seat pulsate.

37

BRISTOL

WHEN I WAKE, I'm disoriented, my eyes lifting to see murky shadows. I think I'm back in the room, the four walls closing in on me.

I see The Mole's blue eyes, staring into my pupils. I jerk my head, drifting back into my abyss, unable to pull myself out of my suffering.

He caught me, I knew he would.

Another gentle tug on my arm, and the blue eyes turn to brown. This time, I notice long eyelashes and a baseball cap staring back at me. The sandy blond hair of The Mole has been replaced with brown hair and olive skin.

Trembling, I blink, my hands moving over my belly, checking to see if the baby's still there. I feel wetness between my legs, liquid pooling there, my thighs covered in stickiness.

My left side feels like a boulder's weighing it down, like I'm smashed underneath something heavy. Gasping, I notice my left arm's twisted at an odd angle, the bone jutting out of the skin. I try to move away from the pressure. Bad choice, since my legs are Jell-O.

"Hi, I'm Max." His voice is almost too soft to understand. "Do you know where you are?"

I don't respond, cradling my arm as I wince at the pain. I try to focus on that, but a cramping sensation starts in my low back and intensifies, my teeth gritting in agony.

His hand clutches me as I try and reach down, feeling between my legs, a dark spot pooling what's left of the nightgown. My eyes are frantic as I realize that the baby's in danger and I'm about two feet from going over another rock wall. The steep drop would no doubt be fatal. His eyes drift down, shocked at the bleeding coming from my lower region.

"I'm pregnant." I manage to croak, trying to sit up.

"You're pregnant?" He's baffled, my body anorexic-looking, my limbs resembling thin sticks.

"You better stay down." The guy named Max puts his hands on my elbow. "I tried to call for an ambulance, but there's no cell service here. I'm gonna walk back out and try again."

"No," I scream, "you can't." I flail, looking around. "Where is he?"

"Who?"

"The Mole, where is he?" A wave of panic propels me forward.

"Argh...." I scream in agony.

"I'm not sure who you're talking about." He's confused. "Were you with someone before you fell? You've got some nasty cuts that will need stitches and..." he examines my dangling left arm, "that's definitely broken. Potentially a concussion."

He tries to keep the horror off his face as he tries not to gasp. "Are these cigarette burns?" My body is covered in scars from The Mole's lighter.

"They're nothing." I murmur.

"They don't look like nothing."

"I need your help." My eyes dart around. "I have to make sure I'm safe from him."

"From whoever did this to you?"

I stare at the sand-colored wall. "Where am I?"

"A ledge on the side of the lava rocks." He points upward. "There's a cliff above us, this is the lower part."

"Honolulu?" I ask. "How far from Waikiki Beach?"

"You're not far from the beach, thirty minutes or so."

"He could come back for me."

"I didn't see anyone come up here."

"Where can I hide? He could be waiting for me." Trying to think through my pain, I ask, "Are there multiple ways up this trail?"

"Yeah, there's a couple paths," he says. "But it's a decent hike, so a lot of people don't go to the top. We're about halfway up. I came up here to hike and camp." He shrugs. "Just my backpack and a sleeping bag."

"Any weapons?"

"I'm not going to hurt you."

Shaking my head, I groan, "No, to protect us from him."

"A hunting knife." He looks at my broken body. "I'm going to go try to reach someone."

"No hospitals," I say.

An unreadable expression crosses his face. "I'll be right back." Terror-stricken, fearful I'll be left here, I whisper, "Please don't leave me, I need help."

"I'm not leaving you, promise." He sets his canteen next to me. "I'll leave this here so you know I'll be back. I've gotta get you and your baby help."

Max starts to walk towards an opening in the cave.

Pausing over his shoulder, he asks, "What's your name, by the way?"

"Bridget... I...I..." I can't breathe, contractions tremoring through my body. "Baby, don't let him take the baby," I manage to say before I lose consciousness.

38

BLAIR

I'M calmer when I get back to my apartment, Priscilla a mere annoyance. I pound on Marge's door, wanting to know her thoughts on this. She answers on the third knock, knowing it's me and not some drunkard from downstairs.

"Hiya, kid, what's up?" Marge is old enough to be my grandma, but she dresses like she's twenty-five and acts it most of the time.

Except when it comes to her business.

Tonight she's wearing a red sequin mini-skirt and a see-through black blouse, black suede boots that stop at her knees.

"It's bingo night," she explains. "I gotta call out the numbers."

I just shake my head.

"You look like you saw a ghost," she says.

I sink down on her worn tan leather couch. Pickles circles around my legs in greeting.

"I pretty much did." I add, "Priscilla."

SHE WHISTLES THROUGH HER TEETH. "Really? Praise be! I thought she'd moved up to her glass house by now, the way she throws stones."

Marge is familiar with Priscilla, the year of AA a constant battle that involved long conversations about my parents, particularly my mother.

I tell her Priscilla's offer.

She sits down on a bar stool and faces me. "What do you want to do?"

I shake my head. "I'm torn. It's not like I haven't looked for Bristol."

"Do you think she's dead?"

"Yes," I say without hesitation.

"Then what will going there accomplish?"

"She wants me to investigate."

"But the FBI, the police, they have. No offense to your skills, kiddo, but what the fuck are you going to do that you haven't or they haven't?"

"I know. That is my dilemma."

"Whatever happened to those boys they accused of kidnapping her?"

"They had to release them. They had no proof." I pick at a nail. "I only found one on Facebook, the other is either in prison, silent, or hates technology."

"You have to do what you think is best."

"What about my job? And our arrangement?" Marge had offered me a job, on the condition that I work at least forty hours a week managing the bar, I don't steal, and I don't date losers. I also can't drink or imbibe on any drugs.

With my menial salary, I get free rent and all the Pepsi products I can stomach.

"Don't worry about your apartment. It's fine." Marge

shrugs her shoulders. "I'm worried about you, kiddo. I don't want you falling off the wagon."

"I hadn't considered that."

"You should." She gives me a tight smile. "If you head down that dark of a path again, can you steer clear of those habits that trip you up?"

Looking at her clock chiming on the wall, I notice the time. "Shit, I gotta get down to the bar." I give Pickles a quick rub and her a peck on the cheek. "Enjoy your bingo numbers."

"Blair?" She cautions as I head out. "Your sister has been missing for ten years. But so have you. Don't harm yourself on the imagination of your mother. You've already paid the price."

I nod, she's right. Not everything in life has a successful outcome. I set the box on the top shelf of my closet and head down to the bar. As I'm pouring drinks and writing down food orders, I consider what Priscilla and Marge both said.

Texting Priscilla on my smoke break later, I thank her for the offer, wish her luck on her chemo, and tell her I'll expedite the money back.

Her only response. "I shouldn't have given up on you, please don't give up on her."

Stubbing out my cigarette angrily with my black boot, her attempt at reverse psychology pissing me off, I block her on my phone. I set boundaries that my therapist would be proud of. I don't need any more messages affirming what we've always known.

I'm a loser.

That night I toss and turn, my nightmares taking on a different form. Usually it's water of some kind I'm drowning in – a bathtub, the lake, an ocean.

Now, I wake up to Bristol being tossed in a shallow

grave, arms reaching up. A nightgown drapes her, the color pink surrounding her face.

Pink roses? I wonder, my forehead clammy.

I slide open my closet doors, pulling the smooth black box out. I wrestle the key from my old jewelry stand, a corner one that's mirrored with drawers clothed in velvet. It was my graduation present from high school from my parents. The key's still hidden in the second drawer from the last, small and tiny, insignificant-looking.

Yet it means the world to me.

Firing up my laptop, I open my own Pandora's box. I look through the names and notes, some photocopied from the police file, others handwritten from myself, Mark, or Goodman. Flipping through pages, I find the orange wristband of the bar we were at - *The Ocean Club,* the club everyone denied seeing us at.

There's a photocopy of a receipt – Will Loomis' eighty-nine dollar bar tab.

The date on the paper says the twenty-fifth. I'm confused, until I remember Will didn't pay the bill, they had to charge it after the fact.

The bartender. The DJ.

Maybe they can still remember something?

It's worth a shot.

I'm microwaving a Hot Pocket, my preferred dinner since I don't like to cook, when my cell rings.

It's an unknown number.

Priscilla.

Another attempt to put me down and guilt trip me. She must've realized I blocked her when it repeatedly went to voicemail.

I'm tempted to ignore the call, except it could be Marge with more questions.

I pick up, but before I can say hello, a man says my name, one I haven't heard since our tense parting when I slid into a taxi all those years ago.

"Blair?"

"Yeah?"

Relief's palpable in his voice. "Thank God you never changed your number."

"I couldn't." I sigh. "In case she ever got found..."

"It's been years with nothing. I know it's the waiting that's the worst."

"My mother seems to think she's alive." I grab a dirty plate out of the sink. "I think she's crazy."

"That's why I'm calling." Mark Matsen lowers his voice.

I wipe it off, rinsing yesterday's crumbs, ignoring the thump of my chest.

"Blair, I have to preface what I'm about to tell you – this isn't public knowledge yet. I only found out since Goodman's replacement called and I do some P.I. work on the side for them."

I grip the counter, the smell of burning ham and cheese filling the small studio.

"A hiker found a girl today. It's believed to be someone who went missing recently, Bridget Masterson."

"Seriously?"

"Yes."

"She's dead?'

"Right now, unconscious."

I inhale sharply. My heart starts palpitating, beating out of my chest as if a marching band is practicing in my sternum.

"But there's more..." He pauses, "Blair? Can you sit down for me?"

Sliding down the counter, hitting the floor with a thud, I rest my head against the marred oak cabinets. "I am now."

"Blair, they found bones. Lots of them that they believe to be from different individuals. They have to go in for examination and testing, but it looks like many have been hidden for years." Mark hesitates. "I'm wondering with the likeness to your sister and where Bridget was found if they might be related."

"So you're saying there's a chance my sister might be... part of the group?" My face drains of color. "She's dead?" I whisper. Saying it aloud after this kind of news feels different than saying it to Priscilla.

This is actual proof.

"No, I'm not saying it's her," Mark reiterates. "There's a possibility, and I wanted you to hear it from me first. I've never given up on this case."

I'm only half-listening, my mind racing. "I need to come there," I say. "I need to find the killer. Did they catch him? Was it Will? Or Nicholas?"

"No suspects yet. A hiker discovered Bridget and a search by investigators led to the discovery in a cave. It was a fluke thing."

"I know *he* did it. And he's just been continuing to kill all these years. That sonofabitch. Think how many girls could've been saved."

"We don't know that for sure."

"I'm coming there." I cross my arms over my chest.

"No, stay put, Blair. I need to be able to contact you and your mother."

"That's what cell phones are for." I sigh. "Did you call her yet?"

"No, I called you first."

"I can't sit and wait for him or his friends to keep taking girls."

"If it's her, you can be on the next plane." Mark promises. "Wait until after the autopsies. They will test for prints, DNA, the works. Let us do our jobs in finding the asshole."

He adds. "Besides, I'm not even there, I'm in the States visiting my daughter and grandchildren, but the department's keeping me in the loop."

I'M NUMB, frustrated at their lack of ability to find the murderer. He's evaded them for at least a decade, maybe more. Who knows how long he's been killing girls?

Priscilla thinks I haven't tried – that I let Bristol die without a fight.

She has no idea the meticulous research I've done, the log of missing persons in Hawaii I've compiled going back two decades.

Some are runaways, others are reported missing but come home, a few are still out there, either displaced by their own accord or because they have no choice.

In 1998, I couldn't find out as much information on potential victims as I can today. The difference is that with time has come advances in technology.

Cameras.

Amber Alerts.

Everything is digital, and human nature prides itself on oversharing.

Twitter.

Facebook.

Instagram.

Snapchat.

Maybe I've been going about this the wrong way. The night of the twenty-fourth is lost. The block of time is too big to reconcile.

If Bridget was taken by the same person, there has to be a link between Bristol and her. Either a hotel, a restaurant, something they both did that put them in harm's way. In his way.

Or maybe it was completely random.

I have no leads with Bristol.

But Bridget's another story.

SHE HAS her own routine and timeline for the night she disappeared. If it's the same person who kidnapped Bristol, there will be commonalities.

I have information bookmarked on her —social media provides a glimpse into her life...but ends a couple hours before she vanished.

I glance over her snapshots. She has the same hair color and eyes, only no freckles. Smooth pale skin. Similarities, both were close in age – she was eighteen at the time of her disappearance a little over two months ago. Both are from small towns. Scanning the news articles, she was visiting Hawaii from Kansas City. Her parents weren't on this trip, she went missing when she was with a group of friends out at the bar. She never returned to their beachside rental. They assumed she had gone home with someone until she never reappeared.

There might not be any ties between the girls, two separate monsters may be responsible, but my gut tells me that's not the case.

Something nags at me...they look a lot alike, more like sisters than Bristol and I do.

The lack of viable leads boggles my mind. But truth is, I haven't focused on anyone else that could have taken my sister because in my mind, there was no one else.

We were with two boys, one notorious for drugging girls.

Will.

39

BRISTOL

BEEPING. All I hear are short, quick warnings.

Words murmur from above me, but exhaustion makes it hard to try and understand. There's a loud commotion, wailing, coming from below or inside me.

Hands press down on my chest, can't they see I'm sleeping?

I drift back into my subconscious, mumbling as I hear my name called.

When I wake up, I expect to see the room instead of a metal bed, the four walls bland and cream-colored. A picture of a cerulean blue ocean stares back at me. My ears crane to hear all the noises – the sound of traffic outside, car horns beeping, the low hum of equipment, and people chattering excitedly.

A television hangs down from the ceiling, except it's flat, unlike the bulky ones from my childhood.

Glancing around, I realize I'm hooked up to machines, IVs, and the metal bed moves up and down, a hospital-grade one. The realization should comfort me, instead I'm immobilized. Does The Mole know I'm here? Is he waiting for me? My eyes dart back and forth, scanning the small room.

A soft knock on the door startles me. The man named Max, my lifesaver, enters with an older gentleman in a white lab coat.

"You're up," the man with glasses and a stethoscope says, "I'm Doctor Peters. You have this young man to thank for saving you and your little boy."

"Ah...I'm not that young." Max laughs. "But forty is the new thirty."

"Little boy?" My voice softens. Instinctively, I reach down with my unbroken arm to my belly, the bump covered by a thin cotton blanket and a plain pink hospital gown. The color pink makes me nauseous. I tighten the material around my middle. "He's alive?" The relief's palpable on my face as I relax against the pillow.

"Close call, you were having back contractions, causing him to be stuck in a perilous position. We got him though. Five pounds, eight ounces later." He pats my knee. "We'll bring him in after you rest. Speaking of giving birth, how're you feeling?"

"Like I just had fifty pounds removed from my body." I shrug. "No big deal." My thoughts drift to the baby boy and The Mole, and a sinking feeling curls in the pit of my stomach. "My baby, is he being guarded?" My mouth twists in concern. "He needs protection."

The doctor and the dark-haired man exchange a look. "What's going on?" I ask.

"Bridget Masterson?" The doctor checks his clipboard, focusing too hard on the paper in front of him.

"Yes, that's me."

His eyes aren't unkind, but his voice betrays doubt. "It can't be you."

"What do you mean?"

"Bridget's only been missing for a couple months. According to her family and friends, she wasn't pregnant at the time of her disappearance."

Gaping at him, I clamp my fingers into the firm mattress.

"Do you know who you are?"

I say nothing, peering between the doctor and Max.

He pats my arm gently. "Don't worry, the authorities have been notified. They can sort this all out. We just want to focus on getting you better."

"Is he here?" I'm frantic. "Don't let him near the baby."

"Who?"

"The Mole." I'm exasperated, rolling my eyes.

"Um...no one is around the baby or you besides myself and our team of nurses. This is a secure floor." Doctor Peters squeezes my hand reassuringly. "The police will want to help you, ask you questions." He gives me a warm smile. "We're so relieved you're safe." Checking my pulse, he makes a few notes on a skinny-looking computer thing, then asks Max to step out in the hall with him, leaving me alone.

I hear their voices, both soft, but the more persistent one belongs to Doctor Peters. He's telling Max he thinks I'm covering for someone who hurt me, clearly the victim of domestic abuse. He's unsure if I'm delusional and manifesting a fake alias because of severe PTSD.

Because I know of Bridget, he speculates I read about her in the paper recently. "Maybe she's doing this to get attention," Doctor Peters offers. "She's obviously been through an extreme amount of trauma."

Straining to hear, they speak in hushed tones, and

unable to make out the rest of their conversation, I close my eyes.

A vivid image takes hold in my mind, The Mole strangles both the baby and I, one in each arm, his choke hold on each of our throats.

Struggling to breathe, I gasp for air, uninterrupted tears wet my cheeks and trail down my neck. The door to the room opens and closes and my lids jerk open, confronting the intruder.

It's Max.

He watches me, his brown eyes darkening. "Bridget?"

I don't answer, looking down at the tremors in my hands.

"Bridget?"

"Yeah?"

"Do you remember your real name?" He asks. "Or are you also a Bridget, just with a different last name?"

Wiping my nose, I don't answer.

He points to the only seat in the room, a plastic blue chair. "Mind if I sit?"

A simple shrug is all I can muster.

"I'm just glad you're safe and you're both..." he stammers, "you and the baby are both okay."

"When can I hold him?"

"Soon, I'm sure." He leans on his elbows. "But right now I'm just trying to figure out why you have Bridget Masterson's ID and debit card on you."

Faking a yawn, I deliberately close my eyes.

"I'll let you sleep, but I just want to let you know I'm here if you need anything. It sounds like you've been through quite an ordeal and need a friend." He stands, stopping at the foot of my bed. "I know you don't know me, but if you have something to hide, you can tell me...or if you need help..."

I remain mute, waiting for the sound of his footsteps on the tile.

Considering my options, being confronted by the police or a complete stranger, albeit one that saved my life, I whisper his name. "Max?"

The steps pause, "Yeah?"

"Thank you for saving our lives." Tears form in the creases of my eyelids. "You have no idea what you saved us from." He stands there, waiting for me to elaborate, but I don't. After a minute of silence, his footfalls echo out of the room, the door silent as it shuts behind him.

I drift in and out of sleep after he leaves, one stop from a social worker introducing herself, another the intrusion of two detectives. I'm asked questions about my injuries, the baby I just gave birth to, and my identity, or lack of one.

"Did you see a doctor during your pregnancy?"

"What was the due date given?"

"Where do you live?

"How old are you?"

"Can you tell us about the burns on your body?"

"In addition to the burns, who physically assaulted you?"

"Do you personally know Bridget Masterson or just read about her?"

I've gotten good at acting after all the years under The Mole's thumb. I play dense, confused, and tongue-tied. Severely underweight, my real age is hidden by the fact I can pass for a fifteen-year-old, the age I'm assumed to be by a round of doctors.

A nurse with a sunny disposition finally brings my baby to me after I refuse to answer any more questions until I can hold him. Tears stream down my cheeks, I didn't think I could cry so hard or feel so attached to a tiny newborn. His miniature hands and feet are swaddled in a blanket, his button nose looks like mine in my baby pictures. I instruct myself not to consider The Mole and what features he might have of his. That's tarnishing this sweet, innocent baby.

Counting his fingers and toes, I squeal as he pushes his little fist in the air, a battle cry following. The nurse smiles at us, giving me pointers as I gently rock him in my one good arm.

Breathing a sigh of relief, I cradle him to my chest.

The moment's bittersweet, my family nowhere in sight at this celebration of life. And really, it's a re-birth for not only being returned to society, but for the new life created.

Questions keep coming from the police, repeating over and over the next week. I make up small details to feed to the detectives, still hiding who I really am.

Max visits every day, a permanent fixture by my side as he keeps an eye on me and the baby. He holds him, cooing and burping him as if it's second nature. I assume he's got his own kids with a wife or girlfriend, but I don't see a ring on his finger. I assume he's being nice, knowing that I'm fragile. He feels sorry for me is all.

The more he sits by my side in the hard plastic chair, the more we talk. I'm careful not to dredge up the past or any details that can tie me to my old life or The Mole. I only allow myself to lie, except for the admission I'm from Nebraska. My focus stays on the present and getting acclimated to the strides that have been made with technology and the Internet.

Everything's slimmer like the television – phones, computers, even the portion sizes of food. He shows me his phone, I'm amazed at the apps and the invention and light-ning speed of what's known as Wi-Fi. Careful not to look anything up about my past, I play crossword and puzzle games.

Max sometimes stays the night, his head lolled back against the chair. When he's there, I sleep better, feel more protected if The Mole comes back. One night I fall asleep, holding my baby boy, his little fist wrapped around my pinky finger. It's the best rest of my life. When I wake up, Max's chest is rising and falling, his snores short and peaceful in the chair beside us.

Some nights are harder when I let my mind wander. I think of Bridget, guilt enveloping me. The other girls that're dead or missing. How many are there? Tears flood my cheeks when I think of Bridget stuck in the room with The Mole.

Eventually, I have to talk, knowing my time's limited, and wanting freedom, I make up a story. Confessing I *am* eighteen, just like they guessed, originally from a small town in Nebraska, and scared of my abusive boyfriend, I flee to Hawaii. They ask why Hawaii, I admit it's as far as I could get from him without leaving the country. I'd only been here a few weeks when I fell off the cliff, everything chaotic in my head from the concussion.

Amazingly Max never tells them I had Bridget's ID, credit, and debit card in my slipper. I attest to the police I pretended to be her because I'm terrified of my ex finding me and Bridget Masterson and I both share the same first name.

They can't disprove this, so they grudgingly release me. The hospital needs my bed and I've got no health insurance, so their hands are tied. I'm required to maintain a place of residence and social work visits for at least six months. This means a local women's shelter to begin with, so a watchful eye can be kept on me and the baby.

The day I'm slated to leave, I'm sitting in the lobby, my eyes glued to the television, making sure there's no evidence that a Bristol Bellamy has been found. Even though my name didn't come up when I mentioned Nebraska, paranoia sets in.

Slumping in my seat, relieved, the focus is on weather, the political climate, and the high-speed chase that involved a pedestrian fatality.

I'm safe, at least for the moment.

Out of the corner of my eye, I see a tall, dark-haired man with olive skin, dressed in business casual clothing, the only thing missing a tie.

He looks frantic, footsteps hurried, his wingtip loafers tapping on the tile floor. Instead of stopping at the nurses station, he continues walking straight towards me.

My heart palpitates, wondering if this is a news reporter coming to get the scoop.

I wring my hands in my lap, anxiety spiking as I think of bolting out another exit.

As the man walks closer, I breathe a sigh of relief at the sight of Max, unrecognizable to me since he's not in gym shorts and a sweatshirt, his usual attire.

"Thank God, Bridget," he sighs. "I'm glad I caught you." He motions to the chair next to me. "Mind if I sit down?"

"Sure," I say.

"I know you're leaving today..." He tilts his head towards the outside, "But I wanted to see if you'd be opposed to my own thoughts about your living situation. I spoke to Doctor Peters and the social worker assigned to your case."

I pick at a ripped cuticle, expecting him to explain his idea. Instead he asks, "Do you need a ride?"

"No, they're providing transportation." I bite my lip. "I'm just waiting for the nurse to come down with the baby. Then a driver will take us to the shelter."

"I'm worried about you adjusting to another new environment." He pauses a moment. "It must be scary to be in a new state, disoriented, and have a newborn to take care of."

"Yeah, but at least I'm away from him." I switch topics. "What're you dressed up for?"

We've never talked about his profession. "Oh, I'm a vet." He glances down at his clothing.

"A veterinarian?"

"Yep, a doctor of the animal kind." He raises a thick brow. "You thought you got saved by a regular guy, not the animal whisperer."

I laugh, slow at first, a genuine smile rising to the occasion.

"I've been meaning to ask you..." He leans back in the chair. "It's been on my mind, bothering me." He taps his fingers on the leather arm rest between us. "I don't want to bother you with it, but I have to know."

He's pensive, his dark eyes clouding over with apprehension.

"Yeah?" I cringe, hoping it's not about The Mole.

"Will you level with me?"

"What do you mean?"

"I found you in a remote area after a nasty fall, you refused to go to the hospital even though you were in labor, looking like you'd been starved and beaten for longer than a few months." He gestures to the revolving door separating us from the outside. "You're scared of someone more dangerous than a high school boyfriend, and you're in hiding. Care to elaborate on any of this?"

My face burns. "No."

"I want to help you, Bridget," he lowers his voice, "if that's your real name, which I don't think it is."

I glance at him warily.

He ignores my hesitation, speaking softly. "I found the ID and credit card of Bridget Masterson in your slipper when I found you. But you've never told me where it came from." He reaches in his back pocket, pulling out the ID.

My heart thuds in my chest, concentrating my focus on my hands.

"I've Googled missing girls in Nebraska..."

I'm unsure what 'Googled' means, but I'm not going to ask.

He reads my mind. "Do you know what 'Google' is?"

"No." I shrug.

"Exactly, bingo." He snaps his fingers. "You haven't been missing for a few months, you've been missing for a lot longer than that. If I had to guess, I'd say at least seven to eight years, maybe more."

"Maybe so..." I shrug. "I wish I could remember, be more helpful."

"I don't know who you are, if you even know, but there's a list of missing girls from Nebraska. He stares at my lowered eyelids. "A ton that start with the letter 'B'."

Careful not to raise my voice or act defensive, I ask. "Why didn't you turn her ID over to the cops?"

"Because there's a lot more to this story than you're telling me. But you've got a name, and you need help." He leans forward, elbows resting on his knees. "And I want you to come live with me for now, to get on your feet."

There's silence as we both collect our thoughts.

"Look...I *want* to help you. Let me help you."

"I don't know you..."

"Understandably, you're scared. I don't pretend to get it or the gravity of what happened to you." He turns to me, compassion in his eyes.

"Max..."

"Google my name, Max Fletcher."

"I don't know how..."

"See, if you're searching for someone, you're definitely going to need my expertise." He runs his hand through his dark, wavy locks. "Especially if you haven't been exposed to technology. We've come a long way since then."

"I don't want to go to the shelter," I say firmly. "I just want to disappear again."

"To where?"

"Away. In hiding. Can you help me with that?" I consider my options. "Is there a bus station?"

"Where will you go?"

"I don't know," I murmur. Biting my lip, the idea of staying with another man frightens me.

Holding up a hand, he says, "You and the baby will have your own bedroom at my place. Plus, you'll need assistance. Doc said it'll be another week or two before you can stop wearing the sling." Before I can answer, the nurse interrupts my dark, troubled memories of the room. She's been a constant presence with both the baby and I, and she's sad to see us go, even though she doesn't know who I am, she's seen the progress we're both making.

I'm relieved he's been a happy baby so far. The stress of our situation and time spent without food and proper medical care nags at me. The nurse gives his tiny head a gentle pat as she tucks him into the crook of Max's arm.

He's right, because my arm's in a sling, I'm incapable of

being on my own yet. Between the women's shelter and his residence, he wins. I need his help if I'm ever going to locate Bridget. That's what the authorities don't know or understand, until she's found, I might as well be her. We're both still missing.

It's time to find The Mole.

40

BRISTOL

FOLLOWING MAX TO HIS VEHICLE, he waves to a tan Jeep, the model unrecognizable from a decade ago. I open the back door, a car seat already installed, prepared even before coming to the hospital. He's more efficient than I am, still clumsy and awkward with a newborn, my healing arm deficient.

When we're settled on the soft leather interior, I glance at him, his eyes focused on the road. "Totally last-minute plan, huh?" I give a slight grin.

"I'm prepared." He shrugs. "Just like when I was hiking. Plus, my best friend has a kid. Him and his wife helped put it in. I had it backwards."

"Didn't they ask what it was for?"

"Yeah, I said I found out I had a child." He snorts, "Illegitimate."

I cringe at the word, thinking of The Mole.

Max notices and instantly apologizes. "Sorry, that was in bad taste."

"It's fine." I give him a tight smile. "Thanks for thinking ahead."

"Just a fair warning, I hope you like dogs." He grins. "My best friend is eighty pounds and golden."

"I love dogs," I say, "I had a dog once upon a time."

"Name? Breed? Boy or girl?"

"Oggie, sheepdog mix, an overprotective and ornery boy."

"Is Oggie still around?"

"No clue." I sigh, my eyes trained on the rear view. "Probably not. That's the thing about time. It doesn't stand still even when we're forced to."

Looking out the window, I'm overwhelmed by the difference in cars, buildings, and people. Some of the chains are still the same, but staring at the booming real estate and oversized signs, I wonder if my hometown has changed this rapidly.

Max pulls onto a tree-lined street, about a mile from the beach. It's a cute two-story bungalow with red clay tiles and Spanish stucco with a wrap-around porch.

He gives me a tour, showing me the white bassinet his friends gave him for the baby. It's already set up with a diaper changing table and plenty of baby clothes and toys.

There's a large, king-size bed, soft and luxurious. Two large picture windows are on either side, covered by sheer aqua curtains. The floors are a dark wood, and a fireplace rests to my left. The intricate carved mantel holds a couple of framed photographs.

I feel bad. Max moved downstairs to a spare bedroom so I can stay in the master. My protests fall on deaf ears. I'd prefer to switch, feeling awful I chased him out of his room.

"There's two of you, it's fine." He points to the large walk-in closet and bathroom that's the size of the room I was in. A large jetted tub and separate shower are decorated in a gray and white bathroom. A white bath robe and plush towels are the opposite of the threadbare cotton ones in the room.

"Thank you." I'm appreciative. "You have no idea how much this means to me."

"We've established you're not Bridget," he asks, "so what should I call you?"

"Call me by her name until she's found." I'm firm. "This way, her name will always be on the tips of our tongue."

"Fair enough." He helps me place the baby in the bassinet, his eyes shut tight as he breathes in and out, softly snoring.

"Houston will be bounding in any minute." Max warns. "We'll have to make sure to keep the door shut so he doesn't wake him."

As if on cue, a bouncing poodle mix comes bounding into the room, his tail furiously wagging. Max laughs, "and right on schedule." He licks my hand, his rough tongue making me laugh. I forgot how much I missed having a pet.

"I'll let you get settled." Max pats his dog on the head. "I'll take Houston with me."

I pause, anxious. "Do you mind leaving the door open?"

"No problem."

"I just don't want to feel stuck," I explain.

"I know." Max gives me a reassuring smile, his even teeth and laid-back demeanor a welcome change of pace from my former life where I was always kept in.

It's weird getting acquainted to a house instead of just four small walls that doubled as my prison cell. Being able to walk between rooms, shower or bathe when I want, consistently go outside, and not refer to Max as 'sir' are all changes from patterns that became ingrained.

AT FIRST, the large rooms overwhelm me, my eyes dart to see what's going on outside of my space.

The ability to breathe fresh air anytime I want is incredible. The first rainstorm enthralls me. Max watches as I let myself out the back patio, the sound of the pounding almost cathartic. I stand outside in the middle of it with no protection as it pours, no umbrella or raincoat, letting it wash over me, the drops tickling my face, soaking my hair. It's like a cleanse to wash away all the bad.

Max stays inside with the baby, his eyes fixedly watching me, but different than how The Mole would stare at me. Max looks at me with concern, opposite of the hostility The Mole had.

It's amazing to be able to walk outside, exercise my legs, and watch my body heal. At least the flesh that can. The internal wounds will take time, if they ever close, and there will be permanent scars. For instance, the idea of being on the sand and near the surf terrifies me. Fearful, I don't wander far from the house, lying in the hammock, swaying by the lemon and orange trees in the backyard, rocking my unnamed baby boy.

One night, I'm fast asleep, or so I think, when I feel hands tugging on me. "Stop," I scream. "You're hurting me, stop touching me, no."

Houston barks, and wet licks cross my cheek.

"Bridget, wake up," a soft voice says above me.

Flicking my eyes open, I'm drenched in sweat, the bed damp underneath me. Disoriented, I gaze around. Houston jumps on the bed, trying to nuzzle his way underneath my arm.

"What's happening?"

"You were having a nightmare." Max switches on the

bedside lamp. "You have them almost every night. They're more like night terrors."

"Would it help if I started shutting the door?" I swallow. "I'm sorry, I don't mean to wake you up."

"I'm not worried about that. I'm concerned about you." He purses his lips, "And I'm afraid I won't be able to help you if you're in danger."

He struggles to find the right words. "I want to help...I just don't know how and it makes me uneasy, that I don't know enough about your situation to know what to do."

"I'm not trying to be difficult." I pull myself into a sitting position, my back resting against the pillows. "I can leave."

"That's not what I'm saying." He sighs. "I care about what happens to you and the baby."

"I appreciate your..."

"Stop," he holds up a hand. "Stop thanking me. I just want to help. But I need you to trust me to help you."

"I can't be helped," I mutter.

His eyes disagree with my statement, they smolder with intensity. "Why won't you name the baby?" he asks. "Don't you think he deserves to have a name?"

Staring open-mouthed, I tug at a loose string on the edge of the comforter. "I do."

He waits for me to continue my sentence.

"But I don't know if I can keep him." I shrug, uncomfortable with discussing this personal struggle out loud. I've been questioning my role and ability as a mother, the stretch of time I've been in hiding has deemed me inadequate to care for a baby, and I have no education, no resources. I've thought of adoption, putting aside my own selfish wants for the better of the little boy. I not only want him to have a good life, I need him to.

He looks at me, baffled, as I meet his eyes, the brown of the irises staring at me.

"What do you mean?"

"Nothing."

"You want to give him up for adoption?" He puts his hands on his knees. "Because you were...violated?"

My mouth twists in a grimace. "Never mind." The baby starts crying, ending our conversation. I rise to grab him, his wails carrying across the large bedroom.

After that, Max learns to be careful not to press me. I'm easily distraught if I feel cornered or forced to re-live all the memories in a short span of time. I know he has questions –

I can tell by the tight line his lips become, his inquisitive glances, and his well-intentioned but sometimes intrusive questions.

The one thing I don't have difficulty asking about is the Internet and how to use it. When I ask Max about the Google search tab on his laptop, he looks at me like I have three heads. Google was born in '98. The Internet was still dial-up and slow, social media wasn't a regular or big thing. Cell phones were still becoming mainstream.

I ask about Myspace and Max falls out of his chair, asking me how old I really am. I've only piqued his curiosity more with my questions and lack of computer knowledge. He shows me basic functions, then finds a free class at the public library for me to take one afternoon. He's arranged child care for the baby so I can attend.

The class is on the latest advances in computer tech-nology and an introduction to the Internet. It's a crash course that lasts three hours, advantageous to someone who's been confined to a room for a decade. Everyone in the group is seventy plus, most are learning about email and Google.

The librarian looks at me with curiosity, her experience not with someone who's twenty-seven. Her eyes widen more when she has to help me set up a free email account.

Afterwards, I go home and boot Max's laptop up. I Google my disappearance, wondering if there's any information dating back to 1998.

There's more articles than I thought I would find available. I'm impressed, my decade of hibernation kept me technologically stunted. I make a list of people who show up as witnesses, the places we went during our short stay, a timeline that's somewhat faulty due to alcohol and roofies.

Blair.

My heartstrings tug at the thought of her.

She's not in California as The Mole told me, at least, not according to any records I find.

No social media accounts come up for her.

I stop searching. If I don't find Bridget, I can't have my family back. It hurts too much to be so close but unable to reach out. I push the loneliness out of the way, focused on finding her.

Bridget Masterson.

Googling her name, I check and see what information comes up, if it's legitimate. I'm not sure how real what I'm reading is or if I'm being scammed.

I know so much about Bridget, her stories might as well be mine, She was all I had to home in on during our time together in the room. She went to school at Kansas State when she suddenly disappeared, a native of the state. I can corroborate this.

Photos show a happy-go-lucky girl, one like I used to be. She's an only child. Her parents cry in pain about the trip she never came home from. Their tearful pleas for her safe return appear on the YouTube channel.

The Sandlot? Hmm...unfamiliar. I wonder if it's close to The Ocean Club.

I have to go back to the bar.

But first, I have some research to do.

A man visiting from San Diego named Peter Riggs was questioned right after my disappearance. He found Blair passed out on the beach. I cover my mouth with my hand, reading his interview with a local newspaper. He told the reporter that he went to get her something to drink and she was gone when he came back. He was worried at first that she went missing too.

My disappearance made the front page for a couple days, then subtly made its way to the back, small paragraphs smashed between natural disasters and local happenings. The caveat was always that I disappeared after a night of binge drinking and could've run away with a boyfriend.

Right. At seventeen, on vacation with my sister.

The investigators talked to the employees at the bar, but they denied seeing us. The owner said he didn't have cameras, there's no mention of the fake IDs, only that our names didn't ring a bell. All they would share without a warrant was that Will had an eighty-nine dollar bar tab from that night and was with two girls, Leslie and Haley.

I'm curious to hear what Peter Riggs has to say.

I set up a Facebook account, using a dummy name and the email account I made in class.

Disbelief furrows my brow as I scroll through tons of the same likeness. There're multiple Peter Riggs. Without having any idea what he looks like, I can only guess his age. He was on vacation with his wife and college-age children, so he must be at least mid-sixties or early seventies by now.

What if he's not alive?

The article mentioned he was jogging on the beach when he found Blair.

I scroll through various runners' groups using his name, nothing.

Looking in San Diego, I Google his name and scan through the options. It amazes me how one search engine can pull up so much information on any person. This would've made my history papers a cinch to complete.

One Peter is a retired teacher, another a police officer, one an internal med doctor.

The retired teacher's deceased. I find the obituary, breathing a sigh of relief when it says he had no kids of his own, only parakeets.

I doubt it's a police officer, since I figured the article would have mentioned his profession as law enforcement.

CLICKING on Peter Riggs in San Diego, California, I pull up his specialty clinic.

There's a man in his mid-forties on the website. My heart sinks, but I decide it couldn't hurt to ask. Maybe they're related?

There's a phone number listed. I sit back on the floor against the bed, letting it ring as I pray this isn't a wild goose chase. Houston comes and lays beside me, his head on my knee.

A woman with a high-pitched voice answers. "Hi, Riggs, Foster, and Chaparral Internists. How can we help you?"

"Hi, I wanted to speak to Dr. Riggs?"

"He doesn't start seeing patients for another hour. I don't believe he's in the office yet, but let me check." She holds a hand over the receiver. I hear muffled yelling, her voice comes back on the line. "Nope, should be here in the next thirty minutes or so."

"Do you know if by any chance his father is around?"

"Dr. Riggs?"

"Yeah – is he also a doctor?"

"He was a dentist."

"*Was?*" I clench my hands around the receiver.

"He's retired, lives in La Jolla,"

I exhale. "It's urgent I get in touch with him. Can you please have Dr. Riggs call me as soon as he gets in?

She pauses. "He has a full schedule today, but I can certainly give him the message."

"Thank you, just tell him it's about a missing person." I leave the house phone number and hang up.

Expecting to not hear from him for a couple of days if ever, I'm surprised when my cell rings with an unknown caller forty minutes later. I've just come back from throwing a load of laundry in the washer, something I had to be taught to do with the savvy machine Max has.

"Hi, this is Peter Riggs calling for Blair..."

"Hi Peter, my name is Blair Bellamy. I met your father on the beach in 1998 while on vacation." I hastily swallow the word. An unexplained disappearance on a beach that results in your life changing doesn't justify the word 'vacation.'

I explain the situation to him. "I just wanted to contact your father, see if he has any details or recollection of that day. I want to follow up as she still hasn't been found."

"Ah, yes, I remember us going to Oahu and Maui then. Sure, let me give you his number. Can you wait a couple minutes? I just want to give him a heads-up you'll be calling."

"Sure," I say. "And thanks."

I PACE THE BARE FLOORS, the hardwood squeaking as I nervously walk off my anxiety. Houston stares at me with his big brown eyes. What if he doesn't remember my sister?

There's no reason he would. To him, we were dumb teenagers making stupid decisions.

Giving Dr. Riggs a fifteen-minute head start to talk to his dad, I dial the number.

He picks up on the first ring. "I've been expecting a call all these years," he whistles.

I'M BEWILDERED. "You have? No one's ever contacted you?"

"No, only the news."

I PRETEND TO BE BLAIR, acting like I'm still hunting for my long-lost sister.

"I wondered what happened to you," he muses. "It was such a weird situation."

"Did you see the articles on my missing sister?"

"Yeah, but we left two days later. I left the police a message that I found you passed out on the beach, but no one returned my call. I figured they either found her or didn't think it was necessary." He sighs. "I should've kept up on it, but I came back home and I'm sorry...life got in the way."

There's a lull.

Peter mentions the 'roofies.'

I'm appalled to read police were concerned my sister

was raped. I might've been trapped, but I didn't want her to have the same fate. The other news channels mention she was drugged. A test upheld it was Rohypnol. "That makes sense with how disoriented you were," he says. "A young girl passed out on the beach is more than a night of drinking."

"Is there anything you remember that you would have told the police now?"

"You were topless. Had lost your shoes and purse."

"Yeah, I remember that," I lie.

"That day I know you got spooked because you thought I was turning you in to the police. I just want you to know – I was only calling the Coast Guard office. If your sister drowned, I wanted them to know she was potentially at risk."

Blair had probably freaked out. "Yeah, we had fake IDs and were worried about getting into trouble."

"But your father – I did speak to him."

"My father?"

"Yeah, I had left him a voicemail when I was at the airport waiting to fly back home. When you used my cell to call their landline, their number was in the call log."

"What did he say?"

"That you were fine but your sister was missing." He continues. "I told him to call me if they needed anything. I explained how I found you. You know, I'm really sorry about your father..." There's a long pause as I wait for him to resume, but the silence drags on, like he's giving me a chance to speak.

"The only reason I know he passed away was because I called to talk to him about a trip I took back to Oahu. This was a couple of years later, a man I took surf lessons from mentioned your missing sister."

My eyes blur as I stop pacing, sitting down on the bed with a thud.

Daddy's dead? I grip the phone, trying not to sob before we hang up.

All I can sputter is, "Really?"

"The guy said he used to live in Honolulu but was sent back home after his best friend was under suspicion for her disappearance. His family was worried he was caught up in a bad crowd."

Forcing myself to pull it together, I ask. "Nicholas Mercer?"

"Yes, that's him."

"What's he doing now?" I wonder out loud.

"Said he lives in Utah. This was years ago, though. Still was coming in the summer months to work so he could continue to surf. Only way his family would let him come back to Oahu. He had to earn money for school."

I thank Peter for his information, condolences, and hang up, stunned.

MY DADDY...YOU would think he'd be the first person I'd search online for information about but I can't, not at the moment.

Swallowing bile and regret, I look instead for Nicholas Mercer, finding a private practice with his name in Salt Lake City. So he did become a dentist, joining the family business. He's married with two children. I wouldn't have recognized him, his frame filled-out now and his blond hair's balding.

The former head of security at The Waterfront, Mark Matsen, comes up in police interviews. He's no longer with hotel security, retired now but still living on Oahu. He's started his own private investigation services, according to a news article from 2005. One of the detectives that interviewed me at the hospital mentioned him, saying Mark was on vacation in the domestic U.S. but would be extremely interested in talking to me when he got back.

I dial the number listed for him, leaving a message.

Will Loomis surprisingly isn't on social media, but is mentioned repeatedly as a person of interest in almost every piece of information I find on the case.

How did The Mole slip a pill in our drinks if he were sitting in a corner? He could've just picked us out and dropped something in a glass before we were served. It was a fairly busy night and we did both go to the bathroom. I realize how easy targets we were. I wonder how many other girls trust their drinks to complete strangers without realizing the cruel intentions of some.

Who else did we see that night that might have insight? The Mole has to be a regular. Maybe an employee can suggest some repeat customers.

The bartender.

What was his name?

I look at the police report.

David Michael Edwards.

Googling him, I find no social media accounts.

I call The Ocean Club, which is now The Sandlot.

Exhaling, I drum my fingers against the keyboard.

Ah, it makes sense now. A piece of the puzzle comes together. Bridget did disappear from the same spot. So this *is* a preferred hangout for the Mole.

The woman who answers the phone remembers him. "Yeah, I used to be a waitress back then. David's no longer employed here, hasn't been since we switched owners recently."

"I'm an old friend from high school. Can you tell me how to get in touch with him?"

Annoyed, the lady says, "I don't know, have you tried social media?"

"Yeah."

"Let me ask the owner," she says.

"Thanks," I say to empty air.

She puts the phone down, shouting at the top of her lungs at a man named Herb. "K, I'm back." She picks up the receiver. "He quit, moved on to another job."

I consider asking where, but she's already hung up the phone.

41

BLAIR

DRIVING TO OMAHA, I catch the red-eye flight to Oahu, not bothering to tell Priscilla where I'm headed. Mark will be surprised when he gets back from his trip to find out I'm here, but I'm not counting on it as pleasant, since he told me to stay put.

The rental car's nondescript, a boring white sedan with four tires and economy fuel. Blending in's important if I'm going to dredge up the past. I don't bother checking into my hotel, an expensive dump not far from where we stayed all those years ago.

Even in the seven years since I've been here, progress has been ongoing, buildings torn down, renovated, and re-named.

The Waterfront is now owned by a large hotel conglomerate.

THE OCEAN CLUB is now called The Sandlot.

Different decor, more of a hipster vibe, appealing to a younger crowd.

Tentatively I walk by it, headed there to take care of my first order of business. My sandals trek through the sand, the beach filled with families, towels, sandcastles, and vendors. I walk up to the tiki hut, knock-off sunglasses and surf boards dangling precariously from hooks.

"What're you doing here?" His voice cracks, recognizing me instantly. "You know you're supposed to stay five hundred yards from me." He's in his early thirties, aging, and not for the better. His once-muscular stature has been replaced with a gut that hangs over his boardshorts, his t-shirt too short for his height. The sun has worn lines across his bronzed skin, making him look years older than he is. There's a scar down his neck, long and jagged.

I try not to stare, curious where it came from. Did his girlfriend slash him with a knife? Did Bristol defend herself against him?

He's wearing Ray-Bans that he pulls up on his head, incredulous.

I smile sweetly. "That ended years ago."

Timid, he darts his eyes around at the beachgoers. "What do you want from me?" He holds his palms out. "I've told you and everyone else, I don't know anything."

"I want my baby sister back."

"I've told you all I know, the cops, your family..." He shakes his head. "You've ruined my life."

"I ruined your life?" I narrow my eyes, incredulous. "I go on a vacation ten years ago with my sister, and only one of us came home."

"Blair...what did you come here for?"

"Justice."

"What do you want me to do?" He pounds the register. "Confess to a crime I didn't commit? I've been carrying guilt around all these years."

"Yeah, because you're guilty."

"No, just because I was the last one to see her alive doesn't make me a murderer." He looks at the ocean, a lone surfer out on the waves. "And now everyone looks at me like I am one."

"No one even remembers her..." I whisper. "That's the problem."

"Everyone remembers." He looks over his shoulder. "I'm working as a mechanic in a second-rate shop because I can't get a job anywhere."

"You were a felon long before I met you."

"Not with those types of accusations." He motions at the cash register. "I still have to teach surf lessons to make ends meet like when I was twenty."

"You were never charged."

"You wanna get coffee?" Will smirks. "Actually, no, you'll throw the scalding pot in my face."

"No, I'm not going anywhere with you." I say. "I'm watching you, and so are they."

"Who?"

"Why Bridget?"

"Huh?" He purses his lip. "Who's Bridget?"

"Where's Nicholas at?" I ask. "You still friends?"

"None of your damn business."

"He still live on the island?"

"No."

"But he was in dental school."

He shakes his head at me, disgusted. "Are you really that selfish?"

"Huh?"

"You think you're the only one whose life changed when Bristol went missing?"

"No, it ruined my parents' lives, too."

"It affected us all, Blair. We were with both of you that night. We were drinking with you. The last ones to see her." He bites his lip. "We all paid the price, believe me."

"How does one person vanish without a trace?"

Turning on his heel, he checks his clipboard, grabs a wetsuit and a whistle.

"Will?" I yell.

He turns his head, looking over his shoulder.

"It will all end when you confess."

"I'm not giving a false confession, Blair," he hollers. "Now get the fuck away from me before I have your crazy ass put in jail for harassment."

42

BRISTOL

AFTER I GET off the phone, I take Houston for a walk down the street, his eyes watchful and protective. We don't venture out too far, staying on the sidewalk and in plain sight of the neighbor's houses.

Max picks up the baby from the sitter and offers to bring take-out back after work. We eat Chinese food, my stomach still adjusting to an Americanized diet, egg drop soup my choice to avoid getting sick. He tells me about some stray kittens that were found in a cardboard box near the beach. They were dropped off by a concerned citizen at his office, and now he is re-homing them. I offer to make some signs.

We talk about my class and he asks me lots of questions on what I learned. My face burns, I must seem so stupid to him. He doesn't make me feel that way, but I'm self-conscious.

Pulling a box out of the kitchen drawer, he surprises me with my own cell phone, my excitement palpable as I open up what is more savvy than anything I've ever owned.

Thanking him profusely, he gives me a quick tutorial on basic functions.

It's for my safety, he says. "I programmed myself in under 'Animal House.'" We both laugh.

Eyeing his watch, he tickles the baby. "I've gotta get going."

"Do you mind if I take a bath?" I ask him as he stands to put on his jacket.

"Not at all." He smiles at me. "I'm going to catch a movie with Dylan." Dylan's his best friend, him and his wife are both doctors and have let us borrow all their old baby stuff.

I'm relieved to be alone. "Enjoy." I climb the stairs, putting the baby in his bassinet, his breathing even as he slumbers.

SITTING down with the laptop and a glass of sparkling apple juice, the idea of drinking wine nauseating, I look up my father, Bruce Bellamy.

I know he's dead but I couldn't comprehend it earlier. It was such a surprise, researching his death wasn't something I could just do. Reading his obituary, tears stream down my cheeks, not only because of sadness, but because of the cause of death. My mouth gapes when it mentions his blood alcohol content being three times the legal limit. I'd never seen my father take a sip in his life.

Is this what happened after I didn't come home?

Shaking, I tell myself it has nothing to do with me, yet I know deep down, it has everything to do with me. Wasn't it Newton's law that said, *'for every action, there is an opposite and equal reaction'*? My disappearance didn't just affect me negatively, it affected everyone that came in contact with me.

Leaving the door open, I start a bath, adding bubbles and warm water, surprised I can even stomach taking one. The water soothes me, and this is a real jetted tub compared to the metal basin, a different experience entirely, one I can separate.

Sinking down, careful to keep my left arm from getting wet, I lean back slowly.

My mind racing, I gnaw at my finger. The stress Daddy must have been under. Yet I was alive this whole time and *he never knew*.

It's just not fair.

Angrily, I pound my fist quietly into the side of the tub, feeling sorry for myself but trying not to wake the baby. Sobbing, it's as if I'm releasing ten years of frustration and sadness. Ripped away from my family and friends, the four walls a prison, I let it all go, my shoulders shaking, my body trembling underneath the scalding water.

HEARING A NOISE, I hold my breath for a second. The baby isn't making any sounds, the monitor silent beside me. I wonder if Houston's chewing on one of his toys.

Sliding down, I try and make myself invisible as heavy footsteps enter the bedroom, the cherry wood thumping underneath.

HOUSTON BARKS FRANTICALLY.

I LOOK UP, my eyes clouded with tears.

He's standing there, arms crossed, looking at me.

It all comes back to me when I see him.

My heart thuds, the next couple of beats slamming into my chest.

Closing my eyes, I sink lower in the water.

43

BRISTOL

"WHAT DO YOU WANT?" I wipe a tear away with the back of my hand, submerging farther into the bubbles so my nakedness and scars aren't visible. I don't want him to see *all* of the burn marks, judge my past even more than he already must.

"Bristol." He takes a small step into the bathroom, leaning against the frame.

A chill tingles down my spine. "What did you just call me?"

"Your real name." He takes another step towards me, the mirrors foggy from the steam. I stare straight ahead at the glass shower wall in front of me, afraid of him noticing the way my lower lip trembles.

"How did you know?" I whisper, avoiding his pensive gaze.

Max lowers himself to the floor, hands resting on his knees.

Taking pity on me, he doesn't try to make eye contact. "I forgot to show you the 'browser history' option on the computer."

I'm confused. "What does that mean?"

"That I could see what you looked at today." He's nonchalant. "Like a log of every site you've visited, everything you've searched."

"You were spying on me?" I furiously thrust my washcloth in the water, angrily twisting it in a knot.

He holds his head held down in shame. "Bristol, why didn't you tell me what happened to you?"

I'm silent for a minute.

"My name's Bridget."

"Bristol Anne Bellamy." He speaks it slowly, emphasizing my first, middle, and last name. "And you're twenty-seven, almost twenty-eight, definitely not eighteen."

"Because..." I say, "I'm not Bristol anymore."

"But you're not Bridget. We've already established that." He hunches forward. "She's dead, right?"

I shudder. "Please don't say that. Not if I can help it." I try and change the subject. "What happened to the movie?"

"Dylan got called in to work a shift. I was going to see if you wanted to go and we could ask my neighbor to watch the baby."

"I'm not feeling well tonight."

"I know. I can see that."

"I'll leave tomorrow. I can go to the shelter."

"Dammit, Bristol, I don't want you to leave. I just want to know what happened to you, how I can help you, who you are, not the façade, but the person you were before you disappeared. You've left me with more questions than answers since I found you on that trail."

"I don't know *who* I am, don't you get it? I have a name. but I've been presumed dead for a decade and my life stopped at seventeen." I burrow my face in my knees, "I don't have the answers, just questions."

I rise, my hands shaking as I hold the edge of the tub for balance. "I'm trying to find a sick pervert who gets off on murdering girls."

Stepping out, I stomp my wet foot on the bath mat. "I've been removed from life and it's like I fell into a pit of blackness for ten years."

"Is this why you don't want the baby?"

"Don't say it that way, don't *you* dare say it that way." I reach down for a towel, wrapping it tight around my chest. "Will you hand me my robe please?"

Max stands, yanking it from the back of the door. "Is it because the baby belongs to him? Is there guilt so you don't want to keep him, to give him a name?"

"Why should I tell you, so you can judge me?" I'm lashing out at him and it's not fair.

"Bristol..." He starts to reach for my hand, but stops himself, scared he'll spook me and I'll shut down completely.

Whispering, I lean on the bathroom counter, my face contorted in the steamy mirror. "I don't know how to care for myself, let alone him."

"Jesus, Bristol, this is..." He runs a hand through his dark hair. "There are no words. Ten years is a long time." I see tears in his eyes as he gives my shoulder a quick squeeze. "I'll leave you alone." He doesn't shut the door, leaving the room instead, I hear his footsteps trailing back downstairs. "Okay," I say to his back.

My hands quiver, the soft cotton robe drawn to my body. Sinking to the floor, my eyes gaze at the white and grey tile, the sleepy labradoodle that's now perched near the small window in the bathroom my protector. He gallantly raises his head to reinforce this.

A few minutes later, I hear a phone ring downstairs,

hushed voices, and then a door slams shut, the silence impenetrable. I'm paranoid, the connotation I have with doors closing reminds me of The Mole.

I decide to get a cup of tea, noticing a handwritten note beside the stove. Max had to rush to his practice to perform emergency surgery on a dog that's been attacked.

Moving restlessly around the house, I can't seem to quiet my mind and body. The tea kettles whistles, my fingers tapping the gray and white Quartz countertops.

The house phone rings, flashing the word 'private'.

"Blair, it's Mark."

"Mark," I exclaim, pretending to be my sister again. "God, it's good to hear your voice."

"Huh? We just spoke…" He sighs. "Please tell me you didn't disregard what I said."

"Why do you say that?"

"Because I just got back in town and heard Will Loomis called in a complaint to the precinct about you."

Wait, what?

What has Blair been doing all this time?

Mark pierces the dead air. "He can get that restraining order reinstated if you keep harassing him."

Lamely, I respond. "Sure."

"Why did you leave me a Hawaii number to call back?" He asks. "If this is about Bridget, we're waiting for forensics. I don't have any updates for you yet."

Wait, Bridget was found? I double over, heaving, as I barely make it to the sink in time to puke. Holding the phone from my ear, I cough and spit up, unable to catch my breath.

"You okay?" I hear him echo into the receiver.

Taking a gulp of tap water, I swallow hard. "Yeah," I whisper.

"There was a girl at a local hospital here but I haven't had a chance to interview her...heard it was a weird situation. She's left the hospital, but the detectives know where she is." He's pensive. "I'll get in touch with her."

"No need. I can fill you in," I offer.

"I knew it." Mark exhales. "You never listen. You're impossible. I told you to wait for my call."

"I couldn't, it's my sister." I tap my fingers impatiently on the counter. "Can you by any chance meet tonight?" I add. "Since I'm in town."

After the shock of my unexpected arrival to the island wears off, along with some choice cuss words on Mark's part, we agree to meet in an hour. Calling Laura the next-door neighbor, who has met the baby a few times, I ask if she'd be okay sitting at the house while he sleeps. Max trusts her implicitly, an older lady that's pushing seventy. She's Houston's dog-sitter and has seven grandchildren between her two kids. She's delighted, telling me she just started a new book and can easily read from over here.

I throw on clothing I don't care to wear –a black dress and strappy leather sandals. Staring at my reflection, weird since for so long I went without the ability to look at myself, I twist my hair up into a knot and swipe on mauve-colored lipstick. It takes a couple tries, I have to wipe it off and reapply, my hands shaking as I trace the outline of my lips. It's more than beginner's nerves, it's dread at hearing about Bridget. Discomfort at going back to the defunct bar, now *The Sandlot.*

I consider leaving Max a note, but I shoot him a quick text instead about where I'm going. If I can speak with Mark in person and determine commonalities between the other missing girls and The Mole, I'll be off to a good start in finding his identity. The popular bar has come up multiple times as a prime locale for disappearances. Even with a name change, maybe the atmosphere will jog memories I've buried for so long.

After greeting Laura when she knocks, I wait on the porch for my ride. Wiping my increasingly sweaty palms on my dress, I wait for a taxi to pick me up. I think about my father, driving aimlessly down the street, alcohol replacing God as his vice. His staunch belief in religion wasn't steadfast enough, my absence causing him to deviate from his path. The thought of him hurting and alone is enough to make me want to curl up in a ball and cry.

44

BRISTOL

I MEET him at a small table in the corner of the bar, The Sandlot is now more of a younger crowd, mid-twenties to early-thirties, the diverse crowd last time replaced by a younger generation. The décor has changed just like the name–from an aquarium and coral reef to a surfer's paradise. Boards from surfing greats like Kelly Slater and Laird Hamilton hang above the bar. The walls are painted in various colors of blue, the paint pantomiming the arches of a rolling wave, at different points the brush ripples off into a breaker effect.

Tonight is live music, punk rockers with bright-colored faux hawks and a preference for leather. They scream into the microphone, their words sound like a never-ending tantrum.

I've never met Mark before, and his shiny bald head and muscular arms fit the career of a security guard, P.I., and ex-military, I learn.

"Mark," I shout over the music.

He turns, his eyes registering confusion. I'm not my dark-haired sister. I'm the one he's been searching for.

Staring in disbelief, his eyes trained on my injured arm. "What the..." Tilting his head, "Bristol? It can't be."

I stand, shaking his hand, "Bristol." It's been so long since I've said my name out loud, it sounds strange to me.

"Are you fucking with me?" He's serious, his eyes moistening. "You better show me some ID."

"I don't have it." I shrug. "It disappeared when I did."

"Is this a joke?" He doesn't know whether to stay or leave.

"Mine's missing, but this is better." Max had given Bridget's ID back to me. I pull it out of my clutch, sliding it across to him. He stares at her picture in shock. "You know her?"

Ignoring his question, I ask. "What happened to her? Where was she found?"

"Near lava rocks, an area called Mermaid Cave."

I brace myself, wringing my hands in my lap. "That was me."

He's puzzled. "You were impersonating her at the hospital?"

"At the beginning." I take a long inhale. "She needs our help," I explain. "She's still locked in a room." His undivided attention's fixated on me as I tell him why I pretended to be her at the hospital. We talk, his familiarity with my case staggering. He's well-versed on the other missing individuals on the island, having lived here so long.

"Have you seen Blair yet?" he asks. "She's been your biggest advocate."

I swallow a lump. "No."

Disappointment crosses his face. "Oh, that's too bad. She's really busted her ass to try and find you. She's never given up hope. I think that's part of why she stayed in Nebraska, it was the only home you both knew."

"What do you mean?" I'm baffled. "Isn't she in Cali? Married with kids?"

"Ha!" He pounds the table with his fist. "No, she's still there. Different town, but still there. She never left."

Settling back in my chair, I feel defeated. "Crap."

"What now?"

"I want to see her and my mom." I brush a piece of hair behind my ear that's fallen out of my twist. "But I need to find Bridget first. If not, she'll die. Either of starvation or from him. He's out there still."

"Why didn't you give him up when you escaped?"

"That's the problem. I never saw where I was being held. It could've been anywhere," I explain. "I wanna tie up this mess and reunite with my family knowing he can't separate us again."

"You say 'him'. So it was a 'he' and you can describe him?"

"Yeah, he never wore a mask or hid his appearance," I describe his yellow tooth, the mole, his blue eyes, sandy hair.

"Did you ever see anyone else?" He plays with the menu in his hand, turning it over, picking it up, putting it down. "Could he have had help?"

"Nope." I shrug. "It was only ever him."

Describing the room in detail as he jots notes on a pad of paper, his fingers try to keep up with my observations. I tell him about the pond and gravesite, remembering the salvage cars and litter. "It was underground," I muse. "At least, it felt that way."

"That's the tricky part. There are so many places, Blair."

"I know. I want to help."

"I hear you."

"What about the other missing girls on the island?"

"There have been lots. Most are runaways that come back or leave permanently. Issues at home, boyfriend troubles, or their own wanderlust."

"But what about the ones that aren't missing on purpose?"

"There have been a couple. I've followed their cases. I tend to hunt for scumbag parents that owe child support or watch spouses that're cheating, not missing girls."

"The fake IDs we had were from two girls, one was Leslie Billings, can you check into her?" I snap my fingers. "The other's Haley, Haley Pritchett."

"I'll look into it," he promises.

The next morning, he calls me with news. Leslie Billings *is* a missing person. No one's seen or heard from her in years.

But she didn't get reported by her family.

She was living in rural Washington in 1992 when she decided to travel to Hawaii for a fresh start at eighteen.

"The reason she never came up as a missing person is because she got married after spending two months in Hawaii. She eloped with an Hawaiian native, her last name changed to Alana. She filed the paperwork but they split, so she took a job at a car dealership here to save money to go back to Washington. She never made it back as far as we know. As for Haley, she's alive, I found her on LinkedIn. She's a massage therapist at a resort in Aspen, Colorado."

"She doesn't fit his type anyway. She's dark-haired."

"True," he agrees.

"How did Leslie come up missing?"

"She didn't show up at the dealership for work. They fired her for no call, no show but also reported her missing."

"Which one?" I ask.

He pauses, keys clicking on his keyboard. "Island Chevy."

My blood turns to ice, the phone heavy in my hand.

"Say it again?" I murmur, gripping the counter.

"Island Chevy, about five minutes from downtown." The cream-colored business card comes to mind.

"There was a card, a business card, in the trash of the bathroom." I fill Mark in on the name of the salesman, Dean Morgan.

"Let's go visit the dealership." Mark's already on it. "He's still working there, his name pops up on their website."

MAX ASKS me where I'm headed, Mark screeching to a halt in a black Dodge Charger in front of the house. "I'm going on an errand," I say, telling him about my meeting with Mark. His hands twist nervously as I tell him I went back to the bar I disappeared from.

"BE CAREFUL," he warns. "You sure you don't need me to go with?"

"I'm going with a retired P.I. that knows my sister."

His gaze sharpens. "Ok, but I'll be at my practice. Call me if you need a ride back or moral support." He gives my shoulder a gentle pat. "Good luck."

I slide into the passenger seat and we speed off, Mark's hands tense on the wheel. We're both lost in our thoughts, wondering if this will lead to a break in the case.

"Dean?" We ask the greeter at the dealership. New cars fill the showroom, the smell of leather and tire wax making me queasy. I'm amazed at all the options and bells and whistles you can buy, but the price tags seem ludicrous.

He's not what I expect, alligator cowboy boots, a brass belt buckle, and a ten-gallon hat. He'd be more at home in the southwest. "Hiya, I'm Dean." He's got a toothpick hanging out of the left side of his mouth. "You get a recommendation for me from a friend?'

"Yeah," Mark says, "I'm trying to remember his name..." He snaps his fingers.

"Your friend?" Dean hee-haws. "Must not be a good one."

"How long have you been in the car business?" Mark asks.

"Twenty-five years." He stands proud. "I retire next year."

"Then I'm glad we caught you," Mark says. "We don't want to buy a car just yet, but we need your help."

"I hear that one all the time." Dean shrugs. "Come into my office."

It's about the size of a closet, and the room makes me claustrophobic. Mark notices, leaving the door open and motioning for me stand in the doorway. He sits on a folding chair in the makeshift office, Dean's desk littered with papers and junk, more Styrofoam coffee cups and fast food paper bags than I can count.

"Explain your business." Dean crosses a leg, ignoring the mess and the buzzing desk phone. I tell Dean the circumstances as he looks in horror at my level gaze.

"All be dammit," he wipes a brow. "Any idea the type of car he has or had?"

"No."

He's crestfallen.

"BUT I CAN DESCRIBE HIM." I give all the details I remember, Dean tapping his boot against the rickety desk, shaking his head, frustrated. "Nobody comes to mind."

"What about Leslie Billings or Leslie Alana?" Mark tries another angle. "She worked here in the early nineties as a receptionist."

"Nope. Doesn't ring a bell."

"She stopped showing up for work." Mark pulls a bulletin of her out of his notepad, it's crumpled up.

"Blonde, blue-eyed?" He scans the black and white copy. "Yep, she was young. Hell, I was too back then." He raises his eyebrows.

"Is there any way to find out what she did here?" Mark asks. "What customers she might've come in contact with, title work, etc.?"

"From then?" Dean shrugs. "Afraid not."

I put my hands on my hips in defeat. "Then how will we ever catch this creep?"

"Let me ask Bill, the service manager. He's been here even longer than I have." Dean stands, knocking off a sheaf of papers on his desk. "Follow me."

Dean leads the way and I follow, my heels clicking on the tile flooring, then the concrete, as we step into the garage stalls where the mechanics work.

An older Hispanic man with a handlebar mustache comes over to greet him, "Dean, what're you doing?"

"Hi George, looking for Bill." George smiles at us, a gold crown winking at me. He points underneath one of the vehicles being serviced. I step around an oil can, almost tripping, when a man says, "You shouldn't be back here."

The voice sounds familiar.

I turn, locking eyes with Will Loomis.

My eyes widen in surprise. "Will?"

He drops the wrench he's holding, it clangs to the ground.

"Bristol?" He looks at me like I'm a ghost coming back to haunt him after all these years.

"Yeah."

"Is that really you?"

"Yes."

"How did..." His bronzed face drains of color. "When did..."

"It was recent..."

"We thought..."

I shake my head. "I know."

"Your sis was asking about you the other day." He stares at me, glued to my reaction. "When was the last time you spoke to her?"

"Blair?" Astonished, I ask, "You saw her?"

He's puzzled. "Yeah, she stopped by the surf hut."

"She's here?" I can't contain my excitement.

"Yeah, she was." He wipes his hands on the rag. "She's been on my trail since you went away. Blamed me for this."

"Oh," I'm speechless. The restraining order must have something to do with it.

"I want to know what happened..." He looks haggard. "Where you've been, why I haven't seen anything on the news or heard from the cops. And here you are, reappearing after all this time."

"Yeah, it's a long story." I don't know how much to tell him, if he'll blow my cover. "I just have some loose ends to tie up and then everyone will know."

"Know what?"

"That I'm alive."

"No one knows?"

I don't answer, my face must give me away. He takes a

deep breath. "Do you know who..."

I lie. "No, I don't."

"Where're you staying?" He scrunches his face up. "I'd like to at least have coffee or something...I need your help... and maybe I can help you."

"My help?"

"To clear my name." He stares at the floor. "No one believes I didn't hurt you. I get you're on your own mission but I've...it's been...rough, is an understatement."

Quickly, he adds, "Not to minimize what's happened to you. Please don't think I'm making light of what happened... I just don't know what happened."

I think about what Will just said about us helping each other. He knows the island and he knows the bar scene, maybe even some of the old employees from The Ocean Club.

Time's not on my side, but I've never had the opportunity to talk to him about the night I went missing. Maybe he can put some of the pieces together for me and we can fill in the blanks together.

Bridget's counting on it.

Maybe other girls as well.

"OKAY," I bite my lip, "let's get together." He pulls a pen out of his work pocket. I give him my number. He doesn't bother with a piece of paper, writing it on his hand.

He nods. "Thank you."

"One condition," I hold up a finger, "no one's to know I'm not missing. Let me tell everyone on my own time."

"Yeah, sure, that's fair." He turns to go back to work, stopping short. He turns back around. "Bristol?"

"Yeah?"

"I'm really happy you're safe." His smile finally reaches the creases, a genuine one. "I've thought about you a lot over the years. I shouldn't have left you alone in your hotel room."

A lump settles in my throat, I can only nod.

He heads back to a waiting vehicle, his shoulders straight instead of hunched over, a bounce in his step. I consider how he must feel, living a life where you're guilty based on public perception because you happened to be in the wrong place at the wrong time.

I WATCH Dean talking to Bill, both are motioning towards the front and pointing to the outside.

"What's happening?" I whisper in Mark's ear.

"Unfortunately jack shit."

Bill greets us, his recollection about the same as Dean's. He remembers Leslie, but he doesn't know what happened to her or anything about her life.

AS I'M LEAVING, Will catches up to me again. Mark walks on ahead, his sunglasses back on his face. I turn to him. "Hey."

"You wanna grab a drink tonight?" Seeing the look on my face, he rubs a hand through his hair. "Shit, I'm sorry, Bristol. A coffee."

A small step back. "I didn't mean to imply anything."

Waving my hand in front of my face, my cheeks burning. Feeling like a socially-awkward freak, I nod.

"Meet you at Zedd's near The Waterfront. They're open until ten. You wanna meet there at eight?"

"Sure." The sooner, the better, I think.

45

BRISTOL

MARK DROPS me back off at Max's. I don't bother to mention to Mark I'm going to see Will later. The baby and Max are gone when I return home. He left a note to call him at the clinic. He sometimes takes the baby with him to hang out while doing paperwork, Houston even has a dog bed there.

I call Max and tell him about my day. "How's the baby?" I ask.

"Him and Houston are bonding, both are checking in clients and learning how to take over the biz." I laugh, thinking of a baby and dog at the front desk, greeting the 'patients' a.k.a. animals who also can't speak. A conversation in baby talk or loud barking and whining.

"It's nice to hear you laugh," Max grins through the phone. "What's on your agenda the rest of the day?

"I'm going to go grab coffee with an old friend tonight," I say.

"You have friends on the island?"

"Yeah, from when I was on vacation."

"Which place? I can give some recommendations if you need one."

"Place called Zedd's. By The Waterfront."

"Zedd's?" He pauses for a second. "I think that coffee shop closed last year. Are you sure?"

"Yep, oh well, if it did, we can always go somewhere else." I shrug.

I hear noises in the background. Lowering his voice, he murmurs, "Hey, I gotta go."

"Okay, see you later." I say.

I start to put down the phone when he offers, "Do you need a ride?"

"No, but thanks. I'm grabbing the trolley that goes around Waikiki Beach. I checked the schedule and should be good."

TAKING A QUICK SHOWER, I eat a light meal, the weight slowly starting to come back on. I'll be going back to the nutritionist in the next couple of weeks to check my progress.

The trolley's actually a double-decker bus. I enjoy sitting on top, the open air calms me, contrary to the room and the four walls that kept me hostage. Heading to the beach early, I stop in a few shops, no particular agenda in mind, just enjoying the sun and people-watching, a new favorite pastime.

A couple minutes before eight, I head to Zedd's, my sandals clicking on the sidewalk as I head to the side entrance. The parking lot's empty tonight. My eyes scan my surroundings, always on the lookout.

"Hey," Will steps out of the shadows. "I don't want to scare you."

I give him my hand, and he shakes it solemnly.

"I just realized this place closed." He shifts from one foot to the other. "I can't keep up with the constant change in real estate." Holding his keys, he points down the street. "You wanna hop in with me? We'll just go to the Starbucks up the road."

Hesitating, I see him giving me a sideways glance.

I don't want to seem skittish, or like I believe he had any part in my disappearance. After all, he wasn't the one in the room with me. I feel stupid for even questioning his innocence.

"Are you still surfing?" I ask as he opens the passenger door of his hot rod for me. I slide in, inhaling the smell of air freshener, stale French fries, and marijuana. His car's filled with empty burger wrappers and napkins, a lighter in the console.

He laughs. "Yeah, not as much for fun, still some lessons, but life gets in the way, especially when you pay bills and gotta act grown up."

We drive down the street, the windows down, the breeze from the Pacific blowing through my hair as I watch the people and streetlamps pass. Will pulls into the Starbucks, my body letting out an internal sigh. I instantly relax – people are inside, some tied to their laptops, others deep in conversation.

Ever the gentleman, he helps me out of the car, walking behind me to the entrance. Halfway there, he pauses and drops down to the ground. Examining his shoelaces, he hollers out to me, "Hey, hold on a sec. Let me get these tied."

I stop and turn around, heading back to him.

"Okay, got it." He stands, brushing his hands on his jeans. "All set."

I'm starting to re-trace my steps when I feel a sharp yank from behind, my hair pulled back roughly, his hand around my neck, a Taser pressed underneath my chin.

STUNNED, I glance over my shoulder at him.

His eyes narrow. "Turn around, get back in the vehicle," he murmurs near my ear, his breath warm and alcohol-scented.

Without making a sound, I turn, passively walking back to the car.

He holds the door again, this time forcefully pushing me in, my head thunking the roof.

"We thought you were dead." He beats his fist on the dash. "He *said* you were dead."

The engine roars to life and he backs out of the spot, hanging a left at the traffic signal. I slide my fingers around the handle, prepared to open it at the red light.

Gripping it for life, I push frantically as we start to idle. It doesn't budge.

Aggressive, I nudge it again, slamming my fist against it, hysteria bubbling over.

Will turns the radio up, blaring AC/DC. "It doesn't open from the inside. Sorry."

I scream, his hand reaching out to choke me. "Shut the fuck up." He squeezes. "You're way too high-maintenance."

"I don't understand..." I cry out. "You're involved?"

He sings along to the music, ignoring my question, hands tapping the steering wheel.

"How? Why?" I ask, my shoulder slamming against the window.

"Money." He shrugs. "And I get to bang pretty young things all the time. That never gets old."

"Who is it?" I'm baffled. "You left me at the hotel..."

"Yes, I did," he grins, "and he followed. I gave him your room key so I could exit and he could enter. Always works like a charm."

"The Mole?"

"Who?" He's confused. "You mean David?"

David. David. Who's David? I don't know a David.

Wait, the bartender from *The Ocean Club*?

My heart beats rapidly, imagining the way he smoothly slid the drink across to me, asking how I liked it, never considering our bartender to be the crux of a kidnapping scheme.

Palms sweating, I wipe them on my thighs, feeling stupid. He was never perched in the corner and I never thought to put two and two together. He concocted our drinks, but I never thought of him as a suspect.

"MONEY, what does money have to do with this?" I ask. "Did my parents pay you a ransom?" I remember Bridget mentioning her rich parents, but mine certainly aren't.

The Mole's obsessed with girls that look like his dead twin – is Will aware of this?

"Sometimes we split the reward money, or ransom from the parents. It's a profitable little racket." He eyes the rear view. "Plus David rewards me with bonuses for helping."

"What about Nicholas?"

"What about him? He's married and lives in Utah."

"Does he know?"

"He knows enough to stay away." He speeds up, getting on an entrance ramp. "You excited to go back home?"

"Home?" I'm doubtful. "You're taking me home?"

"Yeah," he winks, "back to David."

I pound on the door, hurling myself at the metal, screaming in vain. Traffic crowds around us, fairly light, but I still try to make eye contact with other drivers as they whiz by us.

"Scream, baby, no one can hear you."

"So he was right when he said you drugged girls?" I lean my head between my knees.

"Totally, but he helps. Those IDs we sold you...that's my cue to him on who to go after."

"What?"

"Yeah, I give potential girls the missing girls' IDs. That way he knows who to continue to drug."

"You drugged us first?"

"Nah, David has final say. He has his own type of girl so we just get you good and ready for him. You and your sis were already drunken sluts by the time he saw you. You both wanted to jump our bones." He pats my hand. "You really should watch who makes your drinks. I tell the newbies that all the time."

My phone is in my purse, vibrating. I pray he doesn't notice, hoping I can dial 9-1-1 before it's too late.

"There's a lot of girls." I look at the side of his face. "You would've had to start at a young age."

"David's been doing this solo." He turns the radio down. "He's a sick fuck, losing his mom and sister, but he cut me in to the profits, so I turn a blind eye as long as I get paid. I don't ask what he does. Don't ask, don't tell."

He slides his hand up my leg. "You're looking a bit haggard though. Maybe he can slow down this time."

I plead, "Don't make me go back."

"Not my choice."

"Yes, it is. Please," I beg. "Let's talk about this. What if I can get you some money? If it's just about the money, we can figure it out. I know we can."

"Bristol," he squeezes my chin until it hurts. "It's too late. If I don't take you back to him, you'll get us caught."

Wondering if I can sneak my hand into my purse, I decide to make conversation with Will, get him to focus on talking to me about what's been going on for the last decade. He needs to be distracted in order for me to have a chance.

If not, this will be my last taste of freedom. Permanently.

46

BLAIR

I CALL MARK, his voicemail picks up, instructing me to leave my name and number.

Leaving a message, I tell him I'm in town. I don't expect him to call back, a bitter pill to swallow that he thinks I'm still a screw-up.

Setting my phone on the counter of the hotel bar, I sip a Pepsi, content not to drink alcohol, eyeing the chic decor and modern lighting.

My cell vibrates in front of me, shaking in place.

"Hello?"

"Hey, it's me." Mark says.

"Hi, how are you?" I lower my voice. "I'm sorry..." I apologize. "I know I've been a pain in the ass."

"We're okay, Blair." He's resigned. "I just worry about you."

"I know."

Silence.

"I have some news. Gotta make sure you're sitting down first." He's animated as he says this. "Are you ready?"

Mentally I prepare myself for bad news. "Yeah...it's not good, is it?"

"You're never going to believe it."

"Mark, just tell me."

A long pause. "I spoke to your sister."

"What do you mean, *you spoke* to Bristol?" My mouth drops to the floor. The bar stool's sliding underneath me. I lose my balance, catching the edge right before I topple over.

"Mark, you can't play with my emotions like this." I grip the counter as if it can provide life support.

"It's even better. I *saw* her." His voice breaks, emotions overcoming him. "She's alive."

Relieved, I sob and yell at the same time, "Oh my God, are you serious?" I want to sing from the rooftops, break out in dance moves. The other patrons stare at me with curious glances. The bartender checks to see if there's a problem with my drink.

"Where is she?" I'm a tad wounded, wondering why she wouldn't have contacted me first. She probably resents me for leaving her that night. I can't blame her for feeling that way.

He reads my mind. "It's not anything negative. She's trying to catch her kidnapper before he hurts anyone else."

"He's not dead?" My body goes cold. "Who is it? Is there more than one?"

"Whoa, slow down, only one she knows of." He sighs, "But he's alive and has another girl, Bridget Masterson."

"You're letting her try and find him?" My face goes ashen. "You can't be serious, Mark."

"MARK?" I repeat. "Tell me she's not doing this alone."

"She's the only one who knows who it is."

"How dare you?" I cry. "She's my sister, and I already lost her once."

"I'm keeping tabs on her, she just doesn't know it."

"Oh, really, and where is she now?"

"I'd think at home with her friend."

The last remaining color drains from my cheeks. "What friend? What the hell is wrong with you?" I'm about to hang up on him, my anger piquing.

"Blair...she's trying to focus on getting well." He's firm. "She's going to need your support, not your judgment."

"It's not him?" I pause for a minute, clenching and unclenching my fists. "Fine," I concede.

"Good." He whistles. "You'll be reunited with her soon enough."

"Right now's not soon enough." I mutter under my breath.

He promises to call tomorrow, but something I can't put my finger on makes me anxious. Maybe it's the fact she's alive and I want to hold her but I can't.

If I need to reach her, I don't have her number.

Or maybe it's the realization I haven't seen her in ten years and she's still missing when she should be sitting in front of me right now.

I can't sit still.

Swallowing the last of my pop, I leave cash on the bar and head out.

If my sister's on the hunt for her kidnapper, I want to be the one to help. Dammit, she doesn't need to go it alone. We're a team, even if we haven't been in the same room.

I TEXT MARK, relieved when he gives me the address for her present location. Knowing I won't be able to sleep, I decide to scout out the location. A pretty two-story with large windows and a wrap-around porch beckons from a quiet, dead-end street.

Whose place is this? I wonder.

Maybe it's a women's halfway house or something.

Curious, I park down the street, leaving my white rental car in front of a neighbor's house. There's a man in the window, cooing to a baby that's not having it, the wails enough to make the curly-haired dog crawl underneath the coffee table with a sigh.

Peeking in the window, I stare, his eyes are a dead ringer for Bristol's.

Wait...

No.

How long has she been free?

Is this her boyfriend or husband?

I'm frantically trying to shoot off a text to Mark while crouching down beneath pink and orange hibiscus flowers that line the walkway. An overflowing bush scratches against my legs when the red front door swings open with a flourish.

A porch light flips on, illuminating the front steps and wrap-around porch.

Dropping to my knees, I hold my breath.

"Can I help you?" A man stands in the shadows, the baby on his hip, a phone in hand.

I freeze, unsure how to respond.

"Fine, then I'm calling the police." He waves the cord-less in my face.

"Have it your way." Dialing, he presses two buttons

before I shriek, "Wait," bouncing up. Waving my hands in the arm, I motion for him to hang up the phone.

He disconnects, waiting for me to speak.

"Is that your baby?"

"Excuse me?" He frowns. "Are you a reporter? Did Channel Eight send you?"

"The eyes...the nose...they look like my sister's..."

"Your sister?'

"Yeah." I brush my hands on my jeans. "My sister."

"*Who* is?" His snarl turns to a tight-lipped stare.

"Bristol."

"Bristol what?" He's testing me.

"Bristol Anne Bellamy."

He takes a couple steps closer to the edge of the porch. "Blair?"

"Uh-huh."

"Do you want to come in?"

"Very much." I nod, smoothing my hands over my unkempt hair. He backs up a couple steps, waiting for me to walk around him. His eyes scan my face as he points to the front door.

Pausing inside the foyer, I breathe aromas of cinnamon and laundry detergent. The smells give me a feeling of comfort, that Bristol must be all right if she's coming home to this.

The man steps in behind me, shutting the door. "Go ahead and have a seat in the dining room." Realizing he hasn't given me his name, he adds, "Oh, I'm Max Fletcher by the way."

"WHAT'S this little guy's name?" I reach out for the baby's tiny fingers. He can't be very old, under a year.

"The baby."

"You named a baby 'the baby'?"

"Ask your sis." He stares at me, sadness in his eyes. "I'm not getting in the middle of her decision."

Feeling like I've been slapped, I whisper, "It *is* her baby then?"

I SWALLOW the lump in my throat. The baby reaches for me, and I look to Max for permission. "Do you mind?"

"Not at all." The baby lets out one babbling protest, then settles into my arms. I bounce him on my lap, amazed at his tiny feet and hands.

"I'M GOING to shoot her a text. See if she responds that way." He types a quick message on the screen, hitting 'send'.

"Who is she out with?" I ask. "Who does she know here?"

"Maybe Mark, the investigator? The one I read about in the papers...?" He pauses for a moment, a look of dread settling on his face. He runs a hand through his hair. "I told her this place called Zedd's wasn't open..."

"It's not Mark she's with. I just talked to him."

Looking at me with strained eyes, he grimaces. "I wish she wouldn't have gone. I just...she's not answering. I should've asked her who. I just didn't want to pry."

"Max," I whisper, "she could totally be in trouble." I try not to raise my voice, the baby pausing mid-bounce.

Max stares out in the dark. "Surely she will call if she's worried."

"I don't have a good feeling..." My voice trails off. "If

she's trying to save another girl, I'm worried she'd put herself in harm's way."

Mark. He's the best one to help. He did *say* he was watching her. I reach in my pocket for my cell, dialing him, desperately waiting as each ring drones on with no answer.

I hit re-dial, the shrill rings startling the baby. Moving the phone to my other ear, I'm impatient as voicemail picks up again.

"I'm calling 9-1-1," Max mouths at me.

Trying once more, Mark picks up, breathless.

"Where's Bristol?"

"She was going to coffee...what's wrong?"

"He's got her..." That's all I manage to say before the line goes dead.

"Shit," I mumble. His phone must have died.

Max paces the room, talking to Dispatch, halting to glance in my direction. "Can you watch the baby?" He's frantic. "We can't lose her again."

As much as I want to scream at him to let me go, let me find her, I know that both of us searching isn't going to find her any quicker. He lives here and knows the area, I don't.

Someone needs to stay at the house, watch the baby, stay by the phone.

"Maybe we can track location services?" I hear him say into the receiver. He's throwing on a leather jacket and grabbing his keys at the same time when there's a squeal of tires outside.

It's a black sports car with tinted windows. We both peer out as the horn beeps. Max eyes the car suspiciously, holding up a finger to me, the phone still in hand.

Mark sticks his head out the window, honking again, baseball cap on, hands planted firmly on the wheel. "Let's go," he hollers, "move it."

"I'll be back, lock the door." Max thrusts the phone in my hand, running outside to hop in the Charger. The mailbox lifts off its stake and smashes to the ground as Mark wildly backs out.

I hold my breath, unable to come to terms with the fact that my sister might be missing once again.

47

BRISTOL

WILL SPEEDS DOWN THE FREEWAY, going at least eighty-five. I try and make small talk. "Did you get married?" I ask.

"Yeah, she's a royal pain in the ass," he moans. "Not unlike you and your sis." He stares down at my feet, eyeballing my purse. "That's gotta go, no need for a purse where we're headed." My stomach drops to the floor. I reach forward slowly with my trembling right hand, clawing at my handbag.

"If I would've known David was going to keep you for himself, I should've asked to borrow you." He gives me a snide look. "Don't ever get married, it sucks." Grinning, he goes, "But I guess you won't have a chance. You might be the lucky one."

"Hand me your purse," he instructs again, pointing to it. Reaching down, I purposely flip the purse over, lucky that it's not clasped. Stalling, I nudge it with my foot so items start to scatter on the floor. "What about a picture of my son?"

"Are you kidding me?" He frowns at the road. "All of it.

Now." Waiting until he's distracted, swerving around another car, his eyes focused on a cop cruiser behind us, I make my move. Hunching over in the dark, I carefully slide my cell phone into the sling, where it's hidden underneath my arm, guarded by the dark fabric. Sitting up, I pull my purse onto my lap, nonchalant as I watch him switch lanes.

"What about money?" I ask as he yanks it out of my lap.

"What about it?"

"I'll get you whatever you want, name the amount and my family will pay it. They just want me back."

"Then they would've done it before. David said he couldn't get jack from your parents."

I decide to test David and Will's partnership. "That's not true."

He doesn't take the bait, staring straight ahead.

I continue. "I was there."

"Where?"

"My parents gave him a sum of money."

"Bullshit, then he would've let you go." He gives me a sideways glance. "Nice try."

"No, he wouldn't have. He was just baiting them to get more."

"Nah, David wouldn't take money without splitting it. He's dumb, but not that dumb,"

Will says. "I know where he lives, where he keeps the girls."

"I admire your morals." I'm sarcastic. "Well, I heard the phone call. He made me get on

so he could prove I was alive to them." I shrug. "Why do you think I'm free?"

Sneering, he clenches his fists tightly around the wheel. "Stop talking and shut up or

you'll regret it," He waits until there's a clearing in

traffic before he rolls down his window, tossing my purse into the dark freeway behind us. I glance in the mirror, watching it fly through the air and land with a thud, hitting concrete as my items wait to be smacked by the oncoming vehicles.

Exiting the freeway, he hangs a sharp right, barely slowing down for oncoming traffic. I grab the dash, clutching it with my fingers to hold on.

The gravel drive he turns on winds up to a storage facility, a small house next door to it, the yellow paint peeling, one of the house numbers missing. One of the shutters hangs precariously by a corner. A slight breeze could send it crashing. Distraught, I look around the yard – at the junk cars and miscellaneous equipment scattered across the barren grass. My heart sinks. There are no street lamps, just a dim light next to the storage units, a glass front door locked until business tomorrow. A sign has a number to call for after-hours service or emergencies.

Will screeches to a halt, gravel flying as he parks behind the building, a pond in the background, the moon shining over the murky water. Hands trembling, I'm sure there's a graveyard on the property and bodies of the missing. I was so close to freedom, but now I'm back, Will the common denominator yet again.

A steel door with no windows awaits us at the back entrance. His hand tugs on mine as he pulls me across the front seat and drags me out of the car. Rapping hard on the metal with his knuckles, he waits impatiently for someone to answer.

The Mole a.k.a. David.

Blue eyes, sandy hair, orphan, loner, a bona fide murderer and sociopath.

He smiles longingly when he sees me, the yellow tooth peering out.

Clapping his hands, he opens the door wide, welcoming us to hell.

Will pushes me towards the concrete steps leading down to a basement. The hallway, still nothing but pitch-black darkness, terrifies me.

"You already know where to go," The Mole murmurs, holding his flashlight, the beam illuminating the dingy cement floor.

"Where's Bridget?" I shriek, my fist hitting him in the face.

"Whoa, that's enough." Will picks me up from behind, my legs kicking out, as The Mole slaps me across the face, then carries them like a wheelbarrow from behind.

When The Mole pushes the door to the room open, I shudder, my body rejecting this place once more. He pulls the string on the light bulb, and my eyes automatically dart to the bed. Bridget isn't asleep on the mattress but crumpled on the floor, half-naked, wearing a ripped and dirty blue nightgown that's around her waist.

Will suddenly lets go of me, dropping me to the floor. I rush to her side, kneeling down to touch her face. Even in the dark, I can tell her eyelids are purple and mottled, hair hanging past her shoulders, stringy and unwashed.

She's barely conscious. Her eyes flicker in recognition as I grasp her hand. The nails are chewed up, burn marks on her wrists, welts trailing down her buttocks and legs.

"That's enough," The Mole says. "Get away from her. She's mine." He kicks her in the stomach as he stares at her frail body. "But really, she's dead to me." He turns to Will. "Get rid of her, just dump her. She's not worth it. She's too much trouble."

"She has a rich family," Will says. "Let's at least get some money out of her. We can dump her after they pay us."

"Since when did you get so greedy?" The Mole asks. "If we contact them, it opens us up to being found or traced."

"It's always worked for us," Will admonishes. "This is a girl from a wealthy family and you don't want to try? Something's not right with that. Maybe you've had your own business transactions on the side? Possibly without me?"

"What're you trying to say?" The Mole's tone is sharp. "Are you accusing *me* of lying?" He grabs Will by the collar, violently shaking him. Will's muscular, but The Mole is the same height and his grip is lethal. "Don't forget who's in charge here."

"Put me down." Will moans, clutching his throat until he's released. Will shoves him in return, screaming. "You're an inbred freak that's not fit for the public, trailer trash that's meant to live in this dump forever."

Alarm bells go off in my head. I sneak a quick glance at the door. It's not locked, Will came in after The Mole and didn't slide it shut. My insides clench as I watch the two men argue. The Mole's face is crimson, his eyes pop out of his head.

This is my only shot. I have to make a run for it.

Glancing once more at Bridget, then the men, I turn and sprint, my hands grasping the metal slider, pulling it with all my weight. The door moves creakily, lighter than I expected. It bounces to a stop as I push my way out.

48

BRISTOL

THE HALLWAY'S dark and eerie. The sound of silence reminds me how alone I am down here. I remember the bathroom's to the right, a dead end, the stairs in the opposite direction. I pound them two at a time, my breathing ragged as I grab the door that leads out of the back entrance, the metal one that's my last barricade to freedom.

Gripping the handle, I pull.

It doesn't budge.

I push, then pull, frantic, the door already closed, a self-locking mechanism in place, blocking me from the outside.

Sobs wrack my body as I keep pounding on the steel, knuckles turning bloody. My screams fill the air, feet kicking out to hit the door.

Thrusting my fists with raw determination, a fear of being locked in the room again envelopes me. I take short stabs of breath, yelling at the top of my lungs.

A hand reaches out, violently covering my mouth with a soaked rag, tepid breathing in my ear.

The Mole.

He's yelling at Will to help him.

My eyes wide, I try and strike him in the knees, his strength overpowering my still-underweight body. I'm not going down without a fight.

"Don't take her back to the room." Will's holding a cloth over his nose, red leaking through the thin cotton.

"What do you suggest?" The Mole asks.

"Bury them both."

"I'll load her in my truck and you grab the other one," The Mole instructs. "I'll dump them now." He pulls a metal key ring out, flipping through the keys until he finds the right one.

Unlocking the door, he shoves it open with his boot. My head hits the edge as he carries me under his shoulder, my weight not enough to faze him.

The truck's parked in the gravel, mud and dust covering every square inch. The moon reflects off the rusted rims and faded coating.

He doesn't bother to open the passenger door, choosing to dump me in the bed of the pick-up.

My eyes blur, lids flicker open and shut, drifting in and out of lucidness, my face pressed against the cool metal bottom. I think I hear Will's voice, then feel Bridget's body beside me. When I reach out to grasp her, there's nothing but air. The tires crunch under gravel, speeding along as my head thunks against the hard bottom of the truck bed.

My fingers try and grip the uneven surface, but I bounce and groan, head smacking as we hit a pothole. Rough hands reach out to grab me but I swat them away, wanting to remember my childhood as it swims in front of me, the life I left behind when I went missing.

The sound of sirens shrills in the distance, far away,

then closer. They seem to be moving in my direction, blaring as they come nearer.

I want to cover my ears but I can't, the nylon sling shredded but still awkward. Lying there, I have no idea for how long, my mind drifts in and out of reality and a dream-like state. Memories seem to weave together, crisscrossed as they intersect with various points of my life.

All I want is to just see her once more. Hearing my name called, I groan.

"Bristol."

And again. "Bristol, wake up, it's me, Max." My cheeks feel a cool hand caressing them, my hair's being stroked. I like this dream, I don't want to wake up.

Fighting it, I keep my eyes shut.

"You have to wake up, Bristol. Your baby needs you, your sister needs you." A quick intake of breath. "I need you."

"Max?" I moan, my lids fluttering. "Where's Blair?"

"At home with the baby, waiting for you." He squeezes my hand. "Just like she's always been, waiting patiently for you to come home."

WHEN I OPEN MY EYES, I'm being loaded into an ambulance, a paramedic on either side of the stretcher. My hand clasps around his, tears pooling in both our eyes.

I lift my head, noticing Mark on my other side, speaking to police officers, another stretcher holding Bridget a few feet away. She's semi-conscious, and I lay back, relieved. The police are contacting her parents in Kansas to reunite them with their daughter.

Later on at the hospital, a doctor's examining me for

further injuries, her hands poking and prodding at me behind the closed door.

I hear a giggle, one I haven't heard since I was a teenager.

Straining, I wait to hear it again.

Instantly, I'm transported back to the night we got ready together, before we knew what would happen later on that night, when we had all the time in the world.

Gasping, I jump off the exam table, the doctor speaking to me, her words unimportant.

Thrusting the door open, I cry out, "Blair!"

She's waiting for me, Max by her side.

Our eyes lock, both filling with tears. Reaching out, she touches my skin, caressing her hand over my cheekbones, smoothing my hair, and then just as suddenly, pulls me into a hug, her arms wrapped gently around my neck.

"Please don't ever leave me again," she whispers, her tears running down both of our faces.

"I love you."

She squeezes my good arm. "I love you too."

"Thanks for never giving up on me."

Kissing my cheek, she murmurs, "I couldn't, you're the brat of the family."

We stand like this, holding each other, time standing still as people walk around us, curious stares at our reunion, a moment I never thought would come again.

I hug my sister tight to my chest.

When she stands back from me, smiling, she murmurs, "You have the most beautiful baby boy."

"You've met him?"

"Better, I got to hold him. He's with his old nurse right now. She said she helped deliver him."

Grinning, I kiss her cheek. "Can you believe you're an aunt?"

"I couldn't be happier."

The look on Max's face as he watches Blair and I is priceless. Managing only a nod, he gives me a dazzling smile over her shoulder as I watch him tear up.

49

BRISTOL .

I'M RELIEVED I was found in 2008, not 1998, because technology saved my life. Since I had the phone Max gave me, the authorities were able to track the location services from the cell to Will's vehicle. Lucky for me, I was able to conceal the phone in the sling, or I would've ended up with The Mole in unknown parts, this time dead.

Both The Mole and Will are dead, murder-suicide, both in the pick-up during a high-speed chase with Bridget and I in the bed of the truck.

As the police closed in on them, Will shot and killed The Mole as he drove, the truck crashing into a tree when the bullet reached its trajectory, hitting him in the shoulder and then the heart.

Will turned the gun on himself, straight into his mouth, his death immediate. The keys to the storage complex were found in the glove box and the police were able to connect a web of murders that spanned over twenty years. The Mole acted alone for a long period of time, until he met Will Loomis at The Ocean Club.

Will had a thing for drugging and raping girls until The

Mole busted him, threatening to turn him in. That's how they started to conspire together, both for their own selfish desires.

The police searched the storage complex, the yellow house, and another outbuilding. The underground was really the basement of a four-level storage shed. The 'room' is a storage space in the bottom, complete with sound-proofed walls, ceiling, and floor, a perfect place to ensure no one heard his victims. The Mole lives in the yellow house next to the storage complex, where he grew up with his mother and twin sister until she died in the closet.

A search of the property is grueling – besides the cemetery where his mother Jean and sister Marian are buried, there are three other unidentified sets of bones.

BRIDGET IS RESCUED in the nick of time. A head injury caused brain swelling, and she's rushed to the hospital just in time, lying in a coma for a couple of weeks until she's stabilized and able to breathe on her own.

I stay in the hospital a week this time, the doctors and nurses floored that I'm not only back a second time, but this time as myself, a girl that's been missing for a decade.

After I tell my story to the police, I hear from other victims' families. It's surreal, being one of the only two to get away from The Mole and his sadistic years of kidnapping, rape, and murder.

This all weighs on my shoulders, forcing me to deal with survivor's guilt. Why did I live and they died? I ask myself that, but I have to believe that I saved not only mine, but Bridget's life.

One tragic story comes from a victim's mother who asks to visit me after I'm released from the hospital. Her daughter was one of the first known people to encounter David Michael.

Becky Rundahl was a newlywed, starting out her married life in Honolulu with her husband, a military man. She took a job as a waitress to help with the bills and meet new people. Her life was ordinary but happy until she met him, a regular, who ordered coffee, black, no cream, no sugar, no food.

He'd come in and she'd refill his coffee mug over and over.

First she found him endearing. Plus he'd tip well. She'd confide in him, telling him her problems. With a dead-end job and a husband who was married to the military, and no friends on the island, she struggled with isolation.

Perfect for David Michael.

He listened and never made her feel stupid for complaining, just nodded and agreed with her. At least that's what she wrote in her diary.

One morning, he asked her out for a drink.

She declined, her paltry gold wedding band around her finger.

THE NEXT TIME he invited her and her husband out for a glass of wine.

Even though her gut told her to cancel, she didn't have a reason not see him outside of work hours. Plus, he invited her husband. Nothing could go awry with him present.

Except her husband had a last-minute work emergency.

Frustrated, she went solo. She had too many cocktails, her disappointment lessening with each martini.

She started to feel weird, wicked tired, and he suggested they leave, offering graciously to drop her off at home.

Accepting his ride, they stumbled back to his car, but when she woke up, she wasn't in her bed, she was tied up in the back of his trunk.

David Michael had taken her cross necklace, wearing it as his own, placing the gold chain around his neck. This was after he dumped her body in the Pacific.

She lived in the small room for three years, unable to escape, eventually dying of blunt force trauma. He would wear a fake wedding ring at the bar when he was working. He said it put girls at ease that he wasn't hitting on them.

The poor mother learned all story through a meticulous journal. Becky's cross was found around David's neck when he died.

WHEN THE AUTHORITIES searched his paltry home, they found plastic totes that belonged to each of the victims. The items belonging to the girls were considered his 'lucky charms,' as he referred to them. He would mail the victim's family something that belonged to the missing girl, periodically over time, even having them write letters or in my case, sending personal effects like my tooth.

EPILOGUE - BRISTOL

As soon as I'm cleared to travel, Blair and I are ready to go home, this time together, the thought of her flying alone without me not even a thought. We spend our last weeks in Hawaii having long talks that go into the night, Max sometimes shouting at us playfully to shut up so he can sleep, our giggles traveling down the flight of stairs into his room. We have a lot to catch up on and all I want to hear at the beginning are light-hearted stories, nothing heavy. There'll be lots of time for that later.

Max goes home with us, renting a car at the airport. We drive to our hometown, past a monument at the high school dedicated to me. It's surreal, like having a funeral when you aren't dead. I understand, and am flattered, knowing I wasn't forgotten, even at times when I felt that way. The Mole loved to drive that point across to me – that everyone had moved on from my disappearance.

My relationship with Max is starting to blossom into something else, his sweet nature and calming force a positive influence on me. I don't know what the future holds, but I'm falling in love with him, but on my terms, slow and cautious.

Storm clouds scatter across the sky, cotton balls that blanket the cornfields and flat landscape, the smell and view of the ocean a faraway place. Paradise for others was hell for me. Max drives down the long gravel road, pensive, his first time to the Midwest. The scenery's paradoxical compared to Hawaii. Silence lingers between us as we all focus on our own thoughts, getting into our own heads.

The farmhouse still stands after all these years, for better or worse. It reminds me of when I left, yet it became stagnant, just existing...like I had been in that room.

It's depressing. The land and house seem sad and desolate, the panes of glass stare out, paint peeling, screens torn and ripped, the grass ankle deep and growing. No doubt oncoming rain will bring the blades up even more.

My excitement grows as we drive closer. Anticipation growing, I have to sit on my hands to keep from shoving the car door open and sprinting up the porch. It doesn't matter how it looks from the outside. This is home. *My* home.

What matters is that we're all together again, the first step towards healing as a family.

"You okay?" Max gives me a side glance, his brown eyes troubled.

I nod, scared my voice will break if I speak.

Blair leans over the head rest and touches my shoulder. She's in the back with Bruce, who now has a name – a loving tribute to my father. I love him to pieces. My trepidation as a parent has slowly subsided as I've been given the space to nurture not only myself, but also him, thanks to Max. I took a parenting class and have been coming into my own as a mom. I'm by no means close to perfect, but I know I can give him a good life. My confidence is coming back.

The tires sputter over the gravel as we come to a halt. "Do you want me to come in with you?" Max puts the car in park, idling as he peers over the dash.

"Not yet." I shove the door open. "Give us some time." I squeeze his hand, kissing Bruce in the back, and step out, breathing in clean air and manure.

"Take as long as you need." He holds up his coffee mug and the paper, still preferring it to a tablet. "I've got this to entertain me." Houston is at a doggy hotel, no doubt enjoying a life of leisure with other spoiled pets.

I want to run to the front door, just like I did as a child, coming in to show my daddy fireflies in a jar or the dandelion crown Blair and I made. Except Daddy's no longer alive and Mother's a stranger now.

Will she accept me?

It feels weird to knock, but ten years gone is a long time. Hesitating, I put my fist up to the door. It opens before I even pound on it, signaling I'm home.

Home.

Even in disrepair, it's still where I came from.

My mother stands there, clothes drooping, wilting away before my eyes, gaunt circles under her eyes. "Mom?" I tremble.

Her eyes widen dubiously. She pushes her glasses up as they water, looking back at me with my same eyes, the pupils dilating as she stares at me in fascination, then horror.

Gripping the edge of the door, she stammers. "Is this some

kind of a prank? Please tell me this is real, that you're home."

I grip her hands gently in mine. "Hi Mom, I'm home." She wraps her arms around me, and I smell cinnamon and her Elizabeth Taylor perfume. Looking over her shoulder, I rub her thin frame, the tears cascading down both our cheeks.

Ten years.

My eyes scan the small kitchen in disrepair.

"Come on in, honey." It's been so long since I've heard that out of my mom's mouth. I want to bottle it up, record her voice.

She eyes the black sedan outside. "Did you come alone?"

"No."

"Who is with you?" She's curious, her eyes drifting past me.

"My family," I offer.

"Family?" She takes a step back. "You have a *family*?"

I nod, "And of course, Blair."

"Blair's with you?" She touches a hand to her heart. Waving to the car, she takes that as her cue to come inside, wanting to give us a moment in private to reunite.

Blair takes tentative steps, her sneakers slowly making their way up the stoop. "Hi Priscilla," she says.

"Blair." She reaches for a hug, tears streaming down her cheeks. "I can't believe I've got both my girls back." Blair grabs my arm, pulling me into the shared hug, all three of us crying and holding one another.

"Do they want to come in?" Mom's curious as she glances out the kitchen window.

"In due time."

"Let me put on some coffee." She busies herself,

dumping out the old grounds and refilling the ancient machine.

She looks timeworn, her face lined with wrinkles.

I did this to her, I think bitterly. It was selfish of me to not contact them as soon as I escaped. But a voice inside reminds me what The Mole said about hurting them...and Bridget would've been left to die if he hadn't already killed her.

Scared to ask if my bedroom's the same, I peer at the door that leads to the stairs. "You can go on up." Mom gives me a small smile. "It's the same." She wrings her hands. "It's just like you left it when..." She pulls off a necklace, the thin chain holding a silver key.

I manage a wan smile. "What's this?"

"The key to your room."

Taking the stairs two at a time, they creak underneath my feet. The door has a sturdy metal padlock, the heavy wood still covered with the same poster – one with the Wallflowers, a band I used to like. Bob Dylan's son Jakob is the lead singer.

Holding my breath, I slide the key in the lock, removing the padlock.

Slowly, I turn the handle like it will burn me if I go too fast.

Dust mites float in the air, the hardwood still the original from when we moved in. It's polished to a shine, but I'm in awe that everything remains the same, like no time has passed.

The flowered comforter, my desk, bulletin board and pictures.

I'm seventeen again. It's surreal.

I caress a picture of Blair and I as children, our mouths turned up in a smile, best friends when we were younger.

Until we drifted apart.

My cheerleading squad is captured, me in a split position, pom-poms in hand.

I made varsity my first try freshman year.

An 'A' on a geography quiz hangs from the board, a calendar with school reminders and cheer practice, chorus, and debate team. Student council. Every activity is marked in a different color pen – red, green, purple, blue.

Opening the closet doors, I finger my old clothes, the style now retro, smelling of furniture polish and mothballs, my body a different size and shape than back then. At the bottom of the closet, my shoes are stuffed on a wooden shelf, my tennis shoes, cowboy boots, and sandals.

Old leather yearbooks line the top shelf, the other side's still littered with tubes of nail polish, hair brushes and scrunchies, old gum, and instructions on my driving test. I had taken Driver's Ed at sixteen and was just waiting until I had more time to practice.

My mother's voice drifts from the vent below. She's on the phone, her tone muted so I can't make out her words.

I pull my phone out of my purse, texting Max, letting him know that I need some time. He's going to check into the only motel in town and get settled until we're ready for him to come back.

Before I can sit down, I check our old bathroom, the counter stained, the sink rusted and cracked. The shower's unused, no soap or shampoo, the toilet handle still jangly like it used to be back then.

Why hasn't Mom hired anyone to fix it?

A gold chain catches my eye, and I realize it's my 'B' necklace. With shaking hands, I clasp it around my neck, feeling Daddy's presence as I finger the delicate chain.

Peeking in Blair's room, I expect to see her old twin bed, sky blue comforter, and pictures of her favorite bands.

Instead it's a quilting room. An old wooden desk with a sewing machine and rows of fabrics, yarn, and various projects litter the table next to the window.

Nothing remains of Blair.

A bookshelf sits in the corner, filled with Bible stories and trashy romance novels.

Why aren't there any remnants of her in the house?

My heart sinks and I realize the scrutiny Blair's been under all these years, shouldering the blame. I'm not the only one who has suffered.

Walking back into my room, I sink down on the bed, pulling my shoes off, crossing my feet up under me like I did as a teenager, the clear phone with the rainbow wires still beside the bed on my nightstand.

I drift off to sleep, a pillow tucked underneath my head, imagining my childhood, the smell of the pasture, wildflowers, and our Sunday family dinners of pot roast and gravy, or turkey, corn, and mashed potatoes.

For once, I doze off without looking underneath the bed, in the closet, or peeking over my shoulder.

The Mole's dead. Will's dead.

I can finally rest in peace.

Blair comes in a little bit later, busy downstairs talking to Mom, her footsteps heavy compared to my muted ones.

She softly knocks on the door, peeking her head in. "Bristol?"

"Yeah, in here." I groggily motion for her to come to the

bed. "I can't believe she left it the same," I sigh, patting my side.

"I know." Blair stands awkwardly for a moment, looking around.

"Come lie down with me." I hold the covers out to her. She crawls into bed, my hands resting around her waist, spooning her. Her hair smells of lavender and her sweater of nicotine. But most of all, she smells like my sister.

"I missed us," I whisper. "And I'm so sorry you never left, or felt you couldn't move on."

Her shoulders tremble and I feel wetness on her cheeks, the tears mixing with mine. We cry, our bodies shake as we relive the past ten years in ten minutes, a cleanse as we release our feelings.

Later, our mother tiptoes in.

She manages to climb in between us, her arms wrapping around both of our shoulders, her tiny frame fitting perfectly. "I'm so sorry," she wails to Blair. "You deserve so much better than me as a mother."

We all huddle together, sharing stories, crying, time passing fast, unlike the slow passage of time in the room. It's amazing how when you're in the moment how quickly it goes.

I tell my mom about Bruce, what a happy child he is, and she's thrilled to be a grandma, her eyes lighting up at the idea of another child in the house.

We talk about Max and how he rescued me, and we stay like that, our fingers intertwined, until my foot falls asleep, Mom's back spasms, and Blair starts coughing.

And then it's time to get up and rejoin the world.

Blair Post-Epilogue

Today is my first day of class and I'm nervous, wondering what the young, twenty-year olds will think of this old lady in class.

I might be exaggerating a tad, I'm in my early thirties.

Priscilla's set on me finishing college. It's her dying wish to see both her girls complete their education, so she says. I'm only going part-time to start, but the thrill of being back in the classroom, learning, and putting it to use has me excited for the first time in a long time. The community college started a satellite campus for Creighton, so now I can finish what I started, where I began my journey.

I quit the bar and moved back to the farm, trading off with my mother to baby-sit Bruce. Bristol's also working on completing her education, starting first with her GED.

We have a focus on education in this household.

Max and Bristol are engaged to be married and are

looking at houses in Nebraska. He's back in Honolulu, tying up loose ends with his practice and selling the house.

They're thinking Omaha, Max planning to join a veterinary practice or starting one of his own.

We're all trying to make up for lost time and doing the best we can.

And I have my own update on my love life.

Max has a good-looking brother, four years older than him, and we've started to date.

All in all, the Bellamys are doing the best we can.

And in the meantime, I adopted a rescue, Harold the bulldog.

As I'm heading out the door to my car, Priscilla stops me. "Honey, I have something for you." Her hands shake, Daddy's old leather Bible in them.

Confused, I hold it in my hands.

"There's a letter stuck in there," she explains.

"It's not...it's not from him, is it?" I think of the packages and letters from David Michael, wanting to put it to rest.

Priscilla's face drains. "No, no...it's from your father."

I feel a hand clutch at my heart, squeezing my insides.

"I'm sorry." She's genuine, "he wanted you to have this. Left it after...after the accident."

I'm angry, and hurt, but I'm working on forgiveness with Priscilla. We have a long way to go, but I nod, choosing to thank her for the envelope, holding in between my fingers, scared it will be heartbreaking to read, further blame for the past decade.

Waiting until I turn on my engine, it sits on the seat next to me, staring at me in earnest. I can't wait any longer. Before I pull out onto the highway, I gently tear open the envelope. Inside, on my daddy's old church stationary, is a letter typed out to me. Daddy always had the worst hand-writing.

My oldest and wisest Blair,

I raised you and your sister to be good Christians, have decent morals, and repent for

your sins. I've tried to uphold my end of the bargain, choosing to lead by example and not by the old adage of ' do what I say, not what I do.'

Except I've faltered at this as of late.

There's something I have to get off my chest, and I'm a coward for not looking you in the eye and saying it to your face. I love you, and I'm sorry. I've failed you as a father since your sister disappeared.

Please know I don't fault or blame you for your actions. In fact, I admire the steps you took to try and find Bristol, and you showed maturity by involving the authorities and contacting us, as hard as it was to do.

I'm spiraling, and I know you are also fighting your own demons. As I write this, I'm halfway through a bottle of vodka, a source of comfort I never thought I'd reach for. I'm only human, you see. As a parent, you never expect to experi-ence the deepest sorrow of losing a child. In my mind, I've lost both of you. And a third.

You're smart and funny, curious and unique, and I know the lights dimmed in you, as it has for all of us. To witness and be part of what happened, the guilt eats at you. I hate to see you hurt, same goes for your sister.

I've failed because all the values I've tried to teach you, I'm failing at. I've lost my faith

and the ability to see human kindness, as such, it's become an impossible burden to bear. It's not that I can't look at you, it's that I can't stand for you to see how I've lost my way in life and with Jesus Christ.

But as your father, I want you to know I love you. If anything happens to me, you have to

know that I'm proud of you even though I haven't held up my end of the bargain lately.

What I wish for you – stop blaming yourself. There are bad people in this world and we

cross paths with them not by choice, but by circumstance. Maybe even fate.

And when you're ready, I set aside money for you to finish school.

Hold your head high.

Love, Daddy

I'm shocked and saddened, a plethora of emotions over-taking me, sobs wracking my body as the cream paper absorbs some of my tears.

Taking a deep breath, I re-read the letter, gently folding the creases and placing it back in the envelope.

Saying a prayer for my father, I gather my emotions, a smile crossing my face. I touch his old Bible. It's on the seat next to me, my companion. Sliding the envelope in there, a safe spot for his words, I pull out on the highway, ready to start the next chapter of my life.

ABOUT THE AUTHOR

Author Bio

Marin Montgomery is the author of five top-100 Amazon ranked books. A proud native of Iowa, she calls Arizona her 'Zen place.'

When she's not using her overactive imagination to think of her next psych thriller, she can be found hanging with her goldendoodle, Dashiell, binge-watching re-runs of *The Office,* or listening to live music.

To contact Marin, email her at authormarin@gmail.com or follow her on Instagram @marinmont18

Prologue
Talin

"When?" I lean against the doorjamb, crossing my arms. My nakedness a minute ago felt natural and comfortable, now I want to wear a long robe and cover up, hiding my body along with my innermost thoughts.

"Talin." He sighs, running a frustrated hand through his hair. "Let's not do this now." He slides off my bed, the covers rumpled, the decorative pillows tossed in varying degrees across the room. A reminder of a few minutes ago when we lay side by side in unison, not face to face in a stand-off, pitted against one another.

His clothes are folded on the chair in the corner, the exact opposite of mine, which are scattered haphazardly on the floor, a nude bra peeking out from underneath my bed, panties lodged somewhere in the covers, my jeans tossed on the edge of the mirrored dresser.

"I'm not doing this with you anymore." I put my hands

on my hips. I'm going to be strong this time. No more of this back and forth relationship, wavering between my indecisiveness and his empty promises.

He reaches a hand towards me, a peace offering. I swat his hand away. "Talin." He growls.

Twice he's used my real name.

He never uses my real name. He always calls me "Tally", which is what everyone else has nicknamed me.

"This isn't right what you're doing." He throws his arms up in disgust. Or maybe defeat.

"You either."

We stare each other down.

"I'm going to miss my flight." He strides to the corner chair and pulls his boxers out of the neat pile, sliding his white Calvin's on. His gaze never leaves the pouty look on my face.

I shrug.

"Let's not end it like this," he pleads.

"You mean this?" I point towards the bed. "What's *this?* We have nothing more than that bed over there. Let's just end it all together."

"You don't mean that." He tries to hold my stare as he buttons his tan and navy striped shirt, a lock of dark hair falling over his eye. Those chocolate brown eyes I get lost in every time.

"I do. I'm tired of this." I scowl. "I don't want to see you again."

"That's not true."

"It is." I turn to my bathroom. "I'm going to take a shower. You better be gone when I come out."

"You know I have to go."

"Then do that." I swing back around. "Do what you

always do. *Go*. Delete my number. This is over." I stalk through the door, tears pricking my eyes.

I feel his hand reach out for my back, grazing my skin, but I don't acknowledge him. I slam the bathroom door shut, holding my breath as he puts his shoes on, his heavy footsteps echoing on the hardwood floors.

He pauses outside the closed door, only an inch of wood separating us in person but miles in reality.

Twenty-two hundred and seventy miles, to be exact.

I grip the door frame from the other side, resting my cheek against the wood, biting my lip in apprehension.

Will he stay or will he go?

A sigh on his end, as I imagine him pushing his head against the oak, lips curled in resentment.

A quick knuckle slam to the wood.

His footsteps retreat, thudding down the hall.

The front door slams shut in animosity.

After it closes, it confirms how alone I am, and a sob escapes my lips.

My heart sinks, the way it always does when he leaves. Pressing my eyes shut, it's the feeling you get when you're on a rollercoaster, that dizzy head rush that floods your brain at the same time you struggle to breathe. There's a surge of adrenaline kicking in as we soar through the air, every loop faster and more brazen than the last.

That's how we started, six months ago.

The butterflies tickle my stomach, fingers grazing the safety bar that's sheltering me. My eyes dart to the track up ahead and I know it's almost over.

That's today.

No more swoops, upside-down twists, just the final bow, the metal cars shuddering to a stop as they ground to a halt.

The end.

My body feels like that, spent, wishing for the moments that were mere seconds, the ones that passed in a blur.

This will be the last time. It has to be.

Turning the shower on, I pause to stare in the mirror. My white-blonde hair is in knots, sticking up in various places, my green eyes looking dark, sage-like, in the dim light. My mascara's smudged, black rimming the lashes, a combination of sex and tears.

Twenty-seven.

I thought I'd have my shit together at this age.

Relationships?

Always a tumultuous storm. The love of my life is gone, left me almost two years ago, not by choice. He left my engagement ring and a million memories.

Sliding my finger across the simple, wooden mahogany, square-shaped jewelry box my great-grandfather made for my mom that was passed down to me, I finger the simple diamond band nestled in the middle, a reminder of him. The only piece of jewelry I've ever owned of value, the sentimentality worth more than an extravagant price tag.

As I'm smoothing down my wild hair, considering my chipped cerulean blue nail polish and the aftermath of losing a second lover, a thud shudders through the house. It sounds like the front door, a heavy mahogany that closes with a loud bang.

I look in the mirror, leaning on the gray speckled granite to admire my smug reflection.

Of course he didn't want to leave like this.

Maybe this isn't the end.

Maybe he'll come join me in the water and purposely miss his flight.

Stepping in, I close the opaque shower door behind me.

I can't see out of the blurred glass, but I make out a flash of color.

"Reed?"

No answer.

There's a banging against the shower door. I pause, the water hitting me in the face. Tentatively, I slow the water to a trickle, then shut it off completely.

"Reed, are you back?" I holler.

A thump as something raps against the glass with urgency.

I reach for the handle and push, jumping back as he rushes in.

A scream escapes my lips.

Loras.

My rescue cat. An orange tabby with a fluffy white tip on the end of his tail, as if he dipped just the edge in a paint can. He's ancient, at least twelve, his hearing subpar unless it involves catnip and tuna fish. Selective hearing, I guess.

He's meowing, a loud whimper as he steps on the wet tile floor of the stand-up shower.

"Loras," I exclaim. "It's not your bath time." I scoop him up, giving him a snuggle as I set him out, peering my head around the glass.

My bathroom's empty, minus the damn cat and his litter box. I glance down to the other end, to the walk-in closet. It's a straight shot through the bathroom to get to it. Some might find it annoying to not have it in the bedroom, but I prefer the separation. My mad dashes from the shower to the closet mean that I wreak havoc there instead of in my bedroom. The walk-in has a full-length mirror on one wall and built-in shelves on the other, though from the tornado of dresses tossed off hangers, everything's buried underneath the rubble. Loras darts towards his spot on the bottom shelf, his orange fluff disappearing in an instant.

I close the shower door and rub my neck, surprised Reed didn't show back up.

Pulling the metal handle to the right, the blast hits me full force. The stringent water causes me to shut my eyes, blindly grabbing a bar of soap to wash my face, lathering it over my puffy eyes.

Another loud bang.

Loras better not be clawing and dragging the remnants of my wardrobe.

I scrub at my skin, removing traces of make-up.

Bad decisions.

His kiss.

My hand brushes over my mouth. Those lips that grasp onto me like I'm their lifeline. Like he'll drown if I don't reciprocate his touch with a fervent intensity.

Tears start to burn my eyelids, sliding down my cheeks.

I tell myself it's soap in my eyes, counting to ten in my head.

Grabbing the shampoo to lather my hair, I hold the wall with one hand, the bottle in my fist, catching my breath, the culmination of our relationship catching up with me.

Water rinses over my skin as I absentmindedly rub the shampoo into my hair, scrubbing it. I'm pushing too hard, my nails digging into my scalp as if I'm looking for a fight.

I wince, gently rubbing the offended area behind my ear.

A rush of cold air hits my back, signaling the glass door is open.

"What the..." My words stop, crashing to a halt as I feel the smooth touch of a finger on my spine, an automatic shiver down my back.

It's weird though, unnatural, like fabric is covering it up.

"Reed, you're letting the cold air in." I stomp my foot on the slick tiles.

Turning around, the shampoo bottle slips out of my hand, a gasp escaping my lips. When it hits the shower floor, liquid splatters as the plastic top cracks open, the watery pink substance oozing out.

The smooth touch is from a leather glove, the black material covering up a large hand. The rest is dressed head-to-toe in black, down to the Doc Martens on his feet, the yellow stitching synonymous with the brand. I can tell it's a *him* by his stature and the way he stands, an imposing figure hovering over me, at least a foot taller.

His right hand reaches out and grabs my wet hair, pulling it into a ponytail in a single swipe. He doesn't bother to step all the way into the shower, his long arm twisting my slippery strands in his grip, yanking my head back and closer towards him.

I yelp in pain. "Ow."

As I jerk my head in the opposite direction, his other hand reaches for my neck. My feet leave the ground as I'm lifted off the tiled floor. His splayed fingers might as well be a noose. My screams are drowned out by the water spraying me directly in the nose and mouth.

I sputter, trying to catch my breath.

Kicking my feet backwards, I make contact with his knee, which might as well be a steel post. It doesn't even budge as I connect with it.

He drags me towards the edge of the shower, stumbling as he trips over the ledge between the shower and the floor outside of it, a step down across the threshold. We almost go down, his viselike grip loosening around my hair and neck.

I ram my elbow towards his chest, hitting him in the

stomach. Violently, he whips me around, a slap across my face widening my eyes as he first connects with one cheek, then the other. The blows hit me like we're in a sparring contest, except I can't duck his punches.

Tasting the sticky sweetness of blood, it gushes into my mouth, dripping from my nose and cut lip.

A violent shove and I slide across the wet bottom, crashing into the opposite wall, my face making contact with the white subway tiles.

His clothing's now drenched, the water still spurting out from the jets as he becomes a soggy, black mess. He takes a step forward, his heavy boots both firmly planted on the shower floor.

Wrenching my hands from their position on the tile, he twists me around.

Blocking my face, I use my palms to shield myself from this monster.

It's pointless.

He slaps them away.

Reaching out, he grabs my neck with both gloved hands.

I stare at him, looking him up and down, memorizing him, this masked face I can't read.

My body starts to convulse, naked and afraid, as I dig my nails uselessly into the smooth surface of the wall, nothing but the grout to grab ahold of. They slide down the slick wall, polish coming off in protest.

I claw at him, acting like Loras on steroids as I flail my arms.

The floor's wet, and his boots slip as he loses his balance, his grip around my throat loosening.

In order to catch himself, he has to release me and grab for the metal bar.

Now's my chance.

I shove him away from me, catching him off guard as he tumbles.

He's blocking my exit, the difference between me and freedom, my life and living or becoming a statistic.

I push full force, ignoring the bruises forming on my face, the blood, the air supply he cut off, and the purplish welt that's sure to be wrapped around my neck.

His body groans as I pummel his chest with my wet one, one-hundred twenty pounds soaking wet. He's well-built, and it hurts me more than it hurts him. It's like I'm punching a shield of armor.

Pulling my knee up, I try and catch him in the groin.

He connects with my leg, knocking me over. A thud penetrates the white noise of water as my head hits the glass. A sharp crack jolts me, the shooting pain bringing me to my knees.

My eyes see blinding white for a moment, and I close them in protest against the glare.

When I open them, his hand reaches into his back pocket in one fluid movement.

A sliver of metal.

Goosebumps travel down my body. The warm water might as well be ice cold.

He nods at me as if to say 'it's time,' except he never once opens his mouth.

Why? I plead with my eyes. What did I do to deserve this?

He lowers his lids, forcing me against the wall, my back to him. He doesn't want to see me beg, or maybe it's guilt, my tortured eyes and his pained ones.

Gripping my neck to hold me in place, I feel a searing pain in my back as a sharp object enters my flesh. It's as if my lower extremities are being scorched, heat rising up as if I stayed out too long in the sun and acquired a sunburn.

Bile rises suddenly in my throat, the contents of my dinner lost as I choke it up, watching the liquid sluggishly make its way to the drain.

I feel dizzy as the small space spins.

The water suddenly falters, a squeak as he shuts off the lever.

Before I can consider his next move, a second cut snakes around my abdomen to hit my stomach. My mouth twists in horror.

My mind comprehends the pain, the sight, as blood makes its way down my pale skin, a paintbrush slashing burgundy down my pubic bone and then running between my legs. It trails towards my left foot, to the silver toe ring from Mexico, the only time Reed and I made it out of the country.

Looking down, red seeps towards the drain, mixed with the last of the water.

It's like a B-horror movie, the knife connecting with my flesh, over and over again, his frenzied pace showing no mercy. I feel as if I'm being repeatedly punched, with no time to recover in between blows.

Then I go numb. My limbs are visible but useless.

Starting to lose consciousness, my eyes become heavy as my breaths become shallow, each one more of a gasp for air.

I hear Loras screeching, his paws frantic against the steamed shower.

All I can think of, my last cognizant thought, is of him.

And my cat.

Who's going to feed him? He might starve, his extra weight sliding off him as he becomes malnourished, waiting to be fed.

His voice, I want to hear him say my name, but there's only silence.

My eyes bulge, his hands a vise-grip until my lungs fill up with air, the final plunge into one side of my neck.

I go slack, his fingers relaxing around my throat.

Chapter One
Reed

When I slam the door shut to Talin's, I'm fumbling with my laptop bag and the rental car keys.

Instinctively, I reach down in my pocket. It's empty, except for a leather key ring.

My phone's missing.

Gritting my teeth, I exhale.

I shake my head, considering the consequences had I left it at Talin's house.

In Portland.

When I'm supposed to be in Dallas.

Or at least that's the story I told my wife.

I'm pissed and I don't want to go back in the house, to the fight that started that has no good ending.

Pushing the door back open, I stride across the hardwood floor and swipe my phone off the kitchen counter where I set it down. Our dirty dishes are out - we never got around to cleaning up after dinner. I dump the leftovers in a Tupperware container and store it in the fridge, washing out the pots and pans and stacking them in the dishwasher with a bang.

All but the knife.

It needs to be hand-washed.

I clasp it in my hands. It's smooth, brand-new, and sharp.

It could slice an artery, I think. Cause permanent damage.

Before Tally angrily stalked off to the bathroom, we were in bed, tangled up in her sheets, the moments I live for with her fleeting but real. I could barely make out her features in the dark, but I don't need to. Her face is memorized, etched like a scar I can trace but never remove from touch or sight. She has that effect on me, permanency, a lasting impression far after I'd unraveled myself from her body. Her white-blonde hair is spread out around her.

My phone was the cause of the mood tanking. It vibrated, my wife's picture flashing on the screen. She'd been fairly silent this evening, but I owed her and the boys a phone call.

"Do you have to answer?" Tally mumbles. I don't have to look at her, I can feel her pupils drilling into the side of my face, daring me to move from our cocoon.

"Shhh... baby. Go to sleep." I squint at my watch out of habit, unable to see the small numbers on my wrist, the clock on the side table illuminating 9:57 pm in fluorescent green.

"Want me to walk you out?" She rolls over to look at me, the gray satin sheet falling away from her body, the rest of her now naked. Even without light, she's perfect. Smooth supple skin, a few freckles smattered on her chest, pert nipples, a small scar, a keloid from her belly button ring in college.

"Nah, you stay in our bed." I lower my voice. "I'm already missing it." She sighs, but it's not her contented one that comes after sex, it's miffed.

I reach out a hand to touch her arm. It's cool to the touch, raised goosebumps from the ceiling fan circling above our heads. Pulling away slowly, as if the sudden movement will cause a cataclysmic chain of events, I murmur. "Sleep well. I'll text you in the morning."

Backing up, I don't bother to check behind me to see the orange ball of fur curled up on the hardwood floor.

Loras, her obstinate orange cat.

My foot connects with his overweight form, a hiss and then a loud meowing sound as he shoots off into the night. Catching myself, I grab the knob on the bedroom door before crashing into the wood. "Shit," I exclaim.

"What's wrong?" She's rolled over now, her back to me.

"Damn cat." I groan. "Loras never stays in one place long enough."

"Neither do you," she whispers.

"Baby, let's not do this after our night," I soothe.

Her voice has an edge to it. "When are you going to leave, Reed? How much longer?" A shakiness enters her tone, replacing her half-asleep one.

"Not long." I stop listening, the words going in one ear and out the other, this conversation like a re-run, a repeat episode you've seen enough times to know how it ends. The same can be said of this talk.

I'd made vows to one woman I wasn't following and empty promises to another.

"You have to stop asking me to leave," I admonish. "It makes me want to run."

"So run." She abruptly sits up, slamming her feet on the floor. Anger lights up her face, knitting her eyebrows together. "We're always going to be each other's second best."

I know what she means, and I want to shake her like a rag doll. She's in love with the ghost of her ex, and I'm bound by contracts and agreements that supersede my relationship with her. And as much as I want to, as much as I ache when

I leave her bed, the list of responsibilities and priorities hold me back.

I put the knife down.

Phone and laptop bag in hand, I head out the front, slowly closing it behind me so it doesn't slam. Her Craftsman-style home only has one heavy door. She tells me a screen door would ruin the appearance of her bungalow.

I glance back as I walk down the driveway, my rental car parked around the corner. This trip I decided to park it there - less chance of a nosy neighbor commenting on who they see.

Or what they hear.

My shadow follows me into the night as I climb in the nondescript rental, my mind wandering. Sitting in the car, I play with the radio, indecisive on what type of mood I'm in. I decide on some blues as it matches my lonesome demeanor.

Driving around the block a few times, passing Tally's house. It's as if I'm stuck in a loop, my hands clenching the steering wheel in frustration.

I need to distance myself from Mountain Aire Road. Every beginning must have an end, I muse.

A man's walking, his steps hurried as he disappears around the corner. His head's down, but he seems fairly young and he looks familiar. Must be the neighbor on the next street over.

I pull over two streets away, punching her alias in my phone, *Todd.*

She doesn't answer.

I leave a voicemail.

"You're right. This is over. I'm not leaving *my wife* anytime soon. Thanks for the memories. I'm canceling your credit card. Find a new man to antagonize. This is a dead end for both of us."

Before I head to the airport, I stop a few miles from her house on a secluded road that we claimed as ours. We would stop, our hands and mouths frantic, when we couldn't wait even the short distance to her house to have each other.

The thrill of getting caught.

A rush of adrenaline kicks in as I think of how it felt, the sense of calm after we were spent, panting, a quickie in the backseat.

I guess this entire affair has been like that - the potential to make a reckless mistake that results in our being found out.

Punching the steering wheel in anger, I'm filled with remorse. Why, why did she have to push me to leave?

It's for the best, I know. That I get on a plane and go back home and pretend nothing happened here.

My wife is growing suspicious.

I stopped claiming Portland as a business destination when she started asking questions. My work had never taken me to Oregon as much in the past ten years as it did in the last six months.

Flicking off the headlights and reclining my seat, I close my tired eyes, wanting to disappear. I picture the knife on the counter, how both women in my life want more from me than I can give. I'm drained, and it's all because of their constant nagging.

A car horn beeps, forcing me upright. I scan my surroundings. Not much to see in the dark, twinkling lights in the distance. A black pick-up truck passes me, narrowly missing my taillight as it swerves to avoid a collision.

I rub my eyes and squint at the dashboard.

Cursing, I notice the time. It's past eleven, and my flight leaves in less than an hour.

Switching my lights on, I drive to the airport, the freeway not as busy as I expect on a Friday night. Houston is two hours ahead of Portland, and my body never seems to adjust to the time change. Tally and I don't spend our short-lived time sleeping. The red-eye allows me to catch up on some much-needed zzz's. Our focus is on other things in bed.

My eyes barely stay open as I drop off the rental car and take the shuttle to the main terminal.

I'm pushing it, I'm the last passenger to board as the final announcements are made.

The Boeing 747 always leaves me with mixed feelings. When I visit, I'm giddy with excitement, my feet tapping the floor, my hands gripping the arm rests, headphones shutting out the world as I close my eyes and imagine Tally Forrester's face and body.

After I board the plane, for once, it's half-empty, a rare occurrence in this day and age. I plop in my business select seat and shove my laptop bag underneath. Tonight, the plane seems claustrophobic, closing in on me.

Guilt.

I'm tempted to try Tally again from the dummy number I use to contact her. I switch back and forth between her Todd number and an app I pay for that doesn't show up on the wireless bill. If my wife saw how much I talked and Facetimed Todd a.k.a. Tally, it would seem I was gay or having an affair.

I'm sent straight to voicemail.

Guess she got the hint.

And as much as I know we're both going to suffer, what happened tonight is for the best.

I call Meghan as I buckle my seat belt. The flight attendants are walking down the aisle, handing out blankets. I raise my hand in the air and motion for one. I also ask for a stiff drink.

"Hi babe."

"Hey, I didn't know if you were going to answer." She's agitated, no doubt from my lack of communication.

"I'm on the plane now but wanted to say goodnight." I suck in a breath. "How're the twins?"

"Been asleep for hours." I can hear the exasperation through the phone. "You were supposed to let me know what time you got in. I never got your flight itinerary."

"Sorry 'bout that. Should be home by 4 A.M.," I say. "I'll take a taxi or Uber."

"Ok, I'm going to go to bed. The boys will be glad to see their daddy when they wake." She adds, "They miss you."

"I miss them too." The reality is, I bury myself in business trips and purposely choose to stay away from home as much as possible.

A classic avoidance technique.

Part of the continuing argument we have - my Disneyland Dad parenting. I'm never home to know what goes on.

We've been married since our early twenties. It's crazy to think I'm now forty-two and she just hit forty. The flight attendant hands me my drink. For some reason the vodka tonic instantly sours in my stomach, unsettled like my nerves.

I absentmindedly twist my wedding band on my finger. "I'll sleep on the plane so it doesn't disrupt our day tomorrow. We can find something fun to do with Henry and Rolly."

Both of our twins are named after our fathers, the names antiquated, same with our dads, but they both have a rich history where oil and land are concerned. Henry Reed was born four minutes and forty-five seconds before Roland Edgar. Edgar is my brother's name - or should I say, was my brother's name. He died of a heroin overdose in his late twenties. He'd struggled with back problems, unemployment, and addiction. Since he was a kid, he couldn't say no to drugs, pills, alcohol, or women. An addictive personality to say the least.

She says nothing, and I hear subdued breathing.

"We need to talk." She's muffled through the phone. I hear a flight attendant over the loudspeaker make an announcement.

"Megs, I gotta go. We're about to take off."

"K, see you in the morning."

"Love you. Night." I disconnect without waiting for her response, switching my phone to airplane mode.

Absentmindedly, I wipe at a dark spot on my wrist. It looks like a scratch. I push my watch down to cover it.

The airplane circles the runway for a few minutes and then braces for takeoff. At this point in my life, it's a lullaby, the sound of the engines soothing me to sleep as the force of the plane propels us up in the air.

I've got the blanket tucked around my lap, headphones in my ears, white noise that's supposed to relax me. Yet, fifteen minutes later, my eyes fly open, a sense of panic washing over me. My mouth is bone dry, eyes blinking in rapid succession, trying to tamp down the sense of nausea in my belly.

I pull my phone out of my pocket. A picture of my boys is the screensaver on the lock screen, a picture of my wife on the home screen.

In a hidden app, I have pictures of Tally.

I close my eyes, willing myself to think of our first

encounter. I met her six months ago when she stood in front of me in line at a coffee shop. She was reciting a complicated order that ended with 'almond milk' when she knocked her purse off the counter. The contents of her handbag proceeded to roll down the tile floor in all directions. I heard her utter a cuss word under her breath, stumbling over her heels. She leaned down, blonde hair covering her face as she picked up the items she lost - a tube of breath mints, car keys, loose business cards, and lip gloss that had scattered across the floor. Her face turned scarlet red as a tampon spun and landed on the toe of my wingtip loafers. I picked it up and did the best I could not to laugh. "I'm sorry, miss," I said straight-faced. "Is this for a bloody nose?"

She was taken aback at the joke, and a grin spread across her face as the color died down on her cheeks.

We locked eyes.

Her eyes - they took my breath away. I'd never seen that color, perfectly suited to the pale green sheath dress she was wearing.

"I'm sorry." She laughed. "It's one of those mornings." She stood up straight, the contents of her tan leather purse shoved back inside.

The barista impatiently waited for her to collect her wallet and pay her tab, eyeing the line growing behind us.

"Can I buy your drink?" I had asked.

She looked confused.

"Or is that a little forward?" I grinned at her.

"You wanna buy me coffee?" She shrugged. "I'll ditch that guy over there then and sit with you." I looked across the room, and it was my turn to look flabbergasted. I saw a woman in her mid-forties shoving a scone down her gullet and a man that was pushing at least seventy leaning back in his chair, arms crossed.

"Is that your grandpa?" I asked.

"No." She motioned her head towards him. "My boyfriend."

I paused, deciding how to react.

When I hesitated, she reached a hand out and touched my arm just for a second. Only a second, but a tingling sensation followed.

"I'm just kidding. Add your drink to my order and I'll let you pay."

"Your coffee had more syllables than I know what to do with. What was it again?"

She repeated the long, complex drink. Today, I'm proud to say I can recite it in my sleep. A 'skinny iced caramel macchiato with almond milk.'

Not my style.

I ordered my coffee, black, room for cream.

That chance meeting changed everything, for better or for worse.

Chapter Two
Rafael, Elite Transportation Driver

I'm coasting along, rush hour traffic not in effect since it's Sunday, my mind on everything else but the freeway. My wife's threatened divorce again, her screams and the whizzing coffee cup that smashed against the wall this morning her only communication with me. Better than the status quo of silence, I suppose.

My hands grip the leather steering wheel, my first ride of the day. They're almost always airport runs. We contract with a variety of companies, driving employees to and from Portland International Airport.

I sigh, glancing at the concrete jungle this place has become. I settled here twenty-five years ago, adjusting to a rainy climate and hipster mentalities. I grew to love the Cascade Mountains and the vast amount of craft breweries.

Mile marker two-nineteen comes up on my right.

Two miles to go.

I swerve, almost missing my exit, my mind back on Marika, my wife of twenty years. She's battling cancer, brain cancer, and she's angry at the world, especially me. She's tired, depressed, ragged, her body raging.

She's pushing me away due to a terminal prognosis. Forty-five years old. My knuckles turn white, grasping the steering wheel like a lifeline that can hold the fragments of my discombobulated life together. I try not to think about the hospital bills, now in the six-figure range.

People always ask why I chose this profession. The assumption is that driving is boring, the runs like clockwork, the people unmemorable, unless they're rude or display obvious distaste for their drivers.

But I enjoy it. I hear story after story. It's like reading one of those adventure novels that have alternate endings, always a beginning and a middle. Many start with the same idea, just different characters, day in and day out, interchangeable until you have one that really stands out.

That day was today.

I get off at my exit, drumming my fingers to the mindless chatter of talk radio. The debates and arguments that stem from both political sides are too vocal as they lambast each other's viewpoints. Music seems redundant, the same top ten on the popular stations, the oldies I've replayed too many times, the sports channel a recap of games I've already watched.

Following my Google map directions, I head to an older area of the city, one that weaves in and out of destitute areas and gentrification. Like most big cities, one street is filled with well-manicured lawns and pride of ownership, while the other side of the road is littered with vacant eyes and lost souls.

A blur of orange flashing in front of my vehicle brings me back to the present. I slam on my brakes reactively, unsure of what crossed my path.

An animal.

It's a cat, a puffy, overweight feline that can run amazingly fast for its size. It's bright orange with a dab of white fur covering the tail.

I notice it has reddish brown streaks on one side. Even his paws seems to be covered in what looks like dried paint.

It couldn't be blood, could it?

He might be hurt.

Did his paw catch the tire as it flew underneath my vehicle? Or maybe he's feral. I dismiss that idea when I see a blue collar around his neck, where a gold tag hangs from it. Maybe his owner lets him roam the neighborhood and he caught a bird for breakfast.

I slow down to a crawl but before I can stop, he scurries off into a rose bush, the branches shaking as he disappears from sight.

So much for that, I think.

I'm picking up someone from the next street over. The house has a small yard with a patch of grass and a plethora of strategically placed flowers lining the walkway. A couple of flower boxes on the window sills remind me of my grandmother's place.

This is a bungalow, a quaint but adorable-looking house that has a large front porch and character. A *California Craftsman*, I believe they're called, born out of the early nineteen-hundreds. This one has a heavy stone porch column with dormer windows, the house painted olive green with cream trim. Shaker shingles line the top of the low-pitched roof. There is no garage, just an empty concrete slab with an older tan Volvo parked in it.

Glancing at my phone, I double check the address.

My agreed-upon arrival time is 7 A.M. I'm a few minutes early.

I take a glimpse in the rearview mirror and see the same cat strolling up the drive, his deliberate steps towards the porch.

He watches me, alert, as we both stare each other down.

Tapping my fingers on the wheel, I keep one eye trained on him and the other on the front door.

A number is provided with the order and when the clock hits 7:05 on the dash, I call my airport run-it goes to voicemail. I expect to hear a man speaking, except Talin belongs to a young-sounding woman. I don't leave a message.

I open my car door carefully, the cat now standing at the front door, mewing loudly. He stretches out and lays down by the dark-colored mahogany door, three stained glass panels in the upper portion, his tongue licking his paws. I walk towards the front stoop while dialing Talin one more time.

Straight to voicemail. Maybe her phone's off or she overslept.

The cat regards me warily as I take the three steps towards him. He's on a welcome mat, his paws matted with the dark liquid.

My stomach drops. I wish it were paint, but it *looks* like blood.

I swivel to look around the neighborhood. All the homes are similar, small bungalow-style homes that have been remodeled and lovingly restored to a *Leave it to Beaver* suburbia mentality of the idyllic family life. All of the homes are similar, small front yards with flowers and metal mailboxes. The porches are wide, and swings hang from most. This is the kind of street I imagine in black and white images - pre-technology, where families still sat down together for dinner.

Pushing the doorbell, I hear it chime through the house. I try to peep through the two large picture windows, but the shades are drawn.

No answer. I shift from one leg to the other, impatient. We need to get a move on if we're going to stay on schedule.

I notice a brass metal door knocker and bang it against the wood, a loud thump sounding as it slams against the mahogany. The door's ajar, and it's enough to cause it to slowly creak open.

I slam the door shut. I don't want Talin to think I'm trying to enter her house without permission.

I cross my arms, waiting for her hurried footsteps to come to the door. At any moment, she'll acknowledge her ride to the airport.

The house is silent.

A pit forms like a tightly wound ball in my stomach.

Fumbling with my phone, I dial her again. And again. I leave a winded message.

I don't want the neighbors to grow suspicious of a strange man on her porch. Is she married? Maybe a roommate?

My annoyance grows. She probably woke up late and is in the shower.

Jabbing the doorbell, I press it again.

Nothing but the chiming noise.

Stepping off the porch, I check the wooden fence that wraps around the house. The gate is locked. I pause, stopping to eyeball her car. I pull the handle on the driver's side. It's locked. It looks decently clean and organized. The front seat has a pair of sunglasses lying on it. There's a pack of gum on the console.

Checking over my shoulder, I notice a man getting in a cherry red Honda down the street. It might be paranoia, but he seems to stare at me with curiosity.

Her neighbors are probably calling me in as we speak. Me and my nondescript SUV.

I'm trying to decide my next move when the cat lets out an ear-splitting howl. I jump as he butts his nose against the door. His eyes are narrowed at me, as if I'm the reason he's not inside.

I take a deep breath.

Being arrested for breaking and entering isn't an aspiration I have. What if she's inside and I startle her? I'll be fired. My wife and I will be in more dire straits than we already are.

I ignore the cat and head back to my waiting vehicle.

Climbing inside, I call my office to check if they have heard from my client.

The dispatcher, Roseanne, answers. She smokes a pack a day and her voice reflects that in the hoarse way she talks. "Elite Transportation. Rose speaking."

"Hey Rose, it's Rafael. Car seventeen." "Hi Rafael, top of the morning to you." She coughs, hacking up a lung.

"I've got a 7 A.M. that hasn't shown. She's not

answering her phone or door. Name's Talin Forrester. Have we had any cancellations?"

"Lemme check. Please hold." I hear loud, top forty music as she disappears for a minute.

"Nope, no cancellations. Looks like two airport runs for the same company-RGMP Technology Solutions. You've got Talin Forrester and the other customer is Richard Garrett."

"Ok, double checking, address I'm in front of is 1237 E Mountain Aire Road."

"Yep." I hear Rose clicking her keyboard. "Want me to try her?"

"Yes please."

The hold music comes back on. I grimace at the obnoxious lyrics. It's all pop tinged with electronic dance music.

I get back out of the vehicle. The cat circles my leg, groaning. I lean down to touch him, holding the phone between my shoulder and ear. I expect him to run but he freezes, his back arched. I run my eyes over him, checking for contusions. I don't see any open wounds or cuts.

I can smell it now. A metallic odor. A pungent, coppery smell.

Blood.

My fingers start to shake, the phone positioned awkwardly next to my ear. I jerk upright, dropping it. My call with Rose disconnected, the hard plastic case taking the brunt of the fall. I pick it back up and put it in my pocket.

I'm starting to think there's a good reason Talin Forrester isn't answering the door.

She can't.

I feel like I'm falling, my stomach tumbling to my feet. A sense of dread overcomes me and I struggle to breathe. I rest my hand on the doorknob. I want to turn around, go back to my waiting Tahoe, and drive off. Maybe I can go next door, ask a neighbor to check on her or call the police, do a welfare visit.

But what if nothing's wrong and I've made a big deal out of a misplaced woman? Maybe she isn't home. I'm unsure how old she is, but what if she stayed somewhere else last night? She could be running late. Premonition tells me this isn't the case. The skittish cat chatters at the door, unleashing his own epithet. Maybe she forgot to let him in last night and he's starved to death.

Death.

I shake my head. I need to stop thinking everything is related to death. Just because my wife is sick doesn't mean everyone else is about to die. A therapist would tell me I'm transferring my own concerns onto someone else.

Transference, that's it.

The cat startles me when it starts clawing at the door, his paws scratching at the dark wood.

Great, now he's damaging what's hopefully his own front door.

I interrupt him by pushing the handle in, a small click as I haltingly open it.

"Hello?" I yell out. "Mrs. Forrester? Talin?"

I'm instantly overwhelmed by an odor. It's putrid, and it invades my nostrils - filling them with the smell of something rotting. I rub my nose, the cat whizzing past my feet, a blur as it takes off down the hallway.

"Mrs. Forrester?" I call. "Are you here?"

My voice echoes. I'm in a foyer, and light oak hardwood floors cover the entry. There's a beige sofa with multi-colored throw pillows. An ornate grandfather clock sits on a ledge, ticking down the minutes, the seconds.

My brain's on fire, screaming at me to turn back around and exit the house.

Something is not right.

The smell is not natural.

Garbage.

She probably hasn't been home to take out the trash.

Maybe it's leftovers sitting in the fridge.

My eyes drift around the room. There's a stone fireplace with lots of built-ins and nooks and crannies that are filled with various books, decorative vases, and knick-knacks. Gingham print curtains cover the two picture windows that face out the front.

The kitchen is straight ahead, an arched entryway that has patterned black and white tile floors and appliances that are meant to look like they're from another decade. The refrigerator hums. I grasp the door and open it, hoping to see it piled full of leftovers.

A couple bottles of water. Wine. A tub of cream cheese and various accoutrements - mustard, mayo, ketchup. There's a container of leftover pasta - a dish of what looks like Alfredo sauce.

I feel weird going through a stranger's fridge in their own house. I slam it shut quickly, as if the half-eaten slice of cherry cheesecake will reach out and bite me.

There's a small pantry in an alcove. I open the door, the garbage can hidden from view in here. Cat food and kitty litter, along with protein bars and various boxes of pasta and canned goods, line the shelves.

I jump when I hear a thud behind me, and I swivel around in surprise.

Orangie, my new nickname for the cat, his tag too small for me to read, has landed on the speckled granite countertop.

He's walking as if he's on a tightrope, hugging what would be the center of the island.

I see stains on the counter.

How did I miss those?

My throat closes. These are fresh. His paws have new reddish stains on them, now in the shape of his paw prints as he tracks them across the surface.

Pulling my phone out of my pocket, I don't know why, but I snap a quick photo.

Just in case.

I start to quiver. My hands tremble as I reach forward to catch myself on the edge of the counter, evidence that Talin Forrester didn't come home last night wishful thinking.

Does she have children? A crazy ex? Disgruntled colleague? I haven't seen any family photos, and I haven't spotted any toys to suggest a kid lives here.

It's surreal, standing in the house of someone I've never met, their most intimate details on display for me to see. It's as if I'm an extra on the set of a movie, watching what I have no control over, the dialogue and scene already in motion. I'm just waiting for someone to yell '*cut.*'

Just go, I tell myself, go back to the Tahoe and call the police. You don't need to look for trouble. My mama always said you would find trouble if you went looking for it.

I start to stride out of the kitchen but I turn my head to the right, to the hallway that leads to the rest of the rooms.

Holding on to the wall for support, I tentatively step as if I'm stuck slogging through mud, dragging one foot at a time.

"Hello, Talin, I'm your driver. I wanted to come inside and check on you. Your cat seems to think that there's something wrong," I babble. "I hope it's okay I came inside. I'm happy to help you with your luggage. We better get going or you're going to miss your flight."

The first room to the left is open. I hold my breath as I peek inside, my body tense.

Judging by the bare necessities and the feel of stagnation, this must be a guest room. A queen-size bed, made up with a flowered duvet cover, untouched, covered in matching pillows, takes up most of the space. A side table has a small lamp in the shape of a rabbit, with a brand-new looking candle by the amount of wax still in the glass. A small chest of dressers and a flowery painting hang above the bed, with curtains that match the rest of the room covering a small window.

I peek out. I'm looking at the side yard. Her trash cans and some lawn fertilizer are visible.

The closet knobs stare at me.

Someone could be hiding in there.

I inhale at the same time I pull them open, exposing the contents.

Exhaling loudly, windbreakers and extra jackets are hanging, no body shoved in with the clothing or an intruder waiting to pounce. A cardboard box sits on the floor and a clear plastic case filled with pictures is on the shelf above. The pictures that're visible are of a blonde girl, though I can't tell if they're recent photographs.

Her eyes pierce me from their resting spot.

Stepping back into the hall, I pause before I push open the door directly across from the guest room.

Expecting the worst, I cup my hands into fists.

It's a tiny bathroom. A shower curtain with a map of the world hangs over the bathtub. I yank it open. The contents of her shower stall show this bathroom is barely used. A full bottle of shampoo and conditioner along with a new bar of soap rest on the fiberglass enclosure.

The bathroom has old love letters from around the world decorating the walls in gilded frames. One's from Germany, looks to be during World War Two, one is a soldier deployed, and another from high school lovers in Berlin.

Marika would love this. She's a history buff and loves reading historical romance novels. This bathroom has wallpaper, gold and burgundy embossed stripes, giving it a regal look. The hanging towels look unused, as if they've never wiped anyone's hands or face. I inspect them, and a smear covers one edge of the cotton.

It looks to be blood. I pull my hand back as if I've been slapped.

A fleeting image comes to mind. What if they think I had something to do with this? Whatever *this* is?

My mind races. I need to get out of here. Call the cops.

I step back into the hall.

I'm about to go the other direction, head outside, when a low growl followed by a screech reverberates through the small hallway of the bungalow.

The door at the end of the hallway is closed.

My eyes drift down. A bright burgundy stain has seeped underneath the door. The liquid is trailing out, a mass of congealed blood. The dark color contrasts with the light-colored oak flooring. Orangie is lying in it, his cries getting fiercer as he rolls in it.

I tell myself it's spilled Kool-Aid as I start taking steps backward.

Shutting my eyes, my fingers resting lightly on the wall, I keep moving away from the mess. Turning to run, I hesitate.

What if Talin is hurt and needs medical attention ASAP? It could be a matter of life or death. I think of my wife.

Spinning around, I take steps forward. Careful not to step in the blood, I grasp the doorknob, my hand trembling in trepidation.

Slowly I push the door open, my body shaking in fear, unsure what I'm going to encounter.

Or who.

I scream, my voice startling myself and the feline that disappears in a flash of orange, red, and white. My mind takes a second to comprehend the sight in front of me as my eyes drift around the semi-dark bedroom, blinds closed over what is surely a patio door.

Liquid blood has pooled underneath the bloated flesh on the floor.

A body. A naked, dead body, lying on her side. Just a cotton towel covering her face.

It's clearly a woman, who I assume to be my client, Talin Forrester.

One of her hands is clasped, as if she was trying to close her fist around something...or someone.

Her body has a glow, a sheen, as if she just worked out, her skin puffy as if she was filled with helium and expanded into a balloon.

Instinctively I reach out a hand to feel for a pulse, knowing there's no need. Her body is stiff, and rigor mortis has set in. She's a grayish-purple color, unnatural to the living, standard for the dead.

I clamp a hand over my mouth, turning away from the body to vomit. I sink to my knees, careful to avoid descending into the congealed blood.

On her wrist, a thin gold bracelet contrasts with the

snow-white skin, blue nail polish flaking off on her fingers. Defensive wounds cover her hands.

The other arm is laid at her side in a weird angle, as if it was twisted behind her back at one point. I glance behind her to the side table where a picture frame sits. The girl in the photo is gorgeous, model-like, an infectious smile on her face. How she looked in life is not how she looks in death. I see no correlation minus the white-blonde hair.

I carefully push the towel away from her face.

This person is unrecognizable. Dark bruises cover the canvas of her face, cuts jagged across the surface, her nose surely broken.

Multiple stab wounds, I presume by the slash marks that cover her body. I can't count how many, I don't want to count how many. She was a cutting board for her perpetrator, the anger apparent in every gash.

Purplish mottling covers her neck like she had been strangled, the knife not enough.

Her hair's now matted and covered in blood, like she dyed portions of her strands red but couldn't commit.

Her eyes.

I will never forget those eyes.

They will haunt me until I die. Open, rolled back, a dark lucid green. I lay the towel back over her ruined face, gingerly, as if it will heal her when it's pulled back off.

My head swivels around the room to take in my surroundings. The furniture's mirrored, and I can see all angles as I pause and glimpse around the room.

From her wounds and the state of the bed, it looks like there's been a struggle. The gray satin sheets are in disarray. The coverlet's half off the bed, throw pillows scattered all across the room. Or it could just be that she isn't the best housekeeper. Did something happen during sex? An accident? Did a guy freak out and go ape shit on her? Or was this random?

It doesn't look random.

Her clothes are scattered. I notice a once-nude bra peeking out from underneath the bed, discolored now, a pinkish hue. A pair of jeans hang limply over one side of the dresser.

I tiptoe across the room to inspect the side table. There are two, one on each side of the bed. Matching lamps, a set of matches and a candle on one. I peek behind the back of the side table. I see a flowered case still attached to a charger.

Her phone.

My heart sinks.

She probably tried to reach it and couldn't.

I lift it up, my fingers trying to swipe the screen. Her screensaver flashes, a picture of her and a curly, blonde-haired girl.

A passcode's required.

I realize my mistake too late. I'm touching a crime scene, disturbing potential evidence. My wife has CSI and Forensic Files on daily. You'd think I'd know better. What if they think I killed her because my prints are now all over her stuff?

Or what if I contaminated the only evidence linking the killer to her?

Guilt creeps in. The phone clunks on the glass as I drop it on the side table.

My eyes stay above the body as I peer across the room. A trail of blood leads out of another doorway, like an angry paintbrush had trailed across the floor in spatters.

She scooted across the floor to her final resting place.

A movement across the room throws me into a tailspin.

It's the blinds, the air circulating from the ceiling fan causing them to rustle, as if they can soothe away the tragedy. There's a wooden rod that's used to keep the patio door from sliding open. Its purpose is to keep intruders out, I think wryly. Grabbing it, I hold it like a shield in case I have to defend myself.

I pull the blinds away from the patio door. It's closed but unlocked.

Holding my breath, I notice the master bath. The thought of walking through another door, likely finding another body, murder-suicide seems to be prevalent, roots me to the spot.

I clutch my phone in my other hand as I head carefully through the doorway, scared of who might jump out.

It's an en-suite bathroom, and I open and shut my eyes against the nausea building rapidly as I try not to breathe in the stench of death. The floor's damp, the chevron pattern of the rug barely noticeable due to the blood stains. I squint at the shower stall, imagining the attack as I notice chunks of white-blonde hair plugging the drain. There's an emanation of blood and what I guess to be puke, the remnants of brownish-tinged liquid still visible.

Shoving my phone in my back pocket, I pull my shirt over my nostrils, trying to add a layer of protection against the nefarious odor. I walk through the bathroom, careful to watch out for the cat and any signs of life, the rod held tight in my grip. Even the kitty box has speckles of blood intermixed with the chunks of litter. I'm unsure if it's from Orangie's paws or back spatter from the attack.

Either way, it's disturbing.

I pass a large soaking tub, her double sinks, and a laundry hamper. The toilet is housed in its own little room, the door open and the fan on. The last door straight back is a walk-in closet, stuffed to the brim with clothes, shoes, and purses, a large mirror covering one side.

I check to make sure no one's hiding behind the closet door, no feet sticking out from underneath the crammed hangers.

Tears prick my eyes as I notice her suitcase is upright, ready to go for her trip this morning. A trip she would never get to make.

Sinking down in the closet, my back scraping against the door, I crumple as tears stream down my face. Peering at my reflection, I set the rod beside me and fumble to dial 9-1-1.

It takes two times to dial the number, my hands shaking.

"9-1-1. What's your emergency?"

"I...uh...I found a girl."

"Is she injured?"

"Yes." I sob. "She's dead."

"Did you feel for a pulse?"

"Yes, no pulse. She's not breathing."

"Did you administer CPR?"

"No...she's...gone."

"Are you okay?"

"No."

"You're injured?"

"No, I mean, I'm not hurt."

"Can you tell me what happened?"

My voice rises, I become hysterical. "I don't know...she's dead. Dead."

"Where did you find her?"

"In her house."

"Do you know what happened?"

"She's been stabbed multiple times. Choked." I rub a hand over my face.

"Have you touched the body?"

"No." I reconsider. "I mean, just to feel for a pulse."

"Okay, don't move her. I'm sending an officer to the house. Please don't move or touch anything."

I nod into the phone.

"What's your name?

"Rafael. Rafael Hernandez."

"What's the address?"

I start to give my address, stopping mid-sentence. "Wait, that's my home address. I'm picking her up for the airport." A sob escapes my lips. "Her address is..." I pause, fumbling, not remembering the street name. "Mountain View I think. Wait... Aire. Mountain Aire with an 'e'."

"We can trace it."

There's a lapse as I breathe into the phone.

"Sir, I need you to go outside and wait for the officer to arrive."

I gulp. "What if they're still here? I checked the house, but maybe they're hiding in the back?"

"Who?"

"The person who did this."

"Please go out front, don't touch anything, and be careful. I've dispatched the police, and an officer should be there in the next couple minutes."

I sag against the dresser, not mentioning I've touched more than I should have. The woman talks again. "I'll stay on the line with you until the officer arrives."

I'm paralyzed with fear. As much as I try and stand up, the weight of this gruesome discovery keeps me frozen against the door, my eyes darting around the closet, the view of the bathroom in my line of sight in case anyone comes toward me.

It feels like eternity but it's really a few minutes.

Sirens blare as I hold the phone and take deep breaths that are supposed to calm me down according to the dispatcher.

They don't.

I hear the officer's voice before I see him.

"Officer Morse, anybody in here?" A voice yells from inside the house.

"I'm back here," I say, my voice stifled.

He repeats his name.

I try again, this time louder.

"Where?" I hear his voice echo.

"Closet. Master."

I wish I could see how her body affected him, but it's a part of his job, not mine. I wipe the beads of sweat off my forehead, the image of the poor girl ingrained as if she's a permanent fixture on my psyche.

Shutting my eyes, I see her.

I open them and I smell the act of violence, the hate and anger radiating through this house like a bad omen.

"Sir." Officer Morse comes into sight. "I'm going to radio for back-up." His voice is calm, but I can see a glimmer of human kindness, of shock. It's reflected in his blue eyes, his blond hair streaked with gray, betraying his age.

I don't move.

The woman on the other end of the line asks, "Is that the patrolman?"

"Yes." I whisper.

"Okay, Mr. Hernandez, I'm going to disconnect."

I nod, dazed, as I hang up.

"Can you come with me?" The officer motions for me to stand up.

I sigh.

"Sir, are you hurt?" He sees a pained expression on my face.

"No, no, I just..." I'm struggling to find the words. He nods. He understands.

"Is that your vehicle in the driveway?"

"The black Tahoe is my work vehicle."

"Okay, I'm assuming the other one is the victim's?"

I shrug.

Victim?

Of course, she's now a victim. Her name, Talin Forrester, has been replaced with the generic terminology of one that came to her death in an unfortunate incident.

It sounds so cold. And final.

"Do you need help?" His voice is not unkind.

I shake my head, gripping the doorknob with my hand and using it as leverage to pull myself up.

"Let's go outside." He moves his hand toward his belt where his gun rests. I automatically put my hands up in the air. "I'm not armed, I'm not the intruder."

"Do you know the victim?"

"No." I decide to elaborate in case he assumes I'm a suspect. "I just came to pick her up."

"Uber?"

"No, my company, Elite Transportation, contracts with her company for airport runs."

"What time were you slated to pick her up?"

"Seven."

"How did you get inside?"

"The front door was open." I stare at him dumbly. "I found her cat and he wanted in."

"Why don't you have a seat in my squad car and we can talk?"

"I didn't do this." I motion around me.

"I didn't say you did." His tone is gentle. "I need to take your statement. I'm going to secure the premises. Did you go in the back?"

I shake my head no.

He walks me outside, holding the door open as I sink into the leather seat.

I bury my head in my hands.

A nightmare come to life.

Available Now!

Made in the USA
Middletown, DE
29 October 2018